Hunsicker's latest book imagines a frightening scenario: private military contractors—the corporate soldiers usually found roaming the deserts of Iraq and Afghanistan—are operating within the borders of the United States. With a relentless pace and doses of black humor, Hunsicker creates a thrilling combination of What-If with an altogether plausible What-Actually-Might-Be, giving the reader a remarkable post-9/11, War-on-Drugs novel.

> —David Morrell, best-selling author of *First Blood* and *The Brotherhood of the Rose*, co-founder of the International Thriller Writers

The Contractors is the fully loaded model with all the options. With streetwise and wisecracking Jon Cantrell and Piper at the wheel, they take the reader for one hell of a ride through the drug- and crime-ravaged parts of Texas that don't appear on picture postcards or tourist brochures. Hunsicker's eye for detail, sense of place, and his snappy dialogue shine through.

> —Reed Farrel Coleman, three-time Shamus Award–winning author of *Hurt Machine*

The Contractors is film noir without the film, cyberpunk without the cyber. It's a world to lose yourself in, a fascinating tale that lives in shades of grey. The prose is muscular, the images vivid, and the pace relentless. Simply put, Hunsicker kills it.

> —Marcus Sakey, author of *Good People* and host of the Travel Channel's *Hidden City*

THE CONTRACTORS

THE CONTRACTORS

HARRY HUNSICKER

THOMAS & MERCER

Published by Thomas & Mercer, Seattle

www.apub.com

ISBN-13: 9781477808726
ISBN-10: 1477808728
LCCN: 2013906585

To Alison

PART I

"It is clearly cost-effective to have contractors for a variety of things that military people need not do. . . . There are a lot of contractors, a growing number."

 —Secretary of Defense Donald Rumsfeld, Interview, Johns Hopkins University, December 2005

"The border region between Mexico and the US is a war zone right now, virtual anarchy. And war is not pretty, not for anybody. War is an ugly mess, compromises and Faustian pacts for everybody involved."

 —US Senator Stephen McNally, *Meet the Press*, April 2010

- CHAPTER ONE -

The muzzle of the gun is everything. My entire existence, the alpha and omega.

A black circle of emptiness pointing at my chest.

I shiver, skin clammy. My vision tunnels. Sounds become muted.

My memory is brittle, fragments of what used to be, bright images I now recognize as illusions, a reality that never was.

I don't want to die, of course, but I am ready for this to be over.

The lies and deceptions, the running.

They will find us; that's what they do. The grid is too vast, the databases and electronic tentacles reach too far. They'll wave the national security flag, and the pit bulls at Homeland Security will take over.

An image of an Aztec warrior shimmers in my peripheral vision. He stares at me but offers no comment. The room smells of blood and liquor.

I wonder if the warrior is real or if I've been drugged somehow. Perhaps he's more real than I am.

The muzzle of the gun seems to grow larger, and I imagine what the heat from the blast will feel like, a welcome if all-too-brief respite from the cold.

Piper, my lover, is radiant, happy-looking like the day we met. She appears well rested, at peace. Her hair is the color of sunshine, and her skin glows.

"Hello, Jon." She raises the gun a notch higher, aims at my face. "How's it hanging?"

"W-w-where is it?" My voice sounds hollow, far away.

She tilts her head toward the Aztec warrior, her eyes never leaving mine. The shoe box rests on the floor by the warrior's sandaled feet.

Eva Ramirez, her beauty transcending the circumstances, stands by my side, hands raised. She gasps when she sees the cardboard container. Her dark eyes sparkle, unable to hide her hunger for the contents of the box.

Piper aims the gun at her and says, "You want it, don't you, Eva?"

Eva doesn't speak.

"Go ahead and take it." Piper smiles. A long pause. "Just like you took Jon."

No one says anything. Her words swirl between the three of us like smoke from a condemned man's cigarette. The Aztec warrior glistens with sweat.

"They will come for us, yes?" Eva says. "Because of what has happened in the desert and what is in the box, they will never let us rest."

Stress has made her accent more pronounced. She sounds like what she is: a scared young woman from Mexico who finds her days numbered, collateral damage in the wars between the narcotraffickers and the governments on either side of the border.

Piper nods. After a moment, I do the same.

The men in the helicopters will come after whoever has the box. What's inside represents too many loose ends, an icon of a corrupted system marked with the innocuous words "Property of the US Government."

The dead DEA agent lies a few feet in front of the Aztec warrior. Blood pools beneath his body, spills out from his blue windbreaker.

He is my colleague. We have identical badges.

But are we the same? Will we meet similar fates?

"Piper." I hold out one hand. "Give me the gun."

My arm shakes, teeth chatter.

"Choices have been made, Jon." Piper tightens her grip on the weapon. "Every action has a consequence."

"Please." I ease a step closer.

She swings the muzzle toward me. Her trigger finger whitens, and the Aztec warrior smiles.

- CHAPTER TWO -

(*One Week Earlier*)

I was not an honest man, but I was not evil either.

Or so I liked to tell myself, especially when the lies jabbed at me like an aching tooth that couldn't be pulled or sedated away.

No matter.

Introspection was for wussies and Oprah fans.

I locked the dead bolt on the front door of the karaoke bar and shut the blinds.

Almost midnight. The interior was dim, lit only by an exit sign and the fragmented neon glow from the Hispanic nightclub across the parking lot.

Piper, blond hair back in a ponytail, kicked the Korean guy in the ass with one of her pointy-toed boots. The place was empty except for the three of us.

The Korean groaned. He was lying on the floor near an overturned barstool and a couple of his teeth.

"She's only fourteen." Piper stuck the muzzle of her Glock in the guy's ear. "Lisa. That's her name."

Chung Hee was the Korean. He owned the sing-along bar and another business on the back end of the dingy strip center.

He craned his neck around Piper's knee and stared at me, his expression pleading, a little cultural chauvinism that was probably not in his best short-term interest.

"What are you looking at him for?" Piper rapped him on the head with her gun. "I'm the one asking the questions."

Chung Hee's face reddened. He sputtered something in his native tongue.

"You haven't asked him anything yet." I peered between the slats of the blinds.

Nobody outside except for a bouncer in front of the place across the parking lot. Maybe a half dozen vehicles outside the club, all of them speckled with rain from the late summer thunderstorm that had passed by a few minutes earlier.

"What the hell are you talking about?" Piper said.

No squad cars visible, the only worry at this point. Vice, in their unmarked units, didn't work Sunday nights.

"All you've done is pop this guy a couple of times and tell him a name." I let the blinds drop. "You haven't actually asked him a question."

Piper swore and marched across the room to me. "Every time I run a job lately"—she jabbed an index finger at my chest—"you nitpick me to death."

"Hey, don't get pissy." I held up my hands. "I'm just saying."

A shuffling noise behind us.

Chung Hee was crawling toward his cell phone a few feet away.

Piper strode toward the man. I followed. She grabbed the back of his head and jammed the gun under his nose.

"*Where* is Lisa?" She glanced at me, smirked.

"N-no problems with girls. I pay for protection already, yes." Chung Hee held up his hands. "Much, much money. You go now, please."

"You sunuvabitch." Piper reared back the gun for another blow.

I caught her wrist. "We're not interested in anybody else. Just Lisa."

Chung Hee cowered, forearm shielding his face.

Piper struggled against my grip. I held fast, pulled her away. Shoved her toward the bar.

Chung Hee spat some blood on the floor. Maybe another tooth, too.

I knelt beside him and held up the picture of Lisa Sanders, an eighth-grader who the week before had told her stepfather to stick a Miller Lite tallboy where the sun don't shine and stormed out of the family's house in Mesquite, Texas, a blue-collar suburb of Dallas.

"Word is she works for you." I nodded toward the rear of the bar. "Out back, in the modeling studio."

Piper snorted at the phrase. In Korea Town, "modeling studio" was the term du jour for whorehouse.

"You turn over Lisa," I said, "and we'll go away."

Chung Hee was a tough bird. He gave me a gap-toothed smile, blood dribbling down his chin. "Screw you." He shook his head. "I pay for protection. You not get any girl from me."

I sighed.

"Police come." He puffed up. "Mess you up bad. You see."

And then—like he was a Korean Harry Potter who could call down reinforcements from the dark side—a beam of light splintered through the blinds, twitching across the empty bar.

Piper ducked, stared at me.

Outside, a two-way radio blared. Cop talk. Call signs, numbered commands.

The front door rattled. Shoe leather scraped on concrete.

Chung Hee grinned. Scooted backwards.

On the other side of the door, the meaty sound of a palm slapping glass.

"Police." A man's voice. "Anybody in there?"

Chung Hee fought his way to his feet, opened his mouth.

I shoved the barrel of my Glock between his lips. My free hand grabbed his throat. I back-walked him to a tiny alcove on the far side of the bar where the sound equipment was kept.

"I suppose you want me to handle this?" Piper whispered.

"Yeah, that'd be nice." I pressed the Korean into the corner of the narrow space, both of us completely out of view of the front door. "I'm a little busy right now."

By the ambient light from the power buttons on the PA system, I could just see Chung Hee's eyes grow wide as he realized we weren't afraid of the police.

From beyond the alcove, a metallic clank as the dead bolt unlocked.

The blinds on the door rattled. Then, humid air and the muted noise of a city late at night filtered through the empty bar. Tires on rain-slicked asphalt, engines humming on the interstate a few blocks away.

"Hey, guys. How y'all doing?" Piper's cheerful but muffled voice followed by the door shutting behind her as she went outside to talk to the police.

Chung Hee struggled, made a huffing noise.

I stuck the gun in his mouth a little deeper.

He tried to spit it out.

"Suck, don't blow." I winked. "That's just an expression."

He quit fighting. His nostrils flared with each breath.

I stared into his eyes while straining to hear anything from the front.

Piper was good at this sort of thing. She was ex–law enforcement like myself and could talk the cop talk, put them at ease. Didn't hurt either that she was a hottie. Tall and lean, a body built for Commandment-breaking, she looked like a C-list TV star whose name you couldn't remember, or maybe that porn actress who used to date Charlie Sheen back in the nineties.

We'd be okay. Probably.

The air-conditioner kicked on. A bead of perspiration trickled down the small of my back. A sour onion smell wafted off of Chung Hee, the sharp tang of fear.

I started counting in my head.

One Mississippi.

Two Mississippi.

At thirty-seven the blinds rattled again and the door opened. Piper, laughing, told an officer to have a nice night.

Footsteps toward the alcove.

"We're good." She stuck her head in.

I pulled the gun from Chung Hee's mouth. He slumped against the wall.

"Back to the matter at hand." Piper flicked on a tiny overhead light and held up another photo of the missing teen. "Are we gonna do this the hard way or the harder way?"

"I pay good money," Chung Hee said. "Sinclair take every month."

I shook my head, cursed softly.

"Oh, swell," Piper groaned.

Sinclair. The guy who hired us to find Lisa.

- CHAPTER THREE -

Piper and I stood on either side of Chung Hee as he entered a code into the keypad by the front door of the modeling studio.

We were outside, at the rear of the karaoke bar. A light rain continued to fall, coating the city in an oily sheen that hid the decay. This section of the strip center was not visible from the street. The heavy metal barrier clicked open, and the three of us stepped into the foyer.

One way to describe a whorehouse in the Korean part of Dallas would be to talk about the visuals.

The garish red drapes against milk-white, cheaply textured Sheetrock walls. The purple neon that served as molding. Behind the battered Office Depot desk hung a black velvet painting of a naked, apparently Hispanic, Pamela Anderson embracing a tiger.

But the things you could see didn't quite capture the essence of the place as well as what you could smell. This strange combination of tobacco smoke, incense, bleach, and what must have been gallons of cheap perfume, all layered over the faint stench of a locker room.

The pungent aroma of a working brothel.

An Asian woman about forty, a manager/madam type, sat behind the desk. Obviously, we'd encountered each other in the past because she jumped up and called my name.

"Jon Cantrell." She threw an ashtray at my face. "You motherflocker."

The ashtray sailed past me and hit Chung Hee in the nose. He fell to the floor.

"Hello, Sunshine." I aimed my pistol at her. "We've met before, right?"

The woman reached toward an open drawer.

Piper, gun up, flanked to one side and moved in fast. She kicked the drawer shut.

"Easy there, Miss Kitty." She pulled a set of handcuffs from her belt. "Hands on top of your head."

The madam dashed for the door.

Piper was quicker. She holstered her piece on the run, tackled the woman, and handcuffed her in one fluid motion.

I slapped my bracelets on the battered Chung Hee, left him on the floor by the woman.

"She a friend of yours?" Piper pointed to the madam and joined me by the desk.

"We went to different high schools together." I sat down and looked at a yellow pad sitting by a cell phone.

"Jon Cantrell, you big time in trouble." The woman lifted her head from the floor and stared at me. "We pay. No hassle."

"Yeah, yeah. Heard that already." I flipped through the pages. Korean writing and the occasional series of numbers that meant nothing to me.

Piper knelt by our two prisoners. "Where's Lisa?"

The woman spat on the floor.

"Last door on left." Chung Hee smiled, eager to please now.

The madam muttered a few words in Korean, not a happy tone. She looked my way, gave me the stink eye. "You not remember me, Jon Cantrell?"

I shook my head. Scrolled through the call index on the woman's cell phone. Empty.

"You mess with my girls last year," she said. "Claim you a cop."

A vague recollection skittered across my mind and then was gone. The secrets and lies, the people and places, the busts and the busted, all of it ran together.

"That was in Fort Worth." The madam laughed. "You cop here too?"

"How many providers working right now?" I stood. "And how many customers back there?"

"Only two on tonight," Chung Hee said. "No customers right now."

Piper turned to the door behind the desk, the only other exit from the room.

"Wait up." I motioned for her to stop and knelt by the madam. "I remember you now."

The woman on the floor didn't speak.

"One of your girls was overdosing," I said. "I took her to the ER."

The madam shifted her gaze to me and then to the floor. She didn't say anything.

Piper opened the door.

"That girl you call ambulance for," the madam said. "You take good earner. She never come back to work." She paused. "See you around, Jon Cantrell."

I stood and followed Piper into a hall lit only by purple neon. The smell was stronger here. Bad jazz played in the background, like the soundtrack to a 1970s X-rated film.

The last door on the left was half open.

The room was painted cherry red. A black futon on one wall, a dresser on the other. Candles and incense burned on a small table in the corner.

A girl who appeared to be in her teens or early twenties lay on the futon, eyes closed. She wore enough makeup to make Tammy Faye Bakker look like a granola-crunching atheist, and a pink bustier and matching panties.

I compared the photo to her sleeping figure. A pretty close resemblance but hard to be certain under all the makeup. I turned on a penlight, gave her face a closer scrutiny. The nose and dimpled chin were similar enough to be a match. We'd found Lisa Sanders.

Piper sat beside the girl, touched her wrist.

Lisa stirred but didn't wake. Under the glare of the flashlight, she appeared younger than her years but older at the same time.

"She's stoned." Piper held up an amber plastic bottle she'd taken from underneath a pillow. "Opie-dopies."

"Let's get her out of here." I found a robe crumpled in the corner, tossed it on the futon.

Opie-dopies was the street name for a new form of opioid-based painkillers, like Oxycontin but stronger.

"Rise and shine." Piper slapped the girl a couple of times, gentle blows to the cheek.

Lisa licked her lips but didn't open her eyes.

"I remember being this age." Piper propped the girl up, slid an arm into the robe.

I helped with the other side, recollected back to my own teen years. At this girl's age, I'd spent a great deal of time helping my old man track down my mother. Lots of bars and head shops. At least I'd had a father and a mother.

"The court put me with this foster family in Conroe." Piper pulled the girl to her feet. "I'd just started to develop, if you know what I mean."

"Piper." I shook my head. "Leave it alone."

"I shared a room with these two girls from a polygamist family." She cinched the robe around Lisa's waist. "The foster dad started in on the older one first."

I shook my head, made a *shh* sound, soft as the night, tried to derail what was coming next. To no avail.

She shoved Lisa into my arms. "I'm gonna shoot Chung Hee in the crotch."

"No." I grabbed her wrist. "Let's just get the girl out of here."

Lisa stirred, murmured something. Eyelids fluttered.

"Okay, Jon. We'll get her out of here." Piper relaxed, nodding slowly. "We'll take her back to Sinclair, the cop who gets paid off so this place can stay open." She paused. "You want to explain that to me?"

I had no answer.

Together, we carried the fourteen-year-old girl out the back door and into the humid night.

- CHAPTER FOUR -

The hunger gnawed at him, but he didn't eat.

Instead, Senator Stephen McNally pushed away the cold chicken salad and listened to his legislative aide deliver the bad news.

Food held no interest for the Senator. His hunger was of a different stripe, an empty spot in the soul, a burning at the base of his belly that couldn't be slaked by bits of lettuce and grilled meat.

The obsession to win.

In moments like these, Senator McNally hated the craving for success even as he realized he owed his life's achievements to the insatiable desire.

The aide, a smarmy young man prone to wearing bow ties, ran down the list of McNally's colleagues and how they had voted on Senate Bill 994, a modest piece of legislation to which McNally had added a small amendment.

"The Workaholic Senator," that's what the press called him. Certainly fit the current circumstances. Sunday night, nearly Monday, and he was still in his mahogany-paneled office on the third floor of the Hart Senate Office Building on Constitution Avenue, a few hundred yards away from the Capitol.

While the young man droned on, Senator McNally slipped on the cowboy boots he'd removed earlier in the evening.

The boots had been custom-made for him back home, Leddy's in Fort Worth, black snakeskin lowers with matching calfskin uppers. For a Texas politician, they were a cliché, but he didn't care. They were comfortable and stood the test of time, much like his Brioni suits and rose gold Patek Philippe wristwatch. He could afford the best in life, so why not buy it.

The legislative aide finished his report with this summation: SB 994—a highway appropriations request—had failed because of the Senator's addition, a tiny attempt at immigration reform that had earned the enmity of the other Texas senator, heretofore considered an ally, as well as representatives from several other border states.

"The amendment," the aide said. "It was, uh, politically unpalatable."

"Sometimes the right thing isn't the most popular."

The Senator tightened his tie, yanking on the silk, the need to win merging into a low, familiar rage that made his movements jerky.

All the horse-trading he'd done and promises he'd made, assured he would have the votes, only to have SB 994 die because it was *politically unpalatable* to certain fringe elements.

"You know how many underage girls move across international borders every year for the sex business?" McNally took a deep breath, willed himself calm.

"No." The aide shook his head.

The amendment would have automatically given a visa to anyone under the age of eighteen who claimed to be the victim of sex trafficking. The barricade-the-border crowd saw this codicil as a backdoor way to let illegal immigrants stay in the United States.

"The UN estimates around five hundred thousand," McNally said. "But that's based on the FBI's data, which even they admit isn't very accurate. The real number's almost certainly a lot higher."

The aide shrugged, interested only in the abstract, as the young often are.

"Half million or a half dozen," the Senator said. "Doesn't matter too much if you're one of 'em."

"Sir." The aide looked at his watch. "The best political move right now would be to direct your legislative efforts toward the War on Drugs initiatives a-a-and . . ."

The aide's words died on his lips as the Senator fixed him with the blue-eyed, granite stare that made powerful men around the world stammer like school kids.

The border between the United States and Mexico was the hot-button issue this election cycle. Smugglers from either side had made it porous—guns and ammunition going south; drugs and illegal immigrants going north; truckloads of cash headed in both directions. Then there were the never-ending skirmishes between law enforcement and cartel soldiers, gun battles that increasingly were fought on the sovereign soil of the United States.

But if there was one area where no one questioned Senator McNally's intentions, it was the War on Drugs, especially when it came to controlling the border.

Control was everything.

Control would stop the flow of narcotics and enable commerce to thrive, something that would benefit everybody, from the lower-income people on either side of the Rio Grande to the small business owners and ranchers decimated by a decade of drug violence.

SB 994 was the first of McNally's many planned efforts at reasserting control over the border.

And it had failed. And that made Senator Stephen J. McNally angry.

"I, uh, I'm sorry, sir." The aide closed his file. "Will that be all?"

"Yeah, we're done for tonight." The Senator turned off his stare, smiled tightly. "On your way out, tell Patrick to have my private car sent around."

"Your security detail won't like that." The aide stood.

McNally tossed his salad in the wastebasket but didn't reply.

"Before I go, we should talk about your schedule tomorrow." The aide reached for his coat, yawning. "You've got a committee meeting in the morning and then—"

"Fuck the schedule." The Senator stood and slipped the phone in his pocket, aware of the anger smoldering deep inside, a cold burn that made his limbs tingle.

The young aide paused, coat half on, a look of astonishment on his face. The Senator rarely swore.

The Senator didn't care that he'd shocked the young man. He didn't drink or smoke, gamble, or cheat on his wife of nearly four decades. His one passion in life—some might say his vice—was making deals, bringing two sides together to the mutual benefit of both. This passion had allowed him to amass a sizable fortune before entering politics in his later years.

The overwhelming desire to win, ingrained into his DNA, also meant that he hated when transactions failed to come together.

Therefore, he was going to have to make the deal in a different way.

Stopping the flow of children destined for the sex business was just a single aspect, albeit an important one, of his goals for the border.

The aide hurriedly gathered his things and left the room.

Senator McNally watched him go. When he was alone, he pulled an envelope from the top drawer of his desk.

McNally was from North Texas, but he owned a ranch south of San Antonio, a relatively small spread by the standards of the region, about 9,500 acres, a place he used mainly for deer hunting and to escape the glare and soul-numbing grind of DC.

Eighteen months ago, he'd learned firsthand how porous the border was, images he still couldn't shake from his mind.

He'd been alone, meandering in his pickup down a narrow dirt road, a rarely visited section of the ranch, something he did when he needed time and space to think.

In an area where the ranch road veered near the two-lane, farm-to-market highway that bordered his property, he'd rounded a bend and encountered a dust-covered van parked beneath a palm tree.

Two girls stood in the open door of the van. Twins, aged eleven he later learned, from Guanajuato. Their mother was dead. Their father had sold them to satisfy a debt.

One of them was naked, bleeding from places people in polite society didn't talk about. The other girl stood next to her sister, a protective arm around her shoulder.

The Senator stopped, aghast. He reached for his ranch radio and the Smith & Wesson revolver he always brought along during rides around the property.

A man in his late twenties was in the back of the van, lying against a duffel bag full of tidy, plastic-wrapped packages shaped like bricks. He was in a bad way, maybe thirty minutes away from dying as a result of a rattlesnake bite, a not uncommon hazard in the region.

The man was a driver for one of the smuggling operations, a disposable piece of the cartel infrastructure. His shipment contained two items: forty kilos of marijuana, and a pair of prepubescent girls destined for a brothel somewhere on the East Coast. Unfortunately for the latter, he'd decided to sample one of the girls before delivery. Too bad he'd been bitten *after* his abuse of the child.

Senator Stephen J. McNally was an honest individual, hard as iron when it came to business and money, but still fundamentally a player who obeyed the rules of the game. Of course, when your net worth approached the billion-dollar mark, your rules tended to be a little different than those of other people.

Which was why he felt absolutely zero remorse as he watched the trafficker die and made no effort to call the authorities or ease his suffering.

As the man shivered and begged for water—poison from a rattlesnake bite causes a terrible thirst—McNally used the ranch radio to summon his foreman and the foreman's wife, two kind-hearted people who'd been in his employ for years and whom he trusted completely.

While the foreman's wife tended to the immediate needs of the girls, McNally had knelt in front of the smuggler and slowly sipped from a bottle of water. Every few seconds, he held the container in front of the dying man's face, ignoring his pleas for a taste. He tried to fathom the child's terror as she begged the smuggler not to violate her.

When there was about an inch of water left in the bottle, McNally stepped out of the van and made sure the smuggler was watching as he dumped the rest of the liquid in the dirt.

The smuggler died a few minutes later.

The foreman's wife took the girls back to the ranch house while her husband and McNally buried the body of the trafficker in the dusty South Texas soil. They left the van and the bricks of marijuana sitting under the palm tree.

Back at his ranch house, McNally had placed a series of phone calls on a secure line. The first had been to the chief of staff at the Department of Immigration and Customs Enforcement, a golfing buddy. Then, he'd called the head of the FBI, followed by an attorney in Houston who specialized in private adoptions.

The Senator's wealth, political power, and implication that national security was involved meant that by that evening he'd taken legal custody of the two girls, and all the papers were sealed.

After that came a small team of psychologists and doctors from nearby Laughlin Air Force Base in Del Rio, summoned to the ranch by a late Saturday afternoon email from a two-star general at the Pentagon.

McNally's final call had been to the local sheriff, telling him that one of the Senator's hired hands had found a strange van and could the sheriff please come and investigate. The local authorities arrived at dusk, confiscated the van and its contents, and filed the appropriate paperwork with the federal agencies.

And that was that. The end for one particular cartel shipment, a tiny loss that had little direct effect on the organization's bottom line but a huge impact on the way a certain senator from Texas viewed the border.

Now, a year and a half later, the girls were doing well, all things considered. They lived with a family in Virginia, their adoptive father a vice president at one of McNally's banks.

The Senator snapped out of the memory of that day as the door leading into his office opened without a knock, and Patrick Hawkins, his chief of staff, entered.

"You done jacking around with that pussy you call a legislative aide?" Hawkins scratched his crotch with one hand, an absent-minded gesture.

Senator McNally detested the man, as did most people.

Patrick Hawkins was mean and arrogant, loud and foulmouthed, completely amoral. Physically, he was repulsive, blotchy skin, overweight, red-rimmed eyes that were too close together like a rat's. He wore out-of-fashion clothes bought from discount stores and bathed infrequently.

But Hawkins had one of the best political minds in DC, the ability to think three steps ahead of most people, and the ruthlessness to use that skill to crush those that got in his way.

"You don't have to go to the meeting." Hawkins stood in front of the Senator's desk. "Just give me the envelope."

Senator McNally shook his head. "I don't do business without talking to the principals."

"This isn't a hostile takeover of IBM," Hawkins said. "It's just another consulting firm."

The envelope contained a contract between McNally's campaign and the Manzanares Political Consulting Group, a San Diego–based firm specializing in Latino affairs, according to their brochure.

McNally felt tired suddenly, a rare moment of self-doubt. "Where's their office?"

"They're new to DC," Hawkins said. "Got temporary space. North of here, I think."

The Senator didn't reply.

Hawkins sighed. "You're the one who wanted a face-to-face."

"We better get on the road." McNally buttoned his suit coat and felt the hunger lessen just a bit.

A deal was at hand.

- CHAPTER FIVE -

I watched the rain clouds drift away and reveal a moonless sky, dull stars shrouded by smog and the humid atmosphere.

Dallas was a jewel of sorts, a concrete diamond or perhaps a glass emerald, fashioned from brick and sheetrock and a million or so acres of St. Augustine grass, lushly green from too much fertilizer.

Dallas was brilliant gray, dull yellow, and darkly brittle, all at the same time. Fissured through with shiny glass and chrome plating.

At night, the city glowed from the neon-covered bars and the artfully designed lights on the skyscrapers. In the day, she burned with a relentless heat from the near-tropical sun and the troubled energy of her inhabitants, the latter scorching those who got too close to the dark places, the secluded sections of town that made the city tick.

I liked to think of myself as her jeweler, tasked with rooting out the imperfections, correcting the flaws. In rare moments, I recognized the problems inherent in this outlook: in order to do a proper job, shouldn't I also clean the debris from my own psyche, polish the jagged edges of the empty spot at the core of my being? This, I was unable or unwilling to do. Sometimes, usually in periods of extreme stress, I wondered why.

Piper and I helped Lisa into the backseat of the Tahoe that we'd left parked on a side street off of Harry Hines Boulevard, the main drag in Korea Town.

The neighborhood was just inside the inner loop formed by LBJ Freeway, an edgy mix of blue-collar bars and Asian discount stores, places that sold off-brand perfume, leather goods, and cell-phone accessories. In any given block, you could find a meth dealer, a craps game, or a fake Louis Vuitton purse. Or a hooker.

I drove to an all-night Hispanic grocery about a half mile south, across the street from a biker bar where my mom used to score weed back in the day.

On the side of the building by the Dumpsters, I chased off a couple of winos and dug some change from my jeans.

Pay phones were fewer and fewer in the cellular era, but if you dealt with Sinclair, you had to know their remaining locations. I dialed a series of digits from memory, hoping I got it right. Another by-product of the times: who remembers numbers anymore?

A police car passed us, headed north. Rainwater feathered off the back tires.

After three rings, a woman answered. She told me an address and then hung up.

I got back in the Tahoe. The address was on the far east side of town near White Rock Lake, a quiet residential lane called Tranquilla Drive. No traffic this time of night, so we made good time, Piper dozing in the passenger seat.

After about fifteen minutes, Lisa stirred, sat up.

Piper woke at the sound and turned around. "You okay?"

"Where are we?" The girl rubbed her face.

"You're going home," I said.

No response. In the rearview mirror, I could see her eyes get big. And scared.

"You feeling all right?" Piper said.

"Who are you guys?"

"We were hired to get you out of that place," I said.

"My mom. Is she okay?"

I shrugged, exited the freeway at Garland Road.

"We don't know anything about that." Piper glanced at me, an eyebrow raised.

"She's got the lymphoma pretty bad." Lisa stared out the window. After a few miles, she said, "I don't want to go home. My stepdad's such a jerk."

"Nobody's gonna hurt you," Piper said. "We promise."

I started to say something but didn't.

My partner was writing checks we couldn't cover. Our assignment was to get the girl out of the whorehouse, period.

"I was on the street at about your age," Piper said. "You thought it was gonna be better than what you left at home, didn't you?"

The girl made a sound like a sob but not quite.

"Hard to say what's worse." Piper sighed. "The frying pan or the son of a bitch who's stoking the fire."

Nobody spoke.

"The street and places like that, uh, modeling studio." Piper looked in the rear. "That's no kind of life. You understand what I'm saying?"

The girl didn't reply. Piper smiled, reached over the seat and patted her knee. Then she turned back around.

A few minutes later, I said, "You know a guy named Sinclair?"

In the rearview mirror, the girl wiped her eyes and nodded.

"He hired us," Piper said.

"He's my mama's cousin." Lisa stared out the window as the night drifted by. "Takes care of us sometimes when the money gets tight."

I stopped at a light.

"Are you gonna tell Mama about where you found me?" Lisa said.

Piper shook her head. "That's nobody's business but yours."

But we will tell Sinclair about your stepdad, I thought. No sense putting you back in the same situation that caused the problem in the first place.

"Don't even know how I ended up at that place." Lisa bit her lip. Her voice choked with emotion. "I just—I don't know."

The light changed to green, and I pulled away as the girl began to cry again.

- CHAPTER SIX -

Ten minutes later, we arrived at the address.

The street felt almost rural, no curbs or sidewalks but lots of trees towering over low-slung, ranch-style homes on half-acre lots. The cars in the driveways, sometimes a better demographic indicator than the homes themselves, were solidly middle class. Chevys and Hondas, Camrys and minivans.

No lights on except at our destination.

I parked in the driveway behind a Mercedes and two late-model Cadillacs, the only luxury vehicles on the block. Across the street sat a pair of Dallas police cars, empty and dark.

We helped Lisa out and walked her up the sidewalk to the unlocked front door. Inside, a tiny entryway was between a dining room to the right and a small living area to the left. Both rooms were empty, outfitted in the finest furnishings that Sears had to offer circa 1975. The house felt like no one lived there but was occupied nonetheless.

From the rear of the home, down a darkened hallway, came the sound of laughter and men talking amid the soft clink of poker chips. A faint odor of cigar smoke hung in the air.

I glanced around, waited, and a few moments later a

figure appeared from the shadows of the hall.

One of Sinclair's senior flunkies, a slab of gristle named Tommy, part of a motley assortment of lowlifes and ex-police officers usually a couple of hearings away from indictment.

Tommy stunk of cop, the bad kind. He was in his early thirties, about six-five, and carried himself with the air of one who likes to slap around crack whores for fun. He wore Oakley sunglasses even inside, and sported a quarter-inch buzz haircut at odds with his bushy Fu Manchu mustache.

I nodded hello but didn't speak.

He ignored me and Piper and stared at our passenger.

"You must be Lisa," he said. "They were worried about you."

Lisa took a half a step behind Piper but didn't say anything.

"Where's Sinclair?" I said.

"He'll be along. What's your rush?" He sauntered into the dining area and tapped on the door leading to the kitchen. His biceps and shoulders were ropy with muscles, straining the thin material of his Dallas Mavericks T-shirt.

A haggard-looking woman in her forties stepped into the room, clutching a cell phone. She wore blue polyester pants and a platinum-colored wig, her face pale and unhealthy-looking.

Lisa and the woman let out simultaneous cries of joy and ran to each other's arms. After a few moments, they disappeared through the dining room into the kitchen, arm in arm, mother and daughter reunited.

Tommy nodded and smiled. He ran a hand over his Fu Manchu mustache and dabbed the corner of his mouth with his tongue.

Piper stood next to me, hands loose by her side but slightly raised, her guard not down even a little. Tommy had that effect on people.

"You're the find-it man." He nodded toward the kitchen. "Good at it, from what I see."

I shrugged. "It helps when you know the address where to look."

"What about you?" He leered at Piper. "You good at anything special?"

Before she could answer, our employer for the evening emerged from the rear of the house.

Sinclair was in his early sixties with thick mutton chops and a Johnny Cash pompadour dyed the color of original sin, an inky black. A mustache of the same hue but as thin as a piece of string grew just above his upper lip.

"Hear you gave ole Chung Hee a nice little tune-up." He held out an envelope. "I oughta deduct some for his dental work."

The accent was Texas trailer park, as thick as a slab of smoked brisket.

He wore an XXXL beige guayabera shirt that was stretched tight across his girth, shiny gray gabardine trousers, and lizard skin boots with pointy toes.

"The first time you've ever paid full retail." I grabbed the package, tossed it to Piper. "And now you want to renegotiate the fee."

Sinclair was a notorious tightwad. The amount he'd offered seemed high. We should have expected this.

"Never mind." He crossed his arms over his gut. "Money ain't no object when it comes to family."

Tommy licked his mustache and stared at Piper.

"It's all there." She handed me the envelope.

I sat down at the table, put the packet of cash in front of me.

"You expecting dinner?" Sinclair said.

"Up yours, fat man." Piper moved to a corner of the

room, a good vantage point to keep an eye on both entrances and Tommy.

"The mouth on this one." Sinclair sat across from me, shook his head.

Tommy stood motionless with his back to the wall, eyes half closed like he was dozing.

"About tonight," I said. "You didn't tell us everything."

"Like what?" Sinclair pulled a thin cigar with a plastic tip from his pocket and stuck it between his lips.

"Like you're the bagman for that part of town," Piper said.

"I got a lot of business interests that don't concern you." He lit the cigar with a battered Zippo. "Puts food on the table."

"You could have gotten her yourself," I said.

"Chung Hee knows my guys." Sinclair leaned back in his chair. "What are you complaining for? You got paid."

I paused for a moment, trying for a little dramatic effect, and then stuck the money in my pocket. "Don't jack us over the details like that again."

Sinclair could best be described as a snake, except that was unfair to the reptiles of this world. He needed a mild rebuke every now and again in order to keep his fangs in check.

"Or what?" Sinclair chuckled. "You'll quit bugging me for piecemeal jobs?"

I didn't say anything. Neither Piper nor I wanted to do assignments for Sinclair, lying with dogs and fleas and all that. But you have to eat and pay the bills.

"Speaking of jobs," he said, "you remember that warehouse I told you about?"

Sinclair liked to pass on information from time to time in regard to our regular gig. His endgame was always unclear and something I never wanted to know too much about. But the intel he produced was always first-rate.

I nodded.

"Word on the street is it's gonna be up and running pretty soon."

"So I've heard," I said. "We've got that covered."

The warehouse, a way station for contraband, was in our sights already. It was something Sinclair and I both wanted taken out, though for different reasons I suspected. Piper and I were just waiting for confirmation on when it would be operational.

"You sure?" Sinclair said.

"Positive."

People loved to talk, especially when the right leverage was applied. The warehouse was as much of a lock as anything could ever be in our world.

Sinclair smiled for the first time that night.

Footsteps from the hallway.

We all looked up as two uniformed Dallas police officers stopped in the doorway between the foyer and the dining room. Sinclair stood and greeted them. They looked familiar, but both made a point of not noticing me.

Sinclair pulled another envelope from underneath his shirt and gave it to the older of the two cops. "A little something for the coffee pot back at the station house."

"Thanks, Captain." The officer touched the brim of his cap with a forefinger.

After the two policemen had left, Piper said, "You still on the job?"

"Not no more. But once blue, always blue." He stuck the cigar back in his mouth and looked at me. "How's your daddy doing, Jon?"

Nobody spoke for a few moments, an awkward silence.

"Damn shame how that all played out." Sinclair shifted the smoke from one corner of his mouth to the other. "Give him my best. He was a good sheriff, a lawman's lawman."

I nodded, not speaking.

Damn shame was one way to put it.

Sheriffs were elected in Texas, and ten years ago a half kilo of cocaine turned up in the trunk of my old man's squad car a month before the election, an obvious plant.

His long and venerated career in law enforcement kept him from prison, but his days in law enforcement were over, a fact he accepted with his usual stoicism. Underneath his weathered features, the pain was evident to those who knew him, the damaged reputation, the loss of the only occupation he'd ever held, the only thing that mattered. He'd known all along that the job generated enemies, political opponents and others with a vested interest in seeing certain laws enforced in a certain way. He just never imagined they would go that far.

"Let's get." Piper grabbed my arm, propelled me toward the door.

"Wait." Sinclair came up behind us, carrying a shoe box. He handed it to me. Tommy had moved into the hallway as well, watching us depart.

I opened the container and saw a gray plastic device that looked like a radar gun, a pistol grip attached to a tube about the size of a potato chip canister.

The muzzle end had a dish antenna about three inches in diameter. The body had a keypad on top with an LCD screen on the rear, canted at an angle for comfortable reading. Scorch marks ran along one side of the tube. The box smelled like a house fire, acrid and toxic.

"One of my boys found this," he said. "Along with some other stuff."

"What is it?" Piper said.

"Beats me." He shook his head. "But I don't want nothing electronic like that."

Sinclair didn't own a cell phone or a computer. Didn't email. He used pay phones, safe houses, and cutout men to conduct his business, relying on blood kin as intermediaries more often than not.

"Why're you giving it to me?" I said.

"I thought maybe you could sell it." He shrugged. "I'll take a cut of course."

Piper and I weren't fences. We did have certain connections to the federal law enforcement community, direct lines to people who might pay a reward to get something like this—whatever it was—off the street.

"Whatever you do with it," he said, "I wouldn't go turning it on."

"It's a cold day on the Redneck Riviera when I give you a cut of anything." I tucked the box under my arm.

Sinclair shrugged. "Can't blame a body for trying."

"You know why the girl ran away?" I nodded toward the kitchen where Lisa had gone with her mother.

Sinclair didn't answer.

"The stepdad. Not a good situation."

"Never liked that son of a bitch." Sinclair shook his head. "I'll take care of it. Don't you worry."

I opened the door. Piper followed me out. Back in the Tahoe, I started the engine and stared at the dim lights of Sinclair's poker house. The rain started again, a hard drizzle, tiny pellets tapping on the hood of the SUV.

"We gonna sit here all night?" Piper said.

I blinked, erased from my imagination what I had hoped to see, a fourteen-year-old girl with a freshly washed face peering outside.

Instead, Tommy and his bushy Fu Manchu mustache appeared. He stared into the rainy night for a few moments before he shut the curtains. The light went out in the kitchen, and the rain fell harder.

I put the transmission in gear and drove away.

- CHAPTER SEVEN -

Sinclair locked the dead bolt on the front door after the last player left.

The rain had slackened, now just a humid mist that blanketed the city. The darkness promised a hot day when the sun rose, the moisture baking from the damp ground, a dirty, smog-filled steam bath. The month of August made Dallas her bitch, and everybody suffered.

Nobody was left in the house on Tranquilla Drive but a handful of his guards straightening things up and his number two man, Tommy, ridiculous looking in that stupid mustache he insisted on wearing.

Lisa and her mother had been driven home by a uniformed officer, one who owed his continued employment with the Dallas police to the long reach of retired Captain Sinclair. The officer had been given instructions—if Lisa's stepdad was there, feel free to use the billy club.

Sinclair scooped up a stray beer bottle from the floor, tossed it in the garbage.

The city was a gambler's town, built upon the fruits of oil and real estate, two legal, socially sanctioned forms of wagering. Dallas possessed the soul of a showgirl leering over a roulette wheel, waiting to see what turn lady luck would bring.

On any given night there were hundreds of poker tables operating somewhere in the city. Dollar-ante, bring-your-own-malt-liquor games in South Dallas. Soul-patch-wearing hipsters in Uptown, drinking Belgian ale as they sweated the river card on a twenty-buck pot.

The unoccupied but tidy brick home on Tranquilla Drive housed one of about a dozen games Sinclair ran on a weekly basis. Not his most profitable, not his least. The Tranquilla tables were his lowest profile, thus where he spent a lot of time.

He lumbered into the counting room, a bedroom off the kitchen with blackout drapes on the windows and a set of monitors on one wall that showed the surrounding yard and street.

Tommy followed him and stood against the wall, his usual position for the night's count.

A table and a single chair sat in the middle of the room. The furniture had no drawers, no places to hide anything. In the middle of the table sat a pile of rumpled currency, the house cut for the evening. Sinclair locked the door. He sat down and began to sort the money, entering coded notations on a yellow pad.

Ten minutes later he was done. Considering the economy, it was not a small figure, until you factored in the overhead—the booze and food and payroll required to keep an illegal poker game in operation and safe from robbery.

Fortunately, he had other, much more lucrative endeavors in place, businesses that paid extremely well. Unfortunately, with more money came more risk.

The bigger the pot of gold, the more lowlifes out there looking to steal from you. The less obvious hazards were the intangibles, the people who talked too much, the loose ends that needed tidying up for whatever reason.

He needed Cantrell and his little split-tail Piper to take down the warehouse he'd mentioned. They didn't need to know why he wanted it done, or what other business needed doing there. Sinclair didn't want anybody to know about that other business except his closest associate, Tommy.

As if on cue, Tommy tossed a canvas sack on the table.

"I could load up a couple of the boys," he said. "We could take care of the whole thing for you."

Sinclair ignored his underling. The first part would be done by Cantrell and Piper. That was the safest way. He shoveled money into the bag.

Tommy was good at lots of stuff, muscle and loyalty being his two best assets. Unfortunately, extensive brainpower and strategic thinking were not on the list. Tommy, bless his heart, just couldn't quite grasp that the task needed to be kept a secret from their own people.

"The boys." Tommy paused. "You ought to know that they're talking."

Sinclair stopped putting money in the sack. "And exactly what are the boys saying?"

Tommy didn't speak. He scratched his mustache, stared at the floor.

Sinclair's eyes narrowed. A jolt of anger coursed through his gut. He wasn't used to people not answering him.

"The girl at the whorehouse, your cousin's kid." Tommy looked up. "The boys are wondering why you didn't send somebody from our organization to get her back."

Sinclair stifled the ire rising in his stomach. He'd tried earlier to explain it all to Tommy but to no avail.

He didn't use his own crew because he wanted to have a reason for Jon Cantrell to come to his poker house.

He needed to look Cantrell in the eye and hear his voice in person when he asked him about the warehouse. He wanted to know for sure that Cantrell was on track to take down the building. Based on what he'd seen tonight, he felt certain Cantrell was going to deliver.

"How come the boys got time to wonder about stuff like that?" he said. "Receipts're way down. They ought to be hustling, not thinking about shit that don't matter to them."

"C'mon, boss. You know the economy's in the dumper." Tommy shrugged. "People ain't betting like they used to."

"Then people ought to be borrowing more money. Or screwing more of our girls."

Tommy looked back at the floor.

Sinclair was an entrepreneur, a capitalist who made his living by exploiting the weaknesses associated with human desires. One thing decades on the Dallas police force had taught him: the weakness remained constant no matter what the personal cost or economic climate. Receipts were down because his people had gotten lazy.

"You haven't told the boys anything, have you?" Sinclair stood.

Tommy shook his head.

Sinclair closed the canvas sack. His hand shook slightly. He hoped his employee didn't notice.

"There's a fifty-thousand-dollar bounty," Tommy said. "They're gonna hear about that eventually."

Tommy was referring to the reward being offered for a certain item that would be at the warehouse. That other business that would follow Cantrell's business.

"I'll get it, um, her before then." Sinclair stuck the sack under his arm.

The item was a person, a woman.

"But what if you don't?" Tommy said. "What if Cantrell and that little slutbag screw it up?"

Sinclair didn't reply. The room was cool, but a trickle of sweat meandered down the small of his back.

The woman would be in the drug warehouse Jon Cantrell and Piper were set to take down, held captive along with the illegal contents of the building.

When they found the drugs, they would find the woman.

The woman was rumored to have turned state's witness. Unaccountably, she'd been walking around free on bond, an ankle-tracking device her only guard, awaiting arraignment in San Antonio and then transport to West Texas, when she'd disappeared a few days ago.

The event that had caused Sinclair's already-high blood pressure to skyrocket. The trial involved one of the bigger and more deadly border cartels, a fact that neither Sinclair nor Tommy could bring themselves to discuss openly. Even hard men who prided themselves on being fearless had things that caused their stomachs to clench and palms to get sweaty.

Plus there were other forces at work, individuals and agendas that Tommy didn't know about and wouldn't begin to understand. Even if the threat of the cartels magically disappeared, Sinclair would still have to find the witness because these others wanted her located as well.

Sinclair tried to control the tremor in his hands. "Cantrell's a pro. This is what he does."

"We better hope so," Tommy said. "The US Marshals, they're gonna put the word out on the street pretty soon."

Sinclair groaned, tried to keep his cool.

"That much money," Tommy said. "People'll be tripping over each other looking for her."

Sinclair nodded but didn't say anything.

A measly fifty K from the Marshals. He'd pay more than that to get the witness. He'd pay every dime to his name; he had no choice. If he didn't silence the woman, he'd have to pay an even bigger price—his life.

The woman had been kidnapped by a rival cartel because the information she possessed—smuggling routes, safe house locations, code words—was as valuable to another criminal organization as it was to the US government. She was being moved northward, as far away from the border as possible, bundled up with a shipment of contraband. Sinclair knew all this because it was his business to know, a result of his lucrative but risky sideline endeavor.

Since the rival cartel used Dallas as a transportation hub (as they all did), moving product up Interstate 35 for distribution outward like spokes on a wheel, she would soon be in Sinclair's area of operation.

He could have his people get her, of course, just like they could have gotten his cousin's kid back from the Korean pimp. He knew the roads that would be taken, the secret locations used. But to get his people involved would be an admission that the woman had some sort of power over Sinclair's organization, almost as bad as letting her talk in open court.

Plus, there was the danger that came from trying to intercept the kidnappers, soldiers hired especially by the narcotraffickers for their willingness to kill anything that got in the way. Tangling with a crew of cartel gunmen was like wrestling a live electrical wire in a swimming pool full of sharks.

His men would be well aware of the danger, as was Tommy, the one person in his operation with whom he'd trusted a portion of the information about the witness.

Jon Cantrell was aware of the danger, too, but it didn't matter. Cantrell was paid, by Uncle Sam no less, to do very dangerous things.

Such as go into a place full of cartel soldiers.

Sinclair pulled a slip of paper from his pocket. "Here's the address. When Cantrell hits the place the DPD radios are gonna light up and we'll know about it."

Tommy took the paper with the location, a rough section of the city in West Dallas.

"You and me, we'll slide in at that point," Sinclair said, "and take care of her ourselves. Just the two of us."

Sinclair's plan was simple: Get Cantrell and his little hoe-bag of a partner, Piper, to take down a shipment of drugs where the rival cartel had hidden the witness. Let them discover the woman. Let them lead her out into the open, hand-cuffed, on the way to a squad car.

Then Sinclair and Tommy could take care of her, a sniper rifle and a single shot from across the street.

Just another cartel death, one that couldn't be tracked back to Sinclair or to the people Tommy didn't know about, the ones whose phone calls were becoming increasingly insistent in the past few hours. If any blame were to come from the cartel, it would go straight to Jon Cantrell.

He smiled at the thought, allowed himself to feel hopeful.

One of his men knocked on the door, told him they were leaving for the night. Another set of guards was outside, ready to escort the boss off the premises.

"What's her name?" Tommy said.

Sinclair walked toward the door. "Who?"

"The witness."

"What do you care?"

"No reason. The Marshals didn't release a name, just a description."

"Eva Ramirez." Sinclair aimed his index finger at the wall like a gun. "Bang-bang, Eva. Now, you're dead."

- CHAPTER EIGHT -

Piper and I had met for the first time on a Sunday afternoon about six months ago, in a bar on the west side of town, near Love Field.

We'd both been tailing the same guy, a tax cheat and serial adulterer.

I'd been doing a little scut work for a friend who was a criminal investigator with the IRS; Piper had been working for the wife.

The Time Out Tavern was a dim, narrow place, part sports bar, part neighborhood dive. Blacked-out windows, neon beer signs, a handful of tables, and a half dozen TVs, all tuned to the Cowboys game. Piper and I noticed each other immediately, of course, the only two in the crowded place not swilling beer and watching football.

It was obvious to each of us that we were working the same guy. Equally obvious was that we were different from the good-natured crowd of sports fans. The life we led put an edge on you, an extra line or two around the eyes, a face that didn't smile quite as easily or deeply.

We nodded to each other from across the room, a professional courtesy. Then, from my vantage point at the bar,

I watched the train run off the rails and explode in spectacular glory.

The guy we were tailing, a toddler and a pregnant wife at
home, had been on a date. A buxom blond with rhinestones
embedded in her lacquered nails.

When she went to the restroom, he had turned in his
chair and said something to Piper, who was leaning against a
pool table behind him. They were out of earshot.

Piper replied, a few words, an indifferent shrug.

He downed a shot of peppermint schnapps and spoke
again.

Piper shook her head, frowned.

The guy, eyes a little unfocused at this point, said
something else, a belligerent expression on his face. Then
he downed the blond's shot, reached across the aisle, and
squeezed Piper's left breast.

What happened next occurred so fast that it might have
gone unnoticed except for the fact that the pool cue Piper
hit him with broke in two, and the butt end flew across the
room, crashing into the largest of the televisions.

In the ensuing melee, she looked at me, winked, and
then kneed the barely standing philanderer in the crotch.

I was smitten.

We'd both been flush at the time, lots of hundred dollar
bills as well as various badges and official-looking papers, all
of which had smoothed things over in a hurry.

After the ambulance took the injured cheater away, Piper
and I stood together outside the bar and watched the traffic
on Lovers Lane.

"Not that I give a flip," Piper slid on a pair of Ray-Bans,
"but did I screw up your gig?"

"Nah. It's all good."

The guy was in no shape to be traveling overseas as the

IRS had feared. Her actions had just given me an unexpected holiday.

"So what did he say to you?"

"It involved a menthol cough drop and oral sex." She looked at me over the tops of her sunglasses. "Want to get a cup of coffee and I'll tell you more?"

———

Piper and I currently shared a high-rise condo near the center of town, uneasy roommates for the past month or so.

The relationship had burned like a supernova for a few weeks. Our physical connection had been electric, our street personas similar, a couple of smart-mouthed hustlers who cared not one scintilla for what others thought, wreaking havoc across the slimy parts of Dallas.

But this life of ours didn't make for good relationships.

The life didn't usually admit emotionally balanced people inside either, if the truth were to be told, and we were no exception. Piper was an orphan—literally, raised in a group home and then in a succession of foster situations—and I might as well have been. Not a good combination.

We had access to the condo for another week. The guy on the lease—a colleague of sorts—had died, a fact that the Dallas County coroner would not know for another six days.

The Cheyenne was on Mockingbird Lane near the new George W. Bush Library and Museum at Southern Methodist University. The place started out as a Sheraton but fell on hard times, ending up as the world headquarters of an Indian mystic and then a flophouse.

Since then it had been remodeled into a boutique hotel, marble and sleek wood in the lobby, a brightly lit bar that overlooked a pool and row of cabanas. The rear tower had been converted into condominiums, mostly vacant, which is where we were staying.

I waved to the security guard, parked in the garage, and at one forty-five on a rainy Monday morning we stumbled into our two-bedroom apartment on the tenth floor, a transient's home that had all the warmth of an airport Ramada Inn. Neutral colors, bland furniture. Dull prints on the walls.

Piper went to the fridge and grabbed two Carta Blancas. She opened one for herself, handed me the second bottle.

"Not tonight." I put mine on the counter between the kitchen area and dining room.

"I'm too wired to sleep." She paced, swigging from the bottle as she went.

"We've got stuff to do tomorrow at early thirty." I split Sinclair's money into two equal piles, hers and mine.

"It's one beer." She scooped up her stack. "When'd you go Baptist on me?"

After a moment, I picked up the bottle, opened it, and took a long drink, pondering my cut.

Two thousand dollars. Plus the pair of debit cards that had been intended for Katrina victims before being diverted to other uses, each with about five hundred left. A few changes of clothes in my bedroom and a pile of guns, none of which could be sold legally.

Not much to show for nearly four decades on this earth.

"A guy put me on the street when I was a little older than that girl tonight. Tried to turn me out." Piper picked at the label on her bottle. "He was real scum, used to hang around my foster dad."

I didn't say anything. Late night after a job, Piper could take the conversation several different ways. Best to let her chart the course.

"He carried this .44 derringer in a fanny pack," she said. "Tiny little thing."

"Where was this?" I knew that locations were safe to talk about.

"He took me to Waco," she said. "Girls used to work the bars along La Salle Avenue back then."

I nodded, waiting for the next part of the story.

She let the conversation lapse, staring at a spot on the floor. After a few moments, she took a drink and picked up a glossy folder from the coffee table.

The cover of the folder was a collage of snapshots, professionally executed. The photos were all of kids, toddlers up through elementary school. The children represented a slew of ethnicities, most from various Third World countries with hard-to-pronounce names. They were all devastatingly cute, and, according to the text on the cover, available for "adoption" for the low, low cost of only two dollars per week.

Some people drank and gambled. Others collected stamps or needlepointed. Piper sponsored kids in foreign lands. Lots of them.

"So what happened in Waco?" I risked the question that a month ago wouldn't have been necessary. A month ago we would have talked until the sun came up. But that was a different time, a period before we became frightened of this strange feeling that comes from being emotionally intimate with another human being.

"We fought. Yadda-yadda." She drained her beer. "Anyway—long story short—when he kicked me out of the car, I shot his dick off with the .44."

I winced as the darkness slid across her face. Her eyes grew cloudy, more to the story than I would ever know or she'd be able to tell.

"But then I was still on La Salle Avenue." She shook her head. "And I only had one bullet left."

I knew the look well, from the mirror if nowhere else. The singular events of a life on the edge that are best left unremembered, the ones that scar the soul, that no amount of alcohol or therapy will ever take away. I took a long swig of beer anyway.

Piper slid a photo from the folder. "She's adorable, isn't she? Her name is Hasina."

I took the picture.

Hasina did peg pretty high on the precious meter, like, say, an eleven on a scale of ten. She had skin the color of fresh coffee and eyes full of wonder and hope. She appeared to be looking at something beyond the photographer, an expression of amusement on her face.

The back of the picture said Hasina was twenty-three months old and lived in a Catholic charity ward in Uganda, near the Bokora Wildlife Reserve. She liked dolls and coloring books.

"She's cute." I smiled. "What'd you send her?"

"The usual. Plus some clothes and an extra payment." She paused. "Oh, and a bunch of dolls."

Piper always sent just a little extra, no matter how tight money was or how ludicrous the claims of the charity seemed to be. That was part of my attraction to her, a warm soul underneath a cold and dangerous exterior.

I sensed she wanted to talk more about that night in Waco. So I said, "How long were you stuck on La Salle Avenue?"

Piper stared at me without speaking. Her eyes, normally vibrant and alive, were flat and empty. She stood, sauntered to the picture window that overlooked downtown Dallas, the skyscrapers barely visible through the rain.

The dim, washed-out light of the city at night made her look soft and vulnerable, younger than her years. Innocent.

I took a last sip of beer and put down the bottle.

"People do what they have to do." I walked to the window, stood next to her.

"We need this next score," she said. "It's gonna be big."

"Tomorrow." I nodded. "We get the word on the warehouse, and we'll be good to go."

The warehouse was part of our regular line of work, the taxpayer-supported War on Drugs, not associated with Sinclair.

The warehouse was going to be full of contraband, items that needed to be taken off the street. The building was our savior, a cinder block messiah, potentially the biggest payoff of our career. And what we were going to do at the warehouse was entirely legal, sanctioned by the US government, unlike many of our sideline activities for Sinclair.

Neither of us spoke.

"You and me. What happened?" She crossed her arms but didn't elaborate.

I knew the topic, the words she couldn't say. She wanted to ask about us, the future. Unfortunately that's not a good subject for two live-in-the-moment people mired in the damage of their pasts.

Deep down, I wanted to know about us, too. I yearned as she did for a normalcy that would never be ours. Instead, I tried to think about the next day, not the here and now of our respective dysfunctions.

The rain slackened and the skyline became clearer. Reunion Tower glowed a gossamer green on the west side of downtown.

She turned, grabbed the front of my jeans, pulled me close. I let her.

She pressed our lips together, part kiss, part bite. A hand slipped underneath my shirt, cool fingers against my belly.

"We could get a house somewhere." She nipped my bottom lip. "Get out of the game."

A topic we talked about often, leaving The Life, doing something a little more stable that didn't involve people who carry guns and worry about each day being their last. The sticking point that always seemed to mess things up: leaving The Life *together*.

I responded to her embrace and closed my eyes, luxuriated in the warmth of her flesh against mine, the taste of her skin. Then I stopped. "But somebody would screw it up and then where would we be?" My tone was playful.

"That's a good point." She nuzzled my shoulder, reached for my belt. "One of us would be stuck with a house."

I chuckled softly and slid my hand under her shirt, grasped the smooth, contoured perfection that was the small of her back. We kissed again.

She pulled me toward the bedroom, the only area of the apartment that bore any personal mark of the occupants. Framed snapshots of children in foreign lands had been arranged on the top of the chest of drawers. The kids that she'd sponsored, an even dozen at the moment. Hasina would make thirteen.

I resisted for a moment, then followed her.

- CHAPTER NINE -

Washington, DC, at night never ceased to amaze Senator Stephen McNally.

The city inspired awe. She humbled you, made you feel capable of anything, all in the same breath. The purity of the buildings, pale marble bathed in golden lights, the immense potency of the greatest nation in the world barely hidden behind each façade.

New York had more energy. Paris and San Francisco and a dozen other places were more attractive. But for the feeling of raw power—the low hum of influence that affected the entire world—no place beat Washington.

DC was the ultimate city for a deal maker.

Senator Stephen McNally and Patrick Hawkins, his chief of staff, were in the backseat of a gray Ford Expedition, two armed guards in the front. A similar vehicle with four additional security personnel followed close behind.

As the driver sped through the late-night traffic, Senator McNally caught a glimpse of the Capitol on one side and the Washington Monument at the far end of the National Mall on the other. Like always, he felt a tiny lump in his throat to be part of a special group of one hundred women and men, the US Senate, entrusted with governing America.

The guards in both vehicles were employed by one of the Senator's charitable trusts and answered to him alone. His government-provided security detail had been sent home, their protests duly noted.

The driver maneuvered through Columbus Circle and then turned off of Massachusetts Avenue and onto Capitol Street, a major thoroughfare heading north. More buildings, three and four stories of limestone and granite, full of the suckerfish of government: lobbyists and lawyers, pollsters and prostitutes, consultants of every flavor.

"Where are we going?" McNally looked at his chief of staff.

"Maryland." Hawkins pulled out his phone. "Some place called Langley Park."

McNally frowned and shifted in his seat, nervous energy from the day's activities and the failed vote boiling inside of him.

He'd never heard of that area. Most of the influence peddlers made their headquarters, even temporary ones, near the White House on K Street or in Georgetown.

The office buildings gave way to a series of row houses, charming places that had been updated with fresh paint and manicured landscaping.

After a few miles, the Ford veered to the right on Riggs Road, also known as Highway 212, and crossed under a set of railroad tracks, and the neighborhood changed again. The houses became smaller and smaller, the paint jobs less fresh. Small weed-filled yards and driveways with battered cars. The commercial buildings changed, too. Gone were the well-groomed offices, replaced by tired-looking retail centers and worn-down apartments with the style and charisma of a Soviet-era dormitory.

McNally had never been to this part of the District before. He prided himself on being self-sufficient, but for once he was glad to have armed guards around. Ten minutes later, after the driver consulted with Hawkins, the Ford pulled into the parking lot of a small strip center behind an all-night Rite Aid drugstore.

The strip center contained a check-cashing store that advertised in Spanish, a shop called Arcade y Musica Latino, and a restaurant named Mariscos el Ceviche Loco, the last of which was the only place open.

The driver parked in front of the restaurant and looked in the back of the vehicle, awaiting instructions.

Hawkins chuckled. "Who knew there was a barrio inside the Beltway?"

"Where's their office?" The Senator peered out the window. His skin felt tight, palms clammy.

Several groups of young men loitered at either end of the strip center. They were drinking from cans wrapped in paper sacks, roughhousing with each other.

Music blared from the open windows of an early 1980s Chevy Monte Carlo parked by the Dumpster. The car was immaculate, neon green with oversized chrome wheels.

"The restaurant. That's the address they gave me." Hawkins opened his door, exited.

The security guy in the passenger seat got out as well, as did two men from the second Expedition. The security guy from McNally's vehicle surveyed the scene, one hand under his suit coat. After a few moments, he tapped the window, and Senator McNally departed the safety of his SUV.

One of the young men at the end of the building shouted something in Spanish, and several others laughed, made catcalls. No one approached, but the Senator's men tensed, hands underneath their coats.

After it became clear the young men were no immediate threat, Hawkins and a guard from the second vehicle walked on either side of the Senator to the front of the restaurant.

The three men paused at the entrance.

Senator McNally peered through the glass, a moment of hesitation, as he considered what he was doing in this part of town.

His goals were worthy: regain control of the border, increase prosperity (and the tax base) for the region, restore dignity to some of the poorest citizens in the land. And last but certainly not least—win an election.

But, worthy endeavor or not, if you wanted to succeed in today's environment, sometimes you had to use unorthodox methods.

Crack a few eggs so everybody could get a taste of the omelet.

He opened the door and stepped inside.

The place was a mom-and-pop operation, a little more than a fast-food restaurant but not by much. A dirty tile floor, white walls streaked with grease and grime, cracked vinyl chairs and booths. The steamy air smelled glorious, however—tortillas and freshly cooked onions, grilled fish, herbs, the yeasty tang of Mexican beer.

The kitchen was along the back, separated from the dining area by a waist-high barrier that served as a waitress station. The only decorations on the walls were menus and pictures of bullfighters.

A pair of Hispanic men in dirty aprons milled about in the cooking area, banging pots around, arguing in Spanish.

Two men were the dining room, the only customers. They were positioned apart from each other—one with his back to the wall in the rear of the restaurant, the other in a booth a few feet away from him—but were clearly together.

The man at the back of the room was heavyset, vaguely Middle Eastern–looking. He wore a cheap gray suit with the telltale bulge of a shoulder holster under one arm. There was no table in front of him, just an open space and a clear view of both the kitchen and the front door.

The second man, lounging in the booth, was eating a bowl of soup and leafing through the contents of a manila folder. A mug of beer and a cell phone rested on either side of his meal.

The man in the gray suit was built like a linebacker. He was completely still, hands in his lap. His eyes never rested, however, surveying every movement in the restaurant.

Hawkins swore under his breath. Their contact person clearly not anywhere to be seen. He pulled out his phone and sent a text.

An instant later the device resting next to Soup Man's plate vibrated. He glanced at the screen and looked up.

McNally waved off his guard and chief of staff. He strode to the table. Hawkins followed, shaking his head.

The man was in his early forties and the polar opposite of the big guy in the gray suit. He was thin, almost dainty, pale skin dusted with freckles and thick gray hair cut a few inches above the shoulders, bangs swept back. He wore a black velvet jacket, a purple shirt, and a gold Rolex.

Senator McNally sat down across from Soup Man without being invited. Hawkins eased into the booth next to McNally.

McNally said, "We're looking for Raul Fuentes-Manzanares."

Soup Man put down his spoon and said, "He's not here."

The barest trace of a Mexican accent, his voice was low and throaty but feminine, a Latino Lauren Bacall.

"Who the shit are you?" Hawkins pointed to the man's phone. "I thought—"

Soup Man raised a hand. "I am Raul's brother, Ernesto."

"Where's Mister Fuentes-Manzanares?" the Senator said. "We had an appointment."

"He's in the process of moving to the United States." Ernesto stirred his soup with a spoon. "Mexico is not a safe place these days."

"This is not a good way to start off a relationship." McNally gave the man his stare.

Raul Fuentes-Manzanares was part of a very wealthy and powerful Mexican-American family as well as the leader of the Manzanares Political Consulting Group. Descended from Spanish conquistadores, the family had made the bulk of their fortune in manufacturing and mining during the colonial era before going into banking.

"You have such beautiful eyes." Ernesto returned the Senator's gaze. "So blue. Like the sky at Mazatlán in wintertime."

The Senator blinked, sat back.

"Travel is difficult for Raul at the moment. He has a family, small children." Ernesto smiled ruefully. "I, alas, do not. So it was easier for me to be here."

McNally nodded, looked around. "And this is your . . . office."

"We have interests in many different areas," Ernesto said. "This is one of them."

Hawkins glanced at the Senator, shrugged.

McNally squelched the anger that was building inside him. Who the hell did these people think they were, meeting with a US Senator in this rathole of a restaurant?

"You need someone to provide insight into the border region, yes?" Ernesto took a sip of beer. "To advise on getting votes, too?"

McNally didn't reply. After a moment, he nodded, lips tight.

"Do you wish to engage our services, Senator?" Ernesto pushed his food away.

The arrangement was straightforward. For a monthly fee, the Manzanares Political Consulting Group would provide McNally's campaign with expert help in wooing the Hispanic vote in the upcoming election as well as other, unspecified services labeled "miscellaneous."

As a gesture of good faith from both sides, McNally, a member of the Senate Banking Committee, had agreed to sponsor a bill that the Manzanares organization favored. In return, Manzanares would offer immediate help in passing the new immigration legislation.

The bill was simple, a loosening of the rules regarding transactions between banks in the United States and Mexico. As it would be a boon to business, the Senator would have supported the law without the arrangement between his campaign and this new consulting firm. He'd been surprised something similar hadn't passed before.

McNally hesitated for a moment. The urge to win churned his belly. The Hispanic vote was key to an easy victory.

"The election is important, of course," Ernesto said. "But the border region cries out for a man with your influence."

McNally straightened his tie.

Ernesto continued. "Together, we can accomplish much. The immigration issue and the election, that's just the start."

McNally didn't say anything. His eyes drifted across the room. A cockroach crawled along the baseboard. In the kitchen, one of the cooks cranked the volume on a radio,

Mexican rap music, and lit a cigarette. Outside, a siren grew loud and then soft as a police unit passed by.

Ernesto followed the Senator's gaze. "This place makes you nervous?"

"I've seen worse." McNally turned away from the filth of the restaurant. "You should see where I grew up."

The Pleasant Grove section of Dallas. Poverty and crime abounded.

"These people vote, too," Ernesto said. "The legal ones anyway."

No one spoke for a few moments.

"What about in the Senate?" McNally said. "You can get enough votes for SB 994?"

"We have many friends in both houses of Congress, but we also have faith." Ernesto touched a small gold crucifix around his neck. "With faith, one can move mountains."

McNally took a deep breath and pulled the envelope from his pocket. He held it in his hand, rubbed a finger along the edge. The envelope contained a retainer check and the contract between the Senator's campaign and the consulting group, the results of a weeks-long negotiation between Hawkins and the Manzanares people.

"With a leader such as you and our help," Ernesto's voice was soothing, "the United States might regain control of the border and stop this narcotrafficker violence."

Control the border, the Senator's ultimate goal.

A win-win for everybody, his favorite kind of deal.

"Okay." McNally handed over the envelope. "I expect results. And soon."

The man in the gray suit shifted his weight slightly but didn't get up.

"Thank you," Ernesto said. "You won't be disappointed."

McNally nodded, mind moving on to other issues.

"The details of our agreement." Ernesto placed the envelope in his breast pocket. "Perhaps I might have a quick word alone with your chief of staff."

McNally nodded.

Politics was often like sausage—everybody liked the end product, but nobody wanted to see it get made. This was one of those times. Things might be said that a Senator didn't need to hear. Such was the burden of leadership.

Hawkins pointed to the parking lot. "Wait in the car while I talk with our new friend."

McNally had no idea what Ernesto wanted to discuss with his chief of staff and didn't really care. He had an election to win and a border to reclaim for the United States. He slid from the booth, headed toward the exit, his security person holding open the door to the grimy restaurant.

The man in the gray suit watched him go.

McNally had mentally shifted gears, thinking about future legislation and election scenarios and how best to use his new consulting group.

The hunger flamed in his belly, the compulsion to win at all costs stoked once again.

- CHAPTER TEN -

I lived by nickel and dime jobs, a skinny chicken scratching in the dirt for a meal.

The proverbial hand-to-mouth existence, dropping half of what was in the hand on the way to the mouth. Tough to make a living, times being what they were, especially since there wasn't a lot of stimulus money floating around for guys who rough up Korean pimps.

My life didn't used to be this way.

In a time before this, I'd been on the fast track at the Dallas Police Department, the golden child at the Central Patrol Division. I was ex-military, fresh off of a couple of tours in the Middle East. I was also third generation old-school Texas law enforcement, what the country club set would call a scion.

My father had been a county sheriff of some renown.

My grandfather had been a legendary commander in the Texas Department of Public Safety, a man who once told a capo of the New Orleans mob to "Stay the hell out of East Texas or I'll give you a forty-five-caliber enema, too." The capo, so the story goes, had slowly backed out of the room with his hands raised. He made no move to help his underling, the guy trying to set up operations in Texas, a pedophile from Shreveport who was dying from a bullet wound in his rectum. All of this had reportedly occurred in one of the capo's bars in the French Quarter.

Yes, I was going places.

But that was before Costco Barnett and the Night of a Thousand Lap Dances.

Costco was my partner, a functional alcoholic nicknamed after the discount retailer because he once killed a suspected rapist late at night in the produce section. Costco, florid faced and thirty pounds overweight, had nearly three decades on the force and didn't give a damn about much of anything except doing the job the best way he knew how. And strippers.

Good gravy, did Costco Barnett love him some strippers. Something about the concept—money for nakedness—twisted up his sense of reason like Elvis's colon on the day he died.

Which is how we came to be in a topless joint named the Pussycat Lounge on the Night of a Thousand Lap Dances.

In Dallas, a prominent hole in the Bible Belt, the law required dancers to wear pasties. Specifically, the regulation read that the "whole of the performer's nipple shall be covered," a vaguely worded clause open to all sorts of interpretations.

And therein lay the problem. Nipples only? Or the surrounding flesh, the areolas as well? Weighty topics, these legal issues.

Costco Barnett, in no way authorized to conduct such investigations, took it upon himself to be the arbitrator of what was legal nipple coverage. By measuring the pasties with a tiny ruler he carried in the back pocket of his uniform.

On the Night of a Thousand Lap Dances, a promotion

the manager of the Pussycat Lounge dreamed up, Costco downed two boilermakers at the bar while I sipped a Diet Coke. We were both in full uniform. Then he dragged me past the DO NOT ENTER sign and into the dressing area back-stage, a long room full of mirrors and half-naked women, the air thick with cigarette smoke and estrogen.

Costco, a blissful look on his face, whipped out his ruler.

The manager followed us, hopping from one leg to the other.

"Why you jacking with me?" he said. "Tonight of all nights?"

"The law's the law." Costco licked his lips.

The dancers groaned, made catcalls. Their first rodeo with Costco, this was not.

"Here's a couple C-notes." The manager pulled out some bills. "For you and your guy."

"Buzz off." Costco pointed to a platinum blond wearing only a G-string and some flowery perfume. "You first."

The woman's chest was so big it needed its own census tract number.

A closed door was at the back of the dressing room, and I drifted that way. Never did like unopened things since that time in Fallujah.

"Sure, Costco." The blond stood and chuckled, a hand under each enormous breast. "Knock yourself out."

"Ohhh, yeah." My partner slid the ruler under one nip-ple and grabbed a handful of the woman's buttocks.

"Jesus, Costco. You're a pig." The manager shook his head. "Copping a feel and not paying—" He looked my way. "Hey, get the hell away from there."

I put my hand on the knob of the closed door, and the dressing room got quiet except for the pulse of the music from the club. About half the girls decided it was time to get on the floor and hustle one of the thousand lap dances. The other half busied themselves with their makeup and costumes, clearly not wanting any part of the door.

"Take the cash, willya. Get a BJ on the house. Whatever." The manager rushed across the room to me. "But you ain't getting in there."

Costco pushed the blond away and dropped his ruler.

The manager stopped, wiped a tiny layer of sweat from his upper lip, a nervous look in his eyes.

I kept my hand on the knob but didn't turn, waiting to see what my partner did.

Managers of strip clubs did not *ever* tell police officers what they could or could not do, even if one of them was pawing a dancer.

"What did you say?" Costco lumbered over to him, hands on his hips.

"N-n-not tonight, Costco." The manager gulped, then turned to me. "Don't go in there. Please."

My partner nodded at me.

I opened the door and stepped inside a dim area about the size of a motel room. I smelled the smell, saw the child. A baby in diapers and nothing else.

Would I take it back? Never open the door? That's a question that has no answer.

———

The child was about a year old. Hard to tell precisely since he was in a car seat on the floor. His eyes tracked my movements as I stepped in, hand on my gun. He didn't cry or gurgle. Just watched.

It was a storage room. A single fluorescent light flickered overhead, the ballast going bad, keeping the space in gloom.

Stacks of boxes. A leather sofa with a torn cushion. Two card tables covered with beer mugs, pitchers, rolls of toilet paper.

And the smell. Metallic and sulfur. Menthol on top of urine.

"What do you got, partner?" Costco stood in the dressing room, just on the other side of the door.

"Stay outside. Don't let anybody in." I pulled my service weapon and scanned the rest of the room.

The woman was easy to miss at first glance, huddled in the corner, knees under her chin, arms wrapped around her legs.

She was older than your average stripper, maybe thirty-five. Her eyes were closed. Stringy blond hair with a couple inches of dark roots showing. She wore a pair of khaki shorts and a sleeveless T-shirt, her skinny arms and legs at odds with the obviously enhanced breasts pressing against her legs.

"Ma'am." I lowered the gun. "Are you okay?"

She opened her eyes and looked at me without speaking. She just stared, much like the infant. My initial impression: a couple of bump-and-grinds short of a full table dance.

"That your baby?" I nodded toward the car seat.

She blinked and licked her lips but didn't say anything. Her features were coming more into focus as my vision adjusted to the dimness.

Stoned or stupid, hard to tell. Her eyes were glassy, as empty as a church on Monday morning.

"Can you tell me your name?"

She licked her lips again and swallowed. "A-a-are you here for the key?"

"No, ma'am." I holstered my gun. "I'm a police officer. Is that your child?"

"I'll give you the key." She closed her eyes, head tilting to one side. "Just don't hurt my baby."

Noise at the door. Costco eased himself into the room.

"What the hell's going on in here?" He squinted at the woman and then the baby.

"We need an ambulance." I touched my two-way radio.

"No." The manager stood in the doorway. He held a cell phone in one hand.

Costco turned to him. "Again telling us what to do?" He tapped the manager on the chest. "How about you step back and let us do our job?"

"I'm trying to do you a solid." The manager didn't budge. "Don't call this one in. Take a powder; am-scray, you hear me?"

I walked to the car seat, knelt down. The smell was stronger, the light weaker. The child's diaper obviously needed to be changed. But there was something more.

I turned on my flashlight.

"How about I call vice?" Costco shoved the guy back. "And you can expl—"

The sound of his voice disappeared as the door shut, leaving me alone with the woman and her child.

"Please, don't hurt my baby." She tried to stand but couldn't.

The child's legs were greasy from the knees down, like he'd been dipped in suntan oil. Underneath the substance, the skin looked funny, warped or bubbled, a trick of the lighting.

"What the heck?" I leaned closer.

Anyone who's ever been in a war zone or worked as a cop knows how deep the darkness reaches, the bottomless void that allows for actions that have no meaning in the sane world.

Cruelties, both deliberate and not, banal and repugnant at the same time.

The trick for the so-called sane one who desires to avoid sinking into the morass was humor, usually that of the gallows variety. And the trick to the humor was to have your head in the right place when the bad stuff confronts you.

That night, at the Pussycat Lounge, my head was not in the right place.

"Holy crap." I picked up a jar on the floor beside the car seat. Over-the-counter blister cream. "He's been burned."

"I d-d-didn't mean to." The woman stood, finally, and wobbled over. "I was trying to give him a bath but the water was too hot."

I grabbed my walkie-talkie, requested an ambulance and a supervisor, my sergeant. I gave my unit number.

"They cut off my electricity." She began to cry. "But the stove had gas."

The child closed his eyes. His breathing was shallow, a long, slow count between each rise and fall of his chest.

"What's he on?" I touched the baby's throat. The pulse was weak.

"I'm supposed to be in a program." She wiped the tears from her eyes. "Methadone. It's so hard, you know. Getting all the junk out of your system."

"What the hell did you give him?" I pulled her up. "He's stoned off his ass."

"I-I-I just want to get straight," she said. "That make me a bad person?"

"He's a baby, for God's sake." I shoved her against the wall.

She looked at me through a tangle of hair, a sly smile on her lips. "You like it rough, do you?" She giggled, words slurred. "Me too."

The dispatcher called on my radio, loud in the small room: An ambulance was on its way.

"I dig the uniform." She touched my arm. "Maybe you and I could have a little party? Then I'll give you the key."

"The child." I slapped her hand away. "What's he on?"

"Hey, it's all good." She pushed her hair out of her face. "He's been a whiner since day one. Just watered down some of the stuff I take, you know. Mellow him out."

I backhanded her in the mouth. I didn't mean to. It just happened.

Her head whipped back, skull bouncing off the sheet rock. Her teeth bloodied my knuckles.

Costco stepped back in the room.

"You called an ambulance." He shut the door. "I heard it on my radio."

His tone was soft, out of character.

"She boiled the kid like he was a lobster." I wiped my hand with a handkerchief.

The woman groaned.

"You shouldn't a called it in." Costco shook his head. "I think we got a situation here."

"She doped the kid, too." I picked up the car seat. "Little guy's barely breathing."

"You gotta trust me on this." Costco took the carrier from my grip. "We were never here."

"This child has second-degree burns," I said. "He needs to be in a hospital, not a strip joint."

"Ay-yi-yi. What a mess." Costco examined the baby's legs. "All right. We'll let the call stand. But we need to get the hell out of here."

Both of our radios sounded. The ambulance was out front. The dispatcher used my badge number as well as Costco's.

The manager came in the room followed by a uniformed officer around Costco's age, a heavyset man with dyed hair who I knew by reputation but had never met, Captain Sinclair.

"You two stepped in it now." The manager looked at the woman crumpled on the floor, bleeding from her mouth. "This kid's not supposed to exist."

Captain Sinclair's face was blank, but his eyes narrowed as if a great deal of thinking was going on inside his head, various permutations and calculations. He looked at me for a moment before staring at Costco. His cell phone rang, and he left the narrow room to take the call. The manager shook his head and left, too.

Another man entered, sliding into his space. The new arrival was in his late thirties and wore a dark suit, white shirt, and red-striped tie, his hair a buzz cut.

He ignored the woman and child.

"My name's Hollis." He held up an FBI badge. "Which one of you fuckers has the key?"

- CHAPTER ELEVEN -

Piper was in the kitchen making coffee when I woke the next day, a scant few hours after dropping off the girl with her mother and Sinclair at the poker house on Tranquilla.

I yawned and stretched and padded into the living room of our borrowed apartment at the Cheyenne. My sleep had been fitful, filled with images of the injured infant at the strip club years before, the FBI agent Hollis, and half-remembered snippets of my father when he'd been a lawman.

The Dallas skyline was a dull gleam in the morning sun. There were no rain clouds on the horizon, just a pale, blue-gray swath of smog wrapped around the skyscrapers like a dirty river.

Piper poured me a cup and then disappeared into the bathroom.

Two items were on our agenda for that day. One was to interview a CI, a confidential informant we called Rich Dude, our main lead to the warehouse and the money it represented. The other was a personal errand, which I decided to do first. At nine, Piper and I left the apartment and headed south.

Dallas, in all its concrete glory, had grown north, the black gumbo prairies leading to the Red River dotted with strip centers, subdivisions, and the occasional clump of office towers that jutted from the clay soil like glass stalagmites.

The south part of the county, especially to the east, hadn't changed much since the first European settlers had arrived in the middle of the nineteenth century, looking to upsell the natives on cholera and a utopian society called La Réunion.

The terrain was marshy, covered with the post oaks and swamp maples that grew along the Trinity River floodplain, land that was good for crushing spirits and hiding bodies, and not much else.

Twenty minutes later, I turned off a gravel road and maneuvered the Tahoe over the ruts on the packed-dirt driveway that led to a rented double-wide trailer. The home sat under an old bitternut hickory tree that had lost half its limbs during a thunderstorm the year before.

"Damn cell." Piper tossed her phone on the console. "Can't get a signal and we're, what, like only a mile from downtown?"

The five-acre tract was in fact nearly a dozen miles from the city center, just off of South Belt Line Road near the unincorporated town of Kleberg. A dry creek, lined with cottonwoods, ran to one side of the double-wide, the rest of the place overgrown with weeds and brush.

I parked behind a Ford pickup truck that had been new during the last years of the Reagan administration. The rear window was plastered with Police Benevolent Association decals.

Piper and I got out.

The air smelled faintly of river water and dead fish, combined with the pleasant aroma of cut hay from the pasture next door. The place on the other side sold used tires and goats.

I navigated the rickety stairs, Piper right behind me.

A screen door hung by two of its three hinges, large chunks of the screen part missing. TV noise from inside.

I knocked. Odd-sounding footsteps grew louder, metal and flesh. *Clink-step-clink.*

A woman in her late twenties appeared. She wore a print sundress, hair back in a ponytail, a dishrag over one shoulder.

She stepped into the doorway, crutches first. Her left leg was bone white, foot encased in a black Chuck Taylor sneaker. Her right leg was missing.

"Oh." She sounded disappointed. "It's you."

"Guess who brought money." I held up a wad of currency, half my take from last night.

"Doesn't look like much." Tanya was her name, my half sister. "Thought you had a big haul coming in."

"We're working on that later." I opened the door and stepped inside, forcing her to hobble backward. "Probably gonna come together this week."

"Hey, Tanya." Piper followed me in. "How's it going?"

"Cable was screwed up all last night." My sister headed to the kitchen. "And I'm almost out of tampons. So I've had better weeks."

Piper looked at me and mouthed the word, "Ouch."

Tanya and Piper were from the same generation, shared many of the same cultural touchstones. They both had law enforcement backgrounds. They were as close to friends as either one got.

The trailer was wood paneled. Harvest-green, shag carpeting.

The space that served as a kitchen had orange Formica countertops. For some reason, it always smelled like boiled cabbage and onions, no matter what time of day or season.

"The starter on the Ford is going bad." Tanya grabbed a pill bottle from the counter.

I dropped the cash on a pile of bills by the toaster. The top invoice, marked PAST DUE, was from the electric company. I slid another couple of hundreds from my wallet.

Piper opened the refrigerator and pulled out a Snapple.

"And the lady from Medicaid won't call me back." Tanya dumped some pills into a highball glass with the logo for the Sheriffs' Association of Texas on one side.

Her hands were red and scaly, like they'd been rubbed too much.

"I'll stop by her office tomorrow," I said.

Jockeying for the meager resources provided by insurance and disability was often a two-person job.

Piper twisted off the top and took a drink. She pulled out her cell phone and sat down at the kitchen table.

"How long since you've left the house?" I said.

"I went to the store last week." Tanya filled a Diet Coke bottle with water, screwed on the top.

"You know what I mean." I picked up the tumbler of pills. "How long since you've really left."

"Get off my ass, willya." She put the bottle in a canvas sack hanging around her neck.

She'd been a patrol officer and then a homicide investigator with the Fort Worth police department until her mental health and OCD had gotten the better of her. The leg was a recent situation.

I followed her out of the kitchen and into the living room where our father, Frank Cantrell, sat in a recliner in front of the television.

This part of the trailer had a faint odor of decay mingled with the stench of rubbing alcohol and an old man's body too long unwashed.

"Damn carpet-munchers." Dad shook his fist at the television where two women on a daytime talk show were slugging each other.

"Time for your medicine." Tanya placed the bottle of water on a TV tray.

"What happened to your leg?" Frank cocked his head.

"Again with the leg." Tanya hobbled toward the kitchen. "I need to wash my hands."

"Here's your meds, Pop." I put the glass of pills next to the water.

"Who are you?" Frank squinted at me. He wore a dirty khaki uniform, a dented sheriff's badge pinned to the breast pocket. The familiar clothing from long ago seemed to comfort him.

"I'm Jon. Your son."

He had advanced dementia, a condition not unlike Alzheimer's, and only a half pension, grudgingly offered, from Marlin County, the hardscrabble chunk of Texas just to the southeast of Dallas where he'd served as sheriff for twenty-eight years until the whole coke-in-the-trunk fiasco. He took a smorgasbord of meds, some for mental acuity, others for his prostate and blood pressure. All were expensive.

"The hell you say." He squinted at me. "If you're Jon, then tell me where your mom is."

I shook my head, lips tight. The words wouldn't come.

"*Jon's mom* said she was gonna fix me a steak tonight." He banged his TV tray. "Where the hell is she?"

My mother had died two years ago at a commune in Oregon. Tanya's mother had been institutionalized after stabbing a manicurist in Wichita Falls.

Frank, not an easy guy to live with, had a knack for picking women from the spicy side of the menu.

"She's not around right now." I sat across from him in an easy chair. "You hungry?"

"Ah, Jesus." He lumbered to his feet. "I gotta get on patrol."

"Take your medicine first." I opened the water, nudged the pills closer.

"You on the job?" He pointed to the bulge on my hip where the pistol rested covered by my T-shirt. The portion of his mind that still thought like a law enforcement officer worked just fine.

"Yeah." I nodded. "I'm on the job."

"My boy Jon used to be a cop." He swallowed the meds. "Couldn't keep his mouth shut with the feds way back when. He ended up screwed like a three-legged dog."

I leaned back, closed my eyes. Tired now, so very, very tired.

"His mother was the problem." He coughed. "She was a hippie. Damn flower child."

Silence for a while except for bickering voices on the television. I opened my eyes.

"Where the hell is my steak?" Frank pounded the headrest of his chair. "I gotta get to work."

"Listen to me, Pop." I picked up the remote, clicked the mute button. "You're not sheriff anymore."

He stared at me, eyes welling with tears. "W-w-what did you say?"

I bit my lip, tried to control the frustration. The Glock felt heavy on my waist. I wanted to shoot something—anything.

"Hey, you're Jon." He wiped moisture from underneath one eye. "My son."

I nodded. Tried to smile.

"Where's your sister?"

"Tanya's in the kitchen," I said.

"Why? Is it time for dinner?"

My limbs grew heavy. My body ached, a dull throbbing in the middle of my chest.

No place like home.

- CHAPTER TWELVE -

Sinclair blinked, suddenly awake, the phone on his bedside table ringing.

The caller ID told him he'd be better off going back to sleep in the hopes that the whole missing witness issue was a dream. The number belonged to Hawkins, a piece of slime who worked with the other people who wanted the witness found, the ones Tommy didn't know about. Hawkins's employer was a very powerful man, a childhood friend of Sinclair's, now a United States senator. Hawkins and his employer were just more incessant voices clamoring for Eva Ramirez to be found.

He didn't answer. He didn't like to talk to Hawkins under the best of circumstances.

A knock on the bedroom door followed by the muffled voice of Tommy, the only other person on the premises.

"Hey, boss." The man rapped again. "You need to get out here."

Sinclair had spent the night in a vacant apartment he'd leased two years before, using the married name of one of his stepdaughters. The phone and the utilities were registered under an alias.

The last few days he'd stayed in a different place each

night. Motels, a friendly ex-wife's house, apartments like this one. No particular reason, just a nervous twitch at the base of his spine that told him he should keep on the move.

The clock radio on the bedside table read ten a.m. He'd fallen asleep at around four, after finally pushing all thoughts of Eva Ramirez, the missing witness, from his mind. He'd been over the plan a hundred times, tossing and turning. It would work. It had to work.

He lumbered to his feet, reached for a robe. A deep cough rattled his chest, brought up the taste of last night's cigars, sticky on the roof of his mouth. His esophagus burned, the acid reflux acting up again. From the nightstand, he picked up a nickel-plated revolver and dropped it in the pocket of his robe.

The bedroom door opened before he could reach it, and Tommy's hulking figure filled the entryway.

He nodded toward the living room, whispered, "Somebody here to see you."

"Here?" Sinclair cinched his robe.

Tommy nodded, face inscrutable except for a tiny glint of worry in his eyes.

Not a good sign. Sinclair and his crew had the run of the city. Fear wasn't part of their vocabulary. Neither was "unannounced visitor at a safe location." The cartels didn't have the resources in North Texas at the moment to find this place, and Hawkins's people were not local. Besides, dropping in wasn't their style.

The apartment was a two-bedroom unit in a complex that was part of a much larger conglomeration of apartments, what locals called the Village.

Twenty or more complexes, thousands of apartments, all clustered around the intersection of Lovers Lane and Greenville Avenue in Northeast Dallas. Lots of bars and nightclubs in the area. Lots of young, transient people as well. Plenty of turnover among the residents.

Sinclair kept an apartment here for the anonymity, but also because he'd lived in a neighboring complex in the early 1980s, when he'd been a young cop. The older he got, the more he liked to remember back in the day, the women, the parties around the pool, the good times.

This complex was one of the older ones, early seventies vintage. The rooms had shag carpet and ceilings that were stark white with a texture like painted popcorn. The furniture was minimal. A brown sectional couch and glass coffee table in the combo living/dining area. A coffeemaker and cups in the kitchen.

A man in his thirties wearing a blue windbreaker stood in the living room. He was looking out of the sliding glass door that opened onto the second-floor balcony. The balcony overlooked the pool.

The man's name was Keith McCluskey, and he was the absolute last person in the solar system that Sinclair wanted to see at the moment.

"How in the hell did you find this place?" Sinclair walked over and stood beside him.

Both men stared out the window.

"Nice view." McCluskey nodded to the pool.

A pair of blonds were lying on their stomachs by the blue water, stretched out on recliners. Both had elaborate tattoos, tramp stamps, just above their bikini bottoms.

"They work at that new titty joint down the street," Sinclair said. "You want me to introduce you?"

McCluskey shook his head, rubbed his nose with the back of one hand.

"What do you want?" Sinclair yawned. "I'm not exactly receiving visitors at the moment."

"You can't hide from me," McCluskey said. "Never forget that."

"Whatever." Sinclair lumbered over to the couch and sat down.

McCluskey turned away from the window. The badge clipped to his belt identified him as an officer with the Drug Enforcement Administration. He wasn't an actual government employee, however. He worked for a private law enforcement contractor called Paynelowe Industries. That didn't mean the badge wasn't real, however.

"Where's the scanner?" McCluskey hitched his thumbs in his gun belt.

Sinclair didn't reply.

"I know you have it because you're a fucking thief."

"Most people say good morning." Sinclair chuckled. "You start with the insults."

McCluskey rubbed his nose again.

The lines in his face were deep, like they'd been etched in granite by a laser. Dark bags hung under his eyes. His skin was sallow, pupils dilated, whites shot through with red. A portion of one eyebrow was missing, the skin on his forehead blistered above the damaged brow.

Tommy came into the living room. He nodded once. A call had been made.

"Let's talk about this item then." McCluskey pulled an evidence bag from underneath his windbreaker. The clear plastic sack contained a handgun, the distinctive silhouette of a Glock semiautomatic. The black grips were deformed, like they had been melted a little.

Sinclair didn't like where this was headed. He didn't say anything.

"Standard DEA issue, forty caliber," McCluskey said. "A guy who works for you sold it to a federal firearms dealer yesterday at a gun show in Fort Worth."

Sinclair pressed his lips together, resisted the urge to swear. That dumb son of a bitch. He'd told him to toss the gun, not try to peddle it. And certainly not to a dealer.

"The serial number. We keep records, you know," McCluskey said. "The last known location of this weapon was with the scanner."

Sinclair shrugged. "You're looking a little ragged. No wonder, much as your little misadventure with the pipe torched you up. That had to have smarted."

McCluskey touched the spot on his head where his eyebrow was missing, seething.

"You just left me there." He sounded incredulous. "Passed out and smoking. And cleaned out my vehicle."

"At least *someone* thought to call the medics. Made it so you could live to spark it up another day." Sinclair decided to change the subject. "I can get an eight-ball of primo coke here in a few minutes. Then maybe you'd like to meet one of those girls by the pool."

"I am not a drug addict." McCluskey enunciated each syllable precisely. He sniffed, wiped his nose again.

"Of course you're not." Sinclair smiled. "You just, uh, misplaced that scanner doohickey and a bunch of guns and now you're blaming me."

Tommy chuckled. McCluskey didn't reply. His breathing grew ragged, fingers clenched.

Sinclair and the DEA agent were sometimes allies, sometimes enemies. Never friends. Now they were playing a dangerous game, and they both knew it.

On the one hand, federal law enforcement officers, especially crooked ones employed by contractors, couldn't just arrest retired police captains, no matter how checkered the captain's career had been. Retired police brass, even corrupt ones, carried a certain weight in the community, demanded a certain respect.

Added to this was the fact that Tommy, himself an ex-cop, had made a call to the northwest substation, and in a few minutes a half dozen active-duty Dallas police officers would be swarming the apartment. The Blue Tide backs their own; those were the rules.

On the other hand, Keith McCluskey was a credentialed federal agent, able to wield the ungainly but terribly destructive power of Uncle Sam's national law enforcement apparatus—the FBI, Homeland Security, IRS, and so on.

Since both men were bent, they knew that to rely too heavily on their backup resources—the Dallas police for Sinclair; the feds for McCluskey—was to invite disaster, tantamount to suicide. Questions would be asked, official inquiries made. Drug tests administered. So, instead, they danced this particular dance.

Sinclair could always reach out to the man who had called earlier—Hawkins, and by extension his boss, Senator McNally—and have McCluskey taken off the board that way. But that was the nuclear option, and he didn't want to leave a radioactive hole where his business used to be.

McCluskey tucked the damaged gun back under his windbreaker. Then he grabbed an intact Glock from his hip.

Sinclair tensed. Tommy took a step forward and then stopped. Everybody was in uncharted waters now. The dance had changed.

"I need the scanner," McCluskey said. "My ass is on the line for that. Where is it?"

"I ain't got it." Sinclair held up his hands. "Now be cool, and put your gun away."

The device he'd given to Jon Cantrell the night before. Glad he'd thought to get rid of the damn thing.

"I'm gonna find it." McCluskey rubbed his nose with his free hand. "Soon as somebody turns it on, it sends a signal. Don't think you can get away with using it."

Sinclair kept his face blank. He should have figured that something like that was programmed to send a signal out. At least the device was out of his possession. He hoped Cantrell would take his advice and not turn it on.

"I don't even know what you're talking about." He shook his head. "Maybe you oughta switch to downers, mellow out a little."

A thin trickle of blood meandered out of one of McCluskey's nostrils. The agent didn't appear to notice. He gripped the gun tighter, breathing heavily. His index finger curled around the trigger, began to whiten.

"Read my lips, cokehead." Sinclair held his hands higher. "I. Ain't. Got. It."

"You motherfuckasswipesunuvabitch." McCluskey kicked the coffee table. The glass top shattered. Shards scattered around Sinclair's bare feet.

Sinclair inched away on the sofa. He'd been around addicts all his life, knew their mood swings, the dangers inherent in dealing with them.

"Tell me where the scanner is." McCluskey aimed the gun at Sinclair's chest. "I need it." He paused, his voice lower. "I need . . . *her.*"

Tommy had eased his way along the wall when McCluskey kicked the table. Now he was out of sight of the DEA agent. He lunged, grabbed the gun wrist, twisted, wrenched the weapon from the agent's grasp.

McCluskey yelled, swore.

Tommy shoved the DEA agent over the broken remains of the coffee table and onto the sofa.

Sinclair had his revolver out. He launched himself atop

McCluskey on the sofa and used his gun like a set of brass knuckles, rammed the stubby barrel into the man's groin.

McCluskey howled.

"If you weren't a fed," Sinclair said, "I'd rip off your head and shit down your neck."

"Please." The DEA agent was crying now. "T-t-tell me where the scanner is."

Sinclair hopped off the sofa, avoiding the broken glass.

"They're gonna hang me out to dry if I don't find it." McCluskey huddled in the fetal position, whimpering.

"You're having a sucky day, aren't you?" Sinclair tightened his robe. "I'm gonna get you a couple of bumps on the house."

"Listen, okay. I'll make you a deal." McCluskey sat up, cradling his groin. "Keep the scanner. Just tell me where they're gonna be with the witness."

Sinclair didn't reply. The missing woman from San Antonio, Eva Ramirez, the one with the bounty on her head, the single person who could destroy all that he had created. Apparently, the rumors were true. She'd played every side of the fence, including Keith McCluskey's. He wondered if the other stories were accurate as well.

"What do you want with her?" he said. "You working with the US Marshals now, too?"

"Please." McCluskey held up a hand, begging. "I need to find her."

"How come?"

"You wouldn't understand." McCluskey wiped his eyes.

A loud knock on the door. The police had arrived.

"Try me." Sinclair gestured to Tommy to keep the backup outside for a moment more.

"The witness, I have to save her." McCluskey took a ragged breath.

An emotional and chemical turmoil churned deep inside the man, evident in his contorted face and hunched shoulders.

"Save her?" Sinclair raised an eyebrow. "That doesn't sound like good business to me. Sounds personal."

McCluskey didn't reply.

"Jesus H." Sinclair shook his head. "Don't tell me you're in love with her."

- CHAPTER THIRTEEN -

I watched my father weep, powerless to stop him.

"You made Dad cry." Tanya came back in the room, limping on two legs now, the missing right one miraculously regrown.

I ignored her. The walls of the double-wide seemed to be getting closer, falling in on themselves.

"I'm good police." Frank trembled. "You can't tell me different."

"And of course you had to remind him he's not on the job anymore." She shook her head. "Smooth."

Tanya, in addition to terminal bitchiness, agoraphobia, and that thing where you wash your hands all the time, suffered from a rare psychosexual condition called Body Integrity Identity Disorder, or BIID, a disease that manifested itself in an overwhelming desire to amputate a perfectly healthy limb in order to feel normal.

"It's a miracle." I raised my hands, laid the sarcasm on thick. "Your leg's grown back."

Tanya pointed a perfectly healthy middle finger at my face.

Like when a man desires to be a woman and wears female clothing, a BIID sufferer often binds up a limb and acts like an amputee for a period of time.

"Christ, I am tired of this." Tanya massaged her closed eyes with one hand. "You have any idea what it's like living in this house?"

"Here's a thought." I stood. "Why don't you get over the crazies and find a job."

"Ooh, why didn't I think of that?" She wobbled toward me, finger jabbing. "Then who's gonna take care of him?"

We were both silent while our father blubbered. I felt bad for giving her a hard time. She was ill, too, no money for good insurance or the right meds.

Piper wandered into the living room. She sat on the sofa, Snapple in one hand, Pop-Tart in the other. "I just love these family gatherings."

"Get up," I said. "We're leaving."

"And you're not family." Tanya crossed her arms. "Quit acting like it."

Piper paused with the bottle a few inches from her mouth. The smile slid off her face, replaced by a blank expression. She had an emotional hide as thick as rhinoceros skin. Not much could penetrate, except the casual words of someone she considered a friend. Unfortunately, that was what she considered Tanya.

"Don't take it out on her," I said to Tanya. "She's just trying to make a joke."

"We don't need jokes around here." Tanya curled a lip. "We need money."

Piper put the drink and snack down. "I'll be out in the car."

"No." I shook my head. "You stay."

She shifted in her seat but remained on the sofa. She crossed her arms and stared at the floor.

Nobody spoke. Tanya glared at me. I glared back.

After a minute or so Dad cinched his belt tighter. "I'm gonna go on patrol."

"That's probably not a good idea." I grasped his arm, tried to steer him down to his recliner. "Let's do some paperwork inside." I looked around for a magazine or something he could putter with.

"The hell you say." He wrenched free and clomped out of the living room.

"Aren't you going to do anything?" I looked at my sister.

She shrugged. "He wanders around the yard for a while. No harm done."

I listened as the screen door screeched open and then whammed shut. "But—"

"But what?" Tanya interrupted. "So he acts like a cop for a while. You want to screw up what little pleasure he has? It's not like he's in bad physical shape."

Age had clearly taken its toll, but Frank Cantrell was still a formidable individual. Six-three, a stout two hundred plus, and a thick head of gray hair. He looked like the Marlboro Man in a dirty sheriff's uniform.

I slumped my shoulders, shook my head.

"You haven't even asked about him," Tanya said. "Your own dad."

"I meant to . . ." I stopped talking. Nothing about to come out of my mouth would make anything better.

"His mind's dying a little more every day. And I don't have money to pay the electric bill." Tanya shook her head. "That's how he's doing."

"Here's all the cash I've got." I handed her the rest of my take from Sinclair.

Nobody spoke. I stared at the wall of the rented trailer that had the plaques and awards from our father's years in law enforcement.

"There's something you should know." Tanya spoke softly.

I turned, looked at her.

"Dad needs this test. The county clinic told me there were some abnormalities in his blood work."

"Abnormalities?" I said. "What does that mean? What kind of test?"

"Do I look like a doctor?" Tanya said. "Some cancer thing, that kind of test. A biopsy."

"When? What . . ." I struggled to stay calm. "When did you find out? And when were you gonna tell me?"

"Last week." She ran a hand through her hair. "I tried to call you a couple of times."

The messages I had not returned. Because I'd been busy. And because talking to Tanya was like getting the big neck-suck from an emotional vampire with dull teeth.

"Let's take him to the doctor now." I pointed to the door.

"It's an overnight stay at the hospital," she said. "Costs six grand on top of what Medicare's gonna pay."

I didn't say anything.

"You can have my cut from last night," Piper said. "If that helps."

No one spoke. Piper was all about family, even when it wasn't hers. I hoped Tanya felt guilty. Then I felt guilty for thinking that. I rubbed my temples, tried to clear my thoughts.

"Thanks, Piper." I looked at my partner. "But we're still short thousands."

Tanya limped across the room and turned off the television.

"I close this next deal, we'll have the cash," I said to her. "Things are gonna be easier for everybody."

Tanya nodded, a glum look on her face.

Anger and a deep sense of helplessness lashed across my mind. My palms grew sweaty and then cold.

I took several deep breaths, calmed down a little, and shuffled across the room to a picture of Frank Cantrell and Chuck Norris on the set of *Walker, Texas Ranger*. Dad and Chuck were sitting on the hood of a Mercedes Dad had been driving at the time. He'd worked security consulting jobs on the side to supplement the county salary.

The photos clustered on the other side of the room were of the family ranch, long since gone to the bill collectors.

Tanya rubbed her right knee, grimaced. She glanced at Piper. "Sorry about earlier."

Piper nodded, face impassive, the emotional armor back in place.

I wiped dust from a photo of me in a Little League uniform and hoped the Katrina debit cards still worked.

From outside came the sound of glass-pack mufflers, a throaty rumble.

"That's my boyfriend," Tanya said. "You remember the guy I've been going out with?"

"The deputy constable?" I arched an eyebrow. "Did he ever get the gastric bypass?"

Her boyfriend was morbidly obese, a silent indictment of the minimum employment standards used by certain law enforcement agencies.

The engine noise stopped. A car door slammed. Heavy footsteps on the wooden porch. A knock on the screen door. Tanya sighed and sat down.

"Aren't you gonna get let him in?" I said.

She shrugged. "Sometimes, I like to see how long he'll stand there."

Another knock rattled the screen. I shrugged too and moved to the next photo. Frank Cantrell with Willie Nelson in the mid seventies. Willie was in handcuffs.

About a minute later, Tanya's boyfriend waddled into the room. He said hello and blinked a lot.

I felt the anger rise in my throat again, a bitter, foul taste like warm soapy water.

Rage just for its own sake, no purpose, no reason.

Tanya kissed her boyfriend and told me goodbye. Piper and I left. Outside, I opened the driver's door of the Tahoe and hesitated. Piper was already in the passenger side, thumbing her phone, engine running.

The double-wide trailer where my sister and father lived was behind me. The stand of bamboo on the other side of the gravel driveway rustled. I mopped sweat off my face and waited.

A few moments later my father pushed through the cane pole and stepped into the sunlight. His steel-gray eyes were alert now, unlike before.

I shut the door and walked over.

"Hello, Jonathan." He smiled. "When did you get here?"

"I, um, we're just leaving." I held out my hand.

He shook it but didn't speak.

"You feeling okay?"

"Me? Ah, I'm fine." He sighed. "Worried about your sister though. I really put her through the wringer."

"It's okay." I touched his arm.

"I could still work, you know." He squared his shoulders. "I'm a damn good lawman."

I nodded.

"My mind." He stared at the trailer. "It's not that bad most of the time."

"Why don't you go inside," I said. "It's hot out."

"One thing you need to understand." He pointed a finger at my chest. "A man has to provide for his family."

I nodded.

"Hard living with the badge sometimes." He tapped the tarnished shield on his chest. "You know what I mean?"

"I gave Tanya some cash." I wiped my eyes. "Got some more money coming in later this week."

A pair of gulls flew above us, trilling, headed toward the river.

"How's Kmart doing?" he said.

"Who?"

"Your partner."

"Costco." I nodded. "He retired last I heard. Moved down to the coast. Padre Island somewhere."

"But you were here with him the other day."

I shook my head but didn't speak. The last time my dad had seen Costco was about three or four years ago.

He grasped my arm. Pulled me close. I hugged him.

We broke apart, and he looked at me with a quizzical expression on his face.

"What was your name again? You ever met Jonathan, my boy?"

———

I was twelve when I saw my father shoot Bobby Tremont, an alcoholic misogynist who'd been in and out of the local jail a dozen times.

Bobby was a real piece of work—a mean version of Otis, the Mayberry drunk on *The Andy Griffith Show*, crossed with the guy who made Ned Beatty squeal like a pig in *Deliverance*.

For most of his forty-some years in Marlin County, Bobby had been a minor nuisance, relatively speaking, the guy who picked fights on Friday at the honky-tonk on the edge of town and then spent Saturday sitting on a burlap sack of corn in front of the feed store, chewing tobacco and whistling at girls as they walked by.

Every so often the county tried to take his kids away, mostly when the bruises were too prominent to ignore. His wife never pressed charges, even when her arm was broken that one time. She just smiled and told everybody she fell down a lot.

Every place has a person like that. A bad man, but one who skates far enough under the porous radar of the legal system that he avoids the consequences for his actions.

That was before Bobby Tremont discovered cocaine.

In the mid-1980s the drug swept the nation, even backwater towns in the shadow of big cities like Dallas.

One Sunday in January, a raw, blustery day, my father and I were sitting in the café on the square, eating a late breakfast. My mom wasn't around much at that point, something about finding herself at a New Age retreat near Austin, so I was living with Dad, Tanya, and Tanya's mother. Dad had a ranch at the time, a sprawling place with lots of cattle, the best that money could buy. Times were good at the Cantrell household.

The smell of cigarettes, coffee, and fresh-cooked bacon hung in the air of the café. People were eating and laughing, the conversations centered around the sermon they'd just heard, the Cowboys' chances in the playoffs, and cattle prices. Everything was normal. Until Bobby drove up in his rusted pickup and parked in front of the restaurant.

The atmosphere in the room changed when he slammed the door of his truck. The clink of silverware slowed. The voices stilled. Everyone glanced at my father.

The mayor, two tables over, pushed back his chair and walked to our booth, keeping his eyes on the outside. He stood next to my father and said two words: "He's here."

Frank Cantrell, my dad, wore his usual work clothes—a starched khaki uniform shirt, creased Wranglers, and Justin Roper boots. On his hip rested a Ruger double-action revolver chambered in .357 Magnum.

He looked up at the mayor and nodded once. Then he continued to eat.

The mayor stared outside for a few moments and returned to his seat.

The room remained silent.

"What's going on, Dad?" I pushed away my plate of eggs.

"Selfishness." He took a sip of coffee. "That's what."

"Huh?"

"Some people are so ate up with selfishness, they end up killing themselves, one day at a time."

Bobby stood in front of the window of the café, peering in. Breath fogged the glass. His skin was pale, eyes aglow with a fire that I'd never seen before, like a house full of angry people burning in on itself.

"A terrible thing when that happens." Dad stuck a pick between his two front teeth.

"Why's Bobby staring in here?" I pointed to the front. "He looks crazy."

"I suspect the selfishness has gotten so twisted up inside of him, that he's ready for it to be over."

"What does that mean?" I frowned. "I don't understand."

"His wife." Dad sighed. "We found her down by the river last night. Shot in the head with a forty-five."

Bobby shouted something, voice muffled by the glass.

"He's most likely got his granddaddy's army gun under his coat." Dad stood. "The forty-five Colt the old man brought back from the war."

"You're not going out there, are you?" I tried to keep the emotion out of my voice.

In my mind, I knew that's what lawmen did. They went to the dark places and stopped people like Bobby Tremont. In my heart, I didn't want my dad to get hurt.

"You're a smart boy, Jonathan." He tugged at his gun belt. "And law enforcement's an honorable profession. But when you grow up, do something else. Days like this, it ain't no good way to make a living."

The mayor's wife, a heavyset matronly woman, waddled over. She squeezed in next to me and said, "I'll sit here with you while your daddy goes outside."

"Much obliged." Frank Cantrell put on his Stetson and ran two fingers over his bristly mustache. He moved toward the door and stopped.

The room was as quiet as a church basement.

He stepped back to the booth and patted me on the arm.

"See you in a few minutes, Jonathan." He smiled and walked out to face Bobby Tremont.

When it was over, and Bobby lay dead on the concrete outside the café, I knew there was nothing else in my life I wanted to do as much as be a lawman like my father.

- CHAPTER FOURTEEN -

I drove away from the trailer, a lump of emotion welling in my throat. Piper sat quietly next to me.

The dusty road that was my father's life was getting more and more rocky the closer it came to its final destination. Hard traveling on that road. Tough on everybody.

After a few minutes, Piper entered the address of our confidential informant's place into the GPS even though we'd been there several times.

Our other job—the one we did when we weren't rescuing teenage hookers for bent ex-cops like Sinclair—was working for the Drug Enforcement Administration.

We were DEA agents, our windbreakers in the rear seat marked as such in bright yellow on the back.

We had the power to arrest people. Or, if they resisted, use deadly force to subdue them. We were fully credentialed federal law enforcement officers, just like J. Edgar Hoover or the Secret Service guys who guard the president, except for one tiny difference.

Our paychecks came from a private company, not the US Treasury, a firm called Blue Dagger Industries.

We're the new breed of law enforcement, the leaner, more efficient kind, what's known in the trade as outsourced service providers, private contractors who work as public servants.

Maybe you've heard about our international colleagues, the PMCs, short for private military contractors, companies like Blackwater, hired as corporate soldiers for the latest Middle Eastern conflict. We're just like them, only without the scandals. Mostly.

Neither of us spoke as we drove.

At ten thirty, I parked the Tahoe in front of a Mediterranean-style home in the tiny town of Highland Park, a well-to-do residential enclave located in the center of Dallas. The house belonged to our confidential informant, the guy we called Rich Dude.

According to lore, the people who designed Highland Park had been hired because of their earlier success with a similar hamlet on the West Coast, another town-within-a-town called Beverly Hills. Except for the climate and the movie stars, the two places bore a striking resemblance. Expensive homes. Manicured yards. Lots of fashionably dressed white people.

In Rich Dude's driveway: a four-door Maserati, a Mercedes, and a Suburban, the latter plastered with stickers for various athletic teams at the local high school. All three were leased, the payments current on only one.

Piper rang the bell, and a Hispanic woman in a maid's outfit let us in without speaking. She pointed to the back.

Rich Dude was on the phone, standing by the sink in a cavernous area built from stainless steel and marble that looked sort of like a kitchen. He was wearing a peach polo shirt and a complicated gold watch, looking like he'd been born in the Nineteenth Hole Men's Lounge of some hoity-toity country club.

We sat on bar stools at the island that served as a dividing point between the food area and the family room, itself another huge open section dominated by a sixty-inch flat-screen TV mounted over a fireplace.

"You want some coffee?" Piper reached for a Krups in the middle of the island.

I nodded and she poured us each a cup.

Rich Dude hung up, shook his head.

"Happy Monday." I raised my cup to our host and took a sip. It tasted like charred ass.

"They're gonna foreclose." He rubbed his eyes. "The shopping center in McKinney."

"That's what happens when you don't pay the bank," Piper said.

Rich Dude was a real estate developer, a man who lived and died by leverage, the amount borrowed versus the value of the asset. To say Rich Dude was overleveraged was like saying Donald Trump had bad hair.

"It's the damn appraiser's fault." He banged the countertop. "We only needed a hooch more equity on that last project. Just five hundred K."

"And that would have helped on all those other buildings?" I tried to sound sympathetic to the idea of a "hooch" being only a half million dollars.

"You don't understand." Rich Dude was in his late forties but looked twenty years older. His face was gray, the lines around his eyes deeper than they should have been.

"True dat." I pulled out a pen and pad. "Let's get to the business at hand, though. What's the address?"

"You sure this can't be traced back to me?"

"You got a choice?" Piper drummed her fingers on the counter.

"Why'd you bring her?" Rich Dude said. "She gives my wife the creeps."

Piper shrugged. She was wearing a nose ring today and a yellow smiley face T-shirt. The smiley face had a bullet hole between the eyes, blood tickling down either side of the mouth.

"Make with the info." I tapped the pen against the pad. "We don't have all day."

"I want to make sure I understand the structure of our deal." He crossed his arms.

"Look, turdball." Piper rose from her seat. "I got your structure right here—"

"Piper." I touched her arm. "Let me handle this."

"It's not like I want to do business with you people," Rich Dude said.

"You people?" I frowned, my patience wafer-thin. "Did you just say you didn't want to do business with us?"

He didn't speak.

"One call." I pulled out my cell phone, dropped it on the counter. "And all the banks are gonna foreclose on everything. The buildings. The cars." A pause. "Even the house."

Rich Dude clutched his stomach, face grayer than before.

"That's your deal structure," I said. "Or you can give me the address."

We'd been over this before. Rich Dude was going down financially. Not a question of if, but when. I'd found him by accident a few weeks ago and offered the deal. In exchange for some information, one of the banks could be stopped for a few months, buying him a little time to polish the silverware on the *Titanic*. The other part of the deal, the one I'd just mentioned for the first time, was that I could also make all the banks go postal on his loans at any given moment.

A few hundred dollars to my name and I had that kind of power, courtesy of the powers that be at my employer, Blue Dagger Industries. Scary, isn't it?

Before I could say anything else, a woman in a Nike running suit came into the room. She was in her early forties, tanned and fit, a diamond ring as big as a garlic clove on one hand.

Rich Dude's wife.

"Oh." She wrinkled her nose. "You two are here."

Rich Dude had told her we were building contractors, working on their lake house renovations.

A quiet noise rumbled from Piper, part growl, part hiss.

"We'll be gone in a few minutes." I smiled.

The wife paid us about as much attention as she would the gardener's assistant. She handed her husband a gold credit card.

"This doesn't work for some reason. Take care of it before lunch, okay."

Rich Dude nodded, a blank look on his face. She left by the back door.

I slid the pad and pen across the counter.

"I'll call you when I know the time." He scribbled something and pushed it back.

"What do you mean, the time?" I took the pad and stuck it in my pocket. "How about what day?"

"Oh, they took possession early. A couple of days ago," he said. "They're moving stuff today."

"Shit." Piper headed toward the door.

"We'll show ourselves out." I stood, in a hurry now.

"What's the problem?" Rich Dude said. "Why you guys rushing out of here?"

I paused, looked around the expensive house.

"Nice place you've got here," I said. "Enjoy it while you can."

- CHAPTER FIFTEEN -

I already had the address, a warehouse in West Dallas. I'd just been waiting for the day.

Now I had it.

The building was one of twenty or so industrial properties that Rich Dude owned, scattered across Dallas County, most on secluded streets according to the maps we'd already consulted.

"Today is too soon." Piper slammed the passenger door. "What should we do?"

"Get there." I threw the truck into gear. "Fast."

We'd been counting on at least twenty-four hours advance warning in order to set up a stakeout with other freelance Blue Dagger employees.

"What about backup?" She grabbed two dark-blue windbreakers from the rear seat. Shrugged one on and pulled her holstered Glock from the console. She gave the other coat to me.

"There's no time for backup." I sped away from the house. "No sense splitting our commission either."

We were DEA subcontractors, and our employer paid us on a performance basis, in this instance five percent of the estimated street value. Because this was our operation, an entrepreneurial venture, we'd been planning to pay the backup people an hourly fee, not a share of the profit.

The shipment that was headed to Rich Dude's warehouse was reported to have a street value in the five-million-dollar range, meaning that if all went well, Piper and I were going to split a quarter million dollars later tonight, minus some incidental expenses. A nice chunk of change considering the dry spell of late. More than enough to pay for my father's biopsy and for Piper to sponsor an entire banana republic's worth of parentless children.

"Call Milo then." She shifted nervously in her seat. "We can't go in cold."

Milo Miller was an old acquaintance, an impresario of vice and most things illegal as well as a collector of low-life gossip, a TMZ for the criminal set, the Perez Hilton of hoods.

He was also batshit crazy. Nevertheless, she had a point. If that was a hot area, lowlife-wise, then he would know.

I dialed his cell.

He answered after the first ring. "How's my future wife?"

"She's fine." I glanced at Piper. Milo Miller had a crush on her that bordered on pathological.

"Did he call me his future wife again?" Piper raised her voice, leaned toward the phone. "I am not gonna marry you."

"She says hi." I waved at her to be quiet.

"What the hell do you want?" Milo said. "I'm a little busy."

In the background a scream and then music, the volume increasing. KC and the Sunshine Band. "That's the Way I Like It."

I told him the address of the warehouse as I entered it into the dash-mounted GPS. "You got the four-one-one on that part of the world?"

Milo ignored my question. "When are you gonna come work for me?"

"You're a crook. I'm not. It would never work out."

"That part of town is off the reservation," he said. "You should be careful. As in stay away."

"Thanks." I nodded. "Any spec—"

He hung up.

"What did he say?" Piper asked.

"Nothing."

"Why don't I believe you?" She slid the holster into place on her hip. "Why do I ever believe you?"

I turned off of Mockingbird Lane and onto the Dallas Toll Road, a six-lane thoroughfare that ran through the middle of town.

The highway, an old railroad right-of-way, was narrow, just enough room for the lanes of traffic, a barely there shoulder, and a concrete barrier median about a foot wide. The surface ran below the level of much of the city like a canyon filled with roaring autos instead of water.

I headed south, thirty miles over the limit, flitting in and out of traffic, a darting fish among a river of slower moving steel.

Piper grabbed a duffel from the backseat. The bag clanked, our extra hardware. Heckler and Koch MP5 submachine guns, .40 caliber, noise-suppressed. The Ferrari of firearms.

"I've never taken down a shipment this big." She placed an MP5 in her lap.

Her weapon had a tiny sticker on the forearm, a pink peace symbol about the size of a quarter.

I took the Stemmons Freeway and skirted the west side of downtown, past the Old Red Courthouse and the School Book Depository.

"Me neither." I exited at Commerce Street. "You didn't load up with hollow points, did you?"

There weren't many rules for private contractors. Follow all applicable laws, due process, blah-blah. And only use full metal jacket ammo, no expanding bullets.

"Well, duh, I'm using hollow points," she said. "I hit something, I want it to stay down."

The city center lay behind us. Ahead was the county lockup and the Trinity River.

We drove past the jail, crossed the river on the Commerce Street viaduct, and entered West Dallas, a part of town the guidebooks rarely mentioned.

Housing projects and dollar stores, bingo parlors and trailer parks. The grim slice of Dallas where Bonnie and Clyde had gotten their start, born into poverty and destined for early, violent deaths. By the look of things a century later, not much had changed.

On the corner a group of young men in low-riding jeans milled around in front of a burglar-barred convenience store. A couple of guys were passing a bottle in a plastic sack back and forth.

Three blocks later we idled past a vacant cinder block building that looked like it had last been used as a juke joint. The parking lot was asphalt disintegrating into gravel and dirt. On one wall, faded, barely legible lettering read TOMMY'S BLUES CLUB.

"That's the address?" Piper said.

"Yeah." I made the block. "This is it."

The place screamed drug house. Plywood where the windows should have been. Motion detector lights next to small wireless cameras. An elderly Pontiac with new tires and tinted windows, parked at an angle to the front door.

"Where's the warehouse?" She craned her head. "This dump looks like the old bar one of my foster uncles used to take me to."

"There." I pointed to a large metal building that was connected to the rear of the tavern.

The structure was hard to see, bordered by a chain-link fence that was turning into a shrub line from the overgrown hackberry trees and cedars. On the other side of the street were wood-framed houses. Tiny shotgun shacks built in the fifties and not cared for much since.

I kept driving, going through the cross street.

In the next block, I U-turned and headed back the way we came, stopping about two hundred feet from the intersection.

The rear of the warehouse was visible, a large double door that was closed.

Piper said, "They could have an army in there."

"Or not." I backed into the gravel drive of a house with a for-sale sign in the yard. "If the shipment hasn't come in yet."

A row of unkempt trees grew alongside the driveway. The foliage hid the Tahoe from the building, the entrance still visible through their branches.

"Can I tell you something?" She stroked the machine gun like it was a cat.

"Sure."

"I'm gonna quit after this." She took a deep breath, voice quivering. "Use the cash to find my birth parents."

I nodded but didn't speak.

The topic of her real mother and father came up often, especially of late as our relationship became strained, a worn spot in her mind she continued to revisit.

"Then I'm going to visit all those kids I've been sponsoring."

"You'll rack up a lot of airline miles that way." I paused. "Getting out of this line of work, that's not a bad play, though."

An awkward silence.

I cleared my throat. "Maybe, we could, um, visit them together."

"I bet my mom was a ballerina." She spoke hurriedly. "I've got the legs for that, you know."

I nodded in agreement but didn't say anything. My heart was beating faster than normal, not just from the impending takedown of a shipment of drugs. I had just told Piper—in a roundabout fashion—that I would go away with her. That was pretty close to commitment in my world.

"Or maybe she was a writer, like a poet or something." Piper stared out the window. "I like words and stuff."

Every week it was something different, her parents in various improbable roles: mother a schoolteacher or Peace Corps volunteer, father an actor or some other dashing but ultimately tragic vocation.

"If she was a ballerina, then my dad might have been a dance critic," she said. "They had this passionate but brief affair."

"My mother was a hippie and a junkie," I said. "She had her bad qualities, too."

"My mother would have probably tried to help your mother." Piper nodded. "Because that's the way she was in those days."

I didn't reply. These moments were bittersweet. Relationships that might have been, sadness that filled the void instead.

We were silent for a few moments. No movement on the street or at the warehouse.

"One of us needs to do a little recon," she said. "There's probably a window somewhere."

"Rock-paper-scissors?" I balled a fist into my other palm.

"I'm thinking you should go," she said. "On account of it's hot out and I don't want to."

"Let's try that thing Sinclair gave us." I pulled the box from the rear seat and opened it.

The battered instrument looked like one I'd heard about but never seen before. The latest trick in Big Brother's magic show, a device that kept tabs on radio frequency identification cards, the souped-up descendant of the bar code.

A handheld, broad-spectrum RFID scanner, a radar detector for stuff that wasn't moving.

Though the technology was nothing new, ever cheaper components meant that RFID tags, both passive and active, were now in more things than not, and the efficiency and range of the scanners had gotten better as well.

"You think it works?" Piper said.

"Let's find out." I pressed what looked like an On switch.

Sinclair, a technophobe of the first order, had warned me not to activate the device. But what did he know? He could barely figure out a microwave oven.

The screen crackled to life, missing a few pixels. A message from the Department of Homeland Security and the FBI warned that the device was the property of the US government and any unauthorized use or possession would result in imprisonment. No mention of fines.

"So far so good." I pointed the muzzle at a parked car. Pulled the trigger.

The warning on the screen dissolved into a series of squiggly lines, indicating the device was searching. After a few moments a new message appeared. "No Data."

I aimed at a house across the street and pressed the trigger.

More squiggly lines. Then a different screen, two blinking dots next to a code of some sort. Both were hyperlink blue like on a webpage.

"Bingo." I examined the top of the machine and figured out the keypad. Scrolled over to the first item and pressed enter.

The screen dissolved into an antenna sign, indicating information was being transmitted. Then a series of numbers appeared followed by the notation, "Unknown Item—tag assigned to retail outlet—Barnes & Noble."

"Well I'll be a monkey's bunghole." I hit the next hyperlink.

A few seconds later, the screen read the same thing, ending with: "retail outlet—Best Buy."

Piper whistled. "That is so fricking cool."

The information meant that the house across the street contained RFID tags for at least two items, one that had been purchased at Best Buy, one at Barnes and Noble.

"My turn, my turn." Piper grabbed for the scanner. "I want to play with it."

"Let's see what's going on here first." I pushed her away and pointed to the next block.

What looked like a UPS van stopped across the street from the warehouse, and two hard-looking men got out, obviously not employees of the United Parcel Service unless the company had started hiring at the local probation office.

"Scan the truck," Piper said.

I did. Got nothing.

"Should be a bunch of tags in a UPS van." She frowned.

The two men, both armed, judging by the bulges on their hips, walked across the street to the warehouse. They knocked on the door, which opened a crack and admitted them.

"They're waiting on the shipment," Piper said.

"Maybe." I aimed the scanner at the warehouse. "Unless it's already here."

The device took a long time. The squiggly lines seemed to go on forever. When it stopped, the screen filled with links, too many to count, each with the same code. At the bottom a tiny note read, "Scroll down for more items."

Piper exhaled loudly.

I hit one of the links.

The transmit icon followed by the note, "Unknown Item—tag assigned to manufacturer—McCormack Pharmaceutical."

"Winner-winner, chicken dinner." I dropped the scanner on the floor. The shipment was on the premises.

With the advent of medical marijuana dispensaries and the relaxing of drug laws around the country, the cartels had begun to diversify into legal narcotics, hijacking shipments at various places along the route from factory to pharmacy.

Unfortunately for the hijackers, legitimately manufactured products were much easier to track than bales of plant material grown on the sly. Legitimate products left a trail. There were shipping manifests and inventory records to contend with, tax records and video surveillance at the production plant.

And electronic tags.

"Holy crap." Piper shifted in her seat. "This is it."

The two men came out. One pushed a dolly stacked with cardboard boxes. The other held a cut-off shotgun pressed against his leg. He scanned the street and then appeared to relax.

"They're moving the product." I put on my windbreaker.

"Remember," Piper said. "Any problems? The answer is rounds on target."

I nodded but not in agreement, just to shut her up. Her mantra: *rounds on target.* The modern equivalent of "Shoot first; ask questions later."

"Let's do it." Piper grabbed a canvas bag from the floorboard, jumped out.

I got out too. Slung the MP5 strap on a shoulder, snatched the grip with one hand, finger outside the trigger guard. I used the trees and houses as cover until the intersection. Then I headed straight to the warehouse at a gallop.

Piper ran across the street at an angle, flanking the two men, using a pair of abandoned cars as cover. As she went she pulled a Taser from the bag.

The guard wasn't expecting trouble. He didn't realize what was happening until we were about thirty feet away.

He yelled, brought the shotgun up.

Piper was off to his side. She fired the Taser and two barbed hooks connected to the unit's battery embedded themselves in his abdomen.

"DON'T MOVE!" I brought the submachine gun to my shoulder. "POLICE."

The guy behind the dolly looked at his friend jerking around on the ground. He stepped back, hands up.

"Drug Enforcement Administration." I held up a badge.

- CHAPTER SIXTEEN -

Easy operation so far, thanks to the slightly burned scanner.

I cuffed the man who'd been moving the boxes and wondered for a half second where Sinclair had gotten the device. There was no telling. He usually kept a lot of pitchforks simmering in the brimstone.

The guy Piper had juiced with the Taser lay on the ground, twitching like an epileptic meth head as fifty thousand volts of electricity coursed through his body.

I pulled a strip of duct tape off the inside of my windbreaker and slapped it on my guy's mouth. More tape was at the ready, precut, a quick and efficient field bandage for a bleeding GSW if it came to that.

Piper cuffed her prisoner, taped his lips shut.

A small camera was mounted over the doors, just below the eaves of the warehouse. The putty used to hide the wires was still fresh-looking, barely dried.

We were the only people visible on the street. A few cars were parked farther down, beyond where our Tahoe was hidden.

I trotted to the doors and jumped, smashed the camera with the butt of my MP5.

Piper moved to the side of the door and pulled a length of black nylon cord from a pocket of her windbreaker. She looped it around the door handle and then tossed me an olive-drab metal canister about the size of a beer can, a large pull ring on top.

A flashbang grenade, very loud and very bright, designed to disorient but not to wound.

"Take the lock." She tightened her grip on the rope.

I switched the selector lever on my subgun to single shot, fired twice at the dead bolt.

She yanked the cord, jerked the door open.

A three-second fuse.

I pulled the ring, fast-counted onetwothree, and threw the grenade as far as possible inside, aiming for a long, high trajectory.

Piper kicked the door shut.

A nanosecond later a thunderclap erupted from the interior, and slivers of light strobed from the threshold gap.

Piper opened the door, and we dashed inside.

Dust and smoke. Dim light. The air reeked of explosive residue and mold.

The trailer from an eighteen-wheeler sat in the middle of the cavernous space. Open doors faced the entrance to the warehouse and displayed stacks of boxes with a familiar blue and green logo.

Neither of us spoke. Piper went to the right of the trailer, gun up; I headed left.

On my side a few feet away, a guy curled on the floor in the fetal position. He held his hands over his ears and rocked, moaning.

The other end of the trailer was in shadows.

Piper's shoes scraped on concrete from the far side.

Then, her voice: "JON! TWELVE O'CLOCK."

I shouldered the MP5.

A man in a dusty suit staggered into view, tie askew, a gun in one hand, maybe thirty feet away.

"Drop your weapon." I drew a bead on the center of his chest. "Federal agent."

He blinked, lurched toward me. He shook his head, worked his jaws, like he was trying to clear the pressure from his ears.

"DROP YOUR WEAPON." I put the subgun's sight on his middle button.

He fired without aiming. The bullet went wide, struck the wall behind me. The noise made him flinch. He kept walking, blinking, shaking his head.

"Can you hear me?" I tightened my finger on the trigger. "Put. Your weapon. Down."

He let go of the gun and fell to his knees, hands over his ears.

I ran to where he knelt. He teetered, a glazed looked in his eyes. I threw him face down on the floor, bound his hands with a plastic zip tie. Then I trussed the first guy.

"Piper." I stood. "We're clear on the port side."

"Starboard's secure as well." She appeared from the end where we'd entered.

The warehouse was a rectangular box, large enough to hold twenty trailers. Didn't take long to determine there was nothing else in the structure except for two slightly deaf guards and the eighteen-wheeler full of stolen pharmaceuticals. No interior rooms or other hiding spots.

"Tag the shipment and call it in." I pointed toward the other end of the warehouse. "I'm gonna clear the next room, the bar or whatever we saw from outside."

To get credit for a bust, and to get paid, we had to mark the confiscated product with numbered stickers and call the real DEA as soon as possible. No call? No cash.

"Uh-uh." She shook her head. "We go together."

I started toward the front and then stopped. She was right. Safety trumped everything, especially when dealing with the ultraviolent cartels and no backup on the scene.

"Okay." I motioned for her to get behind me. "I'll take the point."

We jogged to the other end of the huge open area, where the only other access point was a dead-bolted metal door. I shot the lock and kicked it open.

Piper went in first, back to the wall, subgun against her shoulder.

I followed, careful to keep the muzzle of my weapon from sweeping her body.

The room was dim, windows covered haphazardly by plywood on the outside, evidently the juke joint we'd seen when we first arrived.

In the middle of the floor sat a couple of cardboard boxes marked McCormack Pharmaceutical. They were next to an old, crumbling bar covered with hundreds of plastic bags that contained what looked like dried grass. The air smelled of mildew and herbs.

Piper looked through a gap in the window covering. "Nobody outside."

"Secure the trailer." I turned toward the shipment. "We're still in hostile terri—"

The woman who stood in the doorway leading to the warehouse and the eighteen-wheeler didn't look very dangerous, but you could never be too careful.

Piper and I aimed.

"DON'T MOVE." I eased to one side, putting distance between my partner and myself.

The woman was about thirty, maybe Hispanic, maybe not. Expensive but filthy clothes. Black hair streaked with dust, olive skin over the high cheekbones of a fashion model. She was pretty except for the dirt on her face and terror in her eyes.

"*Dónde estoy?*" She blinked, licked cracked lips. Where am I?

"*Sus manos,*" Piper said. "*Para arriba.*" Hands up.

"I speak English." The woman leaned against the wall. "Water. Do you have any?"

"What's your name?" I said.

Her eyelids drooped. She fell to the ground.

Piper knelt beside the woman, felt for a heartbeat on her neck. "Pulse is weak and thready."

"Gotta be a kidnapping," I said.

The hostage business was a significant ancillary profit center for the narcotraffickers. We didn't see it much this far north, but that didn't mean it wasn't going on.

"No-no-no-no." The woman opened her eyes.

Her gaze locked on the badge dangling from Piper's neck that had been covered by the windbreaker earlier.

"It's okay." Piper patted her arm. "We'll get you to a hospital."

"W-w-where am I?"

"Dallas," I said. "We're gonna call an ambulance. Everything will be all right."

"No ambulance." She shook her head. "No police."

"Don't worry," I said. "Nobody's going to hurt you."

"You don't understand." She pushed herself up. "They will kill me." She coughed and looked at each of us in turn. "They will kill you."

"Put her in the Tahoe." I looked at Piper. "Give her some water."

"I'm calling in the shipment first." Piper helped the kidnap victim to her feet and hit a few buttons on her cell phone, a text to our DEA supervisor.

A car door slammed outside.

The woman glanced at the front door of the bar and then at me, a terrified look on her face.

Another vehicle door slammed.

The woman staggered toward the back of the room but froze when the voices became clear on the other side of the bar's door.

Men talking in Spanish, getting closer. No time for any of us to get out of the room.

Piper put away her cell phone and moved in front of the woman, gun raised toward the front door.

I hid in the corner and waited.

- CHAPTER SEVENTEEN -

A couple of seconds later, I heard keys rattle, men talking.

The front door of the bar swung open. A shaft of light penetrated the darkened interior. It illuminated the stolen pharmaceuticals but missed me by a wide margin.

Two Hispanic guys in sweatpants and T-shirts, gang tattoos on their forearms, entered.

The last one was talking on a cell in Spanish. He locked the door from the inside.

"Don't move." I sprang from the corner, subgun up. *"Policía."*

The first guy raised one hand but reached for his hip with the other.

The second kept his phone in place and groped under his shirt.

Piper fired a silenced round into a box of stolen drugs.

Gun smoke filled the room. Bits of cardboard floated in the air.

Both men surrendered, arms high. Cell Phone Guy dropped the weapon and cell.

"Hands on top of your head." I swiveled the gun from man to man. "Both of you."

"You're making a big mistake," Cell Phone Guy said.

"Levante sus manos para arriba." Piper fired another silenced round into the carton of drugs.

Outside, another arrival. The screech of tires. More doors slammed. No time to properly search the two suspects.

The kidnapped woman backed against the far wall, shaking.

"On your knees." I moved away from the entrance, attention split between the suspects and whoever else was outside. A dangerous situation.

We'd been lucky to catch the shipment after arrival but before the large-scale distribution began, a period when there had only been a minimal number of guards. The noise outside indicated our luck was changing.

"Quién está fuera?" Piper said. Who is outside?

Neither man answered. They kept their hands up but didn't kneel.

The bar's door splintered. A battering ram plunged inside.

Two guys in blue windbreakers and helmets, an entry team, darted into the bar, carrying submachine guns like mine. They wore thick leather gloves and eye protectors.

They were DEA. A short feeling of relief washed over me followed by a new fear: friendly fire.

I put myself in their heads, tried to see what they saw.

A dazed and disheveled woman crouched by a wall. Two lowlifes, hands up. And two people in dark clothes with weapons aimed in their general direction.

"Freeze." The first one shouldered his gun, swept the room. "DEA agent."

"I'm a cop, DEA too." I dropped my MP5, let it dangle around my shoulder. Hands as high as they would go. "Don't shoot."

"NOBODY MOVE." The second windbreaker was juiced on adrenaline, getting close to the kill-everybody-and-let-God-sort-them-out stage. He jumped to one side like we'd all been trained, covering his partner. He had several smoke grenades and tear gas canisters dangling off his utility belt. The explosive devices were easy to access, but carrying them that way was against the regulations.

"We're all good here." Piper held her hands up. "Everybody's cool. Let's not shoot."

"DON'T MOVE!" The second agent began to shake, face red. He aimed at my nose.

I didn't move. Didn't breathe.

"Two fingers," Windbreaker One said. "Index and thumb. Take the sling and drop the weapons on the floor, both of you."

Piper and I did as requested, very slowly.

Windbreaker One picked up our subguns. "Who are you?"

"We're DEA, same as you." I pointed to the badge dangling around my neck. "Agent Jon Cantrell."

Windbreaker One touched his lapel mic with his free hand and radioed: "Four hostiles plus the subject. Please advise."

"Subject?" I said. "What the hell are you talking about?"

The woman from the shipment moaned. She crossed herself.

Windbreaker Two kept twitching. He lowered his weapon and took Piper's MP5 from his colleague. He touched the peace symbol on the forearm with a gloved finger and giggled.

"Let me call my supervisor," I said. "We can get this all straightened out."

Windbreaker One's radio sounded, words I couldn't understand, something about "follow the special protocol."

He shrugged and nodded to his partner.

Windbreaker Two checked Piper's gun for a round in the chamber. Then he shot both suspects in the head with the silenced weapon, one-two-*thffpt-thffpt*.

Blood and brain matter sprayed across the room as the powerful hollow points did their job. Brass clinked on the floor; the men fell over dead.

My jaw went slack, heart pounded. I struggled to catch my breath.

Windbreaker One smiled.

———

There's one in every crowd, so the saying goes. In any organization, the individual who heads left when everybody else goes right, clueless to the group dynamics, the numbskull who sings when the rest of the crowd is humming. Eager, enthusiastic to a fault.

The military was full of people like that. Sometimes they're called Gung Ho. Other times, crazy. "Dork" is a term that's used a lot in civilian life.

Windbreaker Two was just such an individual.

Brimming with energy that bordered on the psychotic. Marching to the melody of a bugler that only he could hear.

He hopped from foot to foot, laughing as he stared at the two hoods he'd just shot with Piper's gun.

"I love the smell of dead Mexicans in the morning." He yanked a smoke grenade from his belt and held it upward like a sword. "Smells like . . . victory."

"Y-y-you killed them." The woman in the dirty clothes shook like it was cold in the room. "N-n-now you're going to k-k-kill us."

"We've got backup on the way," Piper said. "You need to climb down from the crazy tree."

"Bonus time, baby. We found the witness." Windbreaker Two knelt beside the dead cartel soldiers, rummaged through their pockets.

"Please, let me go." The woman fell to her knees. "I mean you no harm."

Windbreaker One, the saner of the pair, smiled and looked at the woman in the dirty clothes.

"The Marshals got *mucho dinero* on your head." He chuckled. "Plus, we get a big-ass incentive payment for being the first guys on the scene. No way we're letting you go."

Piper and I looked at the woman. A bounty on her? And these guys were contractors?

"What about us?" I said. "We're credentialed. We're cops like you."

"You shot these lowlifes." Windbreaker One shook his head. "I'm sure you can spin a good reason why to the Dallas police and the DA."

"Don't you just love it when you turn a bad guy into worm-dirt?" Windbreaker Two wagged the grenade in my face. "Feels like the world's best boner."

"Put that smoke bomb away, willya." Windbreaker One looked at his colleague. "Remember what happened last ti— Ah, shit."

A small pop followed by a large cloud of smoke.

"Uh-oh." Windbreaker One dropped the canister. "So-orry."

A dense gray fog filled the room, and visibility went from normal to nothing in about a half second.

Piper shouted something I couldn't understand as the woman in the dirty clothes screamed.

A silenced round fired.

In the smoke, I could just make out the figure of Windbreaker One, the closest.

Every ounce of training I had ever received as a law enforcement officer came down to this one truism: Don't shoot one of your own. So I was slow to reach for my Glock. Windbreaker One didn't hesitate. He jabbed my stomach with the muzzle of his MP5. The blow was so hard it felt like the metal of the gun connected with the bone of my spine.

I fell to the floor, tried to remember what breathing felt like.

Smoke and shouts and radio noise. More smoke.

I blacked out.

PART II

"America will never seek a permission slip to defend the security of our people."

   —President George W. Bush,
   State of the Union Address,
   January 20, 2004

"Our values and our belief in God are what made this country great. And one of the values, I believe it's in the Old Testament, is the right to defend ourselves. I'm not just talking about the Second Amendment—your viewers should know by now how I feel about that—I'm talking about our right as a country to defend and secure our borders . . . Yeah, I grew up poor, on the wrong side of the tracks in South Dallas. But one thing I learned in that environment was how to fight, and I am here now, ready to fight for the United States."

   —US Senator Stephen McNally,
   The O'Reilly Factor, October 2011

- CHAPTER EIGHTEEN -

Late morning outside the warehouse in West Dallas.

The muggy air smelled like rotting garbage and diesel fuel. I imagined the stench of blood as well, even though the two dead bodies were inside.

The August sun broke through the scattered clouds long enough to heat up the crumbling asphalt where a half dozen white Tahoes were parked, grill-mounted lights flashing red. The SUVs were just like ours, police suspensions, blue-and-white government plates.

Crime scene tape secured the block and kept out the few locals curious about what was going down. Inside the tape were enough guys in dark suits, windbreakers, and sunglasses to make another *Men in Black* movie.

I stood with my back to the exterior wall of the bar, hands on top of my head, struggling to breathe. My Glock, badge, cell phone, and MP5 lay on the ground next to Piper's subgun, the one used to kill the two thugs. Piper and the strange woman from the shipment had evidently escaped in the confusion.

Windbreakers One and Two were a few yards away by a Tahoe, filling out paperwork.

A guy I took to be their boss stood in front of me.

According to his tag and badge, he was a special agent with the DEA named Keith McCluskey. He was in his mid-thirties and looked like he hadn't slept since grade school. He had a runny nose, and a portion of one eyebrow looked like it had been burned off. Sandy blond hair, lank and flat, tan skin that had gone pale, deep lines in his face.

But his eyes were alert, practically on fire, glowing in their darkened sockets.

Coke or meth? Probably the former, as his teeth looked to be in good condition. If that was the case, he wouldn't be the first narcotics officer to succumb to the lure of the illicit stuff. Sure wouldn't be the last.

He ran his fingers over a blister pack of pills like the bumps of medication were Braille.

Opitrene, the next generation narcotic pain medication, manufactured by McCormack Pharmaceuticals. They were called opie-dopies on the street, about eight bucks a pill depending on the market.

"You know what this is?" McCluskey held up another item, a slim piece of plastic a little smaller than a credit card.

I knew but didn't say. An RFID tag, the device that had triggered the scanner. There was probably one embedded in the cardboard of every carton in the back of the trailer.

"How did you know about this shipment?" He held up the sheet of pills.

I gave him my best thousand-yard stare, a blank expression on my face.

"A couple of freelance contractors," he said. "And you clowns found the big enchilada."

I didn't respond.

It was too soon for the local office to have responded to our call regarding the shipment.

"You don't look familiar," I said. "You a contractor as well?"

The firm I freelanced for had the contract to provide supplemental DEA agents for the Dallas Division. I knew most of the other employees as well as the real DEA agents operating out of the local office.

These guys were part of neither group.

Therefore, they were either real DEA agents from a different field office, highly unlikely, or employees of another, competing law enforcement contracting firm.

A guy in a dark windbreaker approached McCluskey and handed him a file. McCluskey flipped it open and scanned the documents inside.

"You shot two unarmed suspects with hollow points." He read for a few moments and then looked up. "The serial number on the gun with the hollow points goes to your partner."

"I want to talk to my supervisor." I shrugged. "And a lawyer."

"Apparently, this is the same partner who is now aiding and abetting a wanted felon." He shut the file. "How long have you been in contact with Eva Ramirez?"

"Who?"

"The woman in the trailer with the drugs," he said. "Now's not the time to play stupid."

I didn't say anything.

"There's a lot of cash for whoever brings her in." He stepped closer. "Did you think you were gonna screw me out of that? Screw me out of her?"

"I don't know what you're talking—"

McCluskey punched me in the stomach, the same spot as where the muzzle of the submachine gun had hit.

I fell to my knees, tried to detect some oxygen in the

general vicinity of my lungs. Any little bit would do. Stars dotted my vision.

"The scanner." McCluskey knelt beside me. "We picked up two transmissions."

The antenna sign on the screen, they'd triangulated the signal. The amount of resources needed to do that staggered me. Fortunately, I'd turned off the device and left it in the Tahoe hidden down the block, which obviously they hadn't found yet. Sinclair had been right to warn me not to activate the device.

"You appear to have two things in your possession that are very important to me."

I retched, then vomited on the dirty asphalt.

"A classified piece of electronics that is the property of the US government." He rubbed his nose, sniffed. "And a woman named Eva Ramirez, a known associate of several high-ranking cartel members."

"How much coke does it take to get you going in the morning?" I clutched my stomach. "A narc with a drug problem, that is such a cliché."

"You are going to tell me where the scanner is as well as the location of Eva Ramirez." He grabbed a handful of my hair and forced my head up so we were staring at each other.

"If you don't," he said, "then I am going to use a blowtorch on your toes and work my way up."

His matter-of-fact tone was betrayed by the twitch of his feverish eyes. A dot of blood appeared at the base of one nostril.

"Paranoid delusions." I coughed. "Another sign of drug addiction."

"Then you're going to become acquainted with a new Homeland Security program, a little thing we call detain-at-will." He wiped his nose, voice angry now. "Imagine spending the next ten years in Guantanamo Bay."

Before I could come up with a smart-ass reply, his radio squawked, a high-low tone, and an agent approached, whispered in his ear. McCluskey jumped up, looked around.

Sirens in the distance. The other personnel scurried toward their Tahoes. One guy ripped down the crime scene tape. Nobody paid any attention to me.

I struggled to my feet.

McCluskey didn't try to stop me. He pulled the walkie-talkie from his belt and moved a few feet away, speaking into the mouthpiece.

The two agents in the entry team, Windbreaker One and Two, hopped in the closest Tahoe.

In the distance, on the main street, a police car appeared.

McCluskey got in another Tahoe, and all of them sped off in the opposite direction.

I was alone. I grabbed my badge and gun and ran into the bar.

The two dead guys were still there. The room smelled like a copper outhouse—spilled blood, released sphincters—mixed with the acrid tang of the smoke grenade.

I headed to the warehouse, stomach aching not just from the two blows.

Except for dust and rat crap, it was empty.

The trailer was gone.

Five million dollars' worth of opie-dopies disappeared.

I tried to control the mounting panic. After a few moments, I went back outside.

More Dallas police cars than I could count. Three or four white Tahoes. The agent who was our liaison with the regional office of the Drug Enforcement Administration, a man named Phil DeGroot, stood by the front door.

"What the heck's going on here, Jon?" He looked at me. "We've got reports of shots fired. Explosions, too."

Several uniformed police officers entered the bar.

"Piper called in the shipment." He looked up as a Dallas PD helicopter flew over.

A spasm of pain rippled through my abdomen. I clutched my stomach, staggered.

"Well, where is it?" DeGroot caught me so I wouldn't fall.

One of the cops came out. "We've got a crime scene. Two stiffs inside."

"The opie-dopies, what happened to them?" DeGroot said. "And where's Piper?"

I shook my head, felt cold even though the day was brutally hot and getting hotter.

"I have no idea."

- CHAPTER NINETEEN -

The Pussycat Lounge was gone, closed not long after the Night of a Thousand Lap Dances, almost ten years ago. The building had been split into two storefronts, a dialysis center and a payday loan outlet/pawnshop.

Whenever I drove by, I always wondered if you could sell an item in one side to pay for something else in the other.

Over the years, I pieced together the story about the strung-out stripper and the baby with the burned legs.

The guy in the dark suit, Hollis, was a real FBI officer about like I was real employee of the Drug Enforcement Administration. He worked for the domestic division of a company called Paynelowe Industries, a large multinational military contractor based in Alexandria, Virginia. Paynelowe's main source of revenue was supplying armed security consultants for corporate VIPs working in Iraq and Afghanistan. The stateside branch, where Hollis worked, had a contract at the time to staff supplemental positions in the southwest region of the FBI, a tiny tributary in the massive river that was the War on Terror.

The strung-out woman in the storeroom, an alcoholic, drug-addicted stripper, was the mother of the child. The babydaddy—himself a hard-core chemical abuser—was the son of wealth and privilege, the eldest child of a rich man turned US senator.

The key was not really a key, but a thumb drive shaped liked one, the contents of which were the product of one of the stripper's few lucid, self-preserving moments.

The drive contained photos: the babydaddy and the stripper doing the nasty in all sorts of positions and locales, under the influence of various types of substances.

As you can imagine, the Senator—a family values and law-and-order type—was none too pleased about the whole situation. So he called the attorney general and, well, one thing led to another.

Unfortunately, I didn't know any of this when Hollis, a rent-a-badge FBI agent, stepped into the storeroom of the Pussycat Lounge.

All I knew was that I was a Dallas cop who had stumbled upon a child with severely burned legs. The injured child was going to the hospital or I was going to hurt somebody. Badly.

"So which one of you mutts has got the pictures?" Hollis looked at me and Costco. "This key thing?"

I decided to ask the obvious question first. "Why is the FBI involved?"

"The whore's mother." Hollis pointed to the stripper whimpering in the corner. "She's married to an Iranian dude that runs a used car lot in Grand Prairie."

I turned down the volume on my walkie-talkie. "What's that got to do with anything?"

"Iran is a state sponsor of terrorists, dipwad." Hollis rolled his eyes. "That makes this a national security issue."

I didn't reply. The anger welled inside me, a bubble deep down that threatened to burst.

"We don't know anything about a key or any photos," Costco said. "Do we, Jon?"

I shook my head.

Captain Sinclair, possessing the survival instincts of a cockroach, had left the room a few minutes before and not returned. I later found out the owner of the strip club had him on payroll, just as Chung Hee, the owner of the Korean whorehouse, one day would. Unfortunately for the strip club owner, though, there wasn't much Sinclair could do for him with the FBI involved.

"Why don't we take the kid to the hospital and call CPS?" Costco pointed to the infant. "Then you can talk to the stripper about your key or whatever."

"That might have been possible before your partner used the radio and got this little mess logged into the system," Hollis said. "Now we're operating under different rules."

The child woke up. He mewed like a sick kitten, the sound soft but devastating at the same time. The start of the pain.

"We're leaving now." I put my hand on the pistol resting in my Sam Browne belt. "And we're taking the kid."

"I have four agents on the other side of that door." Hollis held up a walkie-talkie. "I don't give them the okay, they're gonna shoot whoever walks out of this room, Dallas Police uniform or not."

A trickle of sweat meandered down Costco's cheek. I squeezed the butt of my gun.

The child began to cry, a mournful wail. The dope the mother had given him was wearing off.

"There's a bureau medical team on their way," Hollis said. "Maybe a half hour out."

"There's a hospital ten minutes away," I said.

"You're new at this, aren't you?" He shook his head.

A dull roar filled my skull. Adrenaline and rage coursed through my system.

"We're cool then," Costco said. "So long as the kid's taken care of." He tugged my arm. "C'mon, Jon. We need to get out of here."

"Not so fast." Hollis held up his hand. "The key. Where is it?"

"We don't have it," I said. "Told you already."

A keening sound from the child, a screech that started at the base of my spine and rose upward.

"My baby." The mother stood, a hand against her bloody nose. "He needs help."

Hollis shoved her back. "Nobody gets anything until I get the pictures."

"P-p-please let me help my baby." She was crying. Blood and mucus mixed with the tears and ran down her face. "I'll give you the photos, just let me help him."

Hollis held out his hand.

"I hid them." She pointed to the child in the carrier. "There."

Costco swore and shook his head. I tried to control the tunnel vision affecting my sight, the cone of anger it projected.

The woman pulled the crying infant gently from the car seat and set him down on one of the tables. She undid the diaper, releasing a sharp ammonia smell, reached under his buttocks.

The child cried harder.

"Criminy, where'd you hide that thing?" Hollis slid on a pair of latex gloves. "You are one sick-ass bitch."

She held up a thumb drive shaped like a key with the logo of a well-known local Realtor on one side, a high-tech gimme advertisement for the wired age.

"You'll get me into rehab?" The woman handed him the thumb drive.

"Sure." Hollis took the device, dropped it into a plastic evidence bag. "Whatever you say."

"And my baby?" She licked her lips. "A doctor's coming for him, right?"

"You got it." Hollis held the walkie-talkie to his ear, his smile as cold as January.

"Then you'll put him into a good foster home? Like we talked about?"

Hollis nodded. There was no trip to rehab in the works. People like Hollis didn't honor deals with marginal members of society like the woman standing in front of us.

The child's cries turned into screams.

"Darn it," said Hollis. "Looks like the medical team's been delayed." He glanced at me and Costco. "You two should get out of here. I'll let them know outside."

"What about the baby?" Costco said.

Hollis shrugged. Not his problem anymore. He'd try, but not very hard.

"Let us take him to the hospital," I said.

"Nope." Hollis shook his head. "This little cluster-fuck has turned into a Homeland Security op now. The kid stays with me."

Calm swept over me at that moment. I pulled out my Dallas Police Department radio and spoke the words that no FBI agent or national security threat could erase.

"Shots fired. Officer down." I rattled off the address for the Pussycat Lounge. "All available units please respond."

"What the hell?" Hollis's face turned pale. "Are you nuts?"

I dropped the radio and pulled the baton from my belt.

The first blow knocked out the teeth on the right side of

his mouth, the heavy wood connecting with a meaty crunch.

Then I hit him again. And again.

After that, things got a little hazy.

And that's how I came to be no longer employed by the Dallas Police Department.

- CHAPTER TWENTY -

I slumped against a hard plastic booth in the Popeyes Fried Chicken on Singleton Boulevard, not far from the warehouse where the shipment had disappeared and a pair of hoods had been killed with Piper's gun. That had been two hours ago.

Piper had disappeared into the white fog and general chaos caused by the grenade, along with the strange woman in the disheveled clothes. I'd thrown up twice more from the smoke and the blow to the gut.

Popeyes was empty of customers except for myself and Phil DeGroot, our DEA supervisor, who was talking to a girl with purple hair behind the cash register.

"What I'm hearing you say is that you don't have a latte machine." Phil stroked his chin.

The girl shook her head, eyes rolling just a tad.

Phil DeGroot was a career bureaucrat. He wore knit ties that weren't long enough, short-sleeved, plaid dress shirts. No-iron Dockers. A Minnesota transplant who liked to go on budget cruises with his wife, Myrna.

"So a cappuccino is out of the question?" Phil chewed his lip, frowned.

"We got, like, decaf." The girl shrugged. "You can put extra sugar in it."

"Tell me about your menu," he said. "Do you have anything that's grilled?"

"Aw, c'mon, Phil. This's a fried chicken joint in West Dallas," I said. "The only thing that's grilled here is the cook's front teeth."

"Hey, that's funny." The girl laughed. "You want some decaf, too?"

I shook my head.

"Something to eat?" Phil looked at me. "You want lunch? My treat."

My stomach was in knots, mostly fear now. Two dead bodies, the missing shipment. I waved him off.

"I'll take a salad and a coffee." Phil paid the girl and then sat down across from me, a steaming cardboard cup in his hand. After a few sips, he looked up, spoke in a quiet voice. "We've got us a little problem here, don't we?"

"The shipment was in the warehouse," I said. "Piper and I both saw it."

"I believe you." Phil dumped a packet of Sweet'N Low in his cup. "Only it's gone now. And so are those other agents you were talking about."

Nobody spoke.

"You tried Piper again?"

I nodded. Seven times now, each call going straight to voice mail.

"Technically speaking, you owe the Drug Enforcement Administration thirteen hundred cartons of Opitrene." He paused for another taste of coffee. "On account of you called it in."

I rubbed my eyes.

"Relax. You're an independent contractor, so it's not like Uncle Sam can garnish your wages."

The girl behind the register called out a number, and Phil slid from the booth and got his salad. When he sat back down, he said, "Of course, you won't be getting paid, either."

"We've got nearly two months into this one." I leaned forward. "You should at least cut loose with some expense money."

"Haven't you read your new contract?" He skewered a tuft of lettuce with a plastic fork. "You opted for lump-sum, performance payments. No expenses, no benefits."

"The other team took the stuff," I said. "The agent in charge was named Keith McCluskey."

"Yeah, we've looked into that." Phil nodded. "He's not a DEA employee either. I'm guessing he's a contractor out of Houston."

"I didn't know Houston contractors had rights in the Dallas region," I said.

"What would I know?" Phil took a bite, chewed thoroughly, swallowed. "I'm just a career DEA agent with twenty-six years' experience."

I massaged my bruised stomach, swallowed a wave of nausea.

"How'd you know about that location?" Phil sliced a tomato.

"A confidential informant."

Rich Dude in his fancy house in Highland Park. Sinclair had told us about a low-level cartel soldier who we'd started following. The soldier had approached Rich Dude about leasing space. We immediately started investigating Rich Dude and used what we learned to lean on him for information about the soldier and his plans for the lease space.

Phil munched another few bites, then pushed his plate away.

"Speaking of Houston. Got an email a day or so ago. One of their scanners has gone missing. Assigned to the company working the South Texas region."

I shrugged, tried to look innocent.

"An outfit you might have heard of," he said. "Paynelowe."

"How'd they get a scanner to lose?" I tried not to think about that name. "Field agents aren't scheduled to get those for another eighteen months."

"Who knows?" He shrugged. "That was the original plan. Had to go through the spook brigade at Langley first."

Neither of us spoke for a few moments.

"Seems Paynelowe's doing overlay work in the Dallas region." Phil drained his coffee cup. "Thought you should be aware of that."

Real DEA agents operated under a regional system designed to keep things organized and sane. Private law enforcement contractors, with their bottom line mentality, had recently lobbied for and won the right to operate more independently. The result, more often than not, was utter confusion on the street.

"Paynelowe." I shook my head. "That explains a lot."

Phil DeGroot clearly had brushed up on my little, all-but-forgotten slice of history with the company, the incident where I bashed in the teeth of a Paynelowe contractor, an FBI agent named Hollis. He also knew of Paynelowe's reputation, as did most law enforcement officers and private contractors. Paynelowe was aggressive to the point of unlawful. Their agents were violent when they didn't need to be, imperious, disrespectful of actual government employees.

I tried Piper's cell again. Nothing.

"The scanner program may not happen as planned." He stuck a toothpick between his front teeth. "The privacy beatniks are all up in arms, some malarkey about *civil rights.*"

"Imagine that." I tried not to sound too sarcastic.

An unmarked Chevy Impala pulled in next to my Tahoe, where the charred scanner sat on the floorboards. Two beefy men in their forties got out. The suits they wore looked like they'd come from the wardrobe department on *Hee Haw.* Homicide investigators.

"Dallas PD wants to talk about those stiffs at the warehouse." Phil watched them walk toward the entrance. "You know these guys, Jon?"

I shook my head. They'd know about me, that's for sure. Mutilate an FBI agent and word gets around.

"Piper's fingerprints were all over the gun." Phil shook his head. "And how many times have I told her not to load up with hollow points?"

He'd obviously saved the most unpleasant topic for last.

"There was an entry team, DEA, like I told you already," I said. "One of them shot the two suspects with Piper's gun. They were both wearing gloves."

"I believe you." He sighed. "Those Paynelowe guys, they play rough. It's gonna be their word against yours." A long pause. "And with your record, well, you know."

I had not told him about the strange woman in the disheveled clothes. Part of me didn't believe she'd really been there. Part of me hoped all of this was a dream. Then I remembered the look in Keith McCluskey's eyes.

"There was another person at the scene." I lowered my voice. "Somebody who saw what happened."

Phil didn't say anything.

"Does the name Eva Ramirez mean anything to you?"

Phil pursed his lips, sucked in a mouthful of air, surprised. The two cops entered the restaurant.

"She disappeared a few days ago," he said. "Set to testify in the Morales trial, the deal in West Texas."

My turn to express surprise. The Morales trial was potentially the biggest strike against Latin American organized crime in a generation. Morales was the number two guy in a major cartel. The thinking was that if he got close enough to going to prison, he might make a deal and turn over the number one guy.

"She's dead by now," Phil said. "That's what everybody's saying."

"We saw her, Piper and me, in the warehouse." I explained briefly. "More importantly, she saw us. Saw who really shot those two guys."

The homicide cops in bad suits stopped at the counter and ordered coffee.

"Me and Myrna have Bible study tonight." He stood. "I've got a ton of paperwork still."

"That's it?" I said. "You're leaving me to deal with these guys alone?"

"I like you, Jon, always have." Phil put his hands on the table, leaned close. "But you make poor choices, get yourself into things that are bad news for everybody."

He shook his head and walked out.

- CHAPTER TWENTY-ONE -

My interview with the two Dallas homicide detectives went about as well as expected.

From the booth in the Popeyes, I tried to explain how two dead guys ended up in the abandoned bar, both killed with my partner's gun. I did not mention the witness, Eva Ramirez. Something told me that now might not be a good time to bring her up. Visions of Sinclair, the crooked ex-cop with the long reach, listening to every word of my supposed confidential interview, danced in my head. Where did he fit in with all of this?

They were homicide investigators so they didn't believe me, as was their way. And since Piper was MIA, they informed me I would be the one indicted once all the paperwork and tests were completed. Oh, happy day.

Fortunately, both of the deceased had extensive criminal histories as well as ties to organized crime, while I possessed a federal law enforcement badge. Unfortunately, the detectives kept wanting to know why my DEA supervisor hadn't stuck around for the initial interview.

I told them again about Keith McCluskey and the other team of agents who seemed to have vanished into the ether.

They didn't write anything down this time, just stared at me. We scheduled a follow-up meeting for the next day, ten in the morning, Dallas police headquarters. A suggestion was made that I bring an attorney and a DEA supervisor.

I scribbled down the details about our next confab on a paper napkin, nodded politely to both men, and left. Outside, I crumpled the napkin into a ball and tossed it on the floor of the Tahoe as I got in the driver's seat. Rule one, Jailhouse School of Law: Never voluntarily enter the police station if you are even remotely suspected of a crime.

I started the engine, took a deep breath, and tried to contain the rising panic. The scanner was sitting on the floorboard in the shoe box where I'd left it.

My federal ID would stall them only so long. Dead bodies meant coroner's reports, referrals to the grand jury. A slow-moving but unstoppable wave of official entanglements was headed my way. Fortunately, the home address on my driver's license and in my personnel file was a condo in Fort Worth, not the borrowed apartment. Tracking me down wouldn't be easy. Piper's records were similar.

I exited the restaurant parking lot. Piper and I had a backup plan, a rendezvous point if things went bad. This certainly qualified. I tried her number again, nothing.

The shotgun houses of West Dallas zoomed by. I pulled onto the freeway, headed back to town. The glass and chrome skyline glistened in the afternoon sun.

The interior of the Tahoe smelled like a house fire, either the residual smoke still in my head from the bar or the charred scanner. Before going to the rendezvous point, I needed to get rid of the thing. None of this would have happened if I hadn't turned it on. If Sinclair hadn't given it to me.

I turned south on Interstate 35, drove past downtown,

and realized I wouldn't have found the drugs or the witness without Sinclair either.

———

The trailer and plot of land where my half sister and father lived was a rental owned by Tanya's ex-sister-in-law, an active-duty noncommissioned officer serving in West Germany.

Tanya and my dad get all their mail at a PO box in Seagoville, a town on the southern border of the county known primarily for being home to a medium-security federal penitentiary. Since it was on the county line, most of the state databases were split, adding an extra layer of difficulty in case anybody wanted to track them down. In other words, the property was virtually untraceable to them and by extension to me.

I turned onto the driveway and stopped. The trailer was barely visible in the distance. Tanya's truck was gone.

Off to the right, a few feet in front of the Tahoe, a narrow path led through the brush.

I left the motor running, got out, and jogged down the trail, the shoe box with the scanner tucked under my arm.

Bamboo intermixed with squat cedar bushes on either side of the trail. At the end of the path sat a storage shed. It was wood-sided, about six feet square, a tin roof.

I opened the door. The interior was full of rusted lawn equipment and smelled of motor oil and insecticide. The floor was rotting plywood.

I found a sheet of plastic, wrapped the shoe box, and then pulled up a corner of the flooring. There was a hollow space, a depression in the dirt that just fit the shoe box. I stuck the package there, replaced the floor, and pushed a broken rototiller over the spot.

Sweat dripped from my face, not just from the heat. I left, mopping my forehead with one hand.

A dog barked in the distance, and a single-engine plane flew overhead not too far away.

I wanted to go see my father. But I didn't.

- CHAPTER TWENTY-TWO -

Nearly ten years ago—maybe a year after the unfortunate incident at the Pussycat Lounge where I encountered Hollis, the FBI contractor—I found myself adrift, both emotionally and professionally, making a subsistence living from the occasional private investigator job.

The pictures on the key-shaped thumb drive had been destroyed, but the debacle at the Pussycat Lounge had ended the only way it could: badly for everybody but the Senator, who was reelected by a landslide.

His son cleaned up for a short period but eventually crashed his Porsche into a house in South Dallas on the way back from a crack dealer. Both car and house were destroyed, and two of the three children asleep in the front bedroom were severely injured. The son served a total of seven hours in jail for his crime. A few months after that, he overdosed and died in a motel room in Galveston.

For assaulting the FBI agent, I was fired but not prosecuted. The media had uncovered Hollis's record during his US Army deployment in Afghanistan, a document that used terms like "excessive civilian casualties" and "unfit for duty" in abundance. A court case would bring all that to light, so the powers that be decided to cut their losses and be satisfied with merely terminating my partner and me. Costco, deep on the wrong side of fifty, took it relatively well even though he was still a couple of years short of his full pension.

The mother of the child with the burned legs never made it to rehab. The EMTs from the ambulance I'd called were finally allowed into the storeroom, and she went to the hospital with her infant. She dried out and detoxed, and her son recovered, though his legs were severely scarred.

Upon her release, she moved in with her mother. She tried to stay clean, but a few months later she'd downed two bottles of Yellow Tail Chardonnay and a hydrocodone and went for a drive with her son in the back of her Hyundai.

When she woke six hours later, she was in the driveway of her mom's house, the keys in one hand, a third empty bottle in the other.

She had no recollection of the day's events. A giant, gaping black hole of unaccounted time. The car was in the same condition as when she left with only an additional twelve miles on the odometer.

Everything was the same, as it should be.

Except her son wasn't in the rear in his car seat.

For years afterward, I would try to understand the emotions that went through her mind at that moment. The horror, the sense of doom.

The child was never seen or heard from again. No corpse turned up. The Amber Alert failed to yield a single lead. Neither did the private detectives that were hired. No ransom note was ever delivered. Nothing. It was as if that baby had never existed. I spent a lot of time and energy tracking down leads but to no avail.

A few months after the child disappeared, I was in a bar near downtown when Costco Barnett, my old partner, came in.

He wore a dark suit, white shirt, and conservative blue tie. He'd lost about forty pounds, and his whiskey tan had faded.

"You're a hard man to find." He ordered a Diet Coke.

"Costco?" I tilted my head, stared at the new image. "What the hell happened to you?"

"Not many people call me that anymore." He held out an FBI badge. "I'm a federal agent now."

"You? A Fed?"

"Yep. Well, a government contractor," he said. "Ever see those guys in Iraq that look like they ought to be at the country club in their khaki pants and button downs, carrying machine guns?"

"The private military contractors?" I said. "The mercenaries?"

"Please." He held an index finger to his lips. "We don't use the *m* word."

"But you're a federal agent?" I couldn't quite get my head around what he was saying.

"I'm both. It's the coming thing." He nodded. "I actually work for a firm called Blue Dagger Industries."

"Blue what?" I ordered another beer.

"Look, dipwad." He pointed a finger at me. "I'm trying to offer you a job. We need warm bodies with law enforcement experience."

"Even with my record?"

We'd both been terminated but, because I had assaulted Hollis, the black marks in my file far outweighed his.

He nodded. "You can't be on salary like me, but you can still make good money."

I didn't say anything. I thought about my life at the moment. Costco nodded, seemed to read my thoughts.

"Blue Dagger would pay you the daily rate," he said. "Plus a 401(k) account and a commission."

"A commission?"

"We need DEA agents. Whatever the street value is of any contraband you seize, we pay you a percentage."

"You're kidding, right?"

"Nope." He shook his head.

"I'd be a federal agent?" I said. "But work for a private company?"

Costco nodded. "Blue Dagger wants you on the team."

I pondered that for a moment. Then, I said, "Why me?"

"Your record." He stared at the pool, chewed on his lip. "It's a good match with the narcs."

I didn't press him. Did he mean my record as a cop, or my record that got me fired as a cop?

"I don't actually do fieldwork," he said. "I'm a recruiter. My commission comes when I sign up guys like you."

Neither of us spoke for a few moments. The implication floated in the smoky air of the bar. Costco was there because I owed him.

"When do I start?" I said.

"Yesterday woulda been good." He straightened his tie. "Get cleaned up and I'll introduce you to your supervisor, Phil DeGroot."

- CHAPTER TWENTY-THREE -

Ernesto Fuentes-Manzanares reviewed the notes from his business trip to the East Coast and his meeting with Senator Stephen McNally. He was sitting in a window seat in first class, a United flight from Dulles to San Diego.

Banco Manzanares Internationale, Ernesto's family business, had entered into an arrangement with a Mexico-based organization with financial concerns in the United States—mainly bridge loans and various cash flow services—and Ernesto had been tasked with due diligence, inspecting facilities and inventory.

His personal guard, a former Mossad agent, occupied the aisle seat, still wearing the same gray suit.

Ernesto carried the envelope Senator McNally had given him in the breast pocket of his velvet blazer. He wore the jacket for the entire flight. The black looked spectacular with the purple of his shirt, so he saw no need to remove it.

When they landed at San Diego International Airport, two freshly washed Suburbans met them at the curb outside the terminal. Both vehicles were armored. The drivers worked for the security division of the La Jolla office of Banco Manzanares.

The first SUV had California plates. Ernesto handed the driver the envelope that Senator McNally had given to him, and the vehicle sped away.

The second Suburban had Mexican plates, and Ernesto and his personal guard slid into the rear seat. A security agent, armed like the driver, rode in the front passenger side.

Before shutting the door, Ernesto took a deep breath of the sea air, marveling at the beauty and balmy temperature of Southern California after the heat and humidity of Washington.

After stopping for Starbucks, they headed south, a straight shot down I-5 to San Ysidro where the interstate breached the Mexican border at the world's busiest land crossing.

A little after lunch, the crossing point wasn't very crowded, only a ten-minute wait in the eight lanes of traffic headed toward Baja California.

They entered Mexico, waved through by a tired-looking border guard, and soon they were on the crowded main thoroughfare heading south, the Paseo de Los Heroes. Except for the billboards for the men's clubs, this part of Mexico looked remarkably like what they had just passed in San Diego, strip malls and office buildings, chain outlets and fast-food restaurants.

Twenty minutes later, the cartel spotters picked them up, just past the Ensenada-Tijuana Highway. Two young men in a late-model Camaro stuck on their tail like a husk on a tamale.

The guard in the front seat looked in the back at Ernesto and his personal security man, the Israeli.

Ernesto finished his coffee and said in Spanish, "Who are they?"

The driver shook his head. "I don't know."

The ex-Mossad guard removed two handguns from a case on the floor of the backseat.

"Pull over then," Ernesto said. "Let's make this quick. I have another flight."

There were too many criminal organizations battling for too little territory, everybody scrambling for market share, trying to earn a peso however they could. Whomever the people in the Camaro worked for, they had obviously spotted a rich-looking target, an armored SUV, and decided to follow for a while, probably calling ahead to set up a hijacking. The Suburban was worth a great deal of money. Wealthy kidnapping victims perhaps even more.

Poor fools, Ernesto thought as his vehicle pulled into the parking lot of a vacant warehouse.

The Camaro stopped behind them at an angle, and the young man in the passenger seat got out, approaching the Suburban.

Ernesto didn't wait. He exited, too, his guard following.

The young man stopped. Arms crossed, an insolent smirk on his face.

"Who do you work for?" Ernesto said.

"What's in the truck?" The young man spat on the ground. "You travel this road, you have to pay a toll to us."

"Your boss." Ernesto pointed at the man. "Who is he?"

"What do you care, *maricón*?" The young man spat again. "Just pay the fucking toll."

Ernesto ignored the insult against his sexual orientation. He said, "Do you work for that imbecile, el Camello?" A pretty safe bet. The Camel was the leader of one of the larger criminal organizations, an outfit that controlled this part of Tijuana.

The smirk slid off the man's face, and he reached under his shirt. One did not slander the leader like that.

Ernesto snapped his fingers, held out his hand. The Israeli guard placed one of the guns in his palm.

"Do you not know who I am?" Ernesto said.

The man paused, a pistol half drawn from his waistband, a fearful look in his eyes. His partner, the driver of the Camaro, got out but made no move toward his friend, a confused expression on his face.

"Did they not give you a list of license plates and a description of vehicles to avoid?" Ernesto said.

The man looked puzzled, vaguely apprehensive. He eased the gun back in his waistband.

Ernesto tossed a business card on the ground. "Go ahead. Pick it up."

The man did as requested. He read the card, began to whimper. The driver got back in the car.

"I am so s-sorry, Señor Manzanares." The man crossed himself. "Please forgive me."

Ernesto shot him in the knee.

The man screamed, fell to the asphalt.

Ernesto handed the gun back to his guard. He walked over to where the thug lay. He looked down at him and said, "I wonder how far you can get on one leg before el Camello finds you."

The man clutched his bleeding knee and wept.

Ernesto sauntered back to the Suburban.

The rest of his journey was uneventful.

- CHAPTER TWENTY-FOUR -

At five o'clock on the day two unarmed cartel soldiers had been killed with Piper's gun, I parked in the side lot of a used bookstore near Live Oak Street and Skillman in Old East Dallas. The bookstore was next to a Luby's cafeteria, a Unitarian church, and a place where you could sell your blood for cash. Across the street was an Irish pub and a Vietnamese restaurant.

The neighborhood was an ethnic stew—urban, part hipster, part senior citizen, part homeless—easy to blend in. The bookstore was our rendezvous point.

Even though the apartment at the Cheyenne was most likely untraceable to us, the smart move was to avoid that locale for the time being. What money I had was in my pocket along with my badge and cell phone, which had my contacts, employment info, and the like. Nothing was left in the apartment that I wouldn't mind losing.

The bookstore was in an old building made from weathered Austin stone, a series of small rooms filled with paperbacks and worn carpet.

I found Piper in the erotica section, alone. She was sitting in an easy chair, reading a paperback edition of a Robert Crais detective novel.

"Took you long enough." She closed the book.

"What happened?" I picked up a worn copy of *The Sensuous Woman.*

"The smoke bomb went off, I ran to the warehouse," she said. "Only it was full of guys in blue windbreakers."

I nodded.

"There was a fire exit on the side. We missed it when we came in. The girl and I went out that way."

"What happened to her?"

Piper closed her eyes, and a wave of fatigue washed across her face.

"The girl? Well, she didn't think much of escaping with me. Packs a mean right hook."

"Ouch."

"It was brushy on that side of the building." She sighed. "I lost her. My phone got broken, too."

A young man in dreadlocks and a Che Guevara T-shirt came into the room. He looked around for a moment and then left.

"There were about a zillion guys in windbreakers out there." Piper hugged herself. "I ran down the alley and hid. Made my way here on foot for a while and then caught a cab."

"The windbreakers were DEA contractors, Paynelowe's people." I filled her in on what had gone down from my end. Told her about the interview with the Dallas homicide detectives and the name of the woman, Eva Ramirez. Relayed the information about the fifty-thousand-dollar bounty and the trial in West Texas of the cartel bigwig.

"So this woman is the only person who can clear us of killing those two hoods?" Piper said. "Clear me, since it was my gun the crazy dude used."

I nodded.

"And we lost the shipment and all that money?"

"Yep." I sat down in the chair next to hers.

"We're screwed eight ways to Sunday." She rubbed her eyes.

"That we are."

Neither of us spoke for a few moments. Then Piper said, "This morning, I got an email about the Tucson office needing Border Patrol agents." She frequented the message boards and Internet sites people like us used to find work. "Two-fifty a day plus a discount at Holiday Inn." She paused. "Come with me, Jon. Let's get out of Texas for a while."

The Dallas Police would inevitably put out a nationwide APB for us over the two dead thugs. But we both had second, almost-legitimate IDs that would let us work as contractors. For a while.

"Let's think this through," I said. "Running away won't fix anything."

"It'll fix it for a while," she said. "Maybe you and I could find something different by then. Maybe the witness, this Eva whatever, will turn up."

"I don't know." I frowned. "You ever been to Arizona in the summer?"

She didn't speak. She pressed her lips together, a jumble of emotions sweeping across her face.

"Going away together to see all the kids you sponsored." I shook my head. "That was one thing. But we need to clear this mess up before we just run off to Arizona."

"So it's okay to run off with me when the times are good?" She arched an eyebrow. "But when the going gets a little rough, you need to think about it?"

"That's not what I meant."

"Am I that damaged?" She shook her head. "You won't even commit in order get out of the crosshairs?" A long pause. "I'm gonna catch a Greyhound day after tomorrow."

"It's not you. There's just—" I stopped, no more words to come that would make sense.

She stood and left. I followed. A handful of customers browsed in the front of the store. We walked past the cashier's stand, and no one paid us any mind.

Outside, we paused on the front steps as the heat and humidity swirled around us.

"The Tahoe's around on the side." I pointed. "Let's get some food and find a place to—" I stopped talking as a pale yellow Bentley pulled into the space facing us, and a man with a buzz cut and a bushy Fu Manchu mustache jumped out of the passenger side.

Tommy, Sinclair's flunky.

He held a pistol pressed against his thigh, out of view from most passersby. He surveyed the parking lot and then tapped the window of the $200,000 car.

Sinclair hefted his bulk from behind the wheel of the Bentley.

"How could you screw up something that easy?" The fat man propped his elbows up on the door frame and roof. "I practically drew you a map."

"The warehouse," I said. "What was your angle on that anyway?"

"Take down a shipment of stolen pills, all you had to do." He rolled his eyes. "You're DEA agents for Pete's sake. That's what you do, ain't it?"

I didn't say anything. This wasn't about pills or other contraband.

"Get in the backseat." Tommy pointed to the ultraexpensive auto with his free hand.

"How did you find us?" Piper asked.

"We're the po-lice," Tommy said. "Now get in the car."

Across the street, the parking lot of the Luby's was full of Dallas PD vehicles, early dinner for the evening shift.

We were armed, but Tommy had the drop on us and there didn't seem much sense in starting a gun battle on a busy public thoroughfare. Besides, the car was air-conditioned.

Piper and I got in the rear.

Sinclair got behind the wheel. Tommy sat in the passenger side and aimed the pistol at me between the two front seats.

Sinclair sighed and turned the AC to high. "Jon, if there was an Olympic Dumbass Team, you'd be captain."

"Nice car," I said. "Is 'Baby Diarrhea Yellow' a custom color, or did they have one on the lot?"

"You have done a whole lot in one day," he said. "You have pissed off an entire Mexican drug cartel, me, and the DEA."

Tommy chuckled.

"And that, my little friend, is a spicy enchilada." He put his hands on the wheel, drummed his fingers. The sunlight glinted off the diamond-crusted Rolex on his wrist. "Oh, and let's not forget the district attorney who's gonna indict you over those two dead hoods."

"We didn't kill anybody," Piper said. "Unfortunately."

"Jon, your daddy and me go way back." Sinclair ignored her. "We stood down a bunch of Bandidos on the county line this one time. He saved my bacon, truth be told."

The Bandidos were a motorcycle gang, a Texas version of Hell's Angels.

"Your daddy was good police," Sinclair said. "You were too, so they tell me, before you went postal on that fed."

I didn't reply.

"So that's the only reason you and me are having a civil conversation right now."

"You don't give a damn about the shipment." I decided to state the obvious. "You're after the witness. Eva Ramirez."

"Bingo." He touched his nose. "And now, because you screwed up, she is on the loose somewhere in our fair city."

"Not to worry," I said. "Pretty sure those Paynelowe guys are gonna find her."

Neither Sinclair nor the goon spoke. The atmosphere in the car grew chilly.

Piper looked at me and shrugged.

"That would be bad, Jon." Sinclair's tone was soft, hard to hear. "Very, very bad."

I didn't say anything.

"You're gonna find her, Jon. You're gonna use your federal badge and track her down, and then you're gonna call Tommy, so we can come get her. We clear on that?"

"Is now a good time to talk about payment for this little service?" Piper said. "I'm thinking a hundred K. Jon, what's your number?"

Sinclair shifted his gaze to my partner. "You remind me of a stripper I used to know. She thought she was funny, too. Had a big time when I had to cut her down to size."

Tommy chuckled.

"As I was saying." Sinclair turned back to me. "You find her and then call me."

"Piper's got a point," I said. "What's in it for us?"

Sinclair didn't respond. The back of his neck grew red.

"She's the only person who can clear us for killing those two guys," I said.

"A video tape," Tommy said. "We get her, and we'll let her do a video that says you two weren't involved."

Sinclair clenched the wheel, knuckles white. After a few moments he nodded.

"You've got a day or so before the DA issues a warrant," Tommy said. "So you better make good time."

"If I knew where your old man was." Sinclair spoke in a whisper. "I'd spell it out just for him about how important it is that you cooperate with me on this issue. You get my meaning?"

I weighed my options, which spanned the gamut from zero to nothing.

"And don't think about going to the US Marshals or the DA with her neither. Or that prissy boss of yours, Phil DeGroot." Sinclair shook his head. "I got eyes and ears everywhere."

Piper and I looked at each other but didn't say anything.

Sinclair popped the locks. "Now get the hell out of my car."

———

They watched Jon and Piper walk around the side of the building to where their government-issued Tahoe was parked.

Sinclair was still behind the wheel, staring at the two people he'd just threatened.

Tommy said, "They're gonna find her and run straight to Phil DeGroot."

Sinclair nodded.

"What should we do?" Tommy asked. "Can't get any of our people involved."

"We get a hold of DeGroot," Sinclair said. "Explain how he *really* needs to cooperate."

Tommy's cell was sitting on the console. It rang, an out-of-state area code, Maryland.

"Who are these people that keep calling?" Tommy punched the End button. "Wish you'd get a cell phone like everybody else."

Sinclair stifled a smart-ass reply. The anger he'd felt for Jon Cantrell dissipated, replaced by fear. The number was associated with Hawkins. Nothing good could come from Hawkins right now.

"That call's about some other stuff I've been working on. None of your business." Sinclair licked his lips. "Bunch of goddamn Yankees."

"They're actually not Yankees in Maryland," Tommy said. "I think that was considered a border state during the Civil War."

"When the fuck did you go to college?" Sinclair wiped his sweaty palms on his pants.

Tommy didn't say anything. He rocked slightly in his seat, frowning.

"Something else on your mind, Einstein?" Sinclair slammed the transmission into reverse.

"DeGroot is a federal agent. A real one." Tommy buckled his seat belt. "We can't be messing with a real live fed."

Sinclair accelerated. "We ain't got no choice."

- CHAPTER TWENTY-FIVE -

Piper and I got in the Tahoe and left the bookstore parking lot.

Neither of us spoke. Piper used my cell phone to check for messages about the Tucson job.

I headed toward the city center. We needed more information and we needed it fast.

Downtown Dallas had once been thriving, luxury hotels and Victorian buildings interspersed with the occasional brothel and gambling den. The vice went underground at the turn of the last century, after which came the flight to suburbia that left the concrete canyons barren, populated by the dregs of society—the bums and drunks and junkies—and the lawyers who fed off the work from the courthouse.

Now tastes had changed, and most of the area was fashionable, an up-and-coming residential neighborhood full of loft apartments, expensive restaurants, and nightclubs.

And one holdover from another era, a place called the Main Street Dash, the kind of bar Dean Martin might have visited if he wanted to go slumming. The establishment wasn't actually on Main Street, but on a side alley a few blocks from city hall and the freeway, next to a soup kitchen and a boarded-up pawnshop.

I parked across the street near where an obese woman in torn hose and a miniskirt leaned against a building. Piper and I got out.

A neon sign flickered over the entryway to the bar, but the D had burned out totally, as had a portion of the H, so if you didn't look too closely it appeared to read MAIN STREET ASS.

I opened the door, and we stepped into the Dash.

Monday evening, the dinner hour, and the place was nearly full, most of the crowd in their fifties or beyond, or maybe just appearing to be that age due to a lot of city miles.

The patrons were a mix of blue and white collars, all of them bleary-eyed, hard-core yet functional drunks. A couple of uniformed cops worked on mugs of beer and shots. A handful of people looked like they'd recently been paroled after serving twenty to life.

In the middle was a horseshoe bar, tended by a peroxide blond old enough to be Dolly Parton's mother. Faded shag carpet covered the walls, dotted with framed photos of B-list celebrities from the sixties.

I let my eyes adjust to the dim lights and my ears to the laughter and clinking glasses.

An old Marvin Gaye song played on the jukebox, "Let's Get It On."

The cops ignored us.

I leaned on the bar, spoke to Dolly Parton. "Is Milo around?"

Piper flanked out, moving to the far side of the room.

"What do you want with Mister Miller?" She peeled a piece of nicotine gum.

I badged her.

She nodded once, stuck the gum in her mouth, and picked up a phone.

I walked to the other side of the horseshoe, sat down near Piper, a barstool between us.

Two minutes later, the door leading to the back opened and a man with scraggly red hair and matching beard stepped into the room.

Milo Miller was built like the kid always picked last for dodgeball, short and scrawny.

The cops sat up a little straighter. Dolly poured a little quicker. The ex-cons backed away.

Except to those who knew him, Milo Miller was about as threatening as a lamppost.

I knew him very well, and I was fearful.

The last time we'd met in person he'd been dressed like Vanilla Ice, but less tasteful.

Now he wore the garb of a Hasidic Jew, black suit with matching wide-brimmed fedora, white shirt, no tie. Curly sideburns and thick glasses with heavy black frames.

His eyes swept the room before settling on Piper. After a few moments, he walked around the bar and sat on the stool between the two of us.

"Jon's a schmuck," he said. "Undying love, Piper. This I pledge to you."

Without being asked, Dolly Parton placed three drinks in front of us, mugs of foaming Budweiser for me and Piper, a sweating bottle of Big Red soft drink for Milo.

Piper groaned and took a swig of beer. She closed her eyes.

"Nice getup," I said. "When did you start going to synagogue?"

"A devout man does not attract the attention of the authorities."

He stroked the scar on his cheek that he'd gotten during one of his stints in juvenile. He'd been twelve at the time.

"Your little foray in West Dallas this morning," he said. "What a mess that was."

Piper opened her eyes. "We didn't kill those two gangbangers."

"Their employers don't see it that way." He patted her hand. "I will of course offer you my protection."

Piper moved her arm. "I can take care of myself."

"In exchange, you would have to lay with me." He leered at her. "In the biblical sense."

Piper curled her lip.

"Let's sign both of you up on Match-dot-com and see what happens," I said. "In the meantime. tell me what you've heard about Sinclair's operation of late."

"In the punch bowl of life," Milo sighed, "Sinclair is a floating turd."

The jukebox changed songs. The Bee Gees, "Stayin' Alive."

"Why do you do business with him?" Milo looked at me. "Any fiefdom in my kingdom I can offer you, yet you want to play with this swine?"

"I'm not going to work for you," I said.

"Oh, yes." He stroked his chin. "Your high ethical standards."

"That's me, a regular Eliot Ness." I took a long pull of beer. "Any idea why Sinclair would be interested in a witness in a big cartel trial?"

Milo didn't reply. His face went blank, eyes empty, devoid of any expression. The silence dragged on, got uncomfortable.

I sipped beer, waited. After about a half minute, I asked the bartender for a bag of pretzels. Hadn't eaten since morning. I was halfway finished with the snack when my friend spoke again.

"I've started a new venture." Milo pulled out a business card. "Miller Law Enforcement Services."

The card had an emblem that look like a cross between the seal for the State of Texas and the US Capitol.

"I have a contract to transport convicts to the penitentiary," he said. "A great way to keep tabs on what the lowlifes are up to."

"But you're a convict." I tried not to sound incredulous. "Now you're a contractor, too?"

"Indicted only." He wagged a finger. "They never proved any of that stuff."

"Back to my original question." I put the card in my pocket. "Sinclair and the cartels?"

He stared at a blank spot on the far wall, the wheels churning, his mind worrying over the answer.

"Some topics," he said. "Questions, they shouldn't be asked."

"This is important, Milo, very important."

"My life, I owe you, Jonathan." He touched my arm. "Walk away from this one."

"The witness can clear us of killing those two thugs." Piper filled him in briefly.

Nobody spoke for a while. Dolly Parton opened another piece of nicotine gum.

"You should leave town," Milo said. "You need money? I have the ten grand I owe you."

I shook my head. "You don't owe me anything."

When I had allegedly saved Milo's life—really nothing more than a well-timed knuckle shot to the crotch of a crooked bookie—I had also enabled him to recover a large sum of money. The ten thousand was a finder's fee, something I had never accepted, preferring to keep our relationship strictly social with only the occasional item of business, usually just the sharing of select tidbits of information.

"Hypothetically speaking." Milo rubbed his eyes. "What if Sinclair provided certain services that aided in the transportation and security of a certain, er, product."

"A crooked ex-cop with his contacts." Piper nodded. "He could be the Shield for North Texas."

Milo clutched his chest. "This term, not to be used in my establishment."

A Shield was a regional position, like a traffic coordinator for the various narcotraffickers. The job title had been created by the cartels in response to the massive, publicity-attracting violence that had plagued the border region, an attempt to keep the peace in the major metropolitan areas north of the border. For a small percentage paid by all the cartels, a Shield ensured that product moved safely through a given area. The Shield also ensured that all disputes were settled in unpopulated areas.

"With Sinclair's track record," I said, "if he gets tied to that sort of an operation, they'd throw him under the jail for life."

Milo nodded. "Now imagine, again hypothetically, if someone like that started skimming."

I closed my eyes and smelled the leather in the Bentley, saw the light glint off the diamonds on Sinclair's Rolex.

Piper said, "Are you telling us—"

"Nothing, this is what I am telling you," Milo said. "You two should leave town."

"But we need to find the witness," Piper said. "We're both going down on a double manslaughter beef if we don't."

"Eva Ramirez," I said. "That's her name."

"Oy." Milo covered his ears. "Enough."

"Can you help us track her down?" I asked.

He didn't reply.

"Anything at all would be a help," I said.

"Nothing is as it seems, Jonathan." He spoke the words softly. "This you must understand."

I sighed. "Make sense, will you?"

"A history lesson." He looked at each of us. "Would you mind listening to one?"

I shrugged. "Whatever ices your cake."

"In World War II, the feds let the mob have a free pass," he said. "Anything they wanted, within reason."

I nodded.

"They ran the ports through the unions. You know this, right?"

I nodded again.

"In exchange, the mob helped the war effort. Secured the harbors, made sure shipments went through easily."

"What's your point?" Piper said.

"What is this mess you are involved in right now?" he said. "What is it called?"

"I don't understand." I arched an eyebrow at Piper. "It's called our job."

"They have a name for it, don't they? The War on Drugs, that's what they call it in the papers."

"Yes," Piper said. "That's what they call it."

"Note the first word." He flexed his hands, examined his fingernails. "*War.*"

"But the war is against drugs," I said. "Why would they make a deal with the dealers? The enemy?"

"Jon's right," Piper said. "That'd be like the feds in World War II making a deal with the Nazis."

"Don't you ever wonder if there's something beyond the cartels?" Milo sighed.

"Why?" I asked. "You know something we don't?"

"No. I'm just a student of history" He finished his soft drink. "The alliances and undercurrents of our world are fascinating."

"Piper and I have become fascinated with staying alive and out of jail," I said.

"Perhaps I can learn something about this Eva person. Call me in the morning."

"Thank you." Piper stood.

"A condo in South Padre." Milo put his hand on her arm. "Run away with me and it's yours."

She plucked his fingers from her flesh, one by one, then headed to the door.

I slid off the barstool and pointed to his outfit. "Do you even believe in God?"

"Last week I'm pretty sure I screwed the Devil himself out of seven whorehouses on the west side of town." He paused. "Does that count?"

- CHAPTER TWENTY-SIX -

We left Milo's bar in the middle of rush hour, the streets and freeways clogged with cars and trucks and blue clouds of exhaust fumes. The grimy skins of the glass towers in downtown fractured the setting sun into a thousand yellow reflections, wedges of light that seemed to have no purpose or focus.

A few blocks from the Main Street Dash, I pulled into a parking lot across the street from the Dallas City Hall, a bizarrely shaped wedge of a building that looked like an upside-down, sand-colored triangle. The spot I'd picked had no camera coverage.

I flipped on the hazard lights and got out. From the back, I retrieved a small toolkit.

Using a screwdriver, I disconnected the power cord from the two-way radio as well as the networked laptop mounted on the transmission hump. Both had the ability to act as transponders, homing devices that broadcast the vehicle's location to whoever had the proper equipment.

Since warrants were about to be issued for us, it would only be a matter of time before Phil DeGroot or the honchos at Blue Dagger demanded the government-issued vehicle back. With the inherent bureaucracy that comes from public agencies interacting with the private sector, this might take weeks. Following the vehicle electronically could be authorized in a few hours, especially by an unscrupulous contractor like Paynelowe who might wave the national security flag.

While I did that, Piper detached a slim piece of plastic about the size of a credit card that was mounted to the windshield by the rearview mirror. The item was a device for electronic toll collection, or ECT, called a TollTag in North Texas. In different parts of the country it had different names: E-ZPass, Smart Tag, and so on.

She ripped it in two, shredding the passive RFID tag it contained.

In the United States, about twenty percent of the quarter-billion passenger vehicles were equipped with an electronic toll collection device of some sort. This percentage was rising as more local governments contracted with private companies to operate public roads as tollways.

Similarly, about twenty percent of the highways were equipped with tag readers, another figure that was increasing each year.

With the right equipment and authorization, a government entity could track a car pretty easily by its ECT device.

But we didn't stop there.

Piper popped the hood, and I went to the front of the Tahoe. She came up beside me and handed me a utility knife.

"You ever done this before?" she said.

"Once." I nodded. "Should last for a day or so."

Not many people had heard about the Transportation Security Act, a little-known piece of legislation drafted by the Republicans, signed by a Democrat, and lobbied for by the auto parts industry. Our concern at the moment was a tiny clause in the act, what was informally called the Loose

Juice Amendment. The clause, like most government initiatives, was a bastardized abortion of a compromise, equal parts inventory control, 9/11 hangover, and pork pie.

The amendment required that all vehicle batteries in the United States manufactured after a certain date be equipped with permanent RFID tags. Removal of the tag was punishable by up to ten years in Club Fed and would disable the battery within twelve to twenty-four hours.

The tags, of course, were registered to the owner of the car or the person who bought the battery. That name would eventually be linked seamlessly to the various criminal and civil databases used by law enforcement.

"There it is." I pointed to a card-size bump on the Sears DieHard, an active tag that emitted a very low-strength signal powered by the auto battery itself.

Piper nodded. "Go for it."

Two months ago, we'd been in a hotel bar in Austin where we'd met a drunk contractor for the National Security Agency. The guy had told us about a new, cheap tag reader that was being mass-produced ostensibly for the Department of Transportation. The device required very little power to function but was still able to beam information to a series of repeaters, which in turn sent the information to the main NSA location, a sprawling campus on the eastern seaboard.

The really chilling part of his drunken tale?

The Department of Transportation, at the behest of Homeland Security, was planning to install the cigarette-pack-sized device on signal lights across the country as well as in select roadside junction boxes, essentially anywhere a steady source of electricity could be found.

This meant that when the system was fully implemented, Uncle Sam could, without using satellites, track a particular vehicle in real time across the United States.

I jammed the blade under the upraised portion and cut. A few seconds later, the tag came free, dangling a series of wires.

"First thing tomorrow." I tossed it in the gutter. "We stop at an auto parts store and get a new battery."

"They'll eventually tie the new one to us, won't they?" Piper packed up our tools.

"Yeah, but it will slow them down a lot."

We got back in the front seat. I took out my cell phone, turned it off, and removed the SIM card from the back.

"There's disposables at the apartment," Piper said.

We kept a supply of untrackable pay-as-you-go phones handy.

"We're not going back to the apartment."

"I've got some cash there, too."

I started the engine but didn't say anything.

"I need to go back to the Cheyenne," she said.

"We'll stop at a Target or something." I pulled out of the parking lot. "Get fresh clothes."

"But the children, the ones I sponsor." She stared straight ahead, voice stiff. "The pictures. Their information."

"They're just photographs." I spoke in a gentle tone. "You've never actually met any of them."

She was silent for a few moments. Then she nodded. "You're right."

"You can get more pictures."

"I know."

I stopped at a light, blinked several times, trying to wake up. The fatigue and extreme stress of the day was catching up with me.

"There's a picture of my mother at the apartment, too," she said.

I turned and stared.

"It's the only thing of hers I've got."

"You never told me."

"Lots I haven't told you." She buckled her belt. "I dream about her sometimes."

From sleeping in the same bed together, I'd ascertained Piper's dreams to be much like mine, cyclones of unexpressed emotion. Fear and rage. Tears.

"I dream of going to the park with her in the springtime for a picnic," she said. "There's tulips everywhere. I'm, oh, maybe a year and a half or two."

"But she gave you up at birth, right?"

"That's what they told me." She sighed. "I wonder sometimes though."

"You should have the picture of your mother," I said.

A police car, lights and sirens blazing, sped through the intersection on the cross street. We both flinched.

"Seems so real, that picnic," Piper said. "The flowers. The toys—there were tons of dolls and stuff. And my mother, I remember she made goose-liver sandwiches."

"Goose liver?"

"With Grey Poupon mustard." Piper smiled. "I can still taste them."

"We'll get the picture. Not sure how, but we'll do it."

"After that, my next memory is nothing but gray." She shook her head. "The orphanage. All I had was this one doll that I remembered from the picnic."

The light changed. I accelerated away from the intersection and downtown Dallas.

"But this girl in the bunk across the room took it. And I never saw it again."

"The picture of your mother," I said. "Where did that come from?"

"My foster family when I was ten. They were actually nice people, not in it for the money from the state." She shuddered a little. "They found it in the file and gave it to me."

I turned a corner, drove past the farmers market, and accelerated onto the freeway.

"Where we gonna stay tonight?" She shifted in her seat, relaxing a little. Her tone of voice and mood shifted as well.

We both subscribed to the same theory: The past was a dangerous place to visit; don't go too often.

I told her what our best option was—one the northern suburbs, maybe Plano. Away from the Dallas police and the inner city where the cartels operated their wholesale businesses. Away from Sinclair.

"Tomorrow, early, we start looking," I said. "If you can get in without being spotted, we'll stop at the Cheyenne too."

"What's gonna happen to us?" She stared out the window as the city passed by.

"We'll find the witness, this Eva Ramirez person." I spoke the words with a conviction that I didn't really feel. "Then we turn her over to Phil DeGroot and get clear on the two dead guys. Maybe collect the reward."

Also on my to-do list: dispose of the scanner I'd hidden on my father's property and find out why a corrupt ex-cop like Sinclair was so interested in the missing witness. Ditto on the cokehead DEA agent, McCluskey. Maybe, if I could learn why the two men were so intent on finding her, we could neutralize the both of them. I tried not to think about my father and his biopsy. His need for cash.

"You are so dense." She shook her head. "I meant us-us."

"Oh, you and me? That *us*?" I pulled onto the freeway on the south side of downtown. "You and me will run away and live happily every after in a cottage with a white picket fence."

"Smart-ass."

"What do you want me to say?"

"I want you to say everything will be all right."

I reached across the console and grasped her hand but didn't speak.

"I've never been in this deep before," she said. "And I'm scared."

I drove north and tried to think of something comforting to say.

- CHAPTER TWENTY-SEVEN -

We woke at dawn in an old motor court motel in Plano, thirty miles north of downtown Dallas. We cleaned up in a mold-ridden bathroom, dressed in fresh clothes we'd bought yesterday with our dwindling supply of cash.

Most of Plano was white-bread suburbia, a farming village transformed during the last part of the twentieth century into Anytown-Subdivision, USA.

The little pocket of town where we spent the night missed the trip to the mall. The clerk at the motel was named Patel, and the restaurant across the parking lot where we ate breakfast was an old Denny's. The manager there was Iranian.

After we ate, I sent Piper to get a battery at the auto parts store the next block over while I called Milo from a pay phone on the side of the restaurant.

"Who the hell is this?" Milo answered after one ring.

"Your pal, Jon."

"Dead to me, that's what Jon is." He hung up.

I drummed my fingers on the Plexiglas cover that shielded the phone and waited. Probably only three pay phones in all of Plano; I was lucky to find one. A tweaker in a flannel shirt appeared from behind the Dumpster and asked if I had any change. I badged him, and he left.

Ninety seconds later, the phone rang.

"Hello," I answered.

"An address and some advice." Milo's voice sounded far away. "That's what I am going to give you."

"Go." I pulled a pen and pad from my pocket.

"Which would you like first?"

"C'mon, Milo. Make with the address, will you?"

"The advice first then." He cleared his throat. "The organization that owned the property in the trailer yesterday at the warehouse."

"The stolen pharmaceuticals?" I said. "The cartel?"

"Jonathan?" He spoke very softly. "We don't use the *c* word."

"Whatever."

"This organization, they are very angry with you over the two missing items, the product and this Eva person." He breathed heavily into the phone. "Their bosses and those above them are angry. You need to leave the area, Jonathan. This is my advice. Leave, in an expedient manner."

"The bosses of the bosses?" I said. "Who's above the head of a cartel?"

"Remember what I told you yesterday."

Milo's hypothetical question from the day before: Don't you ever wonder if there's something beyond the cartels? That little nugget had come after his musings about Sinclair being the Shield, a traffic coordinator for the various narcotraffickers. Which led to his conjecture that perhaps Sinclair had been skimming from the traffic he coordinated.

Piper pulled the Tahoe into a vacant space by the pay phone. The tweaker approached her window. She gave me a thumbs up; the tweaker got a middle finger.

I nodded at her. "Tell me the address, Milo."

After a long pause, he did, a house in South Dallas. Then he hung up.

———

Piper moved to the passenger seat, let me drive.

I entered the address into the GPS and headed south on US Highway 75, Central Expressway, following the instructions issued by the British-sounding voice.

Piper had also bought a new disposable phone at a convenience store, so she set up an email account and logged in to the main contractor job site.

The traffic was heavy, commuters from the far northern suburbs of McKinney and Allen heading toward downtown. After a few frustrating miles, I hit the lights and siren and pulled onto the shoulder. After that, we made good time.

As we skirted the fringes of downtown Dallas, Piper swore and tossed her new phone on the console.

"Our rating has changed," she said. "We're both D-2s."

D-2 was code for "Do not hire, pending criminal investigation."

"The fake IDs," she said. "You think they'll work for the Border Patrol in Tucson?"

"Probably not." I got on Interstate 30.

She swore again.

The highway served as the border between downtown and Oak Cliff, one of the oldest parts of the city. We exited at Sylvan Avenue, a main thoroughfare through the southern section. The first few blocks were filled with remodeled Tudor bungalows, quaint little places on tree-lined streets that surrounded a hospital.

After that the area changed. Some streets were full of restored homes with picture-perfect landscaping. Others contained structures that seemed to be on the verge of collapse: peeling paint, weeds instead of lawns, cars on blocks.

After a couple of miles, I arrived at a narrow street where the homes were small, two-bedrooms at the most. Some brick, some wood, about half had been restored, the others fell along the bell curve between eclectic and crack house.

"This is the place?" Piper said. "Looks like something a tornado blew up here from Austin."

I turned, drove past the address, a corner lot, and checked the address again.

The house resembled a folk art museum that had been turned inside out and then splashed with neon paint. The picket fence surrounding the property had been white-washed in hot pink, the posts topped with overturned coffee cans encrusted in rhinestones. The front yard was concrete, painted green and dotted with metal sculptures made from discarded car parts.

On the side street, I parked and we got out.

A little after nine on a Tuesday morning. Not much traffic, pedestrian or otherwise. A couple of people pulling out of driveways, a couple more getting newspapers.

I opened the gate and threaded my way through the metal sculptures. Piper moved a few feet behind me. We both had our badges clipped to our belts, guns out.

The front door was ajar.

I placed my left hand on the wooden surface and pushed it open the rest of the way.

A living room that might have been from the Addams Family's summer cottage loomed in front of me. A collection of empty birdcages on one side, two suits of armor on the other. Paintings everywhere, abstract oils with vibrant blues and reds, swaths of green.

The cold air spilling out of the entryway smelled like patchouli oil and death.

I stepped inside. Piper flanked out to my right. We didn't speak.

The body lay sprawled in the space where the living area turned into the dining room.

A woman in her thirties. Attractive, even dead. Hispanic, wearing paint-spattered jeans and a faded Jerry Jeff Walker concert T-shirt. She was on her back, head twisted at an odd angle, neck clearly broken.

The house was utterly silent, no movement at all other than dust particles that danced in the shaft of sunlight pouring in from the side windows.

I moved around the corpse and into the dining area. More art, paintings and bronze sculptures.

Piper knelt beside the body for a moment and then looked at me, her face devoid of expression. She mouthed the words: "The witness?"

I shrugged and took a closer look. Could be her. Or a sister. Several of the woman's fingers had been broken, twisted at odd angles. My hunch: she was a relative and the bad guys had been interrogating her, looking for info on the witness.

A floorboard creaked beyond the set of swinging doors on the far wall.

Piper rose. Slid across the room as quietly as possible.

No easy way to proceed. We hand-signaled the action. I'd go first; Piper would come in as backup.

Another creak, softer than before, barely discernible.

I rushed the door. Kicked it open, rolled into a crouch to the left, ending up with my back against a refrigerator.

The kitchen. Empty.

Navy blue tile countertops, worn linoleum floors. Windows formed the back wall, overlooking a rear yard filled with more pieces of art.

A whoosh of air. Movement.

The attack came from behind me, from atop the refrigerator.

Everything fast. No time to think, only react.

I leapt for the other side of the room, twisted, brought the Glock to bear.

A foot kicked the gun from my grip. The weapon clattered across the floor, coming to rest against the baseboard by the sink.

A figure in tight-fitting sweatpants and a narrow tank top.

Olive skin, arms sinewy with muscles. Hair pulled back in a ponytail.

The woman from the warehouse, the kidnap victim. Eva Ramirez.

Piper banged on the swinging door, yelled. A broom had fallen, wedging the door closed.

Eva Ramirez slapped my ear with an open palm, knee headed for my groin.

I rolled away from the crotch shot and fell to the floor, skull ringing from the blow. I kicked and connected with a knee, dropping her, too.

She jumped up at the same time as I did, and we dashed straight at each other, coming together in a lover's embrace, fingers and knees going for pain instead of pleasure.

My palm jammed under her chin, pressed upward as I jerked my face away to avoid the thumb headed for my eye.

She sidestepped my sweep kick and leveraged the momentum to slam me against the countertop, the edge like a knife against my spine.

We broke apart for an instant and then parried blows, a

right this and a left that and every combination in between until everything blurred into a flurry of limbs.

I blocked a hook with my forearm and managed a solid shot to her jaw, rocking her head back. She countered with a kick to the ribs that vaporized the air in my lungs.

No oxygen. Pinpricks of light swirled on the edges of my vision. I staggered back, heard Piper banging on the door harder, the sound of wood splintering.

Eva Ramirez gave no quarter. She moved close for the kill, a trickle of blood at the corner of her mouth. Her foot swung toward my temple just as my head cleared.

I grabbed her ankle and pushed up.

She fell. Landed on her back with a meaty thud that rattled the china in the cabinets.

I jumped on top of her, forearm against her windpipe, our faces only centimeters apart.

She struggled to free herself.

"G-game over." I tried to clear my head, reach for my cuffs. "You're under arrest."

She wriggled harder. Got a hand free. And grabbed my testicles.

The light in the room went from yellow to red to black to white hot. A keening sound filled the air, a locomotive screaming through a high mountain pass. Took a moment to realize the noise was me, shrieking.

Then it was over. Light and sound returned more or less to normal. I was huddled in a ball on the floor of the kitchen, whimpering.

The door leading to the dining room was shattered, chunks of wood lying on the linoleum.

Eva Ramirez was face down, arms behind her as Piper knelt on the small of the suspect's back, slapped on the handcuffs.

"Yo, bitch." Piper pulled the woman to her feet. "You are under arrest."

I groaned.

"You done whining?" Piper slid my gun across the floor with her foot. "We need to get out of here."

I struggled to my knees, grabbed the Glock, holstered it.

"You killed my sister. Tortured her." Eva swore in Spanish. "I hope you burn in hell."

"We didn't kill anybody," Piper said.

"*Los federales.*" Eva spat on the floor. "You are all the same."

"Let's get us some gone." I pushed myself to my feet. "Oww, that smarts."

Piper kicked the rest of the kitchen door away, cleared an easy exit.

"I have money." Eva took a deep breath. "Tell me how much you want to let me go. Name your price."

"A bagrillion dollars." Piper shoved her toward the front of the house. "You got that much?"

I followed them into the dining room.

From the street came the sound of car doors slamming.

Eva Ramirez shook her head. "Too late."

- CHAPTER TWENTY-EIGHT -

I heard men talking from the street in front of the house.

The dining room windows were stained glass, green and violet, surrounding an opaque but color-free center.

"Jon." Piper pointed to a corner of the room where wall met ceiling. "Check it out."

A tiny gray object that didn't belong had been mounted there, about half the size of a matchbook. A wireless sensor, video definitely and maybe sound as well. The device couldn't be seen by anybody entering from the front door. It looked toward the rear of the house and the door leading to the kitchen.

I stepped over the deceased woman, Eva's sister, and eased to the side of the room directly underneath the camera, hopefully out of view. I peered outside through a purple pane.

Two white Tahoes and a handful of men I recognized from the day before were in front of the house.

Paynelowe contractors.

Several held silenced submachine guns. Windbreaker One, the lead man from the entry team yesterday, cradled a grenade launcher in his arms.

"Out the back." I pointed to the kitchen. "Hurry."

Before we'd moved more than a few steps, the window disintegrated as a couple thousand shards of colored glass spewed inward, tiny little daggers that sprayed the room like an aerosol of razors.

The outside noises were louder. Men yelled. A dog barked. Doors slammed.

Then a hiss from inside.

The tear gas grenade had landed on the far side of the dining room. Clouds of noxious fumes wafted toward the ceiling.

Piper shoved the witness toward the back of the house where we'd just come. Both women were coughing.

I covered my mouth and nose with the tail of my T-shirt, ran after them. And tripped over the dead body, Eva's sister. Landed on my hands and knees, jostling my still-tender groin area. Slivers of glass everywhere. I pushed myself to my knees, ignoring the tiny cuts in my palms. Tears streamed down my face.

More noise from the front yard. Men moving, actions on weapons being checked. Another entry team on its way.

The ruined door was across the room, maybe ten feet away.

I lunged toward the entryway leading to the kitchen and the backdoor. Behind me, bullets pockmarked the wall like a contrail following my body.

The kitchen was empty. Piper and Eva were already outside. I sucked in a lungful of relatively fresh air and ran to the open back door.

Piper, her hands zip-tied, was stomach down on the lawn next to Eva.

Windbreaker Two, the guy who had shot the two cartel soldiers with Piper's gun, was at the base of the steps, three feet away. No telling how long we had before the group of agents at the front of the house made their way to the backyard.

He reached for his sidearm.

I rushed him, and we fell to the ground before he could get to his weapon.

One of his hands jammed my chin upward like I'd just done to Eva. The other locked on a wrist, trying to jerk my arm behind my back.

His nails dug into my cheek, a finger headed toward my eye.

I locked my teeth on his thumb and chomped.

"Arrghhh." He jerked his hand free, rolled away.

I scrambled after him, tried to keep the distance between us to an absolute minimum to eliminate the chance for him to use a gun.

He got far enough away to stand, fingers reaching under his coat as he jumped up.

I lunged, tried to ram my head and shoulder through his gut to a point on the other side.

A sound like a punctured tire whistled from his throat as he bent in two, an invisible hand yanking the rear of his belt, and fell, landing by a Weber grill on a small patio. His head snapped back, skull slammed into the concrete with a crunch, a coconut hurled against a stone wall.

He lay still. His legs jerked erratically.

I stood, shaking. Looked over at Piper.

Her eyes were full of a fear that had no name. The hopeless feeling that came from each move, no matter how carefully planned, leaving you in a worse place than before.

A Toyota Prius with the driver's door open sat in the driveway, a McDonald's sack on the front seat. A large bag from the Gap rested on the passenger seat, clothing visible at the top. Eva must have been getting supplies when the Paynelowe crew arrived at her sister's home.

Shouts from inside the house. The entry team from the front was moving our way.

I knelt beside Piper and cut the plastic ties. She jumped up, grabbed her Glock from Windbreaker Two's waistband. Together, we pulled Eva Ramirez to her feet.

"Is he dead?" Eva was staring at the DEA agent.

I didn't answer. Piper and I pulled her toward the rear of the property, the only avenue of escape at the moment.

Bamboo and torpedo grass lined the alley behind the house.

We stopped for a moment behind the garage, out of sight. My heart raced, breath coming in heaves.

The Tahoe was at the end of the alley, only a few yards away.

I strained to hear, searching for a sound from the backyard.

Nothing.

"Let's go." Piper pulled the woman down the narrow roadway.

I followed.

Thirty seconds later, we were in the Tahoe. Eva Ramirez sat in the backseat, hands cuffed in front of her waist, her wrists hooked by a length of chain to a D-link on the floorboard.

I drove away from the street where the Paynelowe crew had just attacked the house.

"Where are you taking me?" Eva said.

"To turn you in." Piper opened a bottle of water, drank half of it. "Collect the reward."

"So you want to die, eh?" The woman shook her head.

I stopped at a light, felt my heart rate start a slow descent to normal. A pair of Dallas police cars, lights on, blew through the intersection heading in the direction of the house we'd just left.

"Y-y-you see what happens to people who get near me." She shook her head. Tears welled in her eyes.

"Sorry about your sister." I accelerated away when the light changed. "If we'd gotten there earlier, maybe it might have played out a little differently."

"How do you say in English?" She wiped her eyes, the movement awkward because of the restraints. "Go fock yourself."

Silence for a few blocks.

"Let's call Phil." Piper finished her water, tossed the bottle on the floor and patted her pockets.

"W-w-who is Phil?" Eva sniffed and leaned back, trying for a tough-girl look.

We ignored her.

"Ah, oh." Piper arched her back, reached for her rear pockets.

"What?"

"My cell phone. It fell out."

I reached for mine, then remembered I had tossed the SIM card so it wouldn't be trackable.

"The new one," Piper said. "It didn't fit my holster. Had it in my back pocket."

"Let's get a replacement." I pulled into a convenience store by the interstate.

Piper didn't move.

I put the transmission into park and swore under my breath.

The cheapest pay-as-you-go phone cost about thirty bucks, and we were out of cash. I'd given most of mine to my sister, used the remainder for a room last night and clothes. Piper had spent the last of her walking-around money to buy breakfast and a new auto battery. We had the Katrina debit cards but those would trigger a hit on the grid when we used them.

"So we use a pay phone." I examined the storefront. Stacks of empty milk crates, a couple of newspaper vending boxes, and a guy sleeping against the wall. No pay phone.

"The apartment." Piper shook her head. "We need to go back."

She was right. We'd left a lot supplies at the Cheyenne. The rest of Piper's money from Sinclair's job. Fresh phones and clothes. Ammo. And, of course, the picture of Piper's mother.

"You haven't used your radio," Eva said. "But you haven't taken me to a field and shot me either."

I looked in the back.

"You're not part of this, are you?" She leaned forward, an excited look on her face. "You are a federal agent who was willing to kill another federal agent."

Piper turned in her seat and looked in the rear as well.

"You can save me," she said. "And yourselves."

Piper and I glanced at each other but didn't speak.

"You must let me go."

"Not a chance," I said.

"You are going to turn me over to the US Marshals, yes?"

I didn't say anything.

"Why do you think I was running away from them?"

"I dunno," Piper said. "Why?"

"They were going to kill me."

"That's not part of the US Marshals mission statement," I said.

"Listen to me, please." She blinked away tears. Her face was pale.

Piper and I glanced at each, shrugged.

"The US Marshals were holding me at a hotel on the River Walk," Eva said. "I told them I wanted to go to the store downstairs and get cigarettes." She shook her head. "*Estúpidos.* I don't even smoke."

"Why'd you run?" I said.

"My sister had called, gave me a coded message: one of the Marshals was employed by the cartel." She paused. "They were going to kill me."

"So you escaped," Piper said.

"Yes. I just walked off."

"But they found you anyway," I said.

"Not the ones you think," she said. "The others."

"Others?" I frowned.

She mentioned the name of a rival cartel, a different organization than the one involved in the trial in West Texas. A competitor who'd found her in San Antonio, realized who she was, and hidden her in the shipment of drugs we'd found yesterday.

I whistled softly. "That was not the day for you to buy lottery tickets."

She didn't reply, clearly not understanding my meaning.

"There's a leak in the US Marshals," Piper said. "That makes this tricky."

"If she's telling the truth." I put the Tahoe in reverse. Backed away from the convenience store.

"The cartels are everywhere," Eva said. "Please, for your own good, just let me go."

"The cartels haven't gotten to Phil," I said.

"Who is Phil? Can he keep me safe?"

Neither Piper nor I said anything. I pulled onto the street and headed toward our apartment.

Eva Ramirez smiled and cried at the same time, breathing hard, hysteria, fatigue, and hopelessness painted across her face. Then she shook her head and leaned back in the seat.

- CHAPTER TWENTY-NINE -

Sinclair tried to control the flutter of panic in his stomach, the sense of things spinning out of control.

The plan, which yesterday had sounded good, seemed like lunacy today: Jon Cantrell and Piper, money-grubbing DEA contractors, would take down a shipment of drugs. The missing witness, kidnapped by the cartel transporting the narcotics, was with the shipment.

Cantrell and Piper, badged up with federal law enforcement credentials, would arrest the cartel guards, risking their skins in the process, and allow Sinclair and Tommy a window of opportunity to eliminate the witness in relative safety.

Unfortunately, lots of things sound good in theory only to fall apart when the time for execution came about.

Sinclair's police contacts had alerted him that Jon and Piper had located the warehouse and secured the shipment. Unfortunately, the cokehead Paynelowe contractor, Keith McCluskey, and his crew of out-of-town DEA agents had barged in, having gotten wind of the witness's location somehow. They started shooting, which allowed Eva Ramirez to disappear, melting into the streets of West Dallas.

For the moment, the flutter in Sinclair's stomach stayed

at a manageable level, a slow drip of fear that kept him alert, wary of danger, like when he'd been a child and his old man had been drinking.

The fear was good in a way, though. It forced him out of what one of his kids called the comfort zone.

Sinclair had spent a lifetime in Dallas County. He knew every back alley and craps game from Cockrell Hill to the slums of Garland. But it had been at least a decade since he'd ventured out to the suburbs, specifically Frisco, located about thirty minutes north of downtown where the Dallas Tollway and State Highway 121 intersected.

In his youth, the area had been nothing but fields of cotton, grain sorghum, and sunflowers, dotted here and there with white clapboard farmhouses. Now the prairie land was covered with concrete and asphalt, fancy strip malls, and a zillion acres of new homes, fanned out in subdivisions with pretentious names.

Sinclair sat in the driver's seat of a Crown Victoria with two hundred thousand miles on the clock, a retired police car. He was in the parking lot of a shopping center with a grocery store at one end and a shuttered Blockbuster video store at the other. The buildings were designed to look like they were from the Texas Hill Country, another place he hadn't visited in decades, rough white stone, tin roofs, cactus landscaping.

Want something done right, you gotta do it yourself, another lesson hard-learned from the back of his old man's hand.

He waited patiently, a cop on stakeout.

About twenty minutes later, a tiny SUV drove across the parking lot. The license plate matched. Behind the wheel sat a red-haired woman in her fifties.

Sinclair smiled and for a few moments the fear went away.

Myrna DeGroot, the wife of the number two agent at the Dallas DEA office, Phil DeGroot, pulled her Toyota Highlander into the parking space directly in front of the dry cleaners.

She exited the SUV, shopping list in one hand, pocketbook in the other.

An old Ford, like the kind the police used, pulled in two spaces away.

"Excuse me, ma'am." A heavyset man got out of the Ford.

His hair was dyed an inky black. He was about sixty, wearing a short-sleeved shirt like a waiter in a Mexican restaurant. In one hand he held a fold-up map, half open. An old-style 35mm film camera dangled around his neck.

She clutched her pocketbook to her chest, tried to smile.

"Sorry, didn't mean to startle you." He smiled. "My name is Sinclair."

She didn't speak. The man had the hard gaze of a cop, a look she knew all too well, eyes that had seen too much for too many years.

"Could you tell me if this road takes you to Southfork?" He pointed to the east-west thoroughfare.

Myrna hesitated. Like most people who called the area home, she'd never been to the ranch that had been home to TV's J. R. Ewing and his family. She knew it was nearby though.

"I'm from Abilene, see, and my wife and me used to watch *Dallas* together." The man paused. He wiped his eyes. "Before she died."

"Let me see your map." The woman relaxed. "Bet I can help."

"You have nice hair." Sinclair spread the map on the hood of the Toyota. "My wife was a redhead too."

Myrna smiled and leaned over the paper.

That was the last thing she remembered.

- CHAPTER THIRTY -

I stopped at the edge of the Cheyenne parking lot by a Dumpster. The Tahoe just fit between the trash receptacle and the wooden privacy fence that surrounded it, concealing us from view.

It was a little before noon on Tuesday. The parking lot was about half full.

We could have gone in the garage, but the remote control needed to access the secure area would leave a record. And there were cameras.

I looked at Piper in the passenger seat. "Don't dawdle."

We stood to collect fifty thousand for turning in Eva Ramirez, but that wasn't like an ATM machine—slide the witness into jail like she was a bank card, get cash back. It would take awhile. In the meantime, we needed all the cash we could get, especially since our contractor status had been downgraded.

"The money and the extra phones." Piper opened the door and got out.

"And the picture," I said.

She shut the door without replying and sauntered toward the condo entrance a hundred feet away from the hotel's front doors. The security guard, an elderly ex-cop, drove by on his golf cart and waved at her. She waved back.

"Please, you should let me go." Eva leaned forward. "I won't tell anybody."

A lock of hair fell across her eyes. She smiled, an eyebrow raised, going for an impish look. She succeeded. She did indeed look like an imp, a seductive one.

I didn't reply. I turned the AC colder. We were in the sun, and the day was getting warmer.

"She's a pretty woman," Eva said. "Are you two together?"

"Shut up." I rubbed my eyes.

"They're going to kill me." She touched my arm. "And you too."

Her fingers were cool and smooth.

I shifted in my seat, easing the pressure on my still-tender groin area.

"They will assume I have told you some secrets, so you must die as well. That's the way this works."

I leaned back, eyes still closed. Tired though it was early in the day.

"Me, I don't fear death." Her voice sounded different, huskier. "But my s-s-sister, she just wanted to paint."

I tried not to imagine what would come next. Tried to think one step at a time. Get the witness in custody. Get her on the record as saying we had nothing to do with shooting the unarmed suspects.

"I made my choices," she said. "Besides, death is everywhere in Mexico."

"Okay, I'll bite." I opened my eyes. "What choices did you make?"

"Do you have someone?" she said. "A lover or a wife?"

I didn't say anything. When you're a cop, it's a good idea to keep your personal life personal when it comes to dealing with people you encounter. Like cons and suspects. And witnesses on the lam.

"My choices." She chuckled without mirth. "Love makes you do funny things." A long pause. "I am glad that relationship is over."

Neither of us spoke for a few moments.

A sharp intake of breath from the backseat.

I opened my eyes.

Three Dallas police cars were clustered by the front entrance under the porte cochere, a couple of hundred yards away. An unmarked Chevy Impala pulled alongside them and a tall man with a bushy Fu Manchu mustache got out. Sinclair's flunky, Tommy, the guy who had been with him in the Bentley yesterday.

"Uh-oh." I reached for my phone to call Piper. Realized neither of us had one, which was why we were here in the first place.

"What is it?" Eva said. "Why are you afraid?"

I opened the door but stopped.

A pair of white Tahoes like mine pulled up to the side entrance of the condo. A group of DEA agents in blue windbreakers jumped out, barged inside. I didn't recognize any of them.

The security guard was an ex-cop. An old guy, he'd been kicking around town for years. I mentally kicked myself for not seeing the connection sooner. He was probably on Sinclair's payroll and had called him as soon as he saw Piper, resulting in Tommy being dispatched to the scene. All of which would have been picked up by Paynelowe's electronic snooping.

Crooked cops were going in one entrance, crooked DEA agents in the other, Piper caught in the middle.

"What are you going to do?" Eva said.

I got out, opened the back door, and recuffed her. Hands in back, still hooked to the D-ring. She protested. I slapped a piece of duct tape over her mouth and left her on the rear floorboard, the engine and AC running.

Then, I jogged to entrance of the garage at the rear of the complex. Once inside I ran toward the freight elevators at the extreme south end, the farthest point away from all the police.

The security guard was heading the opposite direction on his golf cart, looking behind himself every few feet as he maneuvered between a row of parked cars.

I shouted at him to stop.

He stopped. Stared at me, his eyes wide, confused. Then his eyes got bigger, face pale.

I pulled my Glock, took a step closer.

He pressed his lips together, his expression a jumble of emotions: still confused but angry and scared as well. He sped off toward the exit.

I headed to the freight elevator and pressed the button for our floor.

Nothing happened. The system had been shut down, a standard precaution given the police activity.

I pulled out a master key and stuck it in the control lock. Tried again. And waited. The seconds dribbled by, each longer than the previous. Nearly a minute later, a lifetime in a situation such as this, just as I was just about to head for the stairs, the doors closed and the car lifted.

At the tenth floor the elevator opened without making a sound.

I stepped into the hallway, Glock in hand.

Our unit was around two corners, maybe sixty yards

away. There were no other tenants on this floor, and most of the apartments hadn't even been finished out yet, the lingering effects of the recent economic downturn.

The stench of spent cordite and pepper spray filled the air. No noise.

Emotions choked my throat for a moment. Piper, please be okay.

A dark object lay on the carpet at the bend of the hall. It looked like a shoe from my vantage point.

I jogged as quietly as possible to the turn.

The object was a black Reebok. With a foot inside that was attached to a dead guy in a Dallas police uniform.

Two more figures lay just beyond the first in pools of blood that stained the tan carpet. Both wore civilian clothes, weapons by their sides. One of them was Tommy. He groaned, one leg quivering.

I stifled a cough. The pepper spray was thicker in this section of the hall. Also, a layer of smoke hung in the air about chest level, evidence of flashbangs or a huge firefight that had just occurred.

The next corner was about thirty feet away. Our unit lay two doors beyond that.

For no particular reason, I pulled Tommy's cell phone from its holster and stuck it in my pocket. Then I crept forward.

Empty shell casings littered the carpet. Bullet holes dotted the walls.

When I was about five feet from the corner, noise came from around the bend.

The creak of leather, rustle of clothing.

I stopped. Strained to hear more.

Thwat-thwat-thwat.

Three paintballs hit the wall on my left, the angle indicating they'd been fired from beyond the turn of the hallway.

They contained oleoresin capsicum, a substance derived from the hot part of the jalapeño fruit, standard issue for certain DEA personnel. A mist formed as the tissue-thin membrane of the projectile shredded.

I gasped, immediately unable to breathe. Blinked, unable to see. Staggered back. Fire engulfed my nose and eyes, a searing pain. The spray was nowhere near a direct hit but still close enough to be momentarily incapacitating.

The rattle of a machine gun bolt. The thud of silenced bullets hitting sheetrock.

Tears gushed down my face. I coughed, tried not to scream. On my knees, struggled to breathe.

From behind me the squeak of a hinge.

A hand dragged me by the collar.

A door slammed. The air felt different, colder.

The hand kept dragging me, farther away.

Another door slammed, and then I heard nothing.

The pain lessened a smidgen. I blinked away a gallon of tears and saw I was in the bedroom of one of the unoccupied units on our floor, a suite that had never been finished out.

Raw concrete. Gray, unpainted walls. No furniture.

A figure stood over me, barely visible through the tears, as neutral and indistinct as the surroundings. A woman's shape, Piper. She disappeared from view, going toward the hall.

A few seconds later, she dashed back in the room and slammed the door shut.

I tried to speak but couldn't.

Piper jumped on top of me and covered my head.

BOOOM.

A muffled but loud explosion from the hallway, another flashbang.

She rolled off. I blinked, tried to clear my throat. Wiped more tears away.

Piper held her finger over her lips. She leaned closer, whispered in my ear: "Two teams. We're in a crossfire."

From the living area, the sound of a door opening.

Piper and I looked at each other and then turned to the only exit.

The balcony. Ten stories up.

- CHAPTER THIRTY-ONE -

I yanked open the sliding glass door.

Warm air slapped me in the face, easing the sting of the pepper spray a few more notches below scream-bloody-murder-and-scratch-your-eyes-out.

The balcony was a rectangle, about eight feet long by three feet deep. A waist-high metal railing ran along the edges. The view looked east over the emerald canopy that led to White Rock Lake.

Piper followed me out.

Someone banged on the door to the bedroom.

"We have to go down," she said.

The balcony below us was identical to ours.

"Yeah, that's the only option." I pulled the Glock from its holster, wedged it between my hip and the waistband of my jeans.

"I'm terrified of heights," she said.

Muffled gunfire, most likely from the hallway. Not silenced. More of Sinclair's guys or the real police? Either way, I hoped it slowed everybody down.

I stuck the extra mags in my back pocket and connected the Sam Browne pistol belt with the regular one I'd pulled from my waist. Looped the double-length piece of leather through the bottom rung of the railing.

"Lower yourself and I'll catch you." I stepped over the protective barrier. Tried not to think about the dizzying height and the accompanying shakes.

Toes on the edge, I eased my torso down until I was on my haunches, one hand on the railing, the other in a death grip on the leather.

I let go of the metal and pushed out with my feet. Swung away and then back toward the building. Let go. Landed in a heap on the balcony below.

A few seconds later, one of Piper's legs appeared.

I wrapped an arm around her thigh. Grabbed her waistband with my free hand. Inched her body down until we were in an embrace. Then I pulled her in.

"You okay?" I took several deep breaths, trying to lower my galloping heart rate.

"Okay is relative, but I'm fine for the moment."

The apartment on the ninth floor was empty, unfinished as well. The sliding door was not locked. Piper and I rushed through the vacant rooms to the hall entrance. We stopped at the door.

I grabbed the Glock from my waistband, placed an ear on the door, listened. Nothing.

"Did you get everything?" I opened the door.

Piper nodded, followed me out. We took the emergency stairs down, encountered no one. The garage was empty. We jogged to the exit and stopped.

"Where's the car?" Piper said.

"Same place."

"Want to race?" She handed me a new cell phone.

———

I drove without destination, crisscrossing the residential streets on the west side of White Rock Lake, like a patrol cop with nothing to patrol.

Neither of us talked.

Piper was in the passenger seat. Eva Ramirez sat in the back, hands cuffed in front now, hooked again to the D-ring. The duct tape was still across her mouth.

I made a turn and headed east toward the lake.

The closer we got to the shoreline, the nicer the houses. Bungalows became estates, glimpses of sweeping lawns not quite hidden by stone walls.

A few minutes later, on a narrow tree-lined road, I stopped by a cemetery, the wrought-iron fence overgrown with oleanders and Boston ivy. I parked under a towering cedar tree so elderly it must have been planted during Prohibition.

I opened the door and got out. Piper exited as well. The gate to the cemetery was open, and we walked through it.

The place had been freshly mowed but not edged. Weeds grew around the bases of the tombstones. The graves were all old, at least for this part of Texas. The ones nearest indicated deaths from the 1920s.

I sat on a marker for a veteran of the Confederate States of America and pulled out the cell phone I'd taken from Tommy, the guy who worked for Sinclair.

"Where'd you get that?" Piper eased onto a tombstone next to mine.

I told her. "The other DEA agents had to be Paynelowe contractors."

She nodded. "I recognized one from the warehouse yesterday."

"They must have tracked Sinclair's people." I held up Tommy's phone. "Triangulated a cell or something."

After a long pause, he said, "This is some bad mojo we're dealing with."

I scrolled through the numbers in Tommy's cell. Most were local, but a couple were from the 202 area code, Washington, DC. I didn't want to dwell on what that meant.

The last incoming and outgoing calls were to a phone a few digits off of the one we had for Sinclair.

I pressed the Send button.

"Why did you do that?" Piper shook her head.

I motioned for her to be quiet.

A woman's voice answered after one ring. "You take care of it?"

I grunted but didn't speak, evidently something Tommy would not have done. The call ended abruptly.

"So much for that." I shrugged.

Piper handed me one of the backup phones. We programmed each other's new numbers, busywork, each of us trying to come up with something that could get us out of the mess we found ourselves in.

A few moments later, Tommy's phone rang, a private number in the caller ID.

Piper and I looked at each other. She nodded, pointed to the cell.

I clicked the speaker button. "Yeah."

Silence. Heavy, labored breathing. Then, Sinclair's voice: "Where's Tommy?"

"He can't come to the phone right now," I said. "In fact, he's pretty much out of the game on a permanent basis."

Sinclair swore, his voice soft, full of genuine pain. He cleared his throat and said, "That boy was like a son to me."

"Paynelowe had a team at the Cheyenne," I said. "That's not on us."

Sinclair hesitated. Then he spoke again, voice gravelly:

"You have her, don't you?"

I didn't say anything.

"Give her up, Jon, and I'll see that you walk away in one piece."

Piper snorted.

"We'll call it a favor for your daddy," he said. "Bring her to the house on Tranquilla, then you can skiddaddle."

Piper spoke for the first time. "We're supposed to trust you why?"

"The bounty on her is fifty thousand," he said. "I'll double that. Right now, cash money."

I didn't say anything. Piper patted her watch and nodded toward the Tahoe. Every second we were on a phone tied to Sinclair was another second advantage to Paynelowe and their cell trackers.

"All right, you little turd." Sinclair's voice was angry now. "I'll go a hundred grand each."

That was a large sum, even for a crooked ex-cop with delusions of grandeur. Two hundred grand was a whole lot of payoffs from small-time hoods like the Korean pimp. Sinclair was desperate, a condition to which up until now I thought him immune. Milo was right. Sinclair was the Shield, and he wasn't afraid of going to prison. He'd been skimming from the cartels, his clients, the ones he supposedly shielded, and he was afraid of dying. Slowly and painfully.

Sinclair spoke again, voice softer time. "This shit's bigger than you think. Bigger than your little mind can imagine."

Piper was at the gate. She whistled, snapped her fingers. At this point, every second on the line was an exponential increase in our risk.

Sinclair's voice grew frantic. "This ain't just about the damn cartel—"

I dropped the phone next to the Confederate soldier's grave and crushed it with my heel.

At the Tahoe, I slid behind the wheel. Piper was already in the passenger seat.

"You want to call Phil?" She held up a phone. "Or should I?"

"We need to get away from here first." I accelerate down the road.

Eva thrashed in the back, growling beneath her gag.

Piper leaned in the rear and tugged on an end of the duct tape. "If I take this off, will you quit bouncing around?"

Eva nodded. Piper ripped the tape away.

Eva took several deep breaths. Then she said, "What happened back at the apartment?"

I drove, didn't speak.

"They were trying to kill you, weren't they?" She paused. "Because of me."

Piper buckled her belt. "How far should we go before we call Phil?"

"A couple of miles at least."

I had been worried before. Now I was terrified. What if we couldn't get in touch with our DEA supervisor, the one person we trusted? Phil DeGroot was as honest as a Mormon accountant on fresh-long-johns day, but what if Paynelowe had tapped into our phone conversation or even the one I'd just had with Sinclair?

"We're all marked with a bull's-eye," I said. "At least two sides want us dead, one of which has federal IDs."

"You're starting to understand," Eva said. "The DEA and the US Marshals have been compromised."

"Where are you supposed to testify?" I said.

She didn't answer.

"I can tell you." Piper picked up the new cell, a smart phone. She punched a few buttons, waited, punched a few more.

"In West Texas," she said. "A place called Marfa."

I nodded.

A town in the Big Bend region, a hundred miles on the backside of nowhere. But not that far from the battle zones of Juárez.

Eva Ramirez swore.

The lake appeared in front of us. Tiny whitecaps shimmered on its glassy surface. In the distance a pair of sailboats sliced through the gray waters.

I turned south on Lawther, the street that ran along the west side of White Rock Lake. The temporary but false anonymity of the interstate was a few miles away.

"Let me go now and you have a small chance of living," Eva said. "Turn me in or take me to Marfa, and you will die."

"Witnesses should be seen and not heard." I jammed on the gas, headed toward the interstate.

- CHAPTER THIRTY-TWO -

Sinclair refused to carry a cell phone or have an email account.

But he did have a beeper, a holdover from his days as a Dallas police officer, back when the tiny black device had been the cat's meow of gizmos.

His beeper was one of the last available, registered under an alias, and the number only known by a handful of people. One of them was Imogene, the woman who manned the phones at Tranquilla, his de facto base of operations since that thing in South Dallas with the redneck gunrunners from Tyler.

So when Imogene had beeped him with the emergency code, he'd called back immediately using the phone in the office of his current location. Imogene told him about Jon Cantrell's call and the news coming in from his contacts at the Dallas police about the firefight at the Cheyenne Apartments. She also told him there had been a couple of calls from the East Coast, Hawkins in McNally's office, who asked that Sinclair get in touch ASAP. Sinclair had ignored those and phoned Tommy's cell instead. This had confirmed his fears: Tommy was dead, and Jon had the witness and wasn't amenable to selling her.

That left Myrna DeGroot as his fallback option.

Sinclair flicked open a lockback knife and began to clean his fingernails.

He was sprawled on a black leather sofa in a warehouse in East Dallas, not far from the house on Tranquilla. The warehouse was outfitted as a movie studio and used for porn shoots, a relatively new endeavor that Sinclair had invested in. The interior walls had been padded with sound-absorbing material. Large stage lights, now off, hung from the rafters. The only illumination came from a series of fluorescent fixtures mounted on the ceiling.

A round waterbed sat a few feet in front of him, surrounded on three sides by free-standing mirrors that had been placed to simulate walls. The bed had two items on it at the moment: a zebra-skin comforter and a handcuffed Myrna DeGroot.

"Tommy's dead." Sinclair shook his head. "They killed him."

"W-w-who?" Myrna DeGroot wiped away her tears. Her movements were awkward due to the handcuffs. "W-w-why are you doing this to me?"

"That boy was like family. Hired the best lawyer in Dallas for his first indictment."

"Please let me go." Myrna continued to cry. "I won't tell anybody."

"He was as stupid as a carton of hair." Sinclair sighed. "But he was good people. And a hard worker."

The woman opened her mouth to speak but didn't say anything.

Sinclair slid off the couch and approached the bed. He grabbed her jaw and squeezed, forced her eyes to look into his.

"You know who Jon Cantrell is?"

The woman didn't reply. Probably because he had her mouth in such a tight grip. She gurgled instead.

"If Jon Cantrell would just play ball." Sinclair squeezed harder. "You and me wouldn't be stuck here in this damn porn studio."

Myrna DeGroot's lips turned purple and then white.

Sinclair let go.

A few moments later her cell phone rang.

"Bet that's your husband." Sinclair picked it up and smiled. "Showtime."

———

I drove. And drove. Ten minutes later, I parked the Tahoe and grabbed the phone that Piper had retrieved from the Cheyenne.

We were on Grand Avenue, a couple of blocks from Interstate 30, parked in front of Our Ladies of Charity Thrift Store and a taco stand.

"Phil DeGroot is our DEA contact." I looked in the back. "I'm gonna get him to bring us in. We'll be safe with Phil."

"Please, don't call," Eva said. "You've seen for yourself what happens when others know about me."

I hesitated.

Piper snapped her fingers, pointed to the phone.

Eva leaned forward. She propped her chin on the back of my seat, stared into my eyes in the rearview mirror. Her expression was sad and lonely and desperate all at the same time. She bit her lip, wrinkled a brow, and her look changed, vulnerable and alluring, a tad naughty, the lost girl who needed someone to take care of her.

I dialed the number.

He answered after a long time. "This is Phil DeGroot speaking."

"It's Jon."

Nothing except the hiss of an open line. Eva lay her head on my shoulder for a moment, then sat back in the rear seat.

"We're in the deep end," I said. "Sinking fast."

"That's one way to put it."

"We've got the witness." I gave him a short version. "And things are a little, oh, let's say sticky."

"This is an unsecured line." Phil's voice sounded hollow. "Can't you ever follow the rules?"

"Piper and I want to give her to you," I said. "We trust you."

"Probably the safest thing," he said. "Or you could deliver her to Marfa."

A muffled noise from the other end. Static on the line or something else?

I said, "We don't want to make the trip—"

Phil interrupted. "You should turn her over to me. The prosecutor has arranged for a platoon of Marines to guard the courthouse, but getting there's a big problem."

I didn't speak. Phil sounded funny. Why didn't he ask about Piper's sudden return? Maybe that was just the stress of the last few days playing with my head. Or maybe not. For a moment, I debated telling him I also had the scanner, hidden at my father's rented place, but decided not to.

"*Piper* will be glad to hear that," I said. "She's been worried."

"You've done a good job, Jon. Your old man would be really proud of you."

His tone was patronizing, completely out of character. Also, in the years of working together, he'd never once referred to my father. Phil DeGroot was all business, no time for sentiment.

"Yes." I frowned. "Piper and my dad will be happy."

"Let's get the witness squared away," he said. "And we can all go out for dinner or something to celebrate."

Breath caught in my throat. The air-conditioning in the Tahoe felt extra cold all of a sudden. There was out of character, and then there was behavior from *The Twilight Zone*. Phil never wanted to meet outside of work. Never to socialize.

Piper leaned forward, made eye contact. She arched a brow, asked if everything was all right.

"Sure, dinner, that'd be great," I said. "Where should we bring the witness?"

No response. Pings and whistles on the line.

"Write this down." Phil told me an address in East Dallas. "Let's say in about forty-five minutes. How's that?"

I repeated the address, but the line had gone dead.

"We need to roll." I put the truck in gear. "Phil's contaminated."

———

Sinclair wiped his face, enjoyed the slight lessening of the tension in his gut.

Three quarters of an hour until he could rest easy and not worry about those greasy fuckers from south of the Rio Grande or the phone calls from Hawkins.

In the warehouse in East Dallas, Phil DeGroot dropped his cell on the coffee table in front of the leather sofa. He then placed his hands in his lap, near the ornate belt buckle that contained a tiny derringer pistol.

His wife, Myrna, sat on the waterbed. Her red hair hung tangled across her face.

"See there, wasn't that easy?" Sinclair said. "Now all we gotta do is wait."

Phil didn't reply. He inched a finger toward the release button.

"Hypothetically speaking," Sinclair said. "What if Jon were to go to Marfa? What roads do you think he'd take?"

Phil sighed elaborately. He rattled off random highway numbers and reached for the backup gun.

- CHAPTER THIRTY-THREE -

At a stoplight by Fair Park, I sent a text message to Milo Miller, asking him to run a couple of heavyweights to the address in East Dallas. Milo responded immediately. He had people only a few blocks away that he would send over ASAP. It was good to have someone like Milo Miller feel like he was in your debt. I should save more people's lives.

Sending some muscle Phil's way was the least I could do. He was a dork, but a good guy. If he was under the gun, he deserved a chance to get free. Milo would take care of that, no questions asked.

I cut down South Fitzhugh Avenue.

The buildings were old and run down, a stark contrast to the shiny glass towers of downtown barely a mile behind us. Dingy little places housing R&B clubs and fried chicken takeout joints. Apartments that should have been condemned and houses that probably were.

"What happened with Phil?" Piper asked.

I told her, very briefly. Then we were both silent.

"You should have listened to me," Eva said.

After a few moments, Piper touched my arm and spoke one word: "Marfa."

I nodded. A long drive, but we'd be away from Keith McCluskey's crew of Paynelowe DEA contractors. In Marfa, the witness had a good chance of staying alive and being able to attest to the fact that we weren't involved in the slaying of the two thugs at the warehouse. If we took her to the Dallas Police, Sinclair would know within minutes. Also, Marfa represented our best opportunity to collect the bounty money.

Eva swore and kicked the back of the seat. Then she was still.

———

Marfa was west by southwest of the Dallas area, more or less a straight shot on the interstate until Midland, a nine- or ten-hour trip.

After we cleared the county line, I pointed the Tahoe south, the long way.

Hopefully, the safe way.

For a moment, I debated dropping Eva off on a corner and heading north, just disappearing, leaving behind all our problems—the DA in Dallas, Sinclair, the trial in Marfa.

But problems had a way of catching up with you no matter where you went, and running away meant forfeiting the chance for a big cash payout, money I desperately needed for my father.

Both Piper and Eva had fallen asleep, the adrenaline crash and rhythm of tires on the highway like a tranquilizer.

We were on US Interstate 35, the NAFTA superhighway that ran from one end of the country to the other, Laredo in the south, to Duluth, Minnesota, near the Canadian border. One-third of the illicit narcotics consumed in America will have at one point been on I-35, and Piper and I had spent a lot of time patrolling there, working on various drug interdiction programs.

Because of the trafficking activity, and because the highway was the main drag leading away from the largest unsecured border in the world, we needed to get away from I-35 as soon as possible.

Interstate 35 was one big cop-shop, as were all the interstates leading out of Dallas. It was full of Texas highway patrol cars, undercover Homeland Security agents, DEA flimflammers, roving teams from immigration control, and at least three covert CIA operations that I knew about. Then there were all of the local jurisdictions, the sheriffs and Barney Fife types for the towns and counties that straddled the highway.

My plan—and it wasn't much of one—was to exit the interstate at Waxahachie, about thirty miles south of Dallas, and head southwest in the general direction of the Hill Country, zigzagging our way toward the badlands of the Big Bend area.

The opposition would be looking for us on the major highways, the shortest routes; therefore, the smaller the road the better.

At the very least, the narrow, indirect farm-to-market highways were going to be less susceptible to Uncle Sam's various electronic surveillance methods.

Three miles north of Waxahachie, the disposable phone rang, the one Piper had gotten from the Cheyenne, with the number nobody knew.

It buzzed, twice, and then was silent. Piper jerked awake and looked at the screen. Caller ID didn't pick up anything. "What going on?"

"Turn it off." I handed her the phone, exited at a Love's truck stop.

"There's no number." She pressed a button on the device.

"The cell tower on top of the Cheyenne," I said. "They're pinging the SIM cards that were on around the time of the attack."

Tuesday afternoon about one. The truck stop was crowded.

The Tahoe had a half tank, and I didn't want to wait for an opening, so I stopped by the side of the building near the car washes. Away from any cameras.

"I need money," I said.

Piper handed me a wad of bills.

"Give me the phone too."

Eva stirred in the backseat, eyes slowly opening.

I pulled a ball cap from the console and opened the door. "You two make nice while I'm gone."

My windbreaker was in the backseat. My T-shirt was untucked, covering the Glock in my waistband. Most of the blood and grime had been wiped away from my skin.

I stuck the cap on, kept my head low, and entered the building.

The place was a hive of activity. Dozens of travelers scurried about.

One half of the structure was devoted to several fast-food restaurants. The other half was a retail operation only slightly less stocked than the average Walmart.

My shopping list: new disposable phones, over-the-counter pep pills, a case of bottled water, and a five-gallon gas can.

In the restaurant, I ordered three double cheeseburgers, fries, and Cokes. In the restroom, I dumped the cell, after pondering whether I should turn it back on and drop it in the back of a random vehicle outside. Why risk a SWAT team descending on some unsuspecting citizen?

At the register I paid for five gallons of gas as well as all of the other items. Outside, I filled the can with unleaded, keeping my face away from the cameras mounted underneath the canopy.

Ten minutes after leaving, I loaded everything but the burgers in the back of our SUV and hopped into the front seat.

"Lunch time." I plopped the food down on the console. "Anything happen while I was gone?"

Piper was leafing through a glossy folder with a montage of children's pictures on the cover, yet another charity's brochure that promised to "make things better for only a few cents per day." Pamphlets like this ended up stashed all over the apartment and the Tahoe.

"Why are we on this road?" Eva pointed to the south. "This is the highway to Laredo."

Piper put the folder on the floor. She grabbed a sack and unwrapped a sandwich.

I took a big bite of my cheeseburger. Instantly felt better.

"I cannot go to Laredo," Eva said. "Nowhere near the border."

"We're going to Marfa." I took a big swig of Coke. Felt even better.

Sugar and fat: best endorphin triggers ever.

"You don't understand." She shook her head.

"Yeah, we do." Piper spoke with a mouthful of burger. "Cartel bad, border dangerous. Yadda yadda."

"We're taking the long way to get there in one piece." I took another bite. "Go a direct route and they'll find us in two hours."

"When will we arrive?" Eva said.

"We'll hole up for a bit to throw them off." I shrugged. "Two, maybe three days."

Eva nodded. Then she said, "Will you uncuff me so I can eat?"

"You promise not to try anything?" Piper held up the key. Eva nodded, and we believed her.

- CHAPTER THIRTY-FOUR -

Sinclair steered the elderly Crown Victoria around a bus on the freeway. The panicky feeling of events crashing out of control was worse now, a rumble in his gut that competed with the pain from the bullet wound.

Goddam Phil DeGroot and his goddam mouse gun. A little .22 derringer or some shit like that. Where the hell did he have that thing hidden, anyway?

With one hand, Sinclair touched the bandage that covered the tiny hole on the side of his abdomen, really just a graze.

He hoped he'd killed them both, as was his original plan. But he didn't know.

Some new players had arrived on the scene, three large men with baseball bats and guns. Sinclair had barely made it to the Ford, dripping blood.

He'd fired three times. He was pretty sure a round had clipped old Phil in the side of the noggin. Hopefully one had hit his whiny wife, too.

It had been a long time since he'd used a piece for anything other than show. Been even longer since he'd worked the streets.

As he drove, he glanced at Myrna's cell phone. The device had been in his pocket when everything went to shit. It was a complicated model, a large screen above a typewriter keyboard. He wondered how it worked.

The cluster of buildings that formed downtown appeared to the left, including the tower with the big green ball that had been in the opening credits of the TV show *Dallas*. Signs for a number of exits for other highways loomed ahead.

Interstate 30, west to Fort Worth.

Interstate 35, south to Waco.

Sinclair adjusted the sun visor.

Jon Cantrell would most likely take the witness toward Marfa by the fastest route, in this case Interstate 30 to the west.

The exits got closer, and Sinclair debated his move. Finally, at the last instant, he cut across two lanes of traffic and headed south on Interstate 35.

Horns honked behind him. Tires screeched.

Call it a hunch, but that seemed like the smart play at the moment.

Interstate 30 was the shortest route, the expected choice. Therefore, a guy on the run who was reasonably smart, as was Jon, would take the other highway.

Sinclair nodded once, giving himself tentative approval for his snap decision. Something visceral in the back of his head told him that Jon Cantrell would eventually take the back roads, too, a thought to keep in mind.

Once on the southbound highway, he accelerated to eighty. The old car looked enough like an unmarked police unit that he wouldn't be bothered by the DPD. Plus, he still had his captain's badge, the one marked retired. In the trunk, he had a change of clothes and a nice selection of weaponry, a tool for almost any scenario.

He crossed the Trinity River, a trickle of muddy water

set inside a wide channel between two earthen levees. A rumble and sharp stabbing sensation in his gut. He paid no mind to the pain but pulled to the shoulder anyway.

Traffic whizzed by.

He stared at the phone, studied the keys and controls. After a few moments, he dialed the main number for Tranquilla and hit a green button.

The phone rang and rang. Then, Imogene came on the line. She knew about cell devices. She told him what to do. Then she gave him the information he needed. Turns out he had chosen the correct highway.

He smiled and ended the call.

Imogene was aces. Good to know that he now had somebody on the inside.

———

I yawned, took another sip of watery Coke.

Piper sat in the front next to me. She was fiddling with one of the new cell phones.

The cheeseburger sat in my gut like a pound of sand. The fuel it provided was needed, the lethargy not so much.

The farm-to-market road we were on cut through a swath of cropland as flat as week-old beer. Narrow rows of sorghum and wheat grew in precise order, marred only by the occasional fence line that bisected the terrain like a ragged zipper.

No traffic or traffic lights for the past few miles. A house here and there amid acres and acres of farmland under a cloudless pewter sky.

The flatness would change gradually, the fertile fields replaced by rocky soil and then by outcroppings of granite, tufted here and there with cedars and other conifers. Then we'd reach the Hill Country, a broad, elevated plain of small mountains that stretched south into Mexico.

I turned on the radio, the AM band, and found a classic country station.

Tammy Wynette, "Stand by Your Man."

"I hate that song," Piper said.

"Driver's choice." I turned up the volume.

"Should we call Marfa?" She put the cell on the console. "Tell the US Attorney we're on the way?"

We'd left Eva uncuffed, after explaining just how unpleasant we could make the journey for her if she chose to interfere.

"Nah." I shook my head. "Let's surprise him."

"May I use the phone?" Eva said.

"I'm thinking that's a big NO." Piper adjusted the sun visor.

"Would you send a message then?" Eva asked. "I need to tell my mother what happened to my sister."

I sighed.

Piper swore and picked up the phone. "What's the number?"

- CHAPTER THIRTY-FIVE -

Raul Fuentes-Manzanares smiled at what he saw. Then he sighed because of what he heard.

Joy and heartache, together. This was the way of Mexico and had been for centuries.

Raul was CEO of Banco Manzanares Internationale as well as head of the newly formed political consulting company that also bore his family's name.

The joy Raul felt came from watching his youngest daughter as she played with the packing paper and shipping boxes.

She was two years, seven months old and quite possibly the most precious creature God had ever created. She had hair the color of charcoal and a face destined to break hearts, genetic gifts from her beautiful mother. Her creamy skin and emerald-green eyes came from the Manzanares side of the family.

Raul and his daughter were in the family room of his home in the Garza Garcia section of Monterrey, Mexico, an affluent suburb. The stucco house had belonged to Raul's father and grandfather before that. It was relatively modest, four bedrooms on a narrow street with a view of the Sierra

Madre to the south. For security, the home had a high wall topped with broken glass and twenty-four-hour guards.

The heartache came from what Raul heard via the cell phone pressed between his shoulder and ear as he wrapped a vase in a piece of newspaper.

The man on other end of the line was called el Camello, the Camel, for reasons no one could quite remember.

At the moment, el Camello was very angry, so enraged that he used Raul's nickname, something only Raul's closest friends were allowed to do. And el Camello was most definitely not a friend.

Apparently, Raul's hotheaded brother, Ernesto, had injured an employee of el Camello in Tijuana. Two of El Camello's spotters in a Camaro had followed Ernesto's convoy on the Ensenada-Tijuana Highway, a random act. Ernesto had confronted the men. Words were exchanged, followed by gunfire, a round fired into one of the spotter's knees.

Such a waste. So unnecessary. So typical of Ernesto.

Under normal circumstances, this would not have required a call to a man of Raul's standing, but in this instance, the injured individual was the Camel's second cousin once removed, on his mother's side.

While the Camel made vague threats and insulted Ernesto's sexual orientation, Raul listened patiently and watched his daughter play.

Joy and heartache. The sweet and the sour.

When the Camel's rants had run their course, Raul placed the vase in a box and told him that of course, he would make a restitution for the injury and disrespect visited upon his family.

The Camel hung up, and Raul used the house intercom to call his brother, asking for a brief meeting.

These were strange times in Mexico, as evidenced by Raul Fuentes-Manzanares's relationship with el Camello and his organization.

Though neither wanted to admit it, both men needed each other.

The Manzanares clan needed the Camel's organization for safety.

Danger and treachery lurked in each corner of Mexico, a general breakdown in the rule of law and the constraints of civilized society. Kidnappers and other small-time hoods looked to score off wealthy families, petty thieves roamed the streets, drug addicts huddled in every alley.

El Camello needed the Banco Manzanares because his business generated a large amount of cash. Busloads, often in the literal sense.

And, if Raul was to be completely honest, the Banco Manzanares and his family had grown to depend on the money provided by the Camel's patronage of their financial institution.

The current situation was much like the one his grand-father faced during the bank's early years, a time that coincided with America's Prohibition era. There had been many a bootlegger deposit at Banco Manzanares in the 1920s that had been stained by blood or booze.

But cash was cash, then and now, and business was business. Raul couldn't count the times as a child his grandfather had told him that "money is green, no matter how black the heart of the man may be."

So their respective operations became intertwined, everything connected.

A ripple on the Camel's side of the pond affected the tiniest Manzanares lily on the opposite shore, and vice versa. Also, the Camel—unsophisticated in the ways of finance and the upper echelons of society—had come to rely on Raul for advice and counsel as to managing his business and sudden wealth, much like he would with an older brother or mentor.

Ernesto Fuentes-Manzanares, who'd flown on a Banco Manzanares jet from Ensenada to Monterrey earlier in the day, entered the room. He patted his niece on the head and wandered to the wet bar in the corner.

"How was your trip to Washington?" Raul picked up another vase and a piece of newspaper. His tone of voice was clipped.

Ernesto poured a couple of centimeters of scotch into a plastic Flintstones cup belonging to Raul's son, one of the few pieces of glassware not already in a box.

"You are really leaving Mexico?" He stared at the disarray caused by the packing.

Raul nodded.

They'd been over this many times. Moving made sense.

Raul's wife's family had relocated to Newport Beach several years before, and Banco Manzanares had almost as many branches in Southern California as it did in Mexico. The bank also had plans to expand to other locations in the southwestern United States, border towns and other areas primed for growth. Much of the funds for the expansion had been provided by the Camel's business.

"Senator Stephen McNally," Ernesto said. "My feeling is he wants to—how do the Americans put it—change the world."

Raul stopped wrapping the vase, anger bubbling in his stomach.

A brother with a hair-trigger temper. A psychopathic crime boss named the Camel.

And now this—an idealistic politician.

He put the vase down and shook his head, aware of the irony.

If noble-minded leaders hadn't decided to crack down on drug smugglers, forcing them to battle each other, Mexico would be a much safer place today, and he wouldn't be in business with el Camello. Probably.

"His chief of staff, Hawkins, the man we've been dealing with," Ernesto said. "He's better suited to these times and our ways."

Raul threaded his way through the mess and poured himself a scotch.

Neither brother spoke for a few moments.

"We were stopped in Tijuana," Ernesto said.

"I know." Raul took a sip of whiskey. "The man you shot was related to the Camel."

"What a shame." Ernesto didn't sound like he thought it was a shame at all.

Another period of silence. They drank scotch while Raul's daughter popped bubble wrap, laughing uproariously at each tiny explosion.

"The guards foiled a kidnapping attempt yesterday." Raul pointed to his youngest child.

"No." Ernesto gasped, crossed himself. "Such a precious child."

"The Camel's people gave us warning the day before." Raul paused. "And today I had to apologize to him for what you did in Tijuana."

"I am sorry. My temper, it's—" Ernesto rubbed his eyes. "Never mind."

Raul strolled across the room and patted his daughter's head. The anger lessened.

"I am tired of this life, not being who I am," Ernesto said. "I am going away as well."

"New York City." Raul nodded. "Such a vibrant place."

Ernesto had a lover in Manhattan and talked often of leaving Mexico and the family business. He wanted to move to New York where homosexuals did not suffer the persecution that they did in Latin America. Raul could hardly blame him.

"I've taken care of what you asked me to," Ernesto said. "The Senator and our investment in the Camel's organization."

Raul nodded.

"Two days from now." Ernesto put down his glass. "I have a flight from Houston to New York."

Raul looked at the boxes that still needed to be packed and then at the calendar on his smart phone. He was going to have to go to the United States and secure their relationship with this Senator.

McNally thought he was simply getting a consulting firm's services in order to help with an upcoming election.

The other side of the equation was that the consulting firm, a front for the Banco Manzanares and its largest depositor, was gaining the ear of a high-ranking politician's operation, something that would help the bank and the Camel control the anarchy engulfing the border, a desirable turn of events for everyone involved, including Senator Stephen McNally.

He sighed and finished his drink.

If you wanted something done correctly, you had to do it yourself.

PART III

"The global war on drugs has failed, with devastating consequences for individuals and societies around the world."

 —Report of the Global Commission on Drug Policy, June 2011

"The war on drugs is a failure. But that doesn't mean we should stop the fight, at least not right now at this critical juncture. I've seen what drugs do. My s-s-son . . . excuse me, I'm sorry . . . as I was saying, my son died from an overdose. . . . My question to the hawks is this: Where's our compassion? Where's the kindness that America's known for?"

 —US Senator Stephen McNally, *Piers Morgan Tonight*, May 2012

- CHAPTER THIRTY-SIX -

An hour later, I used the smallest road I could find to cut across the western leg of Interstate 35, an underpass by the tiny farming town of Grandview.

Piper had left a message at a number in Houston, the voice on the answering machine that of an elderly woman. She'd said for whoever heard the message to contact the Dallas Police regarding Katherine Ramirez, Eva's sister, and an urgent matter. Under the circumstances, the best we could do.

There were no traffic lights or roadside junction boxes. Nothing electronic that could house an RFID tag reader. Just crumbling blacktop and a concrete embankment that supported the highway leading to Fort Worth. The embankment had been tagged by graffiti, faded, loopy letters that read SENIORS 1997 RULE!

The town itself was a blur, a few white clapboard houses with porch swings, a Dollar General store across from a Dairy Queen, a couple of service stations. A church steeple in the distance. Once on the other side of the city limits, a county sheriff's car passed going the other way. The driver waved. I waved back.

The government Tahoe was going to be a problem the farther we traveled away from large metropolitan areas. I'd switched out our original plates, substituting a backup pair kept for just such an emergency, so the APB for our license number wasn't an immediate problem. We had some breathing room. Hours or days, who knew?

Eventually, they would track us to the purchase of the new battery at the auto parts store in Plano, and the serial number on the RFID tag would be put on high alert at scanners across Texas. Would that happen today or next week? Again, hard to say.

I drove on while the two women slept. Stayed far enough south to skirt Cleburne, a county seat, and Glen Rose, home to Comanche Peak Nuclear Power Plant, both locales most likely full of prying ears and eyes. Stayed well north of Fort Hood, the largest military base in the world, for the same reason.

Radio reception grew patchy, hellfire-and-damnation preachers mixed with country music and a few Spanish-language stations.

Three hours later, after zigzagging across the rocky landscape of Central Texas, I stopped somewhere past Hico at a dilapidated little place called the Alamo General Store, a gas station and barbecue joint that looked like it should have dried up years ago from lack of traffic.

My eyelids were heavy. The diet pills had faded.

The stucco building sat on a flat spot between a pair of limestone bluffs, on a two-lane county road. It was old. Gas pumps from a different era, mechanical dials, faded and worn hoses, sat across from a rack of tires and a soft drink machine that should have been in an antique store.

I parked to the side by the restrooms, near a cluster of hackberry trees that partially shaded an ancient Airstream travel trailer. The odds of this place having a video surveillance system were infinitesimal, but you couldn't be too careful. The odds were zero they would have cameras guarding the toilets.

Piper yawned and stretched. "Where are we?"

"Welcome to Ass-Crack, Texas." I shut off the ignition. "Your turn to drive."

The engine ticked, cooling. Eva was still asleep.

I stretched in my seat. "We should—"

"Gotta hit the head," Piper interrupted, opened her side and jumped out.

". . . get new wheels." I finished the sentence, watched her slam the women's room door.

It had been a calculated risk, the need to get as far from Dallas as possible versus secure transportation.

"How do you plan to get a new vehicle?" Eva yawned in the back, awake now.

"There's a town not too far away." I held up a map. "We can find something there."

Brownwood had a population of about twenty thousand, guaranteeing at least a couple of used car lots where cash would trump the rules about title work and ID verification, items that could be handled at a later date, like, say, never.

I got out of the Tahoe and stretched. Then I opened the rear door.

"We're five miles past the middle of nowhere," I said. "Don't be stupid and try to run."

She nodded and exited the SUV, stretching as well. She wobbled, unsteady on her feet, and fell toward me.

I caught her before she hit the ground, an arm around her torso.

"Sorry." She grasped my shoulder. "My leg was asleep."

I held onto her, helped her stand. She stamped her foot.

Piper came out of the women's restroom.

Eva and I stood by the side of the Tahoe. Eva's head was pressed against my shoulder, my arm around her waist.

"It's a one-holer, no lock on the door." Piper regarded us with a quizzical expression. "The window's nailed shut."

I let go of Eva. "You're gonna be cool, right?"

She nodded. Tested her foot.

"Okay." I pointed to the door.

Eva looked at each of us for a moment and then limped into the bathroom. The door shut.

"Her foot was asleep," I said.

"Did you wake it up for her?"

Neither of us spoke for a moment.

"We're making good time." Piper opened a map, spread it on the hood. "If we're traveling by covered wagon."

"You know as well as me how much heat there's gonna be on the interstate." I sat on the bumper.

"Whatever." Piper opened a bottle of water. "I'm ready for this trip to be over and we've just started."

A midnineties Ford Explorer with peeling tint on the windows rattled to a stop under the canopy by the gas pumps, the only traffic we'd seen in a half hour. The vehicle was faded red except for the rear quarter panel, which was Bondo color.

"I forgot to tell you." Piper arched her back, stretching. "The PI sent me an email. Said there might be a line on my mom."

"What PI?" I looked at her. "What are you talking about?"

"You never listen to me." She took a drink.

The back door of the Ford opened and a woman in her early twenties got out, a cigarette in one hand, a toddler on the opposite hip. She wore goth eye shadow and an orange-and-white striped shirt, a Whataburger uniform. Enough metal studs in her ears to set off an airport detector.

"You hired somebody to look for your mom?" I shook my head. "Oh, Piper. Let it go."

Our access to the most sophisticated databases in the world had failed to yield a single lead to Piper's birth mother. The woman was either in the French Foreign Legion or dead, very likely during childbirth. Yet the lack of information didn't stop Piper from searching, a terminal cancer patient grasping at ever more desperate straws.

The toddler began to cry, and the woman yelled at someone inside the Ford, her voice shrill. She leaned over and stuck the kid back in the truck. Then she yelled some more, an angry conversation with whoever was in the vehicle.

From across the parking lot, a few key terms were audible, evidently a shopping list. Mac-and-cheese. Cigarettes. Maxi-fucking-pads.

"Must be debutante season." I yawned.

The goth woman straightened up and looked around. She had a teardrop tattoo in the corner of one eye and appeared to be missing at least two teeth. She flicked her cigarette away and walked to the women's restroom.

"Somebody's in there." Piper stood. "She'll be out in a second."

Goth Chick didn't hear or care. She entered the restroom and shut the door.

"Just what we need." I got to my feet, shook my head. "A tussle with the locals."

- CHAPTER THIRTY-SEVEN -

I watched as Goth Girl came flying out of the women's restroom, one shoulder of her Whataburger uniform torn.

"What the hell?" She fell to the ground. "Goddamn bitch."

Eva strode out, a foil package the size of a matchbook between thumb and forefinger.

"Hey, that's mine." Goth Girl tried to stand.

Eva placed the sole of one foot against the woman's chest. Shoved her back.

Piper sighed. "Usually I love me a good cat fight."

"What's your problem?" Goth Girl rolled away, stood.

Eva slapped her, hard, an open palm to the cheek.

I winced and approached the two women, wondering how big of a trail this little altercation was going to leave. Initial guesstimate: too damn big.

"Shit. Who the—" Goth Girl covered her face with a forearm, swung wildly with her free hand. "Damn crazy ass—"

Eva grabbed her wrist, slung her back to the ground.

"Do you know why the babies cry in the barrios?" She knelt beside Goth Girl.

Goth Girl didn't speak. She inched backward, eyes wide with fear.

"They're orphans." Eva grabbed the girl's pinky, twisted. "Their parents die because of the *narcotraficantes*."

"Owwww," Goth Girl whined, face scrunched in pain. "You're hurting my finger."

Piper stood next to me. At the word "orphan" she'd tensed.

"The older ones have to beg for food." Eva twisted a little more. "Or worse."

"Pleeease." Goth Girl arched her back. "You're breaking it."

"Just so you could have this." Eva held up the foil package in her free hand.

"Take-it-for-god's-sake-it's-yours," Goth Girl said. "JUST LET GO OF MY FINGER!"

Piper moved to the other side of the two women.

"Enough." I grabbed Eva's shoulder. "You made your point."

"How do you know what my point is?" She pushed my hand away. "You don't know anything about me."

Her eyes were hard, the soft vulnerability that had been there earlier replaced by something brittle and cold. A thousand untold stories lurked beneath the surface, crevices of hurt best left unexposed. In that instant, she reminded me of Piper.

"What happened?" I said.

"She asked if I wanted some." Eva let go of the woman's finger. "Had it out, ready."

"You lying skank." Goth Girl got tough again. "I so wasn't gonna give— Hey, what the hell are you doing?"

"You're under arrest." Piper slapped the bracelets on the woman.

"Oh crap. You guys are the heat?" She struggled against the cuffs. "I totally can't get another bust on my record."

"Time and a place for everything, Piper." I took the foil from Eva's grasp. "And this would not be the most opportune moment for an arrest."

The driver's door of the Explorer opened and a woman in a faded housedress got out.

She was gigantic, the size of a sumo wrestler. Caucasian, age hard to pin down because of the rolls of fat. Somewhere between thirty and fifty. Orange hair, gray roots. A mole the size of a bumblebee on the second of three chins.

"What's going on out here?" She waddled over.

The mole had a tail, a half dozen inch-long whiskers wafting in the breeze.

"Ma'am, get back in your vehicle." I badged her.

"That's my baby." She pointed to Goth Girl.

"Mama, they gonna throw me in jail." Goth Girl was crying.

"You have the right to remain silent." Piper slung the handcuffed woman over the hood of our Tahoe. "Anything you say may be—"

"A word, *por favor*." I grabbed my partner's arm, pushed her toward the small stand of trees growing up against the limestone bluff. She grumbled and stalked away. As she went, I shoved Eva in the backseat and cuffed her.

"What about my daughter?" Sumo Mama said.

"Open your mouth again, and you're both going to jail." I followed Piper behind a tree, out of earshot.

We were in a small clearing along with a couple dozen empty beer cans and an elderly television set with a broken screen.

"What in the heck are you doing?" I opened the foil pack.

Piper's face was blank, eyes empty, the expression she always had when things were seething on the inside.

The foil package contained several small nuggets of opaque material, each about the size of a pencil eraser. Crystal meth. Hillbilly crack.

"Enforcing the law." She held up her badge. "That's what we do, right?"

I dropped the drugs into a small puddle of greasy water, ground them with the sole of my shoe.

"Orphans. Did you hear what she said?" Piper snorted. "What does she know about my life?"

"She wasn't talking about you."

Neither of us spoke for a few moments.

"A day or so longer." I touched her arm. "This will all be over. One way or the other."

"You didn't remember about my mother?" She pushed my hand away.

"You're trying to find your mom; got that. I didn't know you'd hired a PI, that's all."

"Well, I told you." She sniffed, arms crossed.

"I'm sure you did." I rolled my eyes. "And I'm an insensitive jerk for not remembering."

Neither of us spoke for a few moments.

"We could run, you know." I leaned against a tree. "Drop Eva at the next town and hit the road for wherever."

"The money, Jon. We need the cash."

I tried not to think about how long my father had before a biopsy became immaterial.

"This sucks." She brushed back her hair. "We're neck-deep in the bad stuff."

I nodded.

"And we're all alone," she said. "Even when we're together."

- CHAPTER THIRTY-EIGHT -

I surveyed the scene.

Goth Girl was still leaning against the hood of the Tahoe, handcuffed. Sumo Mama stood beside her, a cell phone pressed against her ear. An attendant from the service station was present too, a guy in his fifties wearing a khaki uniform, heavy, black-framed glasses, and a barely there comb-over.

Eva was still cuffed in the back of the truck.

I took the cell phone from the obese woman and pressed End.

"What are you doing?" she said.

"A felony amount of methamphetamine." I gave her back the phone. "That's what your daughter had in her possession."

The attendant gulped. "I need to call my boss."

"No." I aimed a finger at his face. "You're not calling anybody."

Piper uncuffed Goth Girl.

I pointed to the two women. "You're both gonna get back in your vehicle and go home and make sure that kid has a good meal tonight."

They didn't speak.

"If you don't, then I'm coming back and taking both of you to jail."

Sumo Mama nodded. She grabbed Goth Girl's hand and pulled her toward the Ford Explorer and the child waiting inside. The two women got in and sped off.

Piper hopped in the driver's seat of the Tahoe and pulled under the canopy. She began to refuel our tank.

"My cousin." The attendant looked at me. "He's a deputy for this county."

I didn't say anything. We couldn't even stop once in a row without leaving a wake.

"Should I call him?" The attendant scratched his chin.

"No." I shook my head. "That won't be necessary."

———

Ten miles of silence.

I stared outside as the shadows grew long and the afternoon waned. Piper drove.

The hills had become larger, the terrain rockier, the open pastures smaller. The size of the properties had increased as well, farms turned into ranches. Endless stretches of barbed-wire and high game fences, dotted only occasionally with buildings. Stone houses and wooden barns. Rusted windmills. Very little traffic.

"About that, back at the service station," Eva said. "I'm sorry. Didn't mean to cause a problem."

Neither Piper nor I spoke.

"My sister used to work with a charity in Mexico." She paused. "In the barrios, these orphans, they're everywhere."

Piper tensed at the word "orphan" but kept driving. She slowed at a crossroads, a boarded-up stucco building on one corner identified only by a faded Esso sign.

"Let's just forget about it," I said.

"Would you uncuff me at least?"

Piper shrugged so I leaned in the back and unlocked her restraints. The key jammed, and for a couple of seconds we were head to head, her wrists in my hands.

She put her cheek against mine, lips to my ear. She whispered, "I'm sorry. Please don't be mad at me."

Her flesh smelled slightly of sweat and shampoo and something else I couldn't place, an evergreen aroma like freshly chopped rosemary.

I jiggled the key so it worked and removed the cuffs. Then I sat back in the front seat.

"The narcotraffickers, sometimes to make an example, they kill their enemies by overdosing them with meth." Eva rubbed her wrists. "Makes the heart practically explode. A very unpleasant way to die."

"You sound like you don't approve," Piper said. "The cartels, you don't like what they do?"

Eva didn't say anything. Her silence became pronounced, a weary resignation rolling off of her. We continued driving for a while, nothing but the whine of rubber on asphalt.

"Piper, that's your name, yes?" Eva leaned forward.

Piper nodded.

"Do you like the wind?"

Piper didn't respond. Her fingers tensed on the wheel and then relaxed.

"What about you, Jon?" Eva cocked her head. "Do you like the wind? Or perhaps the rain?"

"I don't follow," I said. "What do you mean?"

"The wind blows and the rain falls. But do you like or dislike either?"

Neither of us replied.

"What about when the wind turns into a tornado and

kills an entire village?" Eva said. "Or the rain floods? Do you hate the wind and the rain then?"

"A force of nature." I nodded. "Not something to like or dislike."

"Yes, you understand." Eva nodded.

"That doesn't answer my question though," Piper said.

"The wind is everywhere." Eva sighed. "But you can never see it."

Piper frowned and opened her mouth like she was going to say something. But she didn't. No one spoke again. The minutes and miles droned on as the shadows lengthened. After a while, Eva lay down in the back and went to sleep.

We crossed another highway, larger, two lanes each direction, shoulders on either side.

"Brownwood is that way." I pointed to the right. "We need fresh wheels."

"How you gonna pay for a new ride?" Piper continued driving down a narrow farm-to-market road.

"You should have at least a grand left over from Sinclair's money. Not gonna buy us a fancy car or anything, but we could still get something fresh."

"Private investigators don't work cheap," she said. "Besides, everything's closed by now anyway."

"You spent it all?" I rubbed the bridge of my nose. "What'd you get from the Cheyenne?"

"I have about two hundred left." She paused. "And the picture."

"That's not enough for a car." I swore.

"It was my money," Piper said. "I spent it how I wanted."

"Of course you did." I tried and failed not to sound sarcastic. "Trying to find a dead woman."

She didn't reply.

A couple miles of chilly silence droned by.

"Sorry," I said. "I didn't mean it to come out that way."

"What way did you mean it?"

"Nothing. Never mind."

"It's not your mother, now is it?" Piper swerved around a flattened armadillo in the road. The tires screeched a little; the vehicle swayed.

"It's just that the woman gave you up at birth," I said. "She doesn't want to be found."

"Screw you, Jon." Piper's voice grew husky.

"What are you talking about?" Eva sat up, yawned. "What is wrong?"

"Nothing," I said. "Go back to sleep."

"You two are fighting," Eva said. "A lover's quarrel?"

"Didn't we cover this before?" I looked in the back. "Witnesses should be seen and not heard."

Piper accelerated.

"Men are only interested in one thing." Eva blew a strand of hair out of her face. "Piper, did you know Jon came on to me while you were in the apartment in Dallas?"

Neither Piper nor I replied.

"He winked at me. Stroked my thigh and said something about making the trip to Marfa a fun ride for both of us when we stopped for the night."

Piper slowed and pulled over. She parked on the shoulder next to a six-foot game fence. The fence bordered a field covered with wind-stunted post oaks and bisected by a dry ravine. No other vehicles were visible, nor were any buildings.

She looked in the back. "When I went into the apartment in Dallas this morning, we hadn't decided to go to Marfa yet."

Eva didn't speak. Her bottom lip twitched once and then was still.

Piper turned to me. "Where's the duct tape?"

I opened the console.

"That won't be necessary," Eva said.

Piper took the roll and got out.

"Please don't gag me." Eva looked at each of us. "I won't speak again."

Piper opened the back door.

"Sorry." I shook my head. "We shouldn't have even let you go to the bathroom by yourself."

"Stick your head over here." Piper tore off a chunk of tape. "Don't make me climb in the backseat."

Eva's eyes filled with tears.

"Let's go. Chop-chop." Piper waved the strip of duct tape like it was a handkerchief.

Eva swore, face flushed.

Piper put a foot on the floorboard, prepared to step in. She looked at me and arched an eyebrow.

"All right," I said. "No gag for now."

Eva nodded, wiped her eyes with her manacled hands as Piper returned to the front seat.

We drove in silence. After about ten minutes, Eva said, "You are looking for money? For a new vehicle?"

"That's right." I nodded.

"I have money."

"Really?" I looked in the back.

She wore the same skintight sweatpants and tank top as she'd had on this morning. No place to put a wallet.

"You got an AmEx black card hidden somewhere?" I said.

"Uncuff me." She held up her hands.

I hesitated, shot a glance at Piper, who nodded once. I dug the key from my pocket and unlocked her restraints. I kept my head away from hers, and the key didn't jam this time.

"Thank you." She rubbed her wrists. "I'm going to take off one of my shoes. Okay?"

I nodded.

She removed her right Nike, dug around under the insert for a few moments, then pulled out a tiny roll of pink-and-white papers.

"I have money, just not a lot." She handed me a bill. "Will this enable you to buy a car?"

"You want to help us get to Marfa now?" I took the offered item.

"Are you going to let me go?" she said.

I shook my head.

"Then my only chance for safety is there."

I examined the bill, the currency of a unified European continent.

The euro had originally been pegged at a one-to-one ratio with the dollar. Trade imbalances had resulted in a devaluation of American money, meaning that each euro was worth about one and three-quarters US dollars. Also, the euro had been issued in higher denominations than greenbacks, the largest being the five-hundred-euro note.

Currency marked as five hundred euros was essentially the same thing as a thousand-dollar bill and had become the de facto cash instrument for the movement of large sums of traffickers' money.

I rubbed my fingers over the pink bill, five hundred euros. It had been stamped with a crude insignia, a gold crucifix about the size of a thumbnail. The cartels often trademarked their product with similar symbols, though this design was unfamiliar, and I'd never seen currency marked.

"I have more," Eva said.

I handed the bill to Piper.

Eva tossed a slim packet of currency onto the console. "What will that buy?"

- CHAPTER THIRTY-NINE -

Sinclair touched the bandage and slowed as he approached the service station.

The wound in his side from Phil DeGroot's tiny backup pistol had stopped hurting hours ago. Now it was just a dull throb, not particularly pleasant but not painful either.

Sinclair remembered visiting the Alamo when he'd been five or six. He and Daddy and Mama and his little sister had left their little house in the Pleasant Grove section of Dallas and gone to San Antonio, taking the squirrely little neighbor kid and his mom along, the six of them crammed into his dad's 1950 Dodge Coronet Woody Wagon. He and the neighbor kid had played Davy Crockett, acting like they were killing Mexicans and shit, generally having a fine old time.

The Alamo General Store was nothing like the real Alamo. The walls were plaster, not stone, chipped in places, covered in peeling white paint. The pumps and equipment looked like they were from some old-timey movie.

Sinclair stopped under the rusted canopy, got out, and began filling the Crown Vic with unleaded. While the fuel gurgled, he looked at Myrna DeGroot's cell phone. The screen had a message across the top: OUT OF SERVICE AREA.

He wanted to call Imogene again. They'd talked a couple of hours ago, and she'd told him which road to take. He had done so, stopping at the only service station for miles.

This part of the state was nothing like North or East Texas, a relatively small, heavily populated region criss-crossed with highways. This section of the Hill Country, the western fringe, was vast like a whole other country, but it didn't have very many roads or people. It took a long time to get anywhere, and there were only a few options for heading toward the Big Bend Country. He hoped he was on the right road and would not be forced to double back. He tried to remember the last time he'd been to this part of Texas. Near as he could recollect, it had been never.

The attendant came outside like he was going to help. The man wore heavy black glasses and a thick khaki work shirt.

He nodded hello and then appeared to notice the bloody spot on Sinclair's shirt. He went back inside. Sinclair finished pumping and entered the building.

The inside of the Alamo General Store was empty except for the two of them. Several picnic benches sat by a darkened food counter on one side of the room. The other side had shelves filled with dust-covered sundry goods: toilet paper and motor oil, beef jerky and candy. Mounted deer heads covered the walls, a testament to one of the more popular local pastimes.

"How you doing?" Sinclair sauntered to the cash register.

"Fine." The attendant pushed his glasses back up onto his nose, his face sheened with perspiration even though the air in the store was cool.

"You nervous or something?" Sinclair smiled.

"Are you all right, mister?" The man paused. "Looks like you're bleeding."

"My dog was injured." Sinclair peeled off some bills. "Had to take her to the vet."

"Sorry to hear that." The attendant took the money. "Thought maybe you were in a shootout or something." He chuckled nervously.

"Nah, not me. I don't get out much." Sinclair examined the store. No cameras. "I don't even like guns."

The attendant stared at him, a quizzical expression on his face.

"You get much traffic here?" Sinclair said. "At the Alamo General Store?"

The attendant handed Sinclair his change but didn't say anything. After a moment he shook his head.

"How come you stay open?" Sinclair said.

"Huh?"

"Doesn't look like you make enough money to keep this joint in business." Sinclair touched the elderly cash register.

"I wouldn't know," the attendant said. "This is my cousin's place. He does the books."

"A white Tahoe, government license plates." Sinclair pulled a pack of Juicy Fruit gum from a display on the counter. "You seen one like that here today?"

"They're gone." The attendant held up his hands. "I don't want no trouble, okay."

"What trouble? You and me, we're just talking." Sinclair stuck a piece of gum in his mouth. He tried to keep his voice neutral, hiding the excitement. The trail was fresh.

"My other cousin, he's a deputy, he's gonna be here any minute."

"I'm a cop, too." Sinclair flipped open his wallet.

The attendant's face turned pale.

"How come you called the police?" Sinclair closed his credentials.

"I can read, you know." The attendant blinked several times. "That there badge says you're retired. From Dallas." His voice was hoarse, ragged with fear.

Sinclair didn't speak. He pulled the wad of gum from his mouth and rolled it in a ball.

"W-what do you want, mister?" The attendant gulped. "I don't know nothing about them folks in the white Tahoe."

"Is your mouth dry?" Sinclair leaned over the counter and pressed the chewed gum between the man's lips.

The attendant began to shake. He worked his jaws once and then made a gagging noise.

"I'm looking for the people in the Tahoe." Sinclair drummed his fingers on the counter. "How long ago were they here?"

The attendant flinched. Tears leaked down his chin.

Outside, a county squad car with a single occupant pulled into the station and stopped in front of the Ford, blocking its way. A man in a uniform and straw cowboy hat got out, a revolver on his hip.

Sinclair watched as the deputy walked all around the dust-covered Crown Victoria and then entered the store.

Time was, he'd respect another man with a badge. Time was, he wouldn't have dreamed of doing what he was about to do. But that was before he got in deep with the cartels. Before the angry calls from Hawkins.

"Everything okay in here?" The deputy had a booming voice. "Had a call there was a problem."

Sinclair turned to face the officer, his hand snaked under the tail of his shirt.

"You okay, sir?" The deputy approached the counter. "Looks like you're bleed—"

Sinclair shot him with the nickel-plated revolver, the bullet entering just a little to the left of the man's nose.

The noise was loud in the plaster-walled store. The deputy's straw hat flew off in a slurry of red as he crumpled to the ground.

The attendant cowered, face white, hands over his ears.

Sinclair sat on the counter like it was a bleacher at the baseball game. He ignored the pain in his gut and put an arm around the other man's neck like they were old friends.

The attendant's teeth chattered.

"You were getting ready to tell me about the white Tahoe." Sinclair hugged him close.

- CHAPTER FORTY -

I smoothed the currency on the console of the truck.

Eva's Nikes contained four thousand euros in crumpled bills, almost seven grand US. Enough to pay for my dad's biopsy if Eva were to give it to me and I lived to get back to Dallas, two major uncertainties at the moment. Each bill had the same marking, a stamped silhouette of a crucifix.

The turnoff for Brownwood and a new vehicle had long since been passed.

Piper gripped the steering wheel, her knuckles white, hands at ten and two just like they taught in drivers' ed. The speedometer read eighty-five.

Another two-lane blacktop with even fewer signs of civilization than before. Nothing except the road itself, a lonely ribbon of highway. Cedar trees and mesquites grew along the fence line on either side of the road, intertwining with barbed wire until they appeared as one long curtain of metal and vegetation. We topped a rise, and a khaki-colored plateau unfolded below us, a measureless chunk of Texas rough country. The setting sun caused the clouds along the jagged skyline to look like strands of coral. Spectral, salmon-colored, they seemed to stretch from here to forever. Dusk was coming, and night would soon follow, quicker than expected in the mountainous terrain.

"You're driving too fast," Eva said. "It's dangerous."

"Shut up." Piper accelerated.

"Slow it down, Piper." I stuck the money in my pocket. "Dying young is way overrated."

"The sooner we get there, the better." She eased off. The speed dropped.

I looked in the back at Eva. "Where'd you get this many euros?"

"Girl's gotta look out for herself." She shrugged. "That will buy us a new car?"

"Maybe in France," I said. "Not so much in Texas."

She stared out the window.

"What happened to your accent?" I said. "You speak better English all of a sudden."

"There's a place outside of Brownsville." She stretched a leg out on the backseat. "You can buy anything with euros. *Anything.*"

"I thought you were Mexican." Piper glanced at her in the rearview mirror.

"My mother's American, from Houston. My father's Mexican, from Cuernavaca."

"Who are you exactly?" I said.

"They throw some great parties, the *jefes* do." She stared out the window. "I like to go to parties. Have a good time."

"Morales," I said. "The guy on trial in Marfa. You know him?"

"Did you know they actually have almost half of the Laredo Border Patrol on their payroll?" she said. "I took a briefcase full of money over a couple of times."

We drove in silence for a while.

"Lazaro Morales, the guy on trial," Eva said. "He's in charge of the Texas routes."

I looked in the back.

"He throws good parties, too."

"Is he a friend of yours?" I said.

"He's my husband." She folded a blanket into a pillow, stretched out. "I think I'm gonna sleep for a while."

Piper looked at me. She opened her mouth to speak but didn't say anything.

Our passenger was married to the number two guy in the cartel. And she'd turned state's witness.

———

I debated another diet pill to fight the exhaustion. The excitement that had come from the revelation of Eva's relationship to the trial had faded.

The sun was almost behind the mountains, a bare sliver of yellow still visible on the horizon.

Piper was driving. She blinked a lot, shook her head, trying to stay awake. A while ago, she'd turned on the radio but couldn't find a station. Now a low hiss of static from the speakers filled the vehicle. Eva was still asleep in the backseat.

Popoosh. A muffled sound like a balloon breaking.

Eva sat upright.

The Tahoe rocked, one side tilted down.

Piper swore. Jerked the wheel.

A steep drop-off to the right, a wall of rock to the left.

Sweat had erupted from Piper's forehead by the time she'd wrestled the Tahoe to a stop in the middle of the road.

A switchback turn was a hundred yards ahead. At the bend was a gravel shoulder on the slope side. She idled forward, the remnants of the tire slapping against the road.

"You have a spare?" Eva said.

I nodded, tried to slow my heartbeat, no longer exhausted.

Piper pulled onto the gravel and stopped. The three of us got out.

The tire was shredded, beyond repair.

"You think Triple A can find us out here?" Piper got a bottle of water from the backseat.

I headed to the rear of the truck but stopped.

A chugging noise echoed down the road in the direction we'd just come. Piper and Eva came up behind me. We hadn't seen a car in miles.

A hearse appeared. It had to be at least forty years old, but the condition was hard to discern underneath the layer of road grime. The Texas license plate, muddy as well, looked like the style that hadn't been used in decades, plain black and white.

I slid a hand under my shirt, reached for the Glock.

The vehicle stopped about twenty yards behind the Tahoe and a man in his late fifties got out. He wore a week-old beard and a black suit. White shirt, no tie. Dusty black boots.

"May I be of assistance?" He smiled and walked toward us. His hands were empty except for a small black book.

"Uh, no thanks," I said. "We're not dead yet."

He held up the book. "Perhaps then I could say a prayer for you?"

- CHAPTER FORTY-ONE -

I got the jack out.

Piper leaned against the back bumper, bottle of water in one hand, Glock in the other.

Eva sat on the guardrail a few feet from where I was.

The guy in the black suit stood between our vehicle and the hearse. He paid no attention to Piper's weapon. He opened the slim book and read a few lines silently. Then he closed his eyes and murmured.

The passenger door of the hearse creaked, slowly swung away from its moorings. The waning light and dirt on the window must have been playing an optical trick, because the seat looked empty.

Piper paused with the water halfway to her mouth. I shifted the jack to my left hand. My right reached for the pistol.

"It's all right." The man opened his eyes. He looked at us, then back to his vehicle. "There's nothing to be afraid of."

Neither Piper nor I replied. Eva got off the guardrail and moved back, clearly nervous.

A young woman exited the hearse and approached. She was in her late teens or early twenties and wore a gingham dress that reached to her ankles and wrists, like one of the girls from *Little House on the Prairie*.

Except for the overbite and ears that stuck out too much, she was pretty. She had blue eyes in the middle of a long, angular face, pale skin. Her blond hair was pinned back with a bow that matched the dress.

"This is Sadie, my daughter." He put an arm around the girl's shoulder. "We mean you no harm."

Piper took a drink, watching both father and child.

Sadie held up one hand in a timid wave. She kept her gaze to the side or down, careful not to look anyone in the eyes.

I relaxed and headed to the damaged tire at the front of the Tahoe.

"Why did you stop?" Eva asked the man.

"You were in distress." The man followed me. "It's the right thing to do."

I slid the jack under the front wheel well.

"My name is Angus." He knelt beside me. "Where you headed?"

"Please don't take offense, Angus." I stuck the handle in the jack. "But you need to get away from us."

The man had collar-length blond hair going to gray, slicked back. His eyes were blue like his daughter's.

"Here, let me help." He slid the base of the jack a little straighter under the truck.

I didn't reply. Turned the crank instead.

"Pretty country, ain't it?" Angus stood, patted dust from his knees. "Where y'all from?"

I didn't say anything, continued to work the jack. The front of the Tahoe slowly rose.

"We're trying to see as much of Texas as we can," Angus said. "A family trip."

"In a hearse?" I kept cranking. The damaged tire slowly cleared the ground.

Piper rolled the spare over. "We may have a problem."

Even with no weight on it, the new tire appeared to be low on air.

"Won't make it far on that." Angus clucked his tongue. "I'll follow you to the next town."

"There is no next town." I jammed the lug wrench into place.

The GPS showed virtually nothing for the next seventy-five miles, at least on our present course. We could go back and hit something, but even that would take a long while. This section of Texas was as big as a lot of countries but devoid of people, towns, and roads. Only a couple of ways to get to the Big Bend region and Marfa.

"Then we'll follow you to your destination," Angus said.

Piper shook her head. "I don't think that would be a good idea."

The daughter, Sadie, wandered over.

"You don't by any chance have an air tank in your, uh, vehicle, do you?" I glanced at the man as I spun the wrench. "Maybe a can of Fix-A-Flat?"

Piper melted away from the group. I was the only one who noticed.

"No." Angus shook his head. "We have food though. Do you need supplies?"

"Just air." I removed the last lug nut. Looked at my new cell. No signal.

"Where were you and your daughter planning to stay tonight?" Eva said.

I nodded. Not a bad question.

"Wherever we stop." Angus brushed back his hair. "God provides."

Sadie spoke for the first time. "We have a tent."

Her voice was monotone, like the kid in school every-body knew was slow but hadn't scored bad enough to go to the special-ed classes.

"There's a town up ahead not too far." Angus pointed west. "We're gonna stop there for the night."

"That's strange." I wrestled the spare into place. "Didn't see anything on the map."

"It's not on most maps," Sadie said.

The sun was just a sliver over the western mountain range. An instant later, it was gone. The air was cooler and smelled of juniper and freshly tilled earth and, oddly enough, candle wax.

Piper sauntered back over, eyebrows arched.

"There's a casket in the back." She looked at me. "Which makes sense, seeing as how it's a hearse."

I quit tightening lug nuts, stood up, stared at the new arrivals. Eva took a half step away from the father and daugh-ter. She bumped into me and grasped my arm, a fearful expression on her face.

Piper cocked her head at Angus. "You got a vampire in there?"

"That's my dearly departed wife." He pressed his lips together. A long pause. "It's a family trip, like I said."

"Mama always wanted to see West Texas again." Sadie stared at the spot on the mountains where the sun had been.

Piper whistled softly and sat on the guardrail.

"You mean she's in there now?" Eva said.

I finished tightening the wheel, uncranked the jack.

"Mama's folks are from Balmorhea." Sadie nodded. "We're gonna take her there."

The jack was fully down. The spare tire crumpled, maybe a quarter full. Safe for a few miles if we didn't go too fast, say no speedier than a three-legged armadillo. We were gonna be in bad shape if there wasn't a town up ahead.

"We'll follow you." Angus headed to the hearse.

- CHAPTER FORTY-TWO -

I drove slowly, creeping along the narrow road.

It was completely dark when we arrived nearly an hour later. The headlights reflected off a weather-worn road sign that read SCHWARZEMANN, TEXAS.

The town was not a town, more like a flat spot where two narrow roads intersected. Maybe it had been a town at one point. It certainly wasn't now.

Three buildings total that I could see, clustered around the intersection.

On one corner a mercury lamp hummed on a pole, illuminating a stone farmhouse with a tin roof.

Next to the house sat a three-story brick building with a front porch that ran the length of the structure. The building was old, too, and looked like an office or a hotel. A couple of lights were on inside. Three or four cars were parked in front.

On the opposite corner was a large wooden structure that looked like a barn. Moths buzzed around a bare bulb over the double front doors, lighting a sign that read SCHWARZEMANN HALL in an angular Gothic script.

Eight or ten vehicles were parked on one side of the hall, mostly pickups and a sedan or two.

The Texas Hill Country had been settled in the middle of the nineteenth century by central European immigrants, adventurous young men and women from Slovakia and Poland, sausage makers and brewers from Germany and Bohemia.

They brought with them strange customs. Lederhosen and lager. Pumpernickel bread. And dance halls for their oompah bands, evidently what this barnlike structure was.

We weren't really in the area most maps referred to as the Hill Country at this point, however, more in the mountainous region no one ever visited between there and the Big Bend area. Of course, most maps didn't have any reference to a Schwarzemann, Texas, either.

I stopped in front of the home. The hearse parked beside us.

"Anybody else creeped out?" Piper looked around. "A town that doesn't exist and the McWeirdo family cruising around in the middle of nowhere with mom in a casket."

"They are grieving." Eva leaned forward. "Why does this make you uneasy?"

"Did I say I was uneasy?" Piper cranked her head. "I said I was creeped out."

"I do not understand the difference." Eva frowned.

"Let me whip out my pocket version of Rosetta Stone and find the right term in Spanish."

"Piper," I said. "Let it go."

"Grief is a strange thing," Eva said. "That's all I was saying."

"You calling me strange, bitch?" Piper balled her fists.

"No." Eva shook her head. "'Annoying' would be the term I'd use."

Piper became very still. Her lips twitched.

"Let's all settle down," I said. "Everybody's tired from being on the road all day."

"Settle down?" Piper looked at me. "Did you just tell me that?"

"I didn't mean—"

"Don't stop here," Eva interrupted. "I think I've heard of this place." She paused. "From some people on the other side of the border."

Piper took a deep breath, recovered control.

"Cartel people?" I said.

"We should just keep going." She hugged herself, hands under her arms. "Please, Jon."

"We don't have a choice," I said. "The tire won't make it anywhere else."

"The *sicarios*." She frowned. "They come here, I think."

"Hit men for the narcos," I said. "Here?"

The word *sicario* derived from a Latin term for "dagger men" and meant hired assassin. The cartels employed a lot of *sicarios*.

"Yes." She nodded. "To rest and hide. It's out of the way."

I didn't say anything. Her statement made sense.

In the mountains at the intersection of two narrow roads, the town that wasn't a town served as the very definition of out-of-the-way. But, like an old camping spot in the middle of the wilderness, out-of-the-way places that had resources—water, shelter, a flat spot in the otherwise rocky terrain—tended to attract travelers.

Piper twirled a set of handcuffs around one finger. "The cartels have hit men living on this side of the border?"

Eva looked at both of us strangely like we were slow in the head.

"The narcotraffickers have people everywhere," she said.

Across the street, the door of the dance hall swung open and a figure stepped outside and lit a cigarette.

Knuckles rapped on the driver's window. All three of us jumped.

Angus stood by the door, Sadie a few feet behind him.

The extreme fatigue of the past few days must have taken its toll. I hadn't heard their doors slam or seen them moving.

He tapped again and spoke, words muffled through the glass. "Let's try the dance hall."

I nodded.

He and Sadie wandered across the road.

"He's strapped." Piper peered through the bug-splattered windshield. "He wasn't carrying before."

I stared at Angus as he walked across the road. His coat fit differently than earlier, bulked up around the torso. He held his arms pressed against his sides as he walked. His gait was off too, like he weighed more.

"We're gonna fix the tire. That's all." I opened my door. "Let's make it quick."

"What about her?" Piper pointed in the back.

"I can go with you," Eva said.

"That's not what I had in mind." Piper smiled. She held up the bracelets.

"No, not the cuffs." Eva looked at me. "It's too dangerous."

"Sorry." I shook my head.

"Jon, please." Eva leaned forward. She touched my arm. Her eyes were scared. "She's going to harm me."

"No, she's not." I patted her hand.

"I'm not going to hurt you." Piper had rolled her eyes when I'd touched the witness. She opened the back door and held up the cuffs. "I'm just annoying, remember?"

"NO-NO-NO." Eva shook her head frantically. She tried to climb in the front seat. Her voice was shrill, face terrified.

"It's okay." I grasped her shoulders. Pushed her back. "I know you've had a rough time, but we have to follow the rules from here on out."

She'd been held in protective custody by the US Marshals, marked for death by one cartel, kidnaped by another. "Rough time" was an understatement. She was a magazine cover for the *Post-Traumatic Stress Gazette*.

Eva began to hyperventilate. She quivered like a blade of grass in a storm. Her face grew pale.

"Shhh." I stroked her arm, leaning between the front and the back seats. "It's okay. We're just going across the street."

After a few moments, she calmed down. Her breath slowed. Shoulders slumped.

I nodded to Piper, who attached the restraints. She was quick and efficient about it, cuffs on wrists, not too tight, and a long length of chain hooked to the D-ring on the floor. She shut the door and met me at the front.

I chirped the locks shut. "She's a basket case."

"Do you think I'm annoying?"

Angus and his daughter stood across the road, watching us. They turned and walked into the dance hall.

"No. Of course not." I headed toward the hall. "You got your cell?"

Piper walked beside me. She pulled out her new, disposable phone and held it up. "No coverage."

I looked at mine. The same.

"Eva is trouble," Piper said. "More ways than one."

"Cut her some slack. She's scared for her life."

Piper made a choking noise, a cough that tried to swallow a mouthful of words. "You're unbelievable," she said. "It's like you have a damsel-in-distress fetish."

I ignored her.

We reached the other side of the highway. Angus and Sadie had gone inside.

The guy by the door flicked his cigarette butt into the dark. He was a gringo about forty, a weathered face, callused hands. Faded jeans. A starched, pearl-buttoned shirt, straw Resistol hat.

At that very moment, there were probably a thousand more like him, smoking in front of a thousand different honky-tonks across the state, from Mesquite to Pasadena, Abilene to Longview.

A metal sign was mounted on a pole by the front door, a Texas historical marker.

I stopped to read the text as the thump of music cranked up inside.

"Established in 1869 by German settlers, Schwarzemann was named for the central European mythical creature known as Der schwarze Mann, literally the black man. However, in this context, black did not mean a color. Instead it referred to darkness as Der schwarze Mann was reputed to be an evil entity that lived in the dark regions and preyed on unsuspecting travelers."

"Beautiful." Piper peered over my shoulder. "We're stuck in a town that doesn't exist but was named for the Nazi boogeyman."

The smoking guy stepped back into the dance hall, the door swinging open and a thump of drums and guitars blaring out.

We followed him in.

The place was one open area, maybe a hundred feet by fifty. Except for the stage illumination at the other end, pointing toward the band, it was lit entirely by strands of Christmas lights strung from the rafters over the rows of picnic tables in the middle. A bar and small kitchen area were to one side of the front door.

Sadie sat at the closest table, a pair of longneck bottles in front of her. Angus was nowhere to be seen.

Maybe fifteen people total in the place, scattered about, drinking beer, watching the stage. This was undoubtedly the only entertainment in a fifty-mile radius, meaning probably a quarter of the county was here.

The band was a band in name only. Three slightly out-of-sync players: a lead guitarist-singer, a drummer, and a bass player.

The song ended and another began. An old Charley Pride tune. "Is Anybody Going to San Antone?"

The smoking man walked by, carrying a fresh beer.

I took a step toward him. "Excuse me. Do you know if there's a service station nearby?"

He glanced at me, but walked on.

"You're so charismatic," Piper said. "Such a way with people."

From a side door, Angus entered, carrying a squat cylinder about a foot and a half in diameter. A hose was attached.

"He found air," Piper said.

He approached us and put the object by my feet.

"You should fill your tire and leave," he said.

"Thanks." I picked up the tank.

The front door opened and a cool breeze swept in. The band kept playing. The audience kept listening. But something changed. The air felt charged. The lights seemed brighter, then softer.

"Guess you missed your chance." Angus walked to where his daughter was and sat down.

- CHAPTER FORTY-THREE -

The hair on my arms tickled.

Spend enough years in The Life and you develop an extra layer of perception, a radar for the bent.

It's like a nose for stuff that can't be smelled, or a third eye that can spot a hood by the way he holds his head.

You don't get it from creepy preacher types who cart around dead bodies in their RV hearses. Or from towns named after a German *chupacabra*. No, you get the tingle from something else.

The man was in his late forties. Caucasian, close-cropped gray hair. Starched Wrangler jeans and a denim pearl-button shirt. Lace-up roper boots. And a five-star sheriff's badge pinned to his breast pocket.

He wore a hand-tooled leather belt with a matching holster on his left hip. The holster contained a Colt 1911 with silver and turquoise grips. The weapon was carried ready for shooting, cocked and locked, a strip of leather fastened between the frame and hammer.

I got the feeling that this was a dangerous man, just from the way he shuffled across the floor.

His eyes missed nothing. They swept the room, taking in the band and small audience. His gaze lingered on Angus, who had moved to the table with his daughter.

Then he looked at me and Piper and smiled as the light glinted off the badge.

A girl came from behind the bar and handed him a Coca-Cola in an old-style, returnable bottle. She backed away.

He took a sip and walked over to where we stood.

"Gubmint SUV outside." He looked at the air tank. "With a low tar."

His accent was pure Texas drawl, as country as a John Deere tractor. "Tire" became "tar." "Government" became a sneer, an obscenity of sorts.

I didn't say anything.

"Why you in my part of the world?" His gaze drifted to the bulge on my hip where the Glock was hidden by my shirt.

"You must be the sheriff." I pulled out my credentials.

He peered at them. "D. E. A." He pronounced each letter as a separate word that tasted bad in his mouth.

"We're passing through," I said. "On official business."

He nodded but didn't speak.

A table of people closest to the front entrance stood, leaving half-full beers, and headed to the door.

"Go'on. Fill up your tar." He snapped his fingers at Piper. "Me and your boyfriend is gonna chew the fat."

"Of course. You men talk about manly things." Piper smiled. "I'll go outside and make myself pretty. Then, I'll get barefoot and find a kitchen."

The sheriff squinted at her but didn't speak.

I nodded at her. "I'll be there in a minute." She rolled her eyes but picked up the tank and headed to the door.

The sheriff pointed to a table. "Sit."

While he'd been talking, a pair of men had come inside and moved to either side of the door. They were muscular without being large, fit without appearing to be. Untucked work shirts, hands held loosely at their sides.

Piper walked past them, carrying the tank. They let her go.

The sheriff motioned again to the table.

I could leave now and provoke a confrontation. Or, I could take a seat and hope that I'd be able to get out of this developing situation with a minimum of fuss while Piper recharged the flat.

Leave or go.

I sat.

The man slid onto the bench across from me.

"My name is Sheriff Joe Stepanek." He took a sip of Coke. "You ever hear of me?"

"I'm not from around here."

"Damn straight on that." He nodded. "You're a city boy. I can tell."

"Dallas," I said.

"My daddy came from down around Waco. Used to own him a strip club on the interstate."

Houston belonged to what's left of the Italian mob, mostly the aging wiseguys based in Louisiana. Dallas was still an independent region controlled by local, mom-and-pop thugs like Milo Miller and Sinclair, despite inroads by the Russians advancing across the country from the East Coast. The border region, everything from the Rio Grande to San Antonio, was controlled by the cartels.

That left the central portion of Texas, from Waco on west past where we were at the moment, the heartland of the Lone Star State. This area belonged to the Bohunk Mafia, the crooked descendants of the central European immigrants who built the dance halls and breweries. Apparently, one of their own had entered law enforcement.

"Whatever you got going on," I said, "we're not looking to mess with it."

His eyes grew hard, the color of steel.

I flexed my arm without thinking, touched the butt of the Glock with my elbow.

"Maybe I'll just arrest you for the hell of it," Sheriff Stepanek said. "Traveling judge comes around every week or so. You can make bail then."

The band stopped playing. A canned music track came on, much quieter. The musicians slid out a back exit, and the few people in the audience began to leave by the front door.

I glanced at Angus's table. His daughter was gone. He sat staring at a beer bottle, a wistful look on his face.

Piper came back in, followed by another man who looked like a clone of the two guys by the door.

She sat at the other table, across from Angus, facing us. She splayed three fingers on her knee.

Three more bad guys outside, a total of six. At least. This was going to end in a rough landing no matter what. Might as well increase the airspeed and see if a parachute shook loose.

"You don't have any deputies with you," I said. "That means you're likely the only crooked cop in these parts."

He frowned but didn't respond.

"Your county has the population of Chernobyl right after the meltdown," I said, "But it's relatively close to the border, as the buzzard flies anyway."

Ciudad Acuña was hours from here but the closest crossing point, directly opposite Del Rio on the Rio Grande.

"You are plumb full of yourself, aren't you, boy." He smiled and shook his head.

I decided to bluff with the scant information Eva had provided. Maybe it wasn't the smartest thing to do, but I was tired and didn't really care about being smart anymore.

"But you're not moving product through here. No contraband."

"Keep going." He flexed his fingers, still smiling. "This story you're spinning is better than watching TV."

"Our intel says you're running a bed-and-breakfast for cartel shooters. Letting 'em stage out of here before they go and do a job."

The smile disappeared from his face.

I held up a hand. "Before you get your panties in a wad and start making threats, you need to ask yourself one thing."

"What's that?" His voice was low, hoarse.

"How many more white Tahoes are on their way here right now?"

Piper stood, looked toward the door.

The sheriff's men had started moving our way as another pair entered. These two were Hispanic. They moved like tigers encircling their prey. They flanked out toward the empty stage, trapping us. Nobody paid any attention to the preacher.

Piper reached under her shirt. I did the same as the sheriff grasped his Colt.

Then the lights went out. Darkness except for the all-too-faint illumination from exit signs at either end of the hall.

Feet shuffled. Voices raised in alarm.

From behind me, near Angus, came the tang of metal rubbing on metal.

A quarter second of silence.

Then, a battle started, a climax to a feud that we knew nothing about nor ever would, the end chapter to an unwritten book about a strange man in a hearse and the crooked sheriff of a remote county in West Texas.

Spits of flame filled the room along with the staccato crackle of two or more heavy-caliber weapons.

I dropped to the floor, caught a glimpse of Angus on the way down.

Two side-by-side streams of gunfire illuminated the preacher's face, a gunpowder strobe light, as the pair of machine guns he'd evidently had under his coat fired on full auto. He was aiming at the men who had flanked out, clearly not in our direction. Yet.

Piper was by my side on the ground. We both had our guns out but no targets.

Return fire from the direction of the door. The *pop-pop-pop* of smaller-caliber weapons, semiautomatic pistols. Bullets whizzed over our heads.

Shouts. Someone screamed. The air stunk of spilled beer and burnt cordite.

Then silence.

I grasped Piper's hand and pulled her toward the rear of the building and the exit door the band had used.

"How you doing, Sheriff?" Angus's voice was loud in the stillness. "You on your way to hell yet?"

- CHAPTER FORTY-FOUR -

I ran crouched over, Piper by my side.

The tables in Schwarzemann Hall were arranged in two rows with a wide central aisle running from the front entrance to the stage at the rear.

The exit signs provided just enough light to navigate, a couple of candles in an underground cavern.

Piper and I were halfway to the back of the building when the machine gun fire started again. Quick bursts strafed the other end of the hall.

Glass behind the bar shattered.

People yelled. Fired back.

An alarm of some kind chirped twice and then blared.

We hit the back door and tumbled into the night.

The deep gloom of the bar seemed like a beach at high noon compared to the empty blackness behind the dance hall. Trees canopied this part of the structure, blocking the stars and moon.

I grasped for Piper's hand, found it, pulled her close. Together, we stumbled away.

Inside, the gunfire escalated and then stopped.

We cleared the trees and found ourselves on a gravel road that led upward away from the crossroads where our Tahoe was parked. From where we'd left the witness handcuffed.

Boulders on either side. A crescent moon and a swath of stars overhead.

Shouts from the direction of the dance hall. Footsteps headed our way.

"Let's go." I jogged up the road.

About fifty yards later, a break in the rock appeared on the right, a narrow path leading away.

"Where do you think it goes?" Piper stopped next to me, breathing heavily.

"Does it matter?" I looked behind us.

Two beams of light bounced along the road, shaking like flashlights.

"Wonder if the sheriff had anything to do with Angus's wife croaking?" Piper said.

"Might be a safe bet." I headed down the path. "Did you fill up the tire?"

"Yeah." She moved beside me. "Got that going for us at least."

We trotted as fast as possible down the rock-strewn trail, a small gorge between two tree-covered outcroppings of limestone.

The path ended much too soon, a half minute later, at a narrow plateau dotted with cactus. It was fifty, maybe sixty feet long by about ten feet wide.

Except for the break for the trail where we'd just been, three of the four sides were all rock. The fourth, facing us, was open, a cliff overlooking the dark country below.

The wind blew, rustled our clothes, the pitchy smell of evergreen trees in the air.

"Now what, Batman?" Piper inched to the edge, looked down.

"Don't know." I did the same.

A steep drop, a hundred feet or more.

We both turned and looked down the path we'd just come.

A flashlight bounced in the distance.

"Who are these people?" She stamped her foot. "And why are they after us?"

"The town's a cartel hideout," I said. "Plus, they probably think we came in with Angus."

Schwarzemann was remote enough to be off the DEA radar. No direct route to the border either, so they wouldn't run drugs through here. Just shooters.

The light got closer.

"So that hotel is full of hit men," she said. "Fifty feet from where we left the witness."

"She was okay when you filled the tire?" I squinted at either end of our tiny mesa.

"I guess so." Piper took a step closer to the path, pulled her gun. "I didn't stop and take her pulse though."

"What are you doing?"

"Buying. Time." She aimed her Glock at the light and fired.

Piper's Mantra, once again in action: *when in doubt, put rounds on target.*

The bullet zinged off several rocks, and the light extinguished.

From where we stood, the wall of rock on the left side of the mesa appeared higher. It was flush with the edge, forming one continuous piece where it connected with the flat surface of the mountain. The wall to the right was not flush, a slight gap overlooking the darkness below.

"Let's try this way." I headed to the right, roughly toward the area where we'd left the Tahoe.

A small stand of desert willows grew at the edge of the plateau. By the light of the stars, I could just see a narrow ledge beyond their trunks. In the darkness, the ledge appeared too small to traverse.

Piper and I stopped at the edge. The end of the line.

"I don't want to die in BFE West Texas." She grasped my arm.

"I don't either." I slid my hand into hers. "We got enough ammo, maybe we can hold them off for a while."

"The witness is a hottie." She pushed my hand away. "If I wasn't around, do you think you and her would, well, you know."

"I have my standards." I shook my head. "Marked for death by the cartels doesn't really put me in the mood."

"Standards?" She tapped my chest. "You?"

We didn't move. Didn't speak. Nowhere to go, nothing to say.

Shouts from behind us.

"Why'd you come on this little jaunt anyway?" I said. "You could have just walked away. Disappeared."

I was in it for the money, much-needed cash for my family, an ill father and an obsessive-compulsive half sister. Not to mention that we were both in the hot seat for the two dead men back at the warehouse in Dallas, and Eva Ramirez was the only person who could clear us. Hence the need to get her to Marfa, the best chance of keeping her alive and collecting the bounty.

But Piper was different. After a lifetime in foster institutions and on the street, she had a knack for disappearing, melting away from prying eyes and official ears. She could have just walked. It would have been tricky, and she would have faced long odds, but it could have been done.

"Gotta stand for something, Jon." She slid her gun back in her waistband. "Besides, lots of little children depend on me."

I didn't say anything. A few dollars a month for a kid in Bangladesh did not a mother-child relationship make.

Piper whispered something I couldn't catch, her words lost in the wind. She slid by me, pushed through the drooping limbs of the closest tree, and sidestepped onto the outcropping of rock. A few seconds later, she disappeared around a corner.

I took a deep breath and followed.

Away from the relative safety of the mesa, the wind seemed to blow harder.

I shuffled as quickly as possible, one sliding step followed by another, fingers grasping for slits in the rock.

At ten sidesteps I froze. The ledge had narrowed to a toehold, only a couple of inches wide. The wind blew harder, whipped my sweat-dampened shirt against my torso.

One hand slipped, and I made the mistake of looking down into the blackness.

The height became all-encompassing. Images of what lay at the bottom filled my mind. The rocks and boulders. The broken bones they would cause, the flesh that would tear.

I hyperventilated. Began to shake.

Noise from the mesa where we'd come. Men talking.

I slowed my breathing. Eyes closed, centered myself. Kept going. Slower now but steady.

A couple of minutes later, the ledge grew wider. Another few steps and it became a path several feet across. Then it grew to a broad, flat surface.

Another few seconds and the flat surface turned between two hills and became wider still.

I started to jog, and about a minute after that, the track ended at paved asphalt by a Texas highway marker.

No sounds behind me. Piper was nowhere to be seen.

The road curved to the right in a direction that felt like where we'd left the truck across from the dance hall.

I sprinted, gun in hand.

They were waiting for me around the bend.

Sheriff Stepanek and two men, one holding Piper's neck in the crook of his elbow.

I skidded to a stop, gun up.

"Mister DEA." The sheriff coughed, a wet, hacking sound. "Goddangit, but you brought in a heap of trouble."

His shirt was darker on one side. Moist.

The two men with him appeared unhurt.

I aimed at the sheriff. "Let her go."

"That old boy who's holding her right now." He pointed his Colt at me, wincing a little at the movement. "He's what they call a *sicario*."

Eva had been right. And we'd left her handcuffed right by a nest of cartel shooters.

"He killed an undercover DEA agent in Piedras Negras last week," Stepanek said. "Cut him up into little bits, fed him to a pig."

The second man flanked out, moving away from the *sicario* holding Piper, splitting my targets.

"I like the knife." The *sicario* smiled. "Maybe I cut up you and the chica here."

I aimed at the man on the move, then back to the sheriff. Then back again.

The guy on the move eased toward me, gun in hand.

My limbs were still shaky from the trek across the ledge. Bone-crushing fatigue and adrenaline mixed in my system.

"Shoot him, Jon." Piper's voice was a croak.

"Don't talk, chica." The *sicario* struck her side with his gun, a wicked blow that made her whole body convulse. She groaned and slumped.

I couldn't decide who to take out with the one shot I would have. The sheriff or the closest danger, the guy moving toward me?

Before I could make a decision, Sheriff Stepanek's hat flew off, a strange occurrence because the instant before he hadn't been wearing one.

The hat landed at my feet. It wasn't actually a piece of headgear, more like a piece of head, the top portion of his skull along with a few ounces of brain matter.

The sheriff fell to the ground like a marionette whose strings had been cut.

The guy who'd been approaching me stopped, eyes wide. He stared at the sheriff's skull fragment on the ground.

Through the fatigue, I took this as an opportunity and fired twice, both rounds connecting, one in the chest, the other in his face.

He fell too, dropping his gun in a clatter on the asphalt.

From the darkness at the end of the deserted highway, a figure emerged. Eva, carrying one of the silenced subguns from the Tahoe. She'd managed somehow to get free from her restraints.

The *sicario* holding Piper moved to the other side of the road. His eyes darted back and forth between me and the new arrival, his attention split.

"Let her go." I aimed at his face, the only clear target.

"Ay-yi-yi." He smiled. "Eva *está aquí*."

Eva rattled off a string of Spanish; I caught a couple of swear words.

"*Mucho dinero, sí.*" The *sicario* pulled Piper closer, inching her head up to the level of his, blocking the shot. "Everybody wants the rat dead."

A standoff.

Neither Eva nor I spoke.

I stepped closer.

The *sicario* jammed the muzzle of his gun against Piper's head.

I glanced at Eva, about thirty feet away. She held the MP5 pressed against her shoulder like someone familiar with such a weapon.

"Let her go," I said. "Two against one. You'll never make it."

The *sicario* looked down the road like he was expecting help.

"Your amigos," Eva said. "They're not coming."

The *sicario* took a step to the left and then one to the right. He appeared nervous now.

Eva kept the subgun to her shoulder but didn't move.

I eased in the opposite direction, hoping to draw out the man, make him lower his guard.

The *sicario* shifted his stance, tightened the choke hold on his prisoner, gun not moving.

Phbbt. The spit of a silenced weapon.

The *sicario* screamed. He hopped away on one foot, gun coming away from Piper's temple. His other foot appeared to be missing a few toes, blood spewing out from where they should have been.

Eva fired twice more, both to the chest, and the man fell dead.

Piper jumped away from his corpse, eyes wide, breathing heavily, clutching her side.

I holstered my Glock, rushed next to her. "Are you all right?"

She fell against me, and I eased her down, knelt beside her, holding her. She clutched my arms, taking big gulps of air.

After a few moments, we both looked up.

Eva stood about five feet away, aiming the MP5 at us.

"I had a handcuff key in my pocket," she said.

"You carry one of those all the time?" I asked. "In addition to a stash of euros?"

"My boyfriend is a DEA agent." She shrugged. "There's this game he likes, with the handcuffs."

"You're married to a cartel bigwig." I frowned. "But your boyfriend is a cop?"

"My life is complicated. What can I say?"

"A girl's got to look out for herself." Piper struggled to catch her breath. "Right?"

"You understand." Eva nodded. "*Bueno.*"

"What's his name?" I asked. "Your boyfriend?"

"Always with the questions." She tightened her grip on the gun. "I'm tired of questions."

Nobody spoke for a few moments.

"What happens now?" I stood.

"The tire is fixed on the Tahoe?" Eva asked.

Piper hesitated, then nodded.

"I could take the vehicle, leave you here." Eva smiled. "No one would know for hours. Maybe days."

Piper grabbed my arm, pulled herself to her feet.

"But I won't." Eva tossed me the submachine gun. "We should hurry."

I caught the weapon, slung it over my shoulder, confused. Piper hesitated for a moment before pulling her Glock from the dead sheriff's waistband. Then, the three of us ran toward the tiny town where our vehicle was parked.

- CHAPTER FORTY-FIVE -

Schwarzemann Hall and our Tahoe were about a quarter mile away, down the road from where we left Sheriff Stepanek and the two cartel shooters.

I knew this long before we got there because of the flames.

The dance hall was engulfed. The siding gone, nothing but fire on a wooden skeleton that was the burning frame of the old structure and a blazing roof. Bad wiring, shot-up gas lines, who knows what caused it.

We stopped about thirty yards from the hotel, at the extreme edge of the light from the fire, the town in clear view. After a few moments, it became apparent there wasn't anybody out searching.

All the trucks and sedans that had been parked by the hall were gone.

Across the street, a couple of cars were in front of the hotel, and the hearse was still next to our Tahoe. A tiny figure sat on the open tailgate by the casket. Sadie, Angus's daughter.

"Why did you give me back the gun?" I looked at Eva.

"What's American expression, 'safety in numbers'?" Eva paused. "You think this is the only town where the *sicarios* hide out?"

"What about the hotel?" Piper said. "How many are in there?"

Eva shrugged. "Don't worry about them."

I ejected the magazine from the submachine gun. It was half empty, low fifteen rounds.

"Piper, wait here." I replaced the mag, jogged across the street, and approached the hotel.

Nobody outside. A half dozen empty lawn chairs were on the front porch clustered around a pair of tables.

The front door was open.

I stepped inside, subgun pressed against my shoulder.

A lobby with a cracked tile floor, wobbly ceiling fans. Straight ahead was a check-in counter by the stairs. Behind the counter a peg board with room keys.

To the right was a sitting area. Old leather couches and easy chairs around a wagon wheel coffee table and a big screen TV showing a Mexican soap opera.

The dead bodies were there.

Three Hispanic men wearing jeans and soccer jerseys were sprawled on the furniture and floor. A young woman lay in front of the television, arms stretched out like a crucifix. Another pair of men rested in the corner, one on top of the other.

The volume on the TV increased suddenly, startling me. A political advertisement for US Senator Stephen McNally came on, the good senator prattling on about jobs or immigration or something in pretty passable Spanish.

Some of the corpses had bullet wounds in the head, others in the chest. A smoldering cigarette with two inches of ash sat on the coffee table by an overturned can of Bud Light.

A couple of the *sicarios* had tried to fight back. The woman, a teenager, had a nickel-plated Colt in her grasp. Another clutched a long-barreled revolver to his chest like it was a baby.

The carnage was overpowering, hard to fathom even for someone who'd been in combat. I stared at the macabre scene for a few moments, wondered what was upstairs.

No sound but the cackle of the senator on the television.

I threaded my way between corpses as quietly as possible and picked up the remote from the coffee table. Clicked Mute. Wiped the device with my shirt and dropped it back where it had been. Listened.

Nothing but the groans of an old building in the summer night.

One of the bodies expelled some air, a soft whistle.

I shook my head several times, tried to clear my head of the image in front of me. Then I left.

———

Eva and Piper were by the back of the hearse with Sadie. The dance hall continued to burn, the flames illuminating the intersection and our little cluster of vehicles.

"Where is your father?" Eva touched Sadie on her shoulder.

The girl shook her head but didn't speak.

Piper glanced at me and then at the hotel, an eyebrow raised.

"All of them." I made a slash across my throat with one hand.

Piper blinked several times, clearly trying to process what I had just told her. Then she looked at Eva Ramirez, her eyes wide.

"Did your father come out of the building?" Eva pointed to the fire.

Sadie stared at her, expression blank, and leaned against the casket.

"How many?" Piper pointed to the hotel.

I opened my mouth but didn't say anything. I shook my head.

Eva turned away from the girl by the casket. She looked at Piper and said, "Does it matter how many?"

"You kil—" Piper bit her lip. "You did all of them?"

"Do you know what they would have done to me before they killed me?" Eva asked. "What they would have done to you?"

A tank of some kind exploded near the burning building, throwing off a huge shower of sparks and flames.

"Do you think I want to be like this?" Eva said. "Do you think I chose this life?"

Nobody spoke. The dance hall continued to burn.

"We need to get out of here," I said.

"What about the girl?" Eva pointed to Sadie.

"She should come with us." I ran through the scenarios in my head. The additional complications that would come from having a fourth person on the road.

"I'm not leaving." Sadie shook her head. "Not without Daddy. Not with Mama here."

Piper got two bottles of water from the Tahoe and walked to the rear of the hearse. She handed one to Sadie.

"When did your mother die?" She opened her bottle and took a long drink.

Sadie cocked her head. "W-w-what?"

"Your mother." Piper tapped the coffin. "How long ago did she pass?"

Sadie took a drink of water, wiped her mouth. "A month ago."

"And how old are you?" Piper said.

"Nineteen. Be twenty next February."

"I never knew my mother," Piper said. "So you're pretty lucky that you had all those years with yours."

Sadie frowned, a confused look on her face. Then she nodded slowly.

"What I'm saying is you might think about letting go." Piper drained her bottle.

Nobody spoke for a couple of moments. The fatigue settled on me like a wet coat.

"You need to come with us." I sat beside her on the tailgate. "We can't leave you here."

The girl shook her head. "I gotta find Daddy."

Eva grimaced. Piper pursed her lips, went to the truck.

A portion of the dance hall crashed inward. Sparks billowed out. Flames shot upward.

"We'll come back later," I said. "And look for him then."

"No." She shook her head violently. "No-no-no-no."

Piper returned, unfolded a map, tilted it toward the burning building for light.

"We head south on this road." She pointed to a thin gray line. "Skirt the border the rest of the way to Marfa."

"Yes, that is a good plan." Eva nodded. "There are very few towns on that route."

"But we got to get out of here pronto." Piper folded the map.

"These towns," I said. "Are any of them hideouts for the *sicarios*?"

"Not that I know of." Eva shrugged. "But there's more than one cartel out there."

"That's comforting." Piper stuck the map in her pocket.

"Sadie." I stood up. "You really need to come with us."

"I'm not gonna." She shook her head again. "Daddy's gonna be along in a bit. I got food and stuff. I'll be all right."

Piper and I looked at each other. Piper shook her head slowly.

"Why don't I drive for a while," Eva said. "You two have been through enough."

Nobody spoke for a few moments. A jet of flame shot out from the building. Then Piper said, "Okay. I'll ride shotgun."

- CHAPTER FORTY-SIX -

Sinclair smelled it before he saw it.

Charred wood. Burnt shingles. The unpleasant stench of a fire-damaged building.

He rounded the corner on the narrow road and saw smoke, thin gray ribbons wafting upward in the cool dawn air.

The building was a pile of ash-covered, blackened rubble. A power pole a few yards away remained standing. The trees surrounding the demolished structure had been burned as well. Across the road sat a stone farmhouse and an old hotel, a hearse of all things parked in front of the house.

Sinclair pulled up next to the funeral wagon and got out, gun in hand. He'd been driving all night, running on coffee and the speed tabs he'd scored at a truck stop just outside of Dallas. His side was stiff but not especially painful.

He walked to the rear of the hearse. The tailgate was open, a casket inside.

The girl seemed to materialize from nowhere, appearing next to the back of the vehicle.

Sinclair tensed, brought the gun up, then relaxed.

She was a wisp of a thing, young, maybe the same age as one of his granddaughters, the cross-eyed one who married the Marine. Her skin was pale, eyes red-rimmed and swollen. She wore a calico dress that covered most of her flesh but still outlined the curves of her body.

"Well now. Who might you be?" Sinclair cocked his head.

The girl didn't reply.

"You from around these parts?"

"We were supposed to bury Mama," she said. "I didn't want to come here."

Sinclair peered through the front window of the hearse but didn't see anybody.

"Daddy." The girl sat down on the tailgate. "I don't know where he is."

"Is that your mama in there?" Sinclair pointed to the coffin.

"This was all Daddy's idea." The girl wiped tears from her eyes. "'Unfinished business' what he called it."

"You go to school on the short bus or something?"

The girl frowned. "I don't go to school."

Sinclair pulled out the cell phone and looked at the screen. No signal. Amazing how hooked a person could get on these things. He wanted to get in touch with Imogene to see if he was on the right track. This was the most logical road leading to the Big Bend region and Marfa. Tiny, isolated, threading its way through the mountains far from what constituted a populated area in this desolate chunk of Texas.

But there were other roads after this, choices that could be made. If he picked the wrong path, he'd lose the scent, waste valuable time backtracking and casting about for a fresh lead.

"Have you seen my daddy?" the girl asked.

"Nuh-uh." Sinclair put the phone away. "What's your name?"

"Sadie." She paused. "What's yours?"

He told her and then pointed to the rubble. "What happened over there?"

"I want my daddy." She sobbed, tears streaming down her face. "But I don't think he's coming back."

Sinclair nodded slowly. If her father was anywhere in that pile of burnt crap, there was no way he was alive. He turned toward the hotel. There had to be a phone inside.

"Are you hurt?" Sadie said.

He stopped, looked at her.

"Your shirt's bloody."

He ignored her, walked to the hotel. His side was aching but nothing he couldn't handle.

The inside of the hotel made him forget all about his wound.

Six dead Mexicans in the lobby, plus an old gringo who looked like the clerk on the second floor. Based on the color of the flesh and the number of flies, he estimated they'd died about six or eight hours before. And the phone on the check-in counter didn't have a dial tone.

Outside, he approached the hearse. The girl was still sitting on the tailgate.

"Sadie." He sat beside her. "Do you know what happened inside the hotel?"

"The Mexican lady." She opened a purse and pulled out a tube of lipstick. "Don't tell Daddy about this makeup."

Sinclair watched her smear red lipstick on her lips until she looked like a South Dallas hooker. Then he said, "What Mexican lady?"

"The one with the gun." Sadie produced a compact from the purse.

"Did you see her shoot the men in the hotel?"

"I wonder when Daddy's gonna come back." She powdered her cheeks.

Sinclair didn't reply.

"Sometimes, Daddy likes to punish me by making me wear the makeup." She held a finger up to her lips. "But it's our secret. Don't tell no one."

"I won't say nothing." Sinclair clutched his side against a tiny spasm of pain. "Did you see what kind of vehicle the Mexican lady was in?"

"They asked me to go with them." Sadie closed her purse. "But I couldn't leave Mama and Daddy."

"Who?"

"Them that was here. The Mexican lady and her friends."

Sinclair waited but nothing else was forthcoming. The girl was positively ate up with the stupid syndrome.

"Where you from, Sadie?"

"Near Waco," she said. "My daddy's a preacher there."

Sinclair nodded. "Tell me about the people that were here."

A whip-poor-will cried out from one of the live oaks by the hotel. Sadie sighed loudly and shifted her position on the tailgate, clearly agitated.

Sinclair looked at the casket but didn't say anything.

"There were three of them." She rubbed her nose. "In a white truck."

Sinclair nodded, tried to contain his excitement.

"Can I tell you another secret?" She looked both ways even though the town was deserted.

"Sure."

"I never knew my real mom. This here's my stepmother." She tapped the coffin. "And she was mean to me."

The girl's eyes, just a little bit too far apart, took on a sheen, a glow from somewhere deep inside. Neither spoke for a few moments.

"You seem like a nice person," Sinclair said. "Why would anybody be mean to you?"

Sadie blushed.

"How long ago were the people here?" Sinclair said. "The ones that asked you to go with them."

"You're lucky if you know your real mom." Sadie giggled. "That's what I always say."

Sinclair started to speak but stopped as a wave of pain rippled through his abdomen.

"They was driving a Chevy." Sadie fluffed her hair. "One of them Tahoes."

Sinclair nodded.

"Two ladies and a man. One of the ladies shot them people in the hotel while the other two were in the dance hall."

Neither spoke for a few moments. The sun grew brighter. Shadows on the road dissipated.

"Do you know which way they went?" Sinclair spoke softly, afraid any extra movement would disrupt his insides.

"Daddy and me was real close," Sadie said. "That's why my step-mama didn't like me, you see."

Sinclair nodded.

"Maybe them people in the Chevy know where Daddy is," Sadie said.

"Maybe so." Sinclair peered down the road. "If we knew which way they went, then we could ask them."

"You got a map?" Sadie stood. "I could show you."

- CHAPTER FORTY-SEVEN -

I jerked upright, wide awake but utterly disoriented. An unpleasant, where-the-hell-am-I sensation clattered through my mind.

Threadbare sheets and a polyester comforter slid down my chest. I was naked from the waist up.

A wood-paneled motel room. Worn carpet the color of spoiled avocados. A rumpled bed next to mine. The air smelled like pine cleaner and several decades' worth of stale cigarette smoke.

Running water hissed from behind a door on the far side of the room, next to a counter with a sink under a cracked mirror.

I blinked. Sunlight filtered through the blinds over the air-conditioner.

Piper stood at the foot of the bed, dressed.

"I'm gonna get us breakfast," she said.

The events of the previous night slowly came into focus. Slivers of time drifted back.

After the fire, Eva drove, Piper next to her in the front. Hours and hours into the night on the side roads, putting as much distance as possible between us and the burning dance hall.

Three, maybe four in the morning, we stopped at a motel somewhere past Sonora, on the highway out of Del Rio, a border town that we'd avoided. The vastness of the night had been overpowering. An endless sheet of stars, like glitter from the wings of angels, anchored by the pale wedge of a moon.

"The witness is in the shower." Piper stepped to the door. "I'll be back in ten minutes."

I nodded and looked at the bedside table.

My Glock rested by a cream-colored ashtray marked with a faded stagecoach and the lettering BUENA VISTA MOTOR HOTEL, SOTOL CITY, TEXAS. There was no phone.

I checked the pistol. Loaded, a round in the chamber.

The running water stopped. The bathroom door opened. Steam billowed into the room.

Eva—hair wet, skin damp—stepped out, a towel wrapped around her torso.

"Nice place." My voice was hoarse. "Are the cockroaches friendly?"

"It's the only motel we could find." She ran her fingers through her hair.

I visualized the map, remembered the scuttlebutt from a couple of immigration officers I knew. The road ran parallel to the border a few miles north of the Rio Grande. After Del Rio, the only crossing point—legal or for the most part otherwise—was Presidio, hours away and directly south of Marfa.

The road between here and there was barren and empty, like the surrounding terrain. Safe, for our purposes, as long as our transportation didn't have a breakdown.

I glanced at my watch as Eva pulled a hand towel from the rack by the sink and rubbed her hair. A little after eight in the morning. I'd slept maybe four hours. My eyes were raw. They ached, lids gritty. My limbs felt leaden.

"You had a nightmare last night." Eva looked at me in the mirror. "Shouted something about your father and 'save the child.'"

I had no recollection of anything. I debated calling Tanya to see how Dad was. But I realized the best thing I could do for him was to keep going and get the money.

"This life." Eva stopped drying. "It's no good for any of us."

"How much farther?" I got out of bed. Joints creaked; muscles ached.

My jeans and T-shirt were on the floor. Wallet and phone in the correct pockets. The cell indicated a weak signal.

"We are perhaps four hours away if we take this highway," she said. "How do you say, a straight shot."

I nodded. That was doable. Fill up the tank and eat now. Then don't stop for anything. We'd be there right after lunchtime. I went to the sink, drank a tumbler of lukewarm tap water. Brushed my teeth with one of the tiny brushes we kept in the back of the Tahoe.

"You should see this, though." Eva flipped on an old Magnavox bolted to the dresser.

I walked back across the room, lifted a slat on the blinds, peered out.

The Hill Country had given way to an area that lay between the coastal lushness of the Rio Grande Valley and the mountainous Big Bend region, our ultimate destination.

A high, arid plateau that straddled Mexico and Texas, the Chihuahuan Desert. Rocks and cholla cactus on either side of a dusty two-lane road. Across the street was an old adobe building, a café called the Lonesome Dove Diner.

I turned.

The television warmed up, sound growing louder. The picture was fuzzy, jagged horizontal lines across one of the national morning news shows.

"It will be on in a moment." Eva sat on the bed I had just vacated. She crossed her legs and leaned back on her elbows, the towel riding up her thighs.

The show paused for a commercial break—a guy in a shark costume yakked about the lowest car prices in Del Rio—then cut to the local news.

The anchor wore a green plaid sports coat, brown shirt, and purple tie. His words were muffled due to a faulty speaker on the TV. Something about a double homicide and the Texas Rangers investigating because a law enforcement officer had died.

Then the video ran.

Ambulances and DPS squad cars were parked at the Alamo General Store where we had stopped the day before. Yellow crime scene tape was everywhere.

"The attendant and a deputy sheriff," Eva said. "They were killed about an hour after we were there."

I didn't say anything.

"They are tracking us, yes?"

I looked back out the window.

Piper emerged from the diner across the highway. She held a paper sack in one hand, a cell phone in the other. She walked to the edge of the road and stopped. Placed the phone to her ear.

"The narcos are always worried about satellites." Eva stood. She approached the window. "Maybe the CIA or somebody is watching us from outer space."

Tracking a particular vehicle by satellite was doable but

obscenely expensive, even by the money-doesn't-matter standards of Homeland Security. This was one reason the RFID tags for batteries and the Loose Juice Amendment had come about. I didn't want to tell Eva any of that, however.

"Yes." I let the blinds drop. "They must be using satellites."

My mind was a swirl. How were they following us? Could they have traced the purchase of the new auto battery in Plano to our Tahoe this quickly? And who was Piper talking to?

Eva stepped close to me to get to the window.

I could feel the dampness of the shower on her flesh, smell the soap. Her skin was the color of cinnamon, shoulders dusted with freckles.

She reached for the blind, arm brushing mine.

"So do you love her?" She peered outside.

I didn't reply. I looked away from the swell of her breasts under the thin towel.

"There's a fifty-thousand-dollar bounty for me." She moved closer to get a different viewing angle. "How long would that money last you?"

Her bare shoulder brushed against my bare chest.

"Long enough." I tried to ignore the feel of her skin as it grazed mine.

"Even if we make it to the courthouse," she said, "they will come after you. Revenge is their code."

"I'm gonna get dressed," I said. "We roll in ten minutes."

"There are people above the *jefes*," she said. "Even if you kill the snake by cutting off the head, they create another one."

We were both silent for a few moments. She looked away from the window and stared into my eyes. We held each other's gaze, neither of us willing to break away.

"Do you trust this Piper person?" She pointed outside.

I had no reply, just a sense of weariness and the pinpricks of anger that seemed perpetually close to the surface. A smoky aura floated through my mind, the feeling that always preceded regretful decisions.

"I've hidden some money," she said. "There was so much, it was easy to take some here and there."

I continued to stare into her eyes, felt myself drifting away from reality. She was a beautiful woman, vulnerable yet tough, my favorite blend. I tried to ignore the desire that rose inside me like a river freed from a broken dam.

"They'll give me a new identity after I testify." She caressed my arm with one finger. "But they don't know about the money. No one does."

Her fingers were damp, the feel of her skin electric. The need to touch her flesh ached inside me, a junkie craving the needle-dip into the bubbling spoon.

My weakness, my curse, the darkness deep inside.

Eva leaned closer, pressed her lips against mine. I kissed back, grasped her shoulder.

Noise from the door, a key rattling.

I pushed Eva away. She stepped back, smiled.

Piper stepped inside.

"Am I interrupting anything?" She dropped the bag on the table.

- CHAPTER FORTY-EIGHT -

I hosed off in tepid, rust-colored water, dressed, and scarfed down a chorizo-and-egg burrito, all in seven and a half minutes.

Eva was ready. From inside the room, I chirped open the Tahoe, told her to get in the back while we threw our few things in a duffel bag.

After she left, Piper looked at me, a sly smile on her face.

"A hot tamale, that Eva." She went to the sink and ran some water over a toothbrush. "You looked like a dog in heat when I came in. Maybe next stop, you can tear off a piece."

I strode across the room. Knocked the toothbrush from her fingers.

"Who were you talking to on the phone?" I pointed outside. "Across the street when you came out of the diner."

"You bastard." She pushed me away and cursed, several new phrases involving the sex act and small farm animals.

I pushed back. Then we stopped, both breathing hard.

In the mirror, I caught a glimpse of each of us. Dark circles under our eyes, drawn skin, lines in our faces. Fatigue and stress were taking their toll, making us punch drunk. But I didn't care.

"You haven't answered the question." I nodded to the phone in her pocket.

"Has it come to this?" she said. "We're this far out of the bell curve?"

"They're tracking us," I said. "They took out the place we stopped at yesterday."

"No kidding, Mannix." She shook her head. "Who do you think saw that first?"

I didn't reply.

"I was calling that Texas Ranger from Amarillo, the guy who owed those shylocks the twenty K."

I nodded, understanding now.

A cop with a gambling problem was a bad, sometimes deadly combo. A few weeks before, we'd found the Ranger at a dice game in the back of a Mexican restaurant on Jefferson Boulevard in Oak Cliff, trying to make a payment to a small-time hood who owed us several big-time favors. One conversation led to another and, presto-bingo, the Texas Ranger owed us a chit.

"I was trying to find out how hot we are," she said. "Trying to get us to Marfa in one piece."

"What did he say?"

"Nothing." She shook her head. "I had to leave a message."

Neither of us spoke for a few moments.

"I, uh, I'm sorry."

She ignored my apology. "What were you and Eva talking about when I came in?"

"Nothing." I had never lied to Piper before. It was a white lie, just to keep peace in the Tahoe for the rest of the trip.

Piper didn't reply. She picked up her toothbrush, ran water over the bristles.

I paced the small room. "How did they find us?"

"The tag on the battery?" She shrugged, brushed her teeth, spit. "Who the hell knows?"

"We're about four hours away. One last push."

"So says *your* map."

I picked up my duffel bag.

"My map says we're dead, and we don't even know it." She headed to the door.

———

The motel where we had stayed was like something from a bad slasher movie but not as upscale. Crumbling adobe the color of the sand surrounded the parking lot. A one-eyed attendant in an Iron Maiden concert T-shirt came out to watch us fill up at the service station next door.

"He's gonna remember three people in a white Tahoe." I slid the hose back into place.

"Yep." Piper pulled a handful of cash from her pocket. "That he is."

I got in the driver's seat as she went to pay. When she returned and was ensconced in the passenger side, I put the truck in gear and pulled onto the highway.

Eva said, "Wait."

I idled to a stop and turned in my seat.

"I just wanted to offer my thanks." She touched my arm. "To both of you."

I nodded. Piper didn't move, face blank. She stared at the spot where Eva's fingers had been on my flesh.

"I appreciate the sacrifice you have made," Eva said. "To get me this far."

"It's not about you." I shrugged. "We're in this for the money."

"Yes, of course." Eva nodded. "The money."

Piper turned in her seat. "Tell us how you came to be

bumping uglies with both a DEA agent and a cartel bigwig."

I put the Tahoe in gear and drove west.

Eva stared outside at the desert. "You are interested in my sex life now?"

"No." Piper held up a pair of cuffs. "But if you don't tell me a good story, I'm gonna use these on you."

———

Eva met the man who would become her husband, Lazaro Morales, at a disco in Monterrey four years before. She'd been twenty-seven at the time and cut off from her family because of what her mother called "poor life choices."

Eva's mother, a longtime fan of Dr. Phil, lived in West Houston, working as a life coach and Mary Kay sales associate. Eva's father lived in Cuernavaca, a devout Catholic who refused to grant a divorce. The father had all but given up on his youngest child, calling Eva a *mujerzuela,* a slut.

Eva, a free spirit like her sister but without the artistic talent, had moved to Monterrey because a girlfriend was there. She had a vague notion she would work as a nurse, despite no education in that particular field. Plans and goals weren't a big priority with Eva Ramirez. Parties and good times, these were the important things to her. Enjoy your life and youth, your beauty. Live every day like it might be your last. Because in Mexico, you never could tell. Today might be the final tomorrow.

Unfortunately, nursing jobs for young women with no nursing experience were hard to come by. Money had been tight and expenses high, so Eva, always the prettiest girl in the room, had taken to dating people who had a lot of cash, dashing young men who carried chrome-plated guns in their waistbands and drove late-model Escalades and Suburbans.

The disco where she met Lazaro Morales had a mirrored

ball that hung from the ceiling and a lighted dance floor. A DJ played 1990s pop music, techno tracks from the eighties, and the occasional *conjunto* rap tune, everything loud and rhythmic for the throngs of attractive young people who filled the club. Everywhere, there were martinis and whiskey drinks, champagne in silver buckets, and tiny crystal bowls of caviar.

She'd been dancing with her boyfriend, an up-and-coming lieutenant in the organization that controlled the city.

The boyfriend was her age and owned seven houses. He wore gold Rolexes, three different models, and had a driver for his GMC Denali. He paid the rent for Eva's apartment and gave her a small stipend. Some weekends, always without warning, he whisked her across the border to see her mother in Houston. There, they stayed at the nicest hotels and went shopping at the Galleria for whatever she wanted—Neiman's, Saks Fifth Avenue, Crate and Barrel.

Eva liked her life and her boyfriend, the most confident man she had ever met.

So what if she had to pretend that she didn't notice certain things, the bodyguards and the guns, his sudden disappearances in the night, the occasional sounds of weapons being fired in anger or shrieks of pain from the basement rooms.

The good times were worth it.

She was dancing with her boyfriend to a slow song. Poison, "Every Rose Has Its Thorn." Her head was spinning, the champagne and the light from the mirrored ball reflecting across the disco's floor. These were happy times, the parties that never stopped, money to spend, consequences for the day's decisions that never came.

Smiling, content, she pressed her cheek against her boyfriend's chest, the not-unpleasant aroma of tobacco smoke, sweat, and cologne thick in her nostrils.

Then, in the time it takes for a heart to beat or a thought to form, he was gone.

An empty space on the dance floor.

She was conscious of movement, the touch of his body leaving hers. She opened her eyes, saw a rapidly closing gap in the crowd, the back of his head moving away. Then nothing of him remained.

The lights strobed, blinded her for a moment. The music seemed louder. The safe, familiar sensation of her lover replaced by something else, a feral odor that one of her friends would later call the stench of testosterone.

She looked up and saw a man with eyes the color of a grave, black and endless. He was handsome like a movie star, a cleft chin and a long, thin nose. His body was lean, ropy with muscles. Wavy dark hair.

Eva noticed all this but kept coming back to his eyes, black orbs that missed nothing. His gaze was tender and dangerous, all in the same moment.

He smiled and she felt her knees go weak. Desire like she'd never known roiled inside, but she willed the arousal away. Some might have called her a tramp, but she was faithful. Usually.

Her boyfriend was nowhere to be seen though.

"My name is Lazaro," the man said. "Who are you?"

"Eva." She brushed back her hair.

"Would you like some champagne, Eva?" Lazaro led her to a table in the corner that was surrounded by hard-faced men with their shirts untucked.

In the middle of the table sat a silver bucket full of Dom Perignon, icy cold. Next to the champagne lay a mirror covered with strips of white powder. Several young women who Eva recognized were there as well. Party girls. Young and pretty. Vacuous expressions on their faces. Disposable.

"Would you like a bump?" Lazaro pointed to the cocaine.

Eva shook her head. Beyond the occasional joint, drugs held no sway over her. She didn't like how her heart raced on coke. Didn't want to fall asleep from the opiates.

Lazaro nodded like he approved. He poured Eva a glass of champagne and told her to sit down. She did. She took a sip and asked where her boyfriend was. No one answered. The music got louder and more people joined the party.

Lazaro and Eva married in Mexico City three months later.

She never saw her boyfriend again.

Supposedly, the next week his mother received a package in the mail containing his head. But that was just a rumor.

- CHAPTER FORTY-NINE -

The sandy terrain of West Texas was a blur outside the windows of the helicopter.

Keith McCluskey, DEA contractor and Paynelowe's ops commander for Region 7, turned his back to the others and rubbed the last few grains of cocaine on his gums. He felt good, alive with the possibilities of success. Righteous.

He looked at the picture again. A tourist snapshot, he and Eva Ramirez at the Mexican restaurant on the River Walk in San Antonio, taken a few weeks before, arm in arm.

The sight of Eva, her smiling face, her beauty, made his heart race as much as the coke.

A few more hours and he'd have her in his arms again. His one true love. Then, he'd no longer need the drugs. He'd have successfully completed the mission, retrieving the witness, his darling Eva. She would provide a few nuggets of intel that his supervisors would use to negotiate a new, much more lucrative contract. Details about the new contract were above his pay grade but the numbers were supposed to be huge, the services provided more than just law enforcement contracting. Overrun money and slippage fees had been built into everything so that the executives at Paynelowe and their political patrons could wet their beaks easily.

In exchange for Eva's information, Paynelowe had already given tentative approval to arrange a new identity for her. She would be able to disappear and not risk testifying against the monster that was her husband.

The downside, of course, was that her husband, Lazaro Morales, a cartel leader, would go free because of lack of evidence. Also, McCluskey had yet to retrieve the scanner, the device he had lost.

But such was the way wars went. Sacrifices had to be made for a greater good.

He and Eva would melt away. He had several false identities of his own prepared, along with money skimmed from contract overages, more than enough to last them for a few years until he could figure out a new career path. The divorce papers for his current wife were waiting to be filed.

The plan was going to work. Love would triumph.

McCluskey shifted the headset and mike a little, trying for a more comfortable fit.

The back of the helicopter was loud from the twin turbine engines.

The Chinook had been in use by the US Armed Forces since Vietnam, its primary mission the deployment of heavy artillery and large numbers of troops. The cargo area of this particular aircraft held two ground vehicles and a handful of newly hired Paynelowe contractors dressed as civilians. Jeans and T-shirts, lightweight windbreakers to cover their sidearms.

They were the dregs. Drug abusers and sociopaths. Malcontents.

The op had been arranged on short notice, and the battle plan contained elements designed to please his supervisors. They needed certain equipment to be used, money allocated from select budget items, all part of the negotiating process for a new contract. Unfortunately, this was not a good scenario for designing the most efficient battle plan or getting the best personnel.

Each contractor had a shiny new badge and ID, indicating that he was an agent with the Drug Enforcement Administration.

The men, hired on the cheap because Paynelowe's freelance personnel budget for the year was nearly depleted, were armed with the latest and most expensive in small-arms technology, the Reaper, a catchy name for the acronym REPR, or Rapid Engagement Precision Rifle.

The twelve-inch-barreled firearm looked a little like the standard M-4 army weapon—adjustable buttstock, ventilated forearm—but fired the more deadly 7.62-millimeter round. At the request of Paynelowe's human resources department, each Reaper was equipped with the latest generation Surefire sound suppressor even though the silencer would hinder the bullet's performance, the trade-off deemed acceptable due to the potential liability from workplace hearing loss.

In addition, one of the team carried a Remington 700 sniper rifle that had been outfitted with a Leupold tactical scope. That contractor had been issued earplugs.

The team's mode of ground transportation were two brand new Porsche Cayenne Turbos, $120,000 sport utility vehicles. A Paynelowe subsidiary owned a dealership in South Texas.

Hundreds of thousands for equipment, yet a pittance for the people to operate it all. Budgets and bureaucrats, the scourge of the fighting man since the dawn of time.

McCluskey shook his head at the inefficiency of it all as the pilot's voice sounded over his headphones. Their initial ETA was twelve minutes.

He mentally ran through the checklist one more time. Everything was in place.

The only non-Paynelowe employee on board, a semi-retired FBI contractor from a competing company, lurched down the length of the cargo area, holding on to the straps hung every few feet for balance.

The man had to be sixty, red hair going gray. His face was flushed, a spider web of burst capillaries on his nose. He wore gray Sansabelt pants, a golf shirt stretched to the point of tearing, and black sneakers designed to look like dress shoes. He sat next to McCluskey on the bench seat and plugged in his headset so they could converse.

McCluskey wrinkled his nose at the odor of whiskey. "You've been drinking."

"One of your goon squad just smoked a bowl of hash." The man pulled a pint bottle of Cutty Sark from his back pocket. "And you've got blow all over your face. So don't give me any grief about getting my scotch on."

"That's my demolition expert." McCluskey wiped his face. "Guy can't keep off the weed for one full day without going loony."

The bombers were always the worst. The devastation they wreaked did something to their minds, altered the moral compass a good soldier was supposed to possess.

"What the hell you blowing up out there anyway?" the older man said. "Jackrabbits?"

"A highway." McCluskey tapped a manila folder. "It's part of the battle plan."

"Are you nuts?" The man took another drink.

"Think of it as a link in the food chain. Paynelowe's sister company has the contract for road repair in this state." McCluskey put the folder back into his briefcase. "What was your name again?"

"My friends call me Costco." He put the bottle away. "You can call me Agent Barnett."

"I realize there's some tension between us." McCluskey sniffed. "The merger process is never easy."

Paynelowe was in the midst of a hostile takeover of the other man's company, Blue Dagger Industries.

"Quit trying to squirt Lysol up my butt." Costco crossed his arms. "We're both diving into shit soup. Neither of us is gonna come out smelling very good."

"We'll of course be professional about the business at hand." McCluskey rubbed his nose. He was glad he had another package of cocaine to keep his readiness for the operation high.

Two of the contractors were sitting across the cargo area from McCluskey and Costco, talking on their own intercom system. One obviously said something offensive to the other as both men stood, fists raised, preparing for a fight.

McCluskey motioned to a third, his most reliable subordinate. The subordinate jumped between the other two, calming them down. For the moment at least.

Hopefully, the next group would be better, maybe less psychopathic. After dropping off this bunch, he was to fly to Houston and pick up a new batch of contractors who were being assembled, just in case this squad failed. He didn't want to miss his reunion with Eva, but some things needed his hands-on control, especially with his superiors getting nosy about everything.

"Professional." Costco nodded. "Oh, yeah. I see that."

"I brought you along as a fail-safe, not an operative," McCluskey said. "Don't forget that."

"Really?" Costco cocked his head. "In my mind, I'm here because I got three ex-wives and my AA sponsor was off the grid when I met my fourth."

"What?"

"I sold my soul for a pocketful of coin, dipstick. What's your excuse?"

The chopper banked to the left and tilted downward. McCluskey had no reply. He thought of Eva's body, her limbs intertwined with his. He thought about true love. Emotion choked in his throat.

"This guy we're going after, Jon Cantrell, he used to be a friend of mine." Costco pulled out the whiskey bottle again and drained it. "You make quick work of it or I'll do things to you that make you wish you were being waterboarded instead."

Neither man spoke for a moment, each sizing up the other.

"The package in the front." McCluskey pointed to the forward section of the aircraft. "Took a lot of resources to acquire it. I'd like to know how it's relevant."

"Let's just say I know what buttons to push on Jon Cantrell." Costco rubbed his eyes.

"And what would those be?"

"Your nose is bleeding." Costco smiled. "Altitude getting to you?"

McCluskey grabbed a handkerchief and held it to his face.

"When I get to hell," Costco said, squeezing his knee, "I'll save you a seat next to mine."

- CHAPTER FIFTY -

I worked my jaw, swallowed, trying to clear my ears of pressure.

The temperature gauge in the rearview mirror of the Tahoe read ninety-five. A dry heat to be sure, not unlike an oven.

Was that thunder in the distance?

A faint rumble, a slight disruption to the consciousness of the here and now, like a dream half remembered.

The sky was cloudless, the color of damp cobalt, pale blue and platinum.

Heat waves shimmered on the blacktop. Desert plains lay on either side of the highway, rimmed by a broken line of shallow hills, the remnants of the caldera that formed this particular flat spot ten thousand millennia ago.

We'd been on the road for a while. It was mid-morning, and we were a little under three hours from our destination.

"Did you hear something?" Piper said. "Like a boom?"

I slowed a little. Eighty became seventy.

Eva stirred in the rear seat. She blinked, stretched.

A few miles later, on the western horizon, the line between sky and earth grew indistinct, ethereal. A sand-colored cloud swallowed the ragged boundary between the heavens and the desert, making it difficult to see where one ended and the other began.

"What the hell is that?" I slowed some more.

The two-lane highway we were on was the only passage west. The last turnoff had been about an hour before, a northbound road leading to Interstate 10. The land on either side was privately owned, part of one or more vast ranches contained within the seemingly endless lines of barbed-wire fences.

I tapped a button on the GPS. The next turn-off was a private road that led nowhere, about twenty miles ahead. The cloud was obviously before that.

Eva leaned forward. "They have found us?"

"We don't know that for sure." Piper picked up her subgun from the floorboard.

I eased off the gas as the cloud of what now appeared to be dust grew larger, then wrapped around us. An instant later, the Tahoe broke through and topped a small rise.

"Holy crap," Piper gasped.

I jammed on the brakes, and the truck screeched to a stop.

The road was gone. Disappeared. Adios, Señor Highway.

In its place was a huge, smoking crater.

On the other side were two low hills with flat tops, broad mesas that offered a panoramic view of the hole and the terrain to the east. Of us.

On the hill to the left, maybe five hundred yards away, sat a Chinook helicopter, its massive rotors idle, drooping.

"Hey, Jon." Piper slid the subgun's safety to the fire position. Her voice was calm, almost casual. "How about you get us the hell out of here."

"Roger that." I yanked the transmission into reverse, jammed on the gas.

But not fast enough.

Thunk. The sound of metal crunching like an aluminum can being mashed.

Steam billowed from underneath the hood.

I kept a foot on the accelerator, head craned behind me to peer out the back window.

The next shot hit a tire, and the Tahoe slewed at an angle. The stench of antifreeze and hot rubber filled the inside.

Eva swore. Shouted in Spanish.

Piper slung open the passenger door and rolled out.

"Eva." I popped the transmission into park. "Head for the ditch."

The rear door on my side opened, and she was gone.

I grabbed my subgun, dove out, landed on the road. The heat was ferocious. Pebble-covered asphalt dug into my elbows and knees, the surface as hot as a griddle.

Ching-ching. Ching.

All around me dollops of road surface flew upward like the splatter of asphalt raindrops.

A sniper, dialing in the range.

I ran to the drainage ditch and rolled to the bottom, maybe two or three feet below the grade of the highway. Nothing there but weeds and dust, scant protection from the bullets.

Eva landed on top of me a quarter second later.

I pushed her off and belly-crawled toward the source of the attack. "This way. Keep down."

We were below their line of sight but far from safe. The best tactical move was to keep mobile. The best strategic play, because it was counterintuitive, was to head toward the source of the attack.

After about thirty seconds I stopped, waited for Eva to

catch up. Piper would have gone to the ditch on her side of the Tahoe. For the moment, she was on her own.

The ditch on my side had deepened. A few feet away, a boulder the size of a sedan rested on the ditch bank opposite the highway. The rock was flanked by several smaller chunks of stone and a fringe of cactus.

On my person: one H&K submachine gun with two thirty-round magazines taped together. One Glock, loaded, with one extra fifteen-round magazine. One disposable cell with no coverage at the moment. And a pocketknife.

What I didn't have: water or food. Or a functioning vehicle, though the Tahoe might be able to limp back the way we came for a mile or so.

I crawled to the side of the boulder. Listened.

The sniper appeared to have stopped firing. Nothing but the rustle of weeds from the slight breeze that whispered through the ditch. My face was slick with sweat, arms speckled with dirt.

"Who are they?" Eva crouched next to me. "What should we do?"

"There's a company out of Houston." I struggled to catch my breath. "They have a contract with the DEA to—"

WHOOSH. A loud noise like air forced through a garden hose at high pressure.

I ducked instinctively, covered Eva.

A crash. Metal ripped; glass shattered. Then, an explosion loud enough to rattle fillings as the temperature of the air doubled for a half second.

Fifty feet behind us a fireball rose skyward, followed by a mushroom cloud of black smoke.

So much for the Tahoe.

The smoke shifted direction, pulled by the thermals of

the desert. A dark cloud swirled around us. The air stunk with the odor of gasoline and burnt plastic.

Eva clung to me and blinked away smoke and dust.

I looked at my cell. Still no signal. Not sure who I'd call anyway. Milo Miller back in Dallas? This might be stretching the limits of what Milo owed me, but then again, maybe not. In any event, it was a moot point. I tried to formulate a workable plan.

Thirty seconds stretched to a minute. Neither of us spoke.

The Tahoe continued to smolder, churning out billows of oily smoke.

From behind us came a whistle I recognized. I gave the return signal, two high-pitched calls followed by a low trill.

Piper emerged from the weeds and smoke, running crouched over. She skidded to a stop at the base of the boulder, coughing.

"You okay?" I said.

"The fire." She took a deep breath, wiped her eyes. "Used it as cover to get across the road."

Nobody said anything for a few seconds.

"What do we do?" Eva asked.

"We go forward," I said. "Our only option."

Piper didn't say anything.

"The opposition. Whoever they are." I pointed to the west. "They've got the only transportation for miles."

"So we walk right up to them." Eva hugged her knees to her chest. "And they kill us from a hundred meters out."

I didn't say anything; there was no sense stating the obvious. We were in the deep end, our heads submerged, and the lifeguard was nowhere around.

"Not necessarily," Piper said.

We both looked at her.

"The sniper's a pro." She wiped sweat from her brow. "He's good enough to shoot the tire on a moving vehicle from five or six hundred yards away."

Eva stared at her, face pale, clearly trying to piece it together.

"But he's not good enough to hit any of us when we bailed out?" I finished her thought.

Piper nodded.

"Sinclair's trying to kill you." I looked at Eva. "But these guys want you alive."

Her face drained of what little color it had. She blinked like her eyes didn't work.

"Who are they?" She looked at me. "You were getting ready to tell me."

"The company is called Paynelowe." I paused. "Is your boyfriend a real DEA agent or a contractor?"

The air was very still. The smoke had blown away. Ants crawled in the dirt as a scaly-backed lizard scurried underneath one of the rocks and several bees hummed around a flowering cactus.

"He's a contractor." She licked her lips. "He's from Houston. . . ."

Her voice trailed off as the *whump-whump* of the helicopter grew louder.

- CHAPTER FIFTY-ONE -

Sinclair, behind the wheel of the Crown Victoria, washed down another amphetamine with cold coffee. The inside of his skin felt like electrified velvet. His muscles crackled, the sound of broken glass that only he could hear.

He'd never been much for drugs. Don't get high on your own supply and all that crap. Now he understood what all the kids were talking about.

Sadie sat in the passenger seat. A little after dawn, as they drove, she'd taken a knife and cut off the bottom of her dress so that the hemline came to the middle of her creamy thighs. She'd also ripped off the sleeves so her arms were bare.

The pain in his gut had started to feel different, so he'd asked her to ride along with him for a bit. Just in case he needed somebody to drive. Looking back, he supposed he should have asked if she even knew how to drive.

"I want me a pill." She smacked her lips together. "T'ain't fair you get one but not me."

"That's grown-up medicine." He drained the last of the coffee, purchased the day before.

"I'm a grown-up." She pouted, examined her lips in the mirror. "I'll be nineteen and a half in two months."

343

Her voice had two speeds, monotone and whiny.

"You know what I mean." Sinclair accelerated, slowed, and accelerated again. He was trying to break the monotony of the empty road, an endless blacktop surrounded by desert.

Southwest Texas looked a hell of a lot like the pictures on the evening news of the Middle East. Piles and piles of sand, mounds of rocks. Not as many palm trees though, or exploding camels.

"Where we going anyway?" Sadie shifted in her seat. "I gotta pee-pee."

He'd given her a very abbreviated version of why he was chasing the three people in the Tahoe, but Sadie only seemed to comprehend about half of what she saw or heard. Maybe her real mother had been a boozehound while she was pregnant. Or maybe Sadie had been dropped on her head as a child.

After a while, he'd told her the truth. He needed to make real sure the Mexican lady didn't tell anybody about who he was or what he did. Sadie didn't seem to mind that this implied death or physical harm to the Mexican lady. In fact, she seemed to get off on the idea.

"We're following the helicopter." Sinclair pointed to the west. "Better hold it. We're not stopping for a while."

A gray Chinook with no markings had crossed the road about twenty minutes before. It had been headed south but banked about a half mile past the road and turned to the west, the same way Sinclair was going. The aircraft had then increased its altitude and sped off.

Dollars to donuts that was the cokehead Paynelowe contractor, Keith McCluskey.

"We can't catch no helicopter," Sadie said. "I thought we was after the people in the Tahoe and the Mexican lady."

Sinclair sighed and looked at the cell he had taken from Myrna DeGroot. No signal.

That meant he couldn't call out, couldn't reach Imogene. It also meant he wouldn't get any more calls from Hawkins like he'd received but hadn't answered an hour ago. Scary how they could get this cell number so fast.

This part of Texas was virtually uninhabited, less than one person per square mile. No reason for cell towers. No reason for towns either. Just a single east-west road that led to the target's final destination, Marfa. A perfect place for an attack.

He felt a tingle in his stomach, a rumble above and beyond the speed and the bullet wound. The nervous flutter that came when the fight was close at hand.

The flutter grew louder. Then it became a vision, a cloud of light that enveloped Sinclair in a strange dampness like a cold sauna.

From a long way off came a voice calling his name. A whiny, monotone voice.

"Heeey. Heeey. Are you okaaay?"

The flutter and the cloud disappeared, replaced by a jagged edge of pain so ferocious it was beyond his ability to comprehend. Bile and blood rose in his throat as spikes of agony jackknifed up his spine.

A period of time passed. He opened his eyes. He was still behind the wheel, but the Crown Victoria had somehow parked itself by the side of the road.

"What happened?" Sadie touched his hand. "You're all white and stuff."

There was a wide spot on the shoulder a few yards ahead. The spot led to a break in the fence line where the remnants of a barn lay. The structure was about thirty yards off the highway, the only sign of human habitation they'd seen in a half hour.

"I-I-I don't know." Sinclair heard a strange voice speaking, his own.

The surrounding terrain was sand and rock, partially covered with grass the color of dried wheat, cactus, and the occasional mesquite tree.

The barn was roofless, huge chunks of the walls missing as well. A half dozen mesquites had grown up along the base of the foundation.

The pain eased, and Sinclair drove along the shoulder. He turned onto the rutted path that led around the barn to what used to be the front of the structure, on the side opposite of the highway. He pulled into the building. The wall facing the highway was the most intact, hiding the Ford from any traffic that might go by.

"You're not gonna die, are you?" Sadie licked her lips.

Sinclair slumped in his seat, shook his head.

"You need to go see a doctor," she said.

Sinclair lifted his shirt and stared at the bloodstained bandage on his abdomen.

"No." He let the shirt drop. "I'm fine."

He knew enough rudimentary first aid to know that no major blood vessels had been hit. Nothing structural. Just a little graze that hurt real bad every now and again. As soon as he killed Eva Ramirez he'd find a doctor who wouldn't report a gunshot wound or maybe a veterinarian he could threaten or cajole into treating him.

Sadie didn't say anything.

Sinclair wiped sweat from his face.

"I really gotta go tinkle." Sadie opened her door. "Be right back."

Sinclair covered his face with his hands, took several deep breaths.

A minute or an hour later, someone tugged on his arm. He opened his eyes.

Sadie's face was inches from his. She held a finger in front of her lips and then pointed toward the road.

Sinclair brushed aside the pain and carefully opened the driver's door.

"There's a car," Sadie whispered. "With some soldier men."

Sinclair slid out, eased to his knees, and crawled awkwardly to the rear of the barn. The pain had lessened. He peered through a gap in the wall.

A Porsche sport utility vehicle was parked on the side of the highway about forty feet from the back wall. All the doors were open, and a group of men stood nearby, checking the actions on their weapons.

Even in civilian clothes, they were clearly military. The haircuts and way they carried themselves. The rifles they held, like miniature M-4s but with silencers attached to the muzzles.

There were four of them. They talked quietly among themselves and then got back in the Porsche. The SUV pulled onto the highway and headed west.

Paynelowe operatives, had to be. McCluskey always favored ex-soldiers. That meant he was close by, certainly part of the crew in the helicopter.

Sinclair stood and made his way to the rear of the Ford.

Sadie came up beside him. "What are we gonna do?"

"Time to go hunting." Sinclair opened the trunk and unlocked the biggest of the gun cases. Then, he pulled out a blue-black barrel assembly and a scope.

The Barrett .50 caliber was a huge gun, weighing well over fifteen kilos. In combat, the rifle and its ultra-powerful cartridge were used primarily to stop vehicles or penetrate buildings at long ranges, not to kill enemy personnel. The .50 caliber round was almost six inches long and could shatter cinder block walls or the forged steel of a truck engine from a mile away. The damage it could do to a human body was hard to describe.

He fitted the barrel assembly together with the receiver and pulled a box of ammunition from a duffel bag.

"That's a big bullet." Sadie pointed to the ammo. "You could kill Godzilla with that sucker."

Sinclair slid a cartridge into the breech of the single-shot rifle but left the bolt open.

A gun shop owner back in Dallas with a thing for under-age girls had given him the rifle. The guy had said it was more powerful than a .50 caliber. Sinclair didn't know much about ballistics other than bigger was better.

The rifle was chambered for a little-known round called the .460 Barrett, a .50 caliber case necked down to accept a slightly lighter and much faster .45 caliber bullet. A more accurate projectile that hit with more terminal energy than its big brother. Tommy, may his dumb ass rest in peace, had once shot a cow with the rifle. Damn near blew the thing in two.

"You gonna shoot those guys in the Porsche?"

"You want to take a pill, Sadie?" He popped the lens covers off the scope.

"Yeah." She nodded and twisted a lock of hair in between a thumb and forefinger. "But first I want you to kiss me."

Sinclair stopped what he was doing. "Sadie, darling. I'm old enough to be your grandpa."

"Don't you think I'm good-looking?" She pouted. "My daddy says I'm pretty enough to get the job done."

Sinclair gingerly placed the rifle on the backseat, careful to keep the scope from being jarred. Tommy had sighted-in the finely calibrated optics the week before, six inches high at a thousand yards.

He shut the door, pulled the teenager close, and mashed her face against his.

They stayed that way for a few moments, flesh against flesh, lips pressed together.

When they broke apart, Sadie said, "You know what they say about preachers' kids?"

Sinclair shook his head.

"You shoot your Mexican lady and I'll show you."

He nodded and headed to the front of the car. Sadie scampered after him. He stopped at the driver's door and looked across the roof at her.

"You know how to drive?"

She nodded.

"Why don't I ride shotgun," he said. "Rest up a little."

"Whatever you say, baby." Sadie came around and helped him into the passenger side.

Settled in, Sinclair handed her a pill as she started the engine.

"You ever killed anybody before?" She swallowed the tablet dry.

He looked at her funny but didn't reply.

"It's like flicking a switch." Sadie backed out of the barn. "One minute, they're on. The next, they're off."

"Yeah." Sinclair raised an eyebrow. "How'd you know?"

That was exactly how he'd describe the sensation.

"Lots you don't know about me," she said. "We're gonna have us a ball after that Mexican lady dies."

- CHAPTER FIFTY-TWO -

I scrambled up the ditch and ran toward a low spot in the fence where the top strand had broken. I hopped over, signaled for Eva and Piper to hurry.

The chopper banked, came back for another pass. The aircraft was maybe a thousand feet up, making wide, lazy circles around our general area.

Piper cleared the fence like a gazelle.

Eva's heel caught on the wire, and she fell, landing in the dust, her arm beneath her. She cried out, and I pulled her up. We followed Piper down a cattle trail that led into a stand of mesquites. The trees were squat, close to the ground and thorny, more like shrubs with fancy notions about being something else.

The cover was better than nothing but not by much.

We jogged down the trail away from the highway, trying to avoid the daggers that protruded from each low-hanging branch.

The terrain, which appeared flat from the road, was not. Small depressions sculpted the land, weed-choked draws that led to places where the sporadic rainfall drained, undulations in the earth's surface.

Prickly shrubs and desert yaupons. Texas buckhorn bushes that looked like rosemary but had thorns instead of fragrant needles. Cactus everywhere.

A couple of minutes later, we entered a clearing. In the center was a stock tank full of brackish water, and a couple of salt licks for the cattle that had left hoofprints everywhere.

No breeze at all. The heat was all-encompassing, a fourth, uninvited member of our entourage.

I wiped sweat off my face. Struggled to catch my breath.

Piper, T-shirt wet like she'd been caught in the rain, held up a hand, motioned for us to stop.

A couple of mourning doves whistled overhead.

Piper looked up. "The chopper's gone."

I listened.

Nothing but the buzz of flies around piles of manure.

A path lay on the other side of the clearing. It was wider, two ruts on either side for the wheels of a vehicle, obviously the way the salt licks had been delivered.

Eva rubbed her arm, winced.

"Are you all right?" I touched her shoulder.

Piper clutched her subgun and stared at me. Her face was slick with sweat, eyes filled with something I couldn't place.

Anger and sadness. Regret. *Jealousy?*

"I am fine," Eva said. "Let's keep going."

"Wait." Piper held up her hand.

Eva looked at me, clearly searching for instructions.

Piper put her hands on her hips. "What's your boyfriend's name?"

Eva stared at her. "What are you talking about?"

"The DEA agent," Piper said. "What's his name?"

"Keith. His name is Keith McCluskey."

Piper and I looked at each other.

"You know him?" Eva said.

"Why didn't you ask us about him?" I said. "Or tell us his name before?"

"What does it matter?" She shrugged.

"We're DEA," Piper said. "*Supposedly* on the same team."

"You have to understand." Eva took a deep breath. "There's a line. It separates the narcos and those that fight them."

"You mean the police?" I said. "Law enforcement."

"Yes." She bit her lip, struggling for the right phrase. "And that line, sometimes it's hard to see. Sometimes it disappears."

I nodded. "McCluskey's as bent as a paper clip."

"He breaks the rules, yes. But not in the way you think."

"What do you mean?" Piper said.

"I don't know how to say it."

"Give it a shot," I said.

"Both sides, the narcos and the police, they think they are in the right." She paused. "What's the word in English? It's very . . . *ironic*."

I nodded.

The narcotraffickers were modern-day Robin Hoods. They gave money to the destitute, fed the hungry, clothed the orphans. The police in Mexico were poorly paid and corrupt, oftentimes more dangerous to the citizens than were the criminals.

On the other side of the coin, the DEA and other American law enforcement agencies often let smugglers escape or even gave tacit approval for their continued operation, all in the hope of catching the next man up, the bigger fish. The Bureau of Alcohol, Tobacco, Firearms, and Explosives even allowed smugglers to bring weapons *into* Mexico for the same reason, a clear violation of about a dozen international laws. A little bad now for the greater good later. Right became wrong and then right again. Or did it?

"Why don't you just turn yourself in to McCluskey?" Piper said.

"Because I never want to see him again."

Piper looked at me, an eyebrow arched.

"Keith McCluskey is an addict," Eva said. "Most of the time, he's high on coke and self-righteousness."

"How'd you two meet anyway?" Piper asked.

"I was in Houston," she said. "And I had a kilo of product in my purse."

"You're a mule?" I said.

"I stole it from my husband." She shook her head. "I wanted to sell it and use the money to get away from him. From Mexico. It was the only thing of value I could get."

I stared at the sky where the helicopter had been and decided not to ask her about the money she mentioned back at the motel.

"The parties, they weren't as much fun anymore." She hugged herself. "The violence got worse."

"What happened?" I said.

"One of Keith's associates arrested me when I tried to make the sale." She paused. A trickle of sweat fell from the end of her nose. "Do you know what happens when any-body associated with the organization is arrested by the US authorities?"

"They take away your decoder ring." Piper blew a strand of hair from her face.

No one laughed because there was nothing funny about the situation.

If somebody was arrested, the cartel immediately sus-pected them of talking in exchange for a lighter sentence.

Extreme paranoia formed the narcotrafficker baseline. On the other side of the equation, a person arrested with that much contraband could expect the DEA to threaten serious prison time if they didn't work as an informant. Hello, rock, meet hard place.

She could, of course, have told her husband immediately what had happened, but that would have exposed her theft of the cocaine.

"I was scared," she said. "And Keith was handsome and strong and so confident. He took me to a safe house instead of jail." Eva wiped her face. "He told me what I wanted to hear. There was a way out. All I had to do was trust him."

I nodded. "And you believed him."

She shrugged. "I had no choice."

"How did the boyfriend-girlfriend part come about?" Piper said.

"The next night he took me to a nightclub." Eva smiled. "We met some friends and had such a good time."

"Life's just a party," I said. "What's it matter who's paying the tab?"

"Parties are fun." Eva nodded. "Until they're not."

- CHAPTER FIFTY-THREE -

Sinclair smiled. He told Sadie to slow down.

Keith McCluskey's men in the Porsche hadn't gone far.

They'd been following the SUV for about two miles when a large but thin cloud of dust swirled across the highway, dissipating in the weak summer wind. Then, the helicopter had appeared and flown a few circles around an area south of the road before zooming away.

The driver of the Porsche seemed to know where he was headed. He slowed and then crossed the highway, stopping on the south shoulder.

Sinclair directed her to stop on the north side by a rocky outcropping that jutted from the shoulder about ten feet above the grade of the highway. The tiny hill was flat, topped with a pair of scrawny cedar trees. He estimated they were a little over a half mile away from the minuscule gray figure that was the Porsche.

"What are you doing?" Sadie fidgeted in her seat. "We finally gonna kill somethin'?"

Sinclair pulled a pair of binoculars from the glove compartment. He adjusted the zoom, and the lenses brought the scene into focus.

Two men from the backseat of the Porsche got out and took up position along the fence line, about ten feet away from what looked like an opening that led to a dirt road. They hid themselves in the brush that grew intertwined with the barbed wire, effectively disappearing from view. The vegetation was so thick, Sinclair doubted they'd be visible if he was standing a few feet away.

The Porsche pulled forward and stopped about twenty meters on the other side of the opening. The driver and the fourth man got out and took cover opposite the first two, as invisible as their colleagues.

Sinclair lowered the binoculars and eased himself out of the passenger seat. He figured the chopper had radioed the position of the target to the men in the SUV, and now they were simply waiting.

Sadie got out as well while Sinclair removed the sniper rifle and a portable shooting stand, a foldout seat-and-table combination that was easy to transport.

"What do you want me to do?" Sadie said.

"Use these." He tossed her a pair of earplugs. "It's gonna be loud."

Sadie shoved the plugs in and followed him as he gingerly made his way up the rocky outcropping.

At the top, he paused and caught his breath. The pain in his side pulsated, following no discernible pattern. He ignored the discomfort and opened the shooting platform. Then, he sat, jammed his earplugs into place, and pressed the massive rifle against his shoulder.

"This is gonna be so cool." Sadie stroked the back of his neck. Her voice was muffled due to the hearing protectors.

Sinclair closed one eye and peered through the scope, searching for the target. He closed the bolt, made sure the safety was off.

The magnification of the scope was significantly greater than the binoculars, and everything was clearer and closer. And shakier.

The range finder in the scope indicated the men from the Porsche were over a thousand yards away, nearly three-quarters of a mile. At that distance, with optics this powerful, each beat of the shooter's heart seemed like a minor earthquake, causing the crosshairs to quiver and move slightly off target.

The men waited. Sinclair did too, watching through the scope.

"Can I look?" Sadie said.

"No."

From beyond the fence line, Sinclair thought he could detect a trickle of dust in the air, a fresh disturbance that didn't have anything to do with the earlier cloud. Hard to tell from that far away, maybe a vehicle of some sort moving along the dirt road.

"I want to shoot something, too." Sadie knelt beside him.

His breath caught in his throat as a wave of pain rippled through his stomach.

"You okay?"

"Y-y-yes." He tried to concentrate on the view from his scope. "I'm fine."

She stood.

The dust cloud in the scope grew larger.

Sadie tapped him on the shoulder, fracturing the image into a thousand tremors.

"Behind us. There's somebody coming," she said. "I think it's the police."

- CHAPTER FIFTY-FOUR -

The air around the stock tank seemed to have grown hotter. The cow manure and stale water smelled stronger, the buzz of the horseflies louder.

I checked my cell, saw a weak signal, one bar that came and went.

"Who you gonna call?" Piper said. "The police?"

"I was gonna update my Facebook page." I put the phone away. "Do they have a 'Screwed' status?"

Piper chuckled once, and took off jogging down the path leading away from the stock tank. Eva and I followed.

The track had been headed south, but the road leading away from the water circled back to the east. A hundred yards later, just past a rusted windmill, the road arced to the left again, north in the general direction of the highway.

The three of us jogged and then ran, sweating profusely. Rehydration was going to be an issue sooner rather than later. Each of us glanced repeatedly skyward as we ran, fearful for the return of the chopper.

Another bend in the road and we stopped.

A battered Dodge pickup was parked by a small corral and another windmill, this one functioning.

The truck was old, cracked windscreen, black paint faded to gray, speckled with spots of rust and bare metal.

A man in his thirties with a sun-weathered face and a droopy mustache stood by the front of the truck. He wore a sleeveless denim shirt, a South Texas–style straw hat—low crown in the front, higher in the rear—and a pair of thick-soled cowboy boots that came to his knees.

His jeans were open at the waist; he was in the middle of urinating.

"Howdy." He finished and zipped up.

"We need a ride." I wiped sweat from my eyes. "Can you help us out?"

"Big old chopper overhead." He tilted his hat back. "And you with a fancy machine gun."

"I'm a DEA agent." I badged him. "This is an emergency."

"That a fact?" He spat a stream of tobacco juice onto the ground. "We don't get too many federal emergencies around these parts."

"People are trying to kill us." Eva stepped forward. "Please, we need to get to the nearest town."

He looked at Eva and then at Piper, eyes lingering over the places men like to examine closely.

"Don't get many pretty women here on the ranch." He took a step closer to Eva.

She didn't say anything. Her cheeks were flushed from the heat, damp.

"Crazy stuff I seen coming over the border." The man shook his head. "You wouldn't believe it."

"We need to hurry," I said.

"I ask for help." He shook his head again. "But the Border Patrol's got nobody to send. And now a DEA agent's here?"

"Hey, cowpoke." Piper spoke for the first time. "You know what a euro is?"

The guy frowned. "I ain't stupid."

"Good for you." She stepped forward, bringing the sub-gun up. "Now answer the question."

The cowboy stared at the weapon, eyes wide.

"This is worth nearly a thousand dollars at the currency exchange in San Antonio." I pulled a five-hundred euro bill from my pocket. "There's four more if we can get to a town where we can find a car."

He nodded slowly, pointed to the truck. "Y'all get in the back."

"No." Piper aimed her submachine gun at his head. "Toss the keys instead."

The man gulped. Then he reached in his pocket and dropped a ring in the dirt.

I picked it up.

In the front of the truck was a milk jug full of warm water. I looked longingly at the liquid but didn't take a drink. Instead, I put the container in the shade under a large post oak a few feet from the windmill.

A roll of duct tape sat on the floorboard. I grabbed the tape, bound the cowboy's hands in front of him and then led him over to the tree.

"Sit." I shoved him down.

He leaned against the trunk.

I tossed the keys to Piper. "Where's your knife?" I asked him.

He didn't reply.

"Tell me where your blade is." I knelt so we were eye to eye. "We can't waste any more time."

He hesitated, then said, "My belt. On the right."

I patted him down and found a lockback Spyderco clipped to his waistband. I took the knife and tossed it in the brush about thirty feet on the other side of the windmill. His cell phone was in his shirt pocket, an old-style Motorola with three bars of service. I put it next to the water in the shade.

Piper started the truck, told Eva to get in the middle.

"You should be able to work free from that tape in fifteen or twenty minutes."

"If I was a revenge-minded man," he said, "I might get the notion to hunt you down."

"Don't." I tucked a wad of currency in his shirt pocket. "Here's five thousand euros." I stood and paused, looking down at him. "I'm sorry. Really."

He shook his head and spit in the dirt.

Piper tapped the horn, and I ran to the passenger side.

"You're just going to leave him?" Eva said.

"Yep." I slammed the door, rested my subgun out the open window.

Piper drove. The truck bumped along for a couple hundred yards until the dirt road widened and then ended at a break in the fence line, the highway just beyond.

She stopped, the front of the truck barely through the gap, the fence line bisecting the Dodge between the bed and the cab.

No traffic.

She pulled onto the shoulder slowly.

The fatigue must have caught up with me because it took forever for the significance of what happened then to register.

The engine compartment shredded as a hail of high-powered bullets tore it to pieces.

Steam, fluids, bits of metal flew everywhere.

No sound except for the thud of noise-suppressed weapons amid the crackle and screech of destroyed machinery.

The truck rolled forward another foot or so and stopped, the transmission or motor damaged so severely that any further movement became impossible.

I looked, gun up. No targets.

Piper swore. And raised her hands.

They came from the fence line, a group of men in civilian clothes, assault rifles with silencers aimed at us.

"Throw your guns out." The lead guy was on Piper's side.

We did. Subguns and our Glocks.

"One at time, the driver first," the lead guy said. "Step out with your hands up."

Piper opened the door by sticking her arm outside and grasping the exterior handle. Her other hand was raised. She got out. Eva followed.

"Now you, stud." A man on my side aimed at my head. He had a jagged scar on one cheek, nose to ear.

I did just like Piper, careful to move very slowly.

Scarface threw me on the ground, face down.

Sweat and dust in my eyes. The stench of hot metal and smoking rubber. Gunpowder.

People moving, the clank of weapons. The heat and dirt everywhere.

"Everybody on their knees." A man's voice. "Nice and slow. Hands on your heads."

I blinked away dirt, pushed myself up, knelt. Piper was beside me, kneeling, Eva on her other side.

Two men faced us. Early thirties, crew cuts. Military bearing. One spoke on a radio. The other aimed a stubby assault rifle at us.

The guy with the radio was Scarface. He had eyes the color of concrete in winter, only with less warmth. A rifle sling bisected his torso, the muzzle hanging behind him.

Beyond those two, closer to the highway, stood another pair with similar demeanor.

The guy with the scar put the radio back on his belt.

"We're federal agents." I nodded toward Piper. "DEA."

"What a coincidence." He pulled a wallet from his pocket, flipped it open. "Us, too."

"We've got backup on the way," Piper said.

"No, you don't." Scarface shook his head. "You two have gone rogue. You've got diddly."

Eva didn't say anything.

"I've heard about you, good-looking." Scarface leered at Piper and sat on his haunches in front of us. "We're supposed to turn over the Mex in one piece, but you and your boyfriend we can keep."

His voice had a singsong quality, the tone of somebody who was away from the prying eyes of the authorities and intended to make good use of the time.

"Bet you and my boys can have a nice time together." He caressed her cheek. "A couple of 'em just got out of the stockade in time for this little shindig."

Piper slapped his hand away.

"A fighter." He nodded. "This is gonna be fun."

The guy holding the rifle on us grabbed his crotch with one hand and laughed.

"Before the boss man gets here," Scar Face said, "why don't you and the Mex show us your tits?"

- CHAPTER FIFTY-FIVE -

Sinclair placed the crosshairs in the middle of the Mexican woman's shirt, the kill zone right between her breasts. The reticles of the scope jiggled, refusing to stay in the exact center of the target.

The three people he had followed across Texas were kneeling in a row in front of the ruined pickup, facing his location three-quarters of a mile away. One of their attackers knelt as well, back to the scope. The other attackers were out of view.

Sinclair's angle relative to their positions meant that the guy with his back to the rifle was between Eva Ramirez and Piper. Jon Cantrell, the cause of all this fuss, was a little off to the side.

Four tiny targets in a row, wiggly little blips so far away that the bullet would arrive three or four seconds before the sound did.

His gut rumbled, a fissure of pain followed by stillness.

Unfortunately, he'd only have time to take out Eva, not all of them like he'd planned, but the shot was going to be easy, all things considered. The amount of trigger pressure required to fire the rifle could be measured in ounces. He just needed to time the breaking point between the sear and firing pin with the thump-thump of his heart and the intake of breath.

"It's the sheriff." Sadie stood behind him. "He's parking his car."

Sinclair ignored the crunch of tires on gravel, the sound muffled by his earplugs. He took a breath and held it.

A vehicle door slammed.

Sinclair pressed his finger against the trigger. The crosshairs jiggled back into place.

Footsteps.

Sinclair increased the pressure.

"Hey, what are you doing up there?" A man's voice.

"What should I tell him?" Sadie whispered.

"SIR." The man's voice. "Please back away from your weapon. NOW."

Sinclair directed his mind and body to a still place. The crosshairs slid over the kill zone. He squeezed harder.

"Uh-oh, he's coming up."

The steel of the sear broke free from the trigger. The coiled spring unleashed.

Sadie backed into Sinclair's shoulder at the exact instant the firing pin slammed into the primer. One one-thousandth of a second later, the 400-grain bullet reached the end of the barrel.

Even with earplugs, the sound was horrific, like all the engines at a monster truck rally roaring at once. The grass under the muzzle flattened for three or four feet in every direction.

Sinclair didn't wait to see if he hit the target. He dropped the rifle, jumped up, yanked the nickel-plated revolver from his waistband.

Sadie squealed and pointed to the man in the khaki uniform at the base of the small hill, pistol drawn.

Sinclair tried not to think about the searing pain in his stomach. He shoved the girl away and fired twice at the officer.

After the roar of the Barrett, the report from the .38 was minuscule, like a cap gun. The two bullets did their damage though, both striking the deputy in the chest.

The officer dropped his weapon and clawed at the bloody spot on his chest. He looked at Sinclair for a moment, his mouth formed into a perfect O shape, before falling to the ground.

"Doggone." Sadie fanned her face with one hand. "That was cool beans."

Sinclair clutched his wound, felt the blood on his fingers. He peered at the squad car to verify that there was only one officer on the scene, then went back to the shooting stand and picked up the sniper rifle.

The scope had been jarred when he'd dropped the weapon. The front lens was out of alignment with the muzzle, pointing way to the left. Without recalibrating the scope with the bore, a time-consuming process, there was no way the rifle could function as a long-range weapon now.

Sinclair used it as a telescope nonetheless. What he saw was not good.

- CHAPTER FIFTY-SIX -

Sweat stung my eyes.

I tried to figure a move but none came to me. We'd been relieved of our weapons and were kneeling on a deserted highway with four heavily armed men around us.

That scenario didn't leave too many options.

Scarface pulled a knife from his pocket, flicked it open. He was still sitting on his haunches facing us.

"I got plans for you." He pointed the blade at Piper. "We get done partying, there's a donkey show in Juárez where you're gonna be the sta—"

His torso disappeared.

One instant it was there, the next not.

His shoulders and arms and head remained, along with everything from the waist down. But the middle section, the thoracic cavity and abdomen, all that vanished in a haze of red.

Blood and bones, internal organs, stomach funk. Everything exploded outward like a stick of dynamite in a piñata. All over me, Piper, and Eva.

Nobody moved.

His corpse collapsed on itself as the boom of a heavy-caliber weapon echoed across the desert plains a couple seconds later.

The assault rifle that had been slung over his shoulder landed in front of me, coated in slime and blood.

The closest guy reacted first. He shook his head, blinked away a few stray drops of blood.

I grabbed the dead guy's weapon, rolled over the remains of a lung and some ribs, and fired.

The silenced, three-shot burst started at the closest guy's crotch and worked its way up, ending with a round in his throat. He thumped to the ground like a sack of wet flour.

The third man got a shot off before I could engage. His bullet missed; mine didn't.

The last guy ducked behind the ruined pickup.

Piper, Eva, and I were on the other side.

No time to stand. I rolled back between the two women, stuck the barrel under the truck and emptied the magazine in a spraying motion.

A scream from the other side. Then a groan. Then nothing.

I stood, shaky, wiped blood from my face.

The second attacker had a messenger sack around his shoulder.

I dashed to his prone body and opened the case, grabbed a fresh magazine, reloaded.

Piper ran over, retrieved his rifle, and stood next to me.

Eva got up, breathing hard. She looked at the remains of Scarface, clutched her stomach, and vomited.

"Donkey show, my ass." Piper pulled a strand of intestine from her hair, tossed it away.

Eva retched again.

I patted the pockets of the man who'd been aiming the rifle at us, avoiding the bloody genital area.

"We've got transport now." Piper pointed to the gray SUV on the other side of the fence break.

I pulled a piece of black plastic from his pocket. It was marked with the Porsche emblem. "Here's the key."

Eva leaned against the ruined Dodge, hyperventilating and shaking.

"What the hell do you think happened?" Piper scanned the horizon to the east.

"I'm guessing somebody missed." I walked over to Eva. "You okay?"

"We better roll before they start shooting again." Piper slung the assault rifle over her shoulder.

Eva looked up as I approached. Blood coated her hair and face. She was edging toward hysteria and shock.

"Are you all right?" I said.

"W-w-we could have been killed." She hugged her arms to her side.

"We weren't though." Piper stood by the front of the pickup. "But it's early yet."

Eva looked at both of us. She took a deep breath, evidently pulling strength and resolve from deep within. "You are right. We are alive and that is what matters. Let's go."

Piper nodded, a look on her face that bordered on approval. Together, the three of us jogged to the Porsche.

I chirped the locks open. In the cargo area: a cooler full of bottled water and a large metal container with loaded clips for the two rifles we had commandeered.

"A Reaper. I've heard about these." Piper traced the lettering on the side of her weapon. "That's some serious hardware."

"The man said he was a DEA agent." Eva opened a bottle of water, poured the contents on her face and hair.

"They're contractors. Paynelowe," I said. "Your boyfriend is looking for you. Pulling out all the stops."

"Then who shot at us?" Piper washed her face with spring water.

"Who else is after us?" I said.

"Sinclair." She splashed water on the back of her neck.

"That's my guess." I opened a bottle and rinsed off as much blood and funk as possible. Then I drank two more in a matter of seconds.

"How many people have to die?" Eva stared at the corpses.

"Not as much fun as partying at the disco, is it?" I said.

"I've seen worse." She looked up. "Believe me. It just never gets easier."

We continued to clean up, drinking water, trying to cool down.

"Here's a new issue," Piper said. "We need to head west but there's no road."

"Our new ride is all-wheel drive." I shut the rear of the Porsche. "We'll find a way."

Piper nodded and trudged to the front passenger's seat. Eva got in the rear, and I climbed behind the steering wheel.

The interior of the vehicle smelled like marijuana. A pipe lay on the console next to a two-way radio.

I started the engine, cranked the AC to frigid, and opened the door.

"What are you doing?" Piper said.

I yanked the hood latch and went to the front of the vehicle. The battery wasn't there. I returned to my spot behind the wheel.

"Guy I used to date had one of these," Piper said. "The battery's under the driver's seat. You need a special tool to access it."

"Crap." I drummed the steering wheel.

Piper buckled her belt. "If you were running an op where you blew up a friggin' highway, would you have a tagged battery in your ground transportation?"

"Good point." I put the SUV in gear and drove west.

The crater was around the first bend. The charred hulk of the Tahoe sat about a hundred feet from the edge of the hole.

I maneuvered past the remains and idled toward the spot where the highway ended.

"There." Piper pointed to a dirt track on the right.

"Is that a road?" Eva said.

"Not exactly." I turned. "But it'll do."

The path was not even really a path. More like a flat spot devoid of cactus where the fencing had been ripped away by the explosion.

The SUV's tires rumbled over the dusty terrain. The route led north, a meandering course between mesquites and their thorny limbs.

After a few hundred yards the direction shifted to the west and the ground sloped down to a dry creek bed. I gunned the engine and hit the shallow ravine at an angle, the four wheels churning dirt as we rose to the other side.

"So far so good." Eva nodded.

The handheld radio on the console beeped. A few seconds later a voice: "Hit Man One, Hit Man One. This is Hit Man Two. Please advise status."

Standard military chatter. Not exactly what you'd expect to hear DEA agents use.

Piper picked up the walkie-talkie and pointed the antenna at me. "You want to be Hit Man or should I?"

"What are they saying?" Eva leaned forward.

The radio: "Hit Man One, where are you?"

"They want to know what happened." I took the walkie-talkie.

Radio: "Hit Man One, we heard a big-ass weapon go boom-boom. Please advise status."

"They're gonna figure it out sooner or later," Piper said. "Go ahead and answer."

I pressed the Talk key. "Hit Man One's ejected from the game. Put Godfather on."

The term "Godfather" is typical military nomenclature for the leader of an operation.

No response.

I accelerated.

The remnants of a farmhouse lay ahead. One crumbling half wall and a chimney, stark against the sky like a limbless tree too proud to die.

The path opened onto a dirt road that led away from the house toward the highway.

On the radio: "Jon Cantrell." Not a question.

Piper shrugged, drank some water.

A series of low hills appeared. I stopped by the nearest, motioned to Piper. She got out, pressed the assault rifle to her shoulder and crept around the base. A couple of moments later she returned, nodded once, and hiked to the top.

Eva fidgeted in the rear.

I waited. Stared at the radio. It beeped a couple of times but no one spoke.

A few minutes later, Piper jumped back in the passenger seat.

"The highway is maybe a half mile ahead," she said. "Doesn't look like any hostiles between here and there."

I nodded.

The radio: "This is Godfather." The voice sounded different than before, like it was underwater. "I'm airborne. Excuse the sound quality."

"What's your name, Godfather?" I turned the AC cooler. "You know who I am."

"We've met. Let's leave it at that."

I took a wild shot. "McCluskey, right? From the warehouse?"

No response. Eva swore under her breath.

"So it looks like I've got something you want," I said.

The radio: "What happened to Hit Man One?"

"They're sleeping with the fishes. Somebody else is out there hunting."

"That's not possible," McCluskey/Godfather said. "This is a restricted op."

"Sinclair didn't get that memo."

No response.

I put the car in gear, drove away from the hill.

"Too many people have died over this." McCluskey paused. "There wasn't supposed to be shooting."

"You blew up a road your girlfriend was on," I said, "but you didn't want anybody to pull a trigger?"

"You don't know what fucked is." His voice was choked with anger, mood shifting like a whirlwind. "You think you do. But what's coming your way is in a whole other league."

I thought about possible responses, verbal moves that could be used to our advantage. But nothing came to mind. Reasoning with a drug addict who had the resources to blow up an entire highway just didn't seem like a viable plan.

"One last chance," he said. "Give her up and you can walk away."

"Your man's fighting for you." Piper looked in the back. "Isn't that romantic?"

Eva gripped the back of the seat.

"Sorry, Godfather." I shrugged. "We're gonna keep going."

The radio crackled.

Then, McCluskey's voice, choked with a different emotion: "Is she okay?"

"She's fine." I plucked a bone fragment from my hair. "You can see her in court."

"Please, tell her I love her," he said. "I'm sorry things are going to get bad. You just—"

The radio hissed and made a musical tone, weird harmonics that sounded like a flute. Then, silence, the connection broken or switched.

Eva stared out the window. I turned in my seat, said, "You okay?"

She shrugged, kept staring.

About a minute passed. No sound but the whoosh of the air-conditioning. Then a voice I recognized came on, not scrambled, sounding like it was a few feet away.

"Hey, Jon. This here's your old buddy, Costco. Looks like you're in a heap of trouble."

"Costco?" I said. "I thought you retired."

"I've got a pile of cash for you behind door number one." He paused. "Take the money, Jon. Don't make me open door number two."

- CHAPTER FIFTY-SEVEN -

Sinclair sat behind the wheel of the deputy's squad car, listening to the two-way radio mounted below the dash. The radio system apparently served as the sole emergency communication network for this particular county. There was lots of chatter about the need for an emergency road crew and requests for information on the blast.

The dead deputy lay about thirty feet away, at the base of the small hill from where Sinclair had tried and failed to kill Eva Ramirez.

Eva, along with her protectors, Jon Cantrell and Piper, had disappeared into a cloud of dust, headed west.

Sadie sat in the passenger seat. She was wearing the officer's cowboy hat and playing with his handcuffs.

Sinclair took stock of his situation. He was in the middle of the badlands of West Texas, a hundred miles from the nearest town, and a thousand years removed from where he'd started out. He was unable to reach Imogene, the main contact with his crew in North Texas. He'd now killed two fellow peace officers, men much like himself, something unimaginable in his darkest nightmares.

Back in Dallas, his friend Tommy was dead, as were a half dozen other people in his employ, gunned down in the firefight at the Cheyenne Apartments. The police investigation of the incident, despite his connections, was headed his way.

Jon Cantrell, eaten up with an honest streak as wide as the Cotton Bowl, would deliver Eva Ramirez to Marfa, where she would testify, and the world would know Sinclair worked for the cartels. And the cartels would put the pieces together and learn he skimmed their money. And product.

Hawkins and McNally would be angry as well. They wanted Eva stopped, cost be damned. He'd failed them, and that was almost worse. That meant he'd failed a friend, McNally.

And he had a bullet wound in his side that leaked every time he moved too much.

Voices sounded on the radio in the squad car again, several people talking over each other. One guy, apparently a dispatcher at the sheriff's office, kept asking for the deputy to respond. He wanted to know about the explosion that had been reported on the highway. His tone got more and more frantic with each transmission, and Sadie giggled every time he came on the air.

Sinclair held the deputy's cell in the palm of his hand. The deputy's phone had coverage—unlike Myrna DeGroot's—and had rung several times in the past few minutes. It rang again, and he tossed it in the ditch.

Sadie twirled the cuffs on one finger and leaned across the seat. She kissed Sinclair on the neck and said, "What are we gonna do next?"

He turned. Stared at her stupid overbite, the dull eyes that were too close together. He flexed his fingers several times and then slapped her, a hard backhand on one side of her face.

She yelped, rocked away.

His hand tingled from the blow. He rubbed his fingers.

Sadie cowered in the passenger seat and stared at him.

"I'm going back to Dallas." He got out of the squad car. Lumbered toward the Crown Victoria.

Sadie exited as well. She trailed behind him, one hand pressed against her cheek where he'd hit her.

At the driver's side of the Crown Victoria, he opened the door and stopped, one foot on the floorboard, an arm on the roof. He stared at the empty sky and the vastness of the land that surrounded him. Nothingness as far as he could see.

"What about me?" Sadie asked.

Sinclair ignored her, mentally running through an inventory, his assets, the easily transportable ones. Cash that was hidden. Jewelry and guns. The box of Krugerrands. Bearer bonds from that heist a couple of years back.

No options left. He would have to go on the run, before now an unthinkable scenario.

What was worse, he was going to have to leave Texas, something he'd never done in his sixty-one years. He would go back to Dallas, round up as much money as possible, and hit the road.

"Where am I supposed to go?" Sadie bounced from leg to leg.

"Do I look like I give a shit?" he said.

"I thought you liked me." She grabbed his arm.

"Goddam, but you are stupid." He shoved her hand away.

"You can't just leave me here." She rubbed her face. A long pause. "I got nowhere else to go."

The weight of the nickel-plated revolver felt heavy in his waistband. He flexed his fingers again.

"P-please." She embraced him, chest to chest. "Take me with you."

He didn't reply.

She pulled back, looked into his eyes.

"I'll let you hit me again." She bit her lip and smiled. "I like that sometimes."

- CHAPTER FIFTY-EIGHT -

I wiped sweat off my face, buckled the seat belt. Continued driving down the dirt path that led toward the highway.

An awkward silence in the Porsche.

"Wonder how much money he's got behind door number one," Piper said.

"Jon, please." Eva touched my shoulder. "You can't be seriously considering this?"

I slowed and stopped. The gate that led to the highway was visible about a half mile away. The mesa that had served as a landing pad for the Chinook was in the distance to the east. It was empty. Marfa was about two or so hours to the west.

The radio beeped. Then, Costco's voice: "Turn over the witness, Jon. It's just a package. No sense getting hurt over it."

The package lunged from the rear seat and grabbed for the radio.

Piper shoved her back.

Eva shook her head, a bewildered look on her face. She grasped my shoulder. "*Please.*"

"He's putting on the hard sell." Piper looked at her. "Wonder what you'd bring on the open market?"

Eva didn't speak.

Costco was my former partner, a man to whom I'd trusted my life on numerous occasions. But now he appeared to be working with a drug-addled, crooked DEA contractor named Keith McCluskey.

And then there was the package herself, Eva, the poster child for damaged goods, not all that different from Piper. My favorite flavor, a balm for the rough spot in the corner of my soul. Volatile, enigmatic, more than a little dangerous.

When did life get so complicated? Oh, yeah. Right after the doctor slapped my ass in the delivery room.

"We could hand her over to Costco," Piper said. "And just take a hike."

"WHAT?" Eva leaned forward.

"What about the two dead guys in Dallas?" I said. "The DA's gonna charge us with murder."

"We hit the road for wherever." Piper shrugged. "Can't be as bad as the last twenty-four hours."

"You think Costco will really pay us?" I said.

The image of my father sitting in his recliner filled my mind. Riddled with dementia, needing a biopsy I couldn't afford.

Silence inside the Porsche. Nothing but the hum of the air-conditioning.

I spoke into the radio. "Tell me your location."

"What's yours?" he said. "We'll come to you."

I started to respond but didn't. A new thought in my mind. I put down the walkie-talkie and looked at Piper. "Why would McCluskey be airborne right now?"

"That doesn't make sense." She raised an eyebrow. "He's in charge. Why leave the scene?"

"And wouldn't they need the chopper to transport every-thing away from the middle of nowhere?"

Piper nodded.

"You had a plan," Eva said. "Remember? Take me to Marfa and collect the bounty."

I tried to piece everything together.

"McCluskey's running thin." Piper smiled. "He would have sent more than four people to take us down if he could have."

"And they wouldn't have been stoners." I lowered the window, tossed out the pipe.

Piper pointed to the gate. "Let's make a run for Marfa."

I thought about it for another moment and nodded. Pressed the gas. All four tires spun in the dust.

We were going about forty when we came to the gate, a thin wooden pole reaching from one end of the fence-line to the other.

"Hold on." I slowed a little and cranked the wheel.

The SUV busted through the barrier and rocked to one side, righting itself. The highway to the west was empty. The speedometer ratcheted up. Fifty, sixty, seventy; the Porsche ran like a spotted-ass ape.

At an even one hundred miles per hour, I engaged the cruise control and relaxed a little, taking a drink of water and settling into the plush leather seat.

A few seconds later, we topped a rise.

A gray speck shimmered on the horizon, barely visible in the middle of the road. Whatever it was, it didn't appear to be moving.

I clicked off the cruise control. Piper opened the console and found a pair of binoculars. She pressed them to her eyes and stared out the front window.

"Looks like another Porsche," she said. "And two people standing next to it."

I slowed some more.

"This Costco guy," she said. "Is he a fat-ass?"

I took my foot off the gas and let the Porsche's speed dwindle to a crawl. Then I stopped and took the binoculars. The built-in range finder indicated we were about seven hundred meters away.

Costco 1.0—the old version, fat and drunk-looking— stood next to the rear of a Porsche identical to ours, parked sideways across the center line of the highway. He appeared unarmed. A guy in his twenties holding a rifle, obviously ex-military, stood next to him.

I surveyed the area around the stopped SUV. The surrounding terrain looked like the surface of the moon but not as hospitable. Flat sandy soil, no trees, no hills, only a sprinkling of cactus. No place for anybody to hide, like a location chosen to show there was no ambush in the wings.

"Could we go around whoever that is?" Eva said.

Something glimmered on the asphalt just beyond the SUV.

"Afraid not." I adjusted the binoculars. "They spiked the road."

A chain embedded with nails stretched across the highway, reaching well onto the shoulder on either side.

Costco seemed to realize I was checking out the situation. He stepped away from the Porsche, pointed to the spikes, and then pulled a white handkerchief from his pocket. He held it at arm's length and waved.

Piper squinted. "Is he surrendering?"

"Doubt it." I placed the binoculars on the console, slipped the transmission into drive.

Piper rolled down the passenger window and stuck the muzzle of her rifle outside.

Eva groaned in the backseat, head in her hands.

When we were about a hundred yards away, I stopped, opened the door.

"Wait here."

"Any problems, give me a signal." Piper cracked her door and used the window gap as a rest for the Reaper. "I'll smoke the guy with the weapon first."

I nodded and got out. Then, I approached my old partner, the assault rifle taken from the dead contractor held at the ready. When I was about ten yards away, Costco lowered the white flag, and I stopped.

"Doggone, Jon. What happened to you?" He frowned. "Looks like you been dry-humping old Leatherface from *Texas Chain Saw Massacre*."

"And you look fat and drunk," I said.

The man with the rifle didn't speak. He stood by the rear of the SUV, his hand on the grip of the weapon but the barrel pointed down.

"Paynelowe's buying out our company." Costco sighed. "Sorry I ever got you into this contractor gig."

"Who's doing what?"

"McCluskey's outfit, Paynelowe. They're buying us, Blue Dagger. You and me." He pulled a bottle of whiskey from his pocket. "You're a daily operator so you didn't see the newsletter."

"How much muscle you got in the Porsche?" I nodded at the SUV.

"Just us." He gestured to the second guy with the neck of the bottle. "We don't want to hurt you." He took a long drink, smacked his lips. "You're not gonna take the money, are you?"

I pointed to the chain. "Move the spikes."

"Don't make me open door number two." He took another swig.

"The witness is McCluskey's girlfriend," I said. "And he's operating off the reservation now. We're taking her to the court."

"We flew here in an army chopper," Costco said. "If McCluskey's gone rogue and has that many resources, I'd hate to see how he rolls when he's playing by the rules."

"Don't make me shoot you." I wiped sweat off of my face, gripped the weapon tighter.

The guy with the rifle tensed but didn't raise his gun.

Costco sighed, face drooping. Sixty-odd years of the hard life seemed to press down upon his shoulders all at once. He touched the rear door of the SUV, hesitated, and then turned back to face me.

"I found him," he said.

"Who?"

"The little boy from the storeroom at the Pussycat Lounge. The one with the burned legs."

I didn't speak.

"The mother was a drunk. She lost him, remember?" Costco leaned against the side of the SUV. "Well, I found him."

I remembered all too clearly, every detail. I thought about possible replies. Nothing came to mind.

"Give me the witness," he said, "and I'll give you the kid."

- CHAPTER FIFTY-NINE -

"Are you nuts?" I tried not to laugh.

"Don't make this harder than it needs to be," Costco said.

"That kid's dead, Costco. Long dead."

The child from the storeroom at the Pussycat Lounge would be in middle school by now at the least. He certainly would have turned up if he was still alive.

"He's in the backseat." Costco shook his head. "If you don't play ball, he gets hurt."

"Move the spikes off the road." I pointed to the chain. "Quit with the imaginary threats."

The guy with the rifle at the rear of the SUV flexed his fingers but didn't move.

Costco drained the bottle, tossed it to the side of the road. He crossed his arms and hugged himself, pacing back and forth, agitated.

"Jon, I'm only gonna ask one more time," he said. "Please don't make me do this."

"How far down the hole are you?" I said. "You're bluffing with a pair of twos. Thought you were smarter than that."

"Mister Mastercard and the second ex-wife have got my balls in a big old vise." He stopped pacing, paused. "Jesus, Jon, don't let happen what's coming next. Give up the witness."

"Or what?" I said. "You'll play me for a sucker with a dead kid?"

Neither of us spoke for a few moments.

"You're right. I was bluffing." He sighed heavily. "The kid's not in the back. No idea what happened to him."

"Tell your goon to stand down." I pointed to the armed man at the rear of the SUV. "And move the spikes."

"I am sorry, Jon. So sorry." Costco took one last look at me and opened the rear door of the Porsche.

A man in his late sixties wearing a dirty khaki uniform and a tarnished badge got out, an automatic rifle in his hand.

My father, Frank Cantrell.

Time seemed to stop, my existence split into two separate pieces—before this moment and after. Rescue and escape scenarios ran through my head in a blur, none of them remotely viable given my father's mental condition.

Breath caught in my throat, emotions welled in my chest. I dropped the rifle and sat on the asphalt.

The road surface was hot, but I didn't care. So was hell.

"Frank Cantrell is now a contractor for Paynelowe." Costco walked over and looked down at me. "At least that's what we told him."

"Screw you, Costco." I swallowed my rage. "To hell and back."

"He's a nice old guy," Costco said. "I sure don't want to hurt him. But I will."

I choked down the bile in my throat. My skin was clammy, vision blurry.

"I hoped we weren't gonna get to this stage." He grimaced. "Give me the witness, Jon. And this can all go away."

I didn't say anything. My father clutched the rifle to his chest, an empty look in his eyes. He stared at me, a hard, unknowing gaze. He aimed the gun in my general direction.

"Do the right thing and everybody has a really nice payday. Then you and your dad can go home." Costco handed me a walkie-talkie. "Now call your partner."

I took the radio and glanced at my weapon lying on the pavement.

"Make the call." Costco stood, kicked the rifle away. "I don't want to crank this up another notch."

The guy with the rifle crouched behind the rear of the Porsche. He aimed at our vehicle in the distance. My father continued to stand by the back door of the SUV, weapon in hand.

The walkie-talkie was identical to the one Piper had. Ultra-modern, sleek metal and plastic. A short stubby antenna about three inches long, encased in brushed aluminum.

I held it to my mouth and hesitated.

Costco knelt back down. He placed the muzzle of a pistol on my knee. "Make the damn call."

I pressed the Talk button. "Piper. We're gonna do the transfer here. Bring the witness."

Costco smiled, relaxed a little. The stench of whiskey filled the air between us.

"That was the smart thing to do." He let the muzzle slip from my knee.

I nodded, smiled sheepishly, going for a hangdog expression. Then I jammed the antenna in his eye.

Costco jerked his head to one side, screaming like anybody would when a half-inch-diameter metal rod had been stuck into their eye socket. He dropped the pistol. His eyeball had plopped out and now dangled on one side of his face, a plump, bloody grape attached to a piece of twine.

My father let the gun fall from his grasp and looked from side to side, disoriented, face pale and terrified, the full weight of his dementia kicking in.

The guy behind the SUV jerked his head up to see what was going on. He fired once at me as I rolled away.

The silenced bullet hit Costco in the gut with a big, wet *squoosh*, like a pumpkin had been split open.

Piper, having figured it all out from a hundred yards away, fired a three-shot burst and smoked the guy who'd been behind the Porsche.

Silence. The faint smell of cordite and blood drifted across the road as the empty casing from the dead guy's rifle gleamed in the sun.

I leaned over my former partner.

Costco looked at me with his one remaining eye. Blood bubbled from the massive hole in his stomach. His eye closed, and he died.

I stood, limbs shaky from the adrenaline spurt.

My father had picked up his rifle. He aimed it at me.

"Dad." I held my arms out, palms up. "It's me, Jonathan. Your son."

"H-hands on top of your head." My father pressed the buttstock against his shoulder.

Our SUV, Piper at the wheel, skidded to a stop a few yards behind me.

"You're sick," I said. "You need your medicine. Let me help."

"I am a federal agent." He blinked repeatedly, skin flushed. "With the DEA. Obey my command or I will shoot."

"Dad, this is Jonathan. Remember me?" I spoke slowly. Forced a smile on my face. "Remember when you came to my graduation from the police academy?"

Nobody said anything for a few seconds. My father began to tremble, arms shaking.

"Please." I took a step closer, hand out. "Put the gun down."

"I'm a federal agent." His voice was shrill. "I'M A COP. DAMMIT. Now put your hands on top of your head."

"It's okay." I took another step. "I'm Jonathan, your son."

"W-w-where am I?" He lowered the gun a little. "I don't feel so good."

"Put the rifle down."

"Do you know my son, Jonathan?" He backed toward the Porsche, gun wavering. "He didn't think I could still be a good cop."

I stopped moving. Stared at this strange, sad man who was my father.

He kept the gun aimed at me and got in the driver's seat of the Porsche.

"Dad, stop." I inched forward. "Come with us. We'll get you to a doctor."

He fired. A silenced round zinged off the pavement in front of me. I jumped back.

The door to the Porsche slammed shut, the ignition cranked. The vehicle accelerated away, headed toward the crater in the highway. Toward the nothingness of West Texas.

Piper walked up beside me.

"That was my father." I was shaking. Fear, rage. Hopelessness. "C-costco had my dad."

"I know." She nodded.

"We have to go after him." I pointed down the road. "He's not well."

"We only have one vehicle."

I turned and looked at her. Specks of blood that hadn't

washed off had dried to her skin, rust-colored freckles on her face.

"McCluskey's gonna come back with reinforcements," she said. "And we have to get the witness to Marfa before he does."

"But my dad." I squinted in the direction he'd gone.

Nothing was visible.

My heart seemed to shred inside my chest. A thousand childhood memories flitted through my mind, barbecues and baseball games, learning to ride a bike, fishing trips.

"You're a cop and you have a duty," Piper said. "What do you think he'd want you to do?"

A few moments passed.

I nodded.

She touched my arm and then got into the driver's seat.

I pulled the nail-spiked chain off of the road, got in the passenger side, and pointed west. "Don't stop for anything."

- CHAPTER SIXTY -

The arid flatness of the Chihuahuan Desert slowly gave way to a more elevated area, the beginning of the Davis Mountains, the craggy stepping-stones of the Rockies. The heat dissipated slightly, replaced by a cool, dry air that made the sun appear brighter and the tires hum louder.

We passed through Marathon, a tiny railroad stop that didn't appear to be more than a half dozen blocks long. Nothing but dust-covered adobe and brick homes clustered on either side of an old three-story building called the Gage Hotel.

The next metropolis was Alpine, the biggest city in the region, a college town, maybe six or eight thousand people total. We drove the speed limit, stopped for the signs, yielded where appropriate and didn't see any law enforcement there either.

A roadside marker said Marfa was twenty-five miles to the west. We were less than a half hour away from the courthouse.

"Call the prosecutor." I handed Eva my cell phone. "Tell him we're close but don't say where." I had programmed the number earlier that day.

Eva dialed. She asked to speak to the US attorney.

I tried not to think about my father or where he was at the moment, what he had done when he'd encountered the crater in the road. A full tank of gas in a four-wheel drive vehicle, it was possible that he could have made it to another road somehow. The dementia ebbed and flowed like a tide. He could have hit a lucid period and figured out a way to get back to a town and a doctor. At least this is what I told myself.

Piper locked the cruise control at eighty.

A few miles later Eva said, "Yes, this is Eva Ramirez." She nodded several times, then answered some questions. "Yes . . . yes . . . no." A long pause. "Hold on." She handed the phone to me.

I pressed the device to my ear but didn't speak.

"Hello? This the US attorney." A pause. "To whom am I speaking?"

"This is the taxi driver," I said. "Where do I drop my passenger?"

"Okay, Mister Taxi. How far away are you?"

"We're an hour, maybe an hour and a half out," I said. "Been a lot of road hazards on the way."

"Are you secure at the moment? My security said there's been an explosion on Highway 90. Something about the road blowing up."

"We're good for now," I said. "Where do I take the witness?"

"Are you armed?" he said.

"Affirmative." I paused. "We're also going to be on a BOLO for our run out of Dallas. Take too long to explain why right now."

It seemed like a lifetime ago, but the escape from the Cheyenne Apartments and everything that had led up to that point had generated a lot of carnage, enough to have warranted at the very least a "be on the lookout" notification for all law enforcement statewide. I wanted to deliver the witness safely, but I didn't want to get arrested in the process. This was of course on top of the arrest warrant that had been or was about to be issued in the matter of the two dead men at the warehouse.

"Don't know anything about that," he said. "This deal comes with a get-out-of-jail free card."

A pause long enough that I thought the connection had been broken. Voices in the background. The clink of silverware.

Then the attorney: "I'll be at the courthouse in an hour. My office is on the ground floor."

"What's the address?"

"It's the only courthouse in town. Hope you're not followed. I've got a team of Marshals and that's it."

"What happened to the squad of Marines?" I looked in the back at Eva.

"That was too many uniforms, too close to the border." He sighed. "Didn't play well with the politicos."

I ended the call. Looked at Piper.

"There's not enough security," I said. "Just some Marshals."

She shook her head and accelerated.

- CHAPTER SIXTY-ONE -

I flipped down the sun visor, watched the outskirts of Marfa appear in the distance. A small blip amid the sand and cactus, the mountains looming in the distance.

The town was tiny, population a little over 2,200 according to the city limit sign.

It had originally been a railroad stop, as well as the county seat for Presidio County. But, with the mountain backdrop and the breathtaking but sparse scenery of the Big Bend region, the town had reinvented itself as an arts colony and managed to hang on to some degree of habitation, even after the demise of the rail system as a viable method for moving people and goods.

The houses were colonial style, stucco with pitched tin roofs, and adobe like in New Mexico.

There were two main streets, one of which was the highway we came in on.

Both were wide and empty and only a few blocks long, dominated by polar opposites: art galleries and a couple of upscale-looking restaurants interspersed with the kind of places you'd expect to find in a town with a population in the low four figures—feed stores, a tiny newspaper office, an even tinier city hall.

Initial impression: Marfa looked like a very small cross between Austin and Santa Fe.

A few blocks north of where we'd turn off the highway lay the courthouse, a three-story Victorian building with pale pink walls and white trim.

The structure was across the street from the Paisano Hotel, the headquarters for the cast and crew of *Giant* when the film had been shot in the area more than sixty years before.

"He was at lunch," I said. "Heard silverware."

"Everything's closed." Piper slowed and stopped by a narrow storefront housing a restaurant that looked remarkably upscale for such a small town.

The sign on the window read OPEN THURSDAY THROUGH SATURDAY. It was now Wednesday, early afternoon.

Very little traffic on the street, a few people walking, a couple of pickups slowly driving along.

"The hotel is open." I pointed to the cars parked in front. "Make the block."

Piper turned down a side street.

The courtyard for the Paisano was visible behind a wrought-iron gate and an adobe wall. Dining tables were scattered around a fountain, several groups of people eating lunch.

Two gray Suburbans were parked side by side a few feet down from the gate. One had blue government plates. The other had Louisiana tags.

"Long way from home." Piper kept driving.

"The US Marshals," I said. "Their Special Operation Group is based north of Lake Charles."

"Special what?" Eva spoke for the first time in a long while.

"Kind of like FedEx." Piper slowed for a cross street. "When something absolutely positively can't die, they call in the Special Operation Group."

"It's the Marshals' version of a SWAT team." I looked in the back. "After we make the delivery I'm gonna see if they'll help me look for my dad."

Eva nodded, a blank expression on her face.

"That means they're not contractors," I said. "And they're probably not on the take either."

"One bit of good news." Piper accelerated around a corner and headed toward the courthouse. "Let's do this."

"Are you sure we haven't been followed?" Eva leaned forward, then peered out the rear.

I ignored her. If we'd been followed, they would have hit by now. We'd have certainly seen them coming from a long way off. Whoever had been after us in the desert appeared to be out of the game for the moment.

A few moments later, we arrived at our destination. The sense of relief I was hoping for failed to materialize. I wondered if it ever would.

The building appeared as desolate as the rest of the town. Apparently, this courthouse didn't see much activity during the typical workday.

Piper parked in the front, a half dozen spaces from a Presidio County squad car. Other than that, no vehicles were present.

I shifted in my seat and jammed a couple of fresh magazines in the back of my waistband. Then I fastened my badge to my belt so it was clearly visible.

"We just walk in?" Eva said. "Shouldn't one of you go ahead of me?"

"I'll go first." I opened the door.

"I'm scared." Eva got out.

"Yeah, us, too." Piper exited the SUV and looked down the road.

I shut my door and scanned the area, waiting while the two women grouped at the front of the Porsche.

I started to move toward the front when Eva called out to me softly.

"Your father." She paused. "I am sorry he has gotten mixed up in this."

I didn't reply. Pushed any emotions from my head. Then I nodded once, acknowledging her statement.

To the south of us lay the town's main street, the minuscule commercial district where we'd just been. On the north and east sides of the courthouse were homes with wide front porches and newly planted flower beds. On the west side was a church. Everything was clean and freshly painted, lawns mowed, a West Texas slice of Norman Rockwell's America.

Piper stood by the front of the SUV. She attached a badge to her belt and kept the stubby rifle pressed against her side, muzzle down, hanging off one shoulder. Eva was beside her. After a few moments, Piper nodded at me.

I trotted toward the entrance, a large set of double-paned glass doors. Stepped inside.

The ground floor of the Presidio County Courthouse smelled like a Baptist church. Stale coffee, musty books. The ceilings were high, twelve or fifteen feet, the way things were built in the time before central air. The floor was worn marble that had been polished to a high gleam; the plaster walls were the color of bone.

A woman in her fifties, beehive hairdo and cat's-eye glasses, was walking by the stairs, a file in one hand. She stopped and stared, spending a fair amount of time on the blood in my hair and on my shirt before noticing the badge.

"Where's the US attorney's office?" I said.

She gulped, pointed to a door across from the stairwell. Then she scurried around the corner, looking over her shoulder.

I stuck my head outside. Whistled. Piper and Eva trotted up the sidewalk. When they were about midway, I headed to the office the woman had indicated.

The US attorney's workspace was a large, rectangular room that looked like an English gentlemen's club as imagined by John Wayne. A zebra-skin rug on the floor and a couple of deer mounts on the wall. Bookcases made from dark-stained wood, filled with law volumes. An overstuffed leather sofa and pair of matching easy chairs served as a sitting area opposite an ornately carved partners desk littered with files and papers, a computer and phone on one side.

On the far wall was a narrow door, closed.

A quick whistle from outside, my partner's signal.

I strode back to the entrance. Piper and Eva stood in the hallway. I motioned them inside and then shut the door.

"This is secure?" Piper looked around. "Any old numbnut could walk in here."

Eva moved to the desk, arms crossed. She looked around the room nervously.

Noise from the other side of the room. A toilet flushing.

Piper and I split apart, weapons up.

The door opened and a man in his forties stepped into the room, drying his hands on a paper towel. He wore a dark suit and a red-striped tie.

He smiled, impossibly perfect, blindingly white teeth in a jaw that didn't quite line up correctly, one side off kilter just a tad.

"Jon Cantrell." He tossed the paper towel in a trash can by the desk. "Been a long time."

Indeed. The last time I'd seen this man, his teeth had been scattered on the floor of the storeroom at the Pussycat Lounge. Two Dallas police officers had been pulling a bloody baton from my grip, getting ready to slap the bracelets on me, a fellow officer at the time, as a child with severely burned legs wailed in the background.

"Hollis." I gulped. "What are you doing here?"

"Waiting on you." He turned as the door leading to the hallway opened.

- CHAPTER SIXTY-TWO -

I watched as the US Attorney swept into the office.

Two men in khaki utility pants and matching shirts, holsters strapped to their thighs, trailed in his wake. The men wore five-star badges and ball caps emblazoned with the words "US Marshal."

The attorney wore a glen plaid suit with a bolo-style tie, black cowboy boots polished to a high gleam, and a gold pistol on his waist.

The weapon was visible because he made a great production of placing his hands on his hips, coattails pressed back.

The two marshals moved to either side of the door, both eyeing our badges as well as our disheveled condition.

Eva stared at the pistol and gasped.

"You're early." The US Attorney glanced at her for a moment, took in Piper and her badge, and then stopped on me. "Thought you told me an hour and a half."

"We caught a couple of lights." I shrugged.

"You've met our resident Fed?" The attorney pointed to Hollis.

I nodded.

"We're old friends." Hollis touched the part of his jaw that didn't line up properly.

"And this must be the witness that's gonna nail this case in the grand jury." The attorney took a step toward Eva, who took a step away.

Eva pointed to the pistol. "Why do you have that gun?"

"This is a spoil of war." He pulled the weapon from his holster. "Took it off our suspect."

The pistol was a Colt Government model, the 1911A1. It had been plated in gold, elaborate engraving along the frame. The grips were fashioned from mother-of-pearl.

"Don't worry, Miz Ramirez." He holstered the gun. "I'm not gonna shoot anybody. Unless they need it of course." He laughed at his own non-joke.

"The narcos carry guns like that," Eva said.

"And now I do." The attorney cocked his head. "You gotta problem with that?"

"It took me by surprise, that is all."

A tense silence filled the room.

"Let's have a quick debrief." Hollis pointed toward the east. "There's a dead deputy two counties away, and the conspiracy websites are jabbering about a Chinook helicopter taking people to the FEMA camps or some shit."

"What are you talking about?" Eva said.

"I wasn't speaking to you." Hollis continued to look into my eyes. "Then there's the dance hall in East Jesus that burned down next door to a hotel full of cartel hitmen."

"*Sicarios?*" I looked aghast. "On this side of the border?"

"Killed with a DEA-issued forty caliber submachine gun." He continued. "And a dead sheriff, too."

"What's your function here?" I said. "I missed that newsletter."

"I represent Paynelowe Industries. I am also a national security liaison." He hesitated for a beat. "From the White House."

Piper sighed loudly.

"So what did happen in the desert?" Hollis said.

"Keith McCluskey is what happened," I said. "I believe he works for your company."

"Fuck a duck." The US Attorney kicked the side of his desk. "Him again?"

My suspicions were confirmed. McCluskey was off the reservation, functioning without any mandate from his superiors or the US government. They probably wanted him stopped almost as bad as they wanted Eva to testify.

"Ouch." Hollis shook his head. "Keith McCluskey. That's a situation right there."

"What do you mean?" Piper asked.

"Paynelowe compartmentalized too much," he said. "Gave section heads like McCluskey too much power. Too many dollars."

"You don't know where he is, do you?" I tried to contain my surprise. "No clue what he's up to."

"He's gone native, as they say." Hollis curled a lip. "Operating without any authorization."

"Just a DEA badge and a whole lot of firepower." I whistled softly.

"We have contingency plans for this type of event," Hollis said. "We'll find him."

"He's in a big-ass helicopter," Piper said. "Last we heard, anyway."

"That was him?" Hollis frowned.

"So much for your contingency plans." I explained briefly. "And at some point, he's coming here."

Nobody spoke. One of the Marshals left for a moment and then returned.

Finally, the US Attorney said, "Why here?"

Piper and I looked at Eva.

She shrugged.

"It appears that Keith McCluskey is in love," I said. "With the witness."

"Which reminds me." Piper rubbed her thumb and index finger together. "When do we get paid?"

- CHAPTER SIXTY-THREE -

"Print your name." The US Attorney pointed to the paper. "Then your John Hancock and date."

The document read that whoever signed on the dotted line attested to their true identity and that Eva Ramirez was a witness in the matter of the United States versus Lazaro Morales. The attorney handed a similar document to Piper.

We filled them out and signed.

The attorney scooped up the papers, scanned them both. "As of this moment, Eva Ramirez is in the custody of the US government."

"Do we get a check or cash?" Piper asked.

"Not my department." He nodded and snapped his fingers.

The two Marshals pulled their weapons and aimed at us.

I was beyond exhausted. I was drained, empty of anything, a null set. Still, I started to reach for my gun only to stop, realizing the futility. They had the drop on both of us.

"For the duration of this trial you two are material witnesses," the attorney said. "Hostile, of course."

The Marshals disarmed and restrained us in a matter of seconds.

I swore and struggled against the cuffs. Piper kicked at one of the men but missed.

"I'll take them to the holding area." Hollis stepped forward. "Jon and I could use a little visit."

My stomach clenched. Handcuffed, unarmed. The last thing I needed was a visit with the man whose teeth I had knocked out years before.

Hollis grabbed my elbow in one hand, Piper's in the other. He thrust us toward the hallway.

Eva's face was blank. She watched us go but didn't speak. The door shut.

"That witness is a hot little number." Hollis led us toward the stairs. He spoke to me. "You get a taste of that?"

The beehived clerk with the cat's-eye glasses was walking by again. She gasped and stepped back.

"Dude, your face sure is messed up," Piper said. "If my dog looked like you, I'd shave his butt and teach him to walk backwards."

"A classy chick." Hollis chuckled.

He pushed us downstairs to a basement that smelled of mildew and damp paper. A hallway led to a secure room with cinder block walls and a bank of TV monitors hanging from the ceiling.

There were two iron doors, one we came in, the other leading to the holding area.

Another pair of Marshals and a county deputy were in the room. The deputy sat behind a desk.

Hollis nodded, and the deputy unlocked the entrance to the cells. We stepped inside, and the metal barrier clanged shut. A short hallway led to an open area with two holding pens.

This section of the courthouse, maybe half of the basement, had obviously not been designed as a jail. A walkway ran in front of a long row of bars that were at an odd angle to the exterior walls. Another set of bars ran perpendicular to the first, dividing the area into two large but uneven sections, each roughly the size of a large suburban living room. Both sides had several beds and what must have been a bathroom behind a closed door in the corner.

The unit on the right was smaller and appeared to be occupied. The bed was rumpled. Clothes and pizza boxes lay on the floor.

The one on the left was clearly vacant. Hollis opened the door on that side, and shoved us in. Then he locked it.

"Turn around." He held up handcuff keys.

We did, and he removed the bracelets.

This was not going as expected. No beat down. No romantic encounters with a cattle prod.

"Not your typical jail accommodations, is it?" Hollis said. "Your suite mate must be in the shower. Cleanest hood I've ever seen."

"Who?" I rubbed my wrist.

"Lazaro Morales. The guest of honor, so to speak."

"I want a lawyer." Piper grabbed the bars.

"Shut up." Hollis looked both ways. Then he smiled at me and touched his crooked face. "Our personal tally sheet isn't balanced yet. Business comes first."

The holding area was still empty, just like when we arrived seconds before.

"Here." He pulled a pistol from the small of his back and handed it to me, butt first.

I didn't touch it. A couple thousand tricks and bad scenarios played out in my mind.

"It's not gonna bite. Take it, willya?" He held up a ring. "And here's the key too."

"What are you doing?" I said.

"Morales has got a lot of good intel to offer up." Hollis looked around again, lowered his voice. "Let's just say I want to double-down on the fact that he lives until your witness testifies and we've got him by the short hairs."

"You think there's somebody out there who can take him out?" I said.

"The NSA reported unusual cell chatter at the crossing south of here." He shrugged. "That asswipe of an attorney upstairs is not in the loop on this either. Just you two and me."

"And you trust us?" I still had not taken the items offered. "You trust *me*?"

"And don't forget Keith McCluskey." Hollis ignored my statement. "He's got a lot of firepower at his disposal. If you're right and he's coming back here . . ." He rolled his eyes.

"Jon, let's not overanalyze," Piper said. "Take the gun and the keys."

"Listen to your partner. I have to trust you on this." Hollis shook his head.

I took the gun and keys.

"Besides, you're a damn sight more honest than your father."

"What the hell does that mean?"

"Oh, jeez." Piper sat on one of the beds, looked at Hollis. "Don't get him wound up on Dad."

"You haven't figured it out?" Hollis buttoned his coat. "Great. You're honest but dumb."

"What are you talking about?" I stuck the pistol in my waistband, covered by my shirt.

"Those drugs they found in your father's squad car."

I didn't say anything.

"They weren't planted," he said. "Your old man was in bed with the traffickers way back when."

- CHAPTER SIXTY-FOUR -

I stared at the floor in the makeshift jail cell, not really seeing. My mind churned—Frank Cantrell, my father—a cartel
employee?

Piper looked around. "This is nicer than the bedbug
sanctuary last night."

I didn't say anything.

"For what it's worth, I am sorry." She craned her head
like she was listening.

"Huh?" I frowned. "What do you mean?"

"About your old man. I'm sorry you had to hear that
about him."

I wanted to say something but had no words. Cartel
employee or not, the thought of my father, not of sound
mind, alone in the vastness of Texas, filled me with dread.

"He seems like a nice guy," she said. "And he tried to be
a good father, didn't he?"

Around the corner of the hallway came the sound of a
door clanging shut as Hollis left.

I didn't say anything.

"You turned out more or less okay," she said. "That says
something about him as a person, right?"

I was in a jail cell in West Texas. Dead broke, wanted for half a dozen felonies. Trending toward "less okay" at the moment.

"Let's get out of here." She pointed to the door.

"What are you talking about?" I rubbed a finger over the teeth of the key Hollis had given me.

"We're not gonna get paid," she said. "Plus, they're probably going to stick us with all the crimes that went down on the trip out here."

I stared at her, tried to make sense of her words. Fatigue settled over me like depression at an old folks' home.

A row of squat windows, secured from the exterior by bars, lined the top of the far wall. They were about shoulder high in relation to the basement floor but appeared to be at ground level with the outside.

"The suit with the screwed-up mouth gave us a present." Piper grasped my arm, pulled me close. "Let's use it. Get out of here while the US Attorney's still sorting things out."

"W-w-where would we go?" I looked at the key.

"*We* wouldn't go anywhere," she said. "We would get out of here with that key, and then *me* would hit the road."

"I don't understand."

"At the motel this morning. I was looking in the window when you kissed Eva."

The blood drained from my face. She nodded knowingly.

"You don't understand." I shook my head. "She kissed me—"

Noise from the other cell.

The door in the corner opened and Lazaro Morales appeared, sauntering out like a hustler entering a pool hall, his presence filling the room with an undercurrent of energy that was hard to define. It certainly wasn't his clothes. He was dressed like a border town street thug—black jeans, red Puma sneakers, and a yellow polo shirt with oversized numerals on each sleeve.

"Look at what we got here. A lady to keep me company." Morales strolled across the room, eyes on Piper. "*Tu eres muy bonita.*"

Piper crossed her arms.

"I know a place in Acapulco." He slipped his hands through the bars between our cells, forearms on the cross beam. "Overlooks the cliffs. The best *ceviche* in the world."

He had a face designed by Michelangelo, but inspired by Clooney and Depp. Smooth, dimpled cheeks, chiseled chin, wavy black hair. Long silky lashes over eyes that were the color of smoke except when the light hit them at a certain angle. Then they were black like midnight in winter.

"Your boyfriend looks like a cop," Morales said. "Why does a *señorita bonita* like you hang with somebody like that?"

In the space of a few seconds, the new arrival had filled the basement with confidence and charisma. Not hard to see how he'd risen in the ranks of the cartel. Or how a naive party girl like Eva had fallen for him. If circumstances had played out a little differently, he could have been a politician or a CEO of a Fortune 500 company.

"What's your name, cop?" He pointed a finger at me. "Why you locked up?"

I ignored his questions. "How did they catch you?"

"A traitor." He sucked at a tooth, lip curling. "To be dealt with at a later date, you can bet on that."

Piper cleared her throat. "You, uh, seem awful sure you're getting out of here."

"A voice like an angel to match the body. You and me, we could have a good time." Morales laced his fingers together, flexed the knuckles. "Tell me this, angel. You ever seen a billion dollars in cash?"

Piper didn't reply.

"That much money takes up this whole room." He paused. "Now guess how many rooms I've got, angel?"

From outside, the sound of car doors slamming. Lots of them, very loud like the occupants were in a hurry. Piper and I looked at each other but didn't speak. New arrivals didn't bode well for any of us. Our suite mate didn't seem to notice.

"You're the prize," I said. "I wouldn't count on taking a walk."

More doors slammed. Shouts.

I strode to the window, fearful now. Piper stayed by the cell door.

"It's been arranged already, *comprendes*?" Morales stepped from the bars, yawned and stretched. "Guy from Washington came down and everything."

"Washington, DC?" I stopped at the window. "Talking to you?"

"The family's going to get some new leadership at the top after I get out." He ran a hand through his hair, preening. "Diego *me prometió*." He spoke the last under his breath, a wave of hostility rolling off each syllable. He was angry and had let something slip. Diego, whoever that was, had made him a promise.

"Who is Diego?" I said. "Is he the leader of the cartel?"

"*Cállate la boca*." Morales pointed a finger at me. "Fucking narc. I know your type. I'm not talking to you."

He'd just told me to shut up; I'd hit a nerve. His face had contorted with anger.

"What if you don't get out?" Piper said. "What if they convict you?"

"They need a witness." He smiled, recovered his easy manner. "And they ain't got one."

Piper started to speak but I held up my hand.

"Listen to me. This is important," I said. "We're trying to keep you alive."

He stared at me, not understanding.

"Who did you meet with from DC?" I couldn't say why this was important. I had no way to know what his answer would tell me. There was an unseen layer to everything, and I wondered if this might be only the part that was visible— somebody from Washington.

"My English, it's not so good." He held his hands out, palms up. "I'm just a businessman. The gringos arrested me for no reason."

More noise from the town square.

I stared outside, the angle of view awkward due to the basement elevation of the window.

A Chevy dealership's worth of white Tahoes was in the parking area. A dozen or so men in blue windbreakers were clustered around the Porsche we'd been driving. Each man carried a submachine gun. One of them was Keith McCluskey.

"They're here." I took several deep breaths.

"Who?" Morales plopped down on his bed, stretched out. Not a care in the world.

"Is it the team that was after the witness?" Piper dashed to the window, peered out. "Ooh, crap. Looks like it is."

"What witness?" Morales sat up. Maybe a slight care now.

"The one we brought here to testify against you," I said.

Morales stood.

One of the US Marshals guarding the courthouse walked across the lawn toward the squad of DEA contractors.

"This is not good," Piper said. "They're everywhere."

"They start shooting, we need to be away from the windows." I pulled out the gun Hollis had given me. "Maybe that interior room."

Morales stared at the weapon. "I'll give you a million dollars for that."

I glanced at him. "You got it on you right now?"

"Hey, I'm good for it." He slicked back his hair with one hand. "How come you got a gun anyway?"

"A guy upstairs asked us to keep you alive until the trial." I fished out the key to our door.

"Never happen." He shook his head, paused. "Who's this witness, huh?"

"It just got more complicated." Piper, still peering outside, tapped my shoulder. "There's another crew coming in."

The *pop-pop-pop* of gunfire. Yelling.

"I think they're from Mexico." She turned to me. "The clothes, the weapons."

I dropped the keys, swore. Looked back outside.

Two crews of gunmen.

Keith McCluskey's DEA agents and a squad of heavily armed Hispanic men. The DEA agents were clearly not expecting trouble. They were trying to snatch the witness because their boss was in love. They would use badges and intimidation, followed by violence. But even rogue contractors wouldn't kill indiscriminately in a courthouse square.

The crew from Mexico was different. They didn't care about badges or casualties. Violence was their default option. Plus they were here for something else, and it didn't take a lot of expertise in the ways of narcotraffickers to figure out what that was. They were here to stop any potential leaks in the organization—that is, the accused, Lazaro Morales, and the witness, Eva Ramirez. They were a hit squad, *sicarios*. A safe bet: they were Diego's men, whoever he was.

"That's not possible." Morales ran to his window. "They wouldn't come this far across the river. They . . ." His voice trailed off.

I picked up the key, dashed across the room, and jammed it into the lock on our cell door. From the inside, the action was difficult due to the angle.

"Five million dollars for the gun." Morales scampered to the bars that separated us, reached for me. "Okay, ten million."

Piper rushed beside me. "Hurry it up, willya."

"I'm good for the money." Morales clawed at my shirt. "Please."

I finally opened the door and stepped into the hall.

More gunfire from outside. One of the basement windows shattered.

"What about Mister Slimeball?" Piper pointed to the other cell. "We can't just leave him here."

"The chica's right." Lazaro nodded. "A stray bullet could kill me."

"Give me your belt." I aimed at him.

He hesitated and then pulled off his braided leather belt.

I tossed Piper the key. "Open his door."

She did as instructed.

"Hands on your head. Walk out very slowly."

Lazaro placed his palms on the top of his scalp and shuffled into the hall.

I threw him against the far wall, bound his hands with the belt.

"The interior room where the deputy was," I said. "That's the most secure place."

"It's gonna be crowded." Piper shoved the prisoner down the hall. "Those US Marshals, Hollis, Eva."

"Eva?" Morales said. "Eva who?"

"Your wife," I said, "Eva Ramirez, that's who."

"She's here?" Morales had a stunned look on his face.

"Yep." Piper nodded. "And boy is she gonna be pissed when I tell her you asked me out on a date."

- CHAPTER SIXTY-FIVE -

We ran away from the cells and the gunfire, Lazaro Morales between us, and slid to a stop at the entrance to the holding area. The iron barrier was closed, locked from the other side.

"Officer needs assistance." I banged on the metal with the barrel of the gun and then stuck it in my waistband. "Hurry it up."

The door swung inward, and the Presidio County deputy who'd earlier been sitting at the desk in the basement room stood in the entryway, weapon drawn.

"How did you get out of your cell?" He aimed at me. "We're under attack. Courthouse is in lockdown."

"We're undercover DEA agents," I said. "What's your contingency plan for something like this?"

"You're supposed to be in custody." He began to shake, the muzzle of his gun wobbling. He looked at Morales. "And he's the guy on trial. H–he can't be out of his cell."

Despite the training required to be an accredited Texas law enforcement officer, not to mention the FBI briefings and Homeland Security seminars, the current situation was clearly outside the realm of his experience or ability to react to properly.

"There's a crew from Mexico outside." I pointed to the bank of monitors on the wall above his desk. "The cells here were never designed to be cells. They're exposed to gunfire."

"W-w-what should we do?"

"We need to make this room as airtight as possible." Piper pointed to the interior chamber where the deputy had been.

"I already called the sheriff." He lowered his gun. "We've never had anything like this happen around here."

One of the screens flared white and then went dark. I pushed our way in, dragging Morales along.

"Unless the sheriff's got a platoon of Green Berets, he's not gonna be much help." I pulled my weapon out. "How many access points are there to this floor?"

Before he could answer, across the room the door leading to upstairs flew open and the US Attorney stepped into the basement, dragging Eva with him. Hollis entered right behind them.

Eva gasped, covered her mouth. She stared at her husband.

"Eva?" Morales said. *"Estás aquí?"*

"What the hell's going on?" The US Attorney aimed the gold-plated Colt at me. "Drop that gun."

"No." I pointed the muzzle at his face.

"Where the hell did you get a pistol?" the attorney said.

"I gave it to him," Hollis said. "Now everybody needs to be calm. There's backup on the way."

"You gave a prisoner a pistol?" The US Attorney sounded incredulous. He lowered the Colt, stared at Hollis.

"How bad is it up top?" I nodded at the monitors. "How many are there?"

A rattle of automatic gunfire sounded, muffled but close.

The deputy kicked the door leading upstairs shut, bolted the lock.

"It's a shitstorm is how bad it is." Hollis pulled out a pistol.

"How many?" I asked.

"Don't know, maybe thirty total." Hollis wiped sweat from his upper lip. "Looks like McCluskey and some of his guys are mixing it up with a squad of cartel shooters."

"*Your* guys," I said. "McCluskey's people are Paynelowe employees. Same as you."

Hollis didn't reply.

"Contractors. What a mess." The US Attorney holstered the Colt. "You guys are nothing but trouble."

Eva slumped against the wall. "They're going to kill us all."

"Not without a fight," I said.

"Eva, I missed you, baby." Morales smiled at her. "Been so long since we've seen each other."

"Shut up, Lazaro." She sneered at her husband. "This is all your fault."

"Please, baby, help me." He struggled against the restraints on his hands.

"You're a field operative." Hollis looked at me. "What's our best move at this point?"

"This is the most secure room," I said. "We stay here until reinforcements arrive."

"Oh, that's just dandy." The attorney shook his head. "More Paynelowe contractors, that's our reinforcements."

"They're legitimate," Hollis said. "No rogue operators."

"Whatever." The US Attorney rolled his eyes.

"Enough talk," I said. "How much firepower do we have access to down here?"

"There's some shotguns and a couple of pistols in the cabinet." The deputy pointed to a metal storage locker behind the desk, a push-button combination dial on the front.

An explosion, like a grenade, from outside.

"She needs a weapon." I pointed to Piper. "This is gonna get worse before it gets better."

"Yeah." Hollis nodded. "Give her a shotgun."

The deputy scampered to the locker and punched in a series of numbers. He opened the door, tossed a black Remington to Piper.

"What about me?" Eva said. "I want a gun, too."

"Yes, me too." Morales moved across the room.

"Shut up." I shoved the drug smuggler away. "Sit in the corner and be quiet."

"They're here to kill me," he said. "And you have me tied up."

"No weapon for the guy on trial." The US Attorney accepted a shotgun from the deputy. He jacked a round into the chamber.

"What about my wife? They're going to kill her as well." Morales paused. "I thought Americans were fair. No gun, that's not fair."

"He's right. They will try to kill me, too." Eva grasped my arm. "I need a gun."

"Give me the Colt." I pointed to the gold pistol on the US Attorney's hip.

He hesitated and then handed it over.

Eva did need a piece. The more firepower we had, the better.

"Don't do it," Piper said. "Don't give a gun to her."

I held it out.

"Thank you." Eva reached for the weapon. "I must be able to defend myself."

"Follow the rules on this one, Jon." Piper's voice was frantic. "We have enough firepower down here to hold them off if we secure the doors."

Lazaro Morales smiled, and I realized nothing was as it seemed.

I pulled the gun back.

But not fast enough.

Eva grabbed it and smiled.

The pistol was a .38 Super, basically a turbocharged nine-millimeter, the preferred cartridge for Mexican criminals since it was illegal for citizens of that country to own weapons chambered for military rounds.

The sound of the report was horrendous in the narrow confines of the basement room, the explosion echoing against the cinder block walls.

The US Attorney's head snapped back as the bullet penetrated the soft spot just below his cheekbone.

Lazaro Morales jumped to his feet, grinning.

Eva fired twice more. Twin licks of flame. The blasts, softer this time.

Hollis fell to the ground as the deputy sprung a leak and a red stream jetted from his chest.

"Kill him." Lazaro Morales nodded to me.

Everything was in slow motion, languid. My vision tunneled. My muscles seemed disconnected from my bones, working at odds with each other.

I raised the shotgun. The barrel moved like it was underwater, sluggish.

Next to me, Piper shouted, her words indistinct, muffled by cotton.

Eons of time passed, a thousand tiny years between life and death. I kept raising the gun, millimeter by millimeter. Piper was faster, a bolt of lightning in comparison. She had her shotgun about halfway up.

Eva fired, muzzle aimed at my partner.

Boom. Noise was loud again.

Piper fell.

"NOOO." I yanked my weapon toward Eva. Slapped the trigger.

Nothing. I struggled for the safety.

From a long way off, down an empty, dark tunnel, the barrel of Eva's gun came toward my head. I tried to move but couldn't. The sense of powerlessness was total.

Then, nothing but red and a strange smell of melted candles in a distant room.

I blinked away blood. Sounds were returning to normal. My skull ached. I was on the floor, face up.

Eva stood next to me, holding a cell phone in front of my face.

"The girl at the first place we stopped. The one who fought with me over the meth," she said. "I took this from her."

I groaned. Couldn't move. Stomach nauseous. Head dizzy.

The Alamo Service Station. We had neglected to search Eva after her encounter with the goth woman in the Whataburger uniform.

"I organized the attack with our people outside." She knelt, stroked my face. "I'm sorry things couldn't have been different."

My voice returned. "P-p-piper. Y-y-you killed Piper."

"You did love her." Eva nodded. "Just as I suspected."

Lazaro Morales appeared behind his wife. His hands were free.

"*Vámanos.*" He touched her shoulder.

"Goodbye, Jon." She stood. "You're a nice man. I'm not going to kill you."

"*P-p-piper.*" I blinked, tried to stop the double vision.

"No." Morales wagged a finger. "Kill him. You must."

Eva hesitated. She raised the gold-plated gun and stared at me down the barrel. Sadness filled her eyes.

"Noooo." I held up a hand as if it would stop a bullet.

She nodded. "*Sí.*"

Then she turned, jammed the muzzle against her husband's chest, and pulled the trigger.

I didn't remember anything after that.

PART IV

"It is with the utmost humility that I accept my party's nomination for president. The time has come for this nation to reclaim her compassion, for the labels which separate us to disappear. . . . Yes, that's correct. I accept in the name of all peace-loving peoples in the Americas. Now is the moment for every person in this hemisphere who loves freedom to come together in a spirit of unity and harmony, and for each of us to reach for the shining star of opportunity that is our collective destiny."

   —US Senator Stephen McNally,
     party convention, July 2012

McNally Leads by Eight Points — New polls indicate the charismatic and increasingly moderate US Senator Stephen McNally has an apparently insurmountable lead over his opponent. Establishing what amounts to a coalition of voters, members of the left and right wings of both parties have embraced McNally's message of hope and economic prosperity.

   —The Associated Press, August 2012

- CHAPTER SIXTY-SIX -

Paynelowe flew in style.

Their bird, a Gulfstream V, had plush leather seats, dark lacquered wood trim, and hunter green carpet embroidered with the company's logo, a bloody claw superimposed over a pair of crossed swords.

Piper and I sat in the rear in overstuffed swivel chairs. I had a bandage on my temple from where Eva Ramirez had struck me with the gold-plated Colt.

The bullet Eva had fired at Piper had hit the breech of the latter's shotgun and split apart, copper-clad shards of lead splintering off, slicing several furrows along Piper's right hand and arm, which had been holding the weapon.

These wounds were minor and had been bandaged by a Paynelowe medical team who had arrived at the courthouse within a few minutes after the gun battle ended.

The flight attendant on the Gulfstream was about twenty-five and looked like she could have been an alternate on the Norwegian bikini team. She wore a skirt that came to midthigh, a matching blouse, and a push-up bra.

It was about four on the afternoon of the attack, and we were airborne.

She served us a late lunch: herb-crusted salmon, aspar-
agus in a balsamic vinaigrette sauce, and rosemary-roasted
new potatoes. All washed down with a nice Sauvignon Blanc
and mineral water. Piper, grumpy from being shot, called her
a sky whore, so we didn't get any coffee, which would have
been nice.

My father was still missing in the badlands of West Texas,
at least according to the people who had transported us to the
airport.

Lazaro Morales, the number two man in one of the most
powerful criminal organizations in the western hemisphere,
had died, taking with him the secrets he possessed about the
inner workings of the cartel as well as any chance of nabbing
the leader.

His wife, Eva Ramirez, had disappeared along with the
survivors of a crew of heavily armed men who had arrived
from Mexico that morning at the town of Presidio, the only
crossing point in the five-hundred-mile stretch of territory
between El Paso and Piedras Negras. Presidio was lightly
guarded by the Border Patrol and accessible to the rest of
Texas only by a two-lane highway that ran north to Marfa.
A straight shot in and out.

Eva's boyfriend, Keith McCluskey, a corrupt, drug-
addicted DEA contractor, had disappeared as well and was
presumed dead. The remnants of his rogue band of Paynelowe
operatives had surrendered to Hollis's group of slightly more
legitimate law enforcement contractors.

The US Attorney for the West Texas region was dead, as
were three US Marshals, a county deputy, four Paynelowe
contractors, and a half dozen Mexican nationals. The
wounded had been airlifted to Midland and El Paso, the
locations of the closest trauma centers.

About an hour ago, the plane had picked us up at the

Marfa airport for the flight back to Dallas Love Field, where our arraignment for various and sundry crimes awaited.

Obviously, the easy cleanup for this entire mess would be for Piper and me to disappear down a hole somewhere. No chance then for us to tell our side of the story.

But with a body count this high, stretching across the breadth of Texas, the national media had jumped on the story like a hobo on a ham sandwich, meaning the smart move for everybody concerned (except us) was to find a scapegoat suitable for sacrifice.

The collateral carnage was staggering. Eva Ramirez's sister. The firefight at the Cheyenne Apartments back in Dallas. God knows how many in the badlands of West Texas.

I wiped my mouth on a linen napkin, stifled a belch. The salmon had been excellent. My appetite had been surprising, given the physical and emotional turmoil of the past few hours.

"So Eva Ramirez was a shooter," I said. "Sent to take out her husband."

Hollis, ribs bruised from the round that had hit his bulletproof vest, had explained earlier. As a witness, Eva would be lightly guarded yet in the same courthouse and holding area as her husband. That way she could either take him out herself, a pretty big undertaking, or, more likely, coordinate an attack from the outside.

Hollis nodded.

"They were gonna bring people across the Rio Grande." I shook my head. "To attack a federal court?"

"They did just that. And what about the shooters in that little town, Schwarzemann?" He paused. "These are dangerous times. That's why our contract is going to be bigger next year."

The pilot's voice sounded over the speaker, telling us to buckle our seat belts.

"His own wife," Piper said. "Wonder what leverage they used to get her to play ball."

"Fucking animals." Hollis shook his head. "They'll use anybody."

Piper made a huffing noise, drained her wineglass.

"You were gonna let a baby with burned legs scream in agony," I said to Hollis. "Don't go high-and-mighty on me."

The flight attendant took our trays.

"And you work as a DEA agent," he said. "But you still don't understand the realities of the War on Drugs."

I didn't reply.

"Riddle me this." Piper looked at Hollis. "How did you jerkoffs let a cokehead like McCluskey have access to all those guns and personnel?"

"That policy is under rev—"

"I wasn't finished." Piper pointed a finger at his face. "And then let the cokehead fly around the state in a freaking Chinook helicopter?"

Hollis shook his head but didn't speak. He bit a lip and looked out the window as the green-brown mass of Central Texas slid by.

I closed my eyes. The food and wine had made me sleepy, which was the point. Get me to lower my guard. Then I remembered the exploding highway and my father who was still missing. I opened my eyes, guard not lowered even a little bit.

The interior of the plane was silent except for the drone of the engines.

"You both spent a period of time alone with two cartel members." Hollis continued to stare out the window. "We're going to want to know everything they told you."

The Gulfstream banked to one side and began its descent.

"Morales," Piper said. "How did you snag him?"

"A lucky break. One of his guys blabbed when he crossed at Presidio to see a girlfriend." Hollis looked at her. "The Texas Rangers arrested him."

"And Eva," Piper said. "How did she end up being a witness?"

"She came to us. Dropped in out of the blue in San Antonio. Kept talking about how she wanted to get out of the life."

"She played you," I said.

"Like a cheap guitar." Hollis nodded. "We didn't know about her relationship with McCluskey either. Turns out he was trying to arrange a new identity for her using Paynelowe resources."

Piper chuckled.

"Did he really bust her with a kilo of coke?" I asked.

"Probably," Hollis said. "But he was operating independently so we don't know for sure."

"She took out all those shooters at the hotel." I shook my head. "A stone-cold killer."

"Not surprising. The best intel we've got at the moment indicates they were with a rival cartel," Hollis said. "And their bosses had a shoot-on-sight order out for her head."

"I don't understand," Piper said.

"The other cartel didn't want Morales to start talking about them. Which he might have done if she'd testified against him."

"But Morales's boss, Diego somebody," I said. "He sent her to kill Morales."

Hollis shook his head. "*El jefe*'s name is not Diego. It's some hard-to-pronounce Indian name. Guy goes by el Camello, the Camel, of all things. They love the shit out of the animals down there."

"Camel, donkey, whatever." I sighed. "The boss man

wanted her to take out Morales so he wouldn't testify. Seems like the other cartels would want the same thing—"

"The others cartels didn't know what she was up to." Hollis shrugged. "She was deep undercover, not unlike the way we do agents sometimes."

I didn't say anything.

"Apparently, McCluskey misappropriated some Paynelowe funds," Hollis said. "He had this big plan to run away with Eva and live happily ever after."

"Another round of parties," Piper said. "Eva would have liked that."

"Where are you taking us when we land?" I asked.

"Dallas County Jail." Hollis tightened his seat belt. "Sucks to be you, doesn't it?"

The angle of the descent increased. The smoggy silhouette of the Dallas skyline was now visible. Reunion Tower and the massive white arches of the new bridge across the Trinity River.

The plane circled; the engine noise grew louder. Hollis leaned forward, motioned us closer.

"The scanner you used," he said. "We need it back."

I shrugged.

"Retrieving that device is an action item at the next NSA department head meeting."

"What the hell does that mean?"

"That means it's beyond serious."

"We don't have it," Piper said.

"My boss lied to the NSA. Told them Paynelowe had already recovered the scanner." Hollis rubbed his eyes. "And the NSA went ahead with the software update."

"Oops-a-daisy." Piper raised her eyebrows. "Now tell me what you're talking about."

He explained briefly. The software update meant the scanners could read the tags on auto batteries as well as the magnetic strips on the driver's licenses in all fifty states. All of which could then be tied to every criminal and civil database in the country.

I tried to fathom the enormity of what that meant. A single agent in the field could point a scanner at an individual and learn everything about that person with the push of a button.

"We'll get it from you." He buttoned his coat. "One way or the other."

The whine of the engines changed pitch. The tarmac rushed closer.

"A couple of ex-cops." Hollis chuckled. "Hope they don't leave you in general population very long."

- CHAPTER SIXTY-SEVEN -

We landed without incident and taxied to a restricted hangar on the west side of the airport. The Gulfstream cut through a line of Southwest Airlines planes, the orange-and-blue Boeings likely filled with daily commuters heading home to San Antonio or Houston.

As the door of the Gulfstream opened and a wave of steamy air rushed inside, two guards from the forward area of the plane cuffed our hands in front and linked the restraints to chains around our waists. Then they led us out, one in front, the second behind.

Hollis brought up the rear, lugging a duffel bag full of our personal effects: wallets, cell phones, badges, and the two Reaper rifles we'd been carrying. The bag was sealed with a yellow evidence tag.

A dozen or more men in navy blue utility pants and matching shirts stood guard on the tarmac. They carried MP5 submachine guns and wore vests with yellow stenciled signs Velcroed on the back that read DEA AGENT.

Six or eight Dallas police cars were parked in a loose semicircle around the area between the plane's door and a large white panel van. The van had blue government license plates, metal lattice over the rear windows, and oversized run-flat tires bulging from the wheel wells.

One of the outside guards opened the rear doors of the vehicle.

Hollis came around from behind us and tossed the duffel bag inside. Then he waited.

The guard by the door of the van and two of his colleagues hopped in after the bag as the pair of agents from the plane led us over, a short trip of about twenty yards.

"We're not gonna do very well in jail," Piper said as she walked beside me.

"No. I don't suppose we will." I scanned the surroundings.

Nothing but uniforms and official vehicles. Zero options. The chains that bound me rattled as I walked.

At the rear of the van, the guards stopped by Hollis. He ignored Piper and held a tri-folded piece of paper in front of my face.

"You know what this is?" he said.

A jet took off, screamed across the sky above us. After it passed, I shook my head.

"It's a brochure for a company that makes a do-it-yourself Lucite paperweight kit."

I didn't say anything.

"When this is all finished and we get the scanner back," he touched the off-kilter part of his jaw, "I'm gonna take your balls and make a paperweight out of them."

I kept my face impassive, didn't react.

"Just to be clear," he said. "I am not speaking metaphorically." He snapped his fingers at the guards. "Load 'em up."

The two agents from the plane shoved us inside and slammed the door shut as we lay on the floor.

The interior of the van was all metal. Bench seats ran along either side. The three new guards sat at the far end and made no move to secure our restraints to the D-rings attached to the seats, as was standard protocol.

A video camera was mounted in the corner, allowing the driver and anybody riding shotgun to see what was going on.

"Gonna be a rough ride today." Guard One pulled on a pair of heavy leather gloves.

The van pulled away from the plane, accelerated, rocking a little.

"Expect lots of turbulence." Guard Two slid a blackjack from his rear pocket.

The van turned. Piper and I, still on the bare metal floor, rolled to one side.

The guards held on to the canvas straps hanging from the ceiling as the van shimmied over a rough spot and then sped up. I couldn't see out but figured we were on Denton Drive, the western boundary of the airport. The street led south toward Interstate 35, which in turn was a straight shot to the county jail. All in, maybe a ten-minute ride. Ten *long* minutes.

Guard One staggered toward us, smacking a fist into his palm. Then he fell over, landing with a painful-sounding thud on one of the bench seats as the vehicle took a sharp turn to the right.

The van sped over a bumpy road, rocking on its heavy shocks and safe-but-uncomfortable tires. Piper and I bounced and rolled, along with Guard One. The other two held on and tried to stay upright.

A voice blared on a speaker: "This is the driver. We've got a mechanical situation. Need to stop. I've called for backup."

"What the hell?" Guard One managed to stand as the van rattled to a halt.

The voice on the speaker: "We're gonna secure the cargo area. Wait for another transport." From the front came the sound of a door slamming.

The three guards looked at each other, obviously confused.

Piper and I managed to sit up, cross-legged on the floor of the van.

The rear doors swung open and a figure in a blue uniform and DEA ball cap stood backlit by the afternoon sun.

"Oy vey. What's going on here? Everything okay?"

Milo Miller stepped inside, tilting the ball cap a little to one side. "A new van is about five minutes away."

Our friend, the mobster and occasional government contractor, had trimmed his beard, cut off the curly sideburns.

"What the hell's going on?" Guard One said. "The rear door's supposed to stay locked no matter what."

"Change of plans." Milo shot him in the crotch with a Taser.

The guard's toes extended so hard and fast that his head hit the metal ceiling. His back arched like he was possessed, eyes wide and bulging. Then he fell to the floor and screamed.

Milo dropped the Taser and pulled two more from his belt like a cowboy gunfighter. He zapped the remaining guards before they could react.

They dropped and flopped. Moaned, twitched.

"Let's go." Milo jerked a thumb toward the outside.

Piper and I hopped to the street. Milo pulled a key ring from his pocket and unlocked our restraints as a gray Honda minivan pulled up behind the prisoner transport.

The neighborhood immediately west of Love Field was airport barrio, full of tiny, wood-framed houses on narrow overgrown lots. Virtually everybody who lived in the area was Latino, first-generation immigrants working two jobs until they could get enough cash together to move to a better, less noisy part of Dallas.

Late Thursday afternoon, and it was beer-thirty. A small

crowd of people had gathered on either side of the street to see what was going on. Several of the men were drinking cans of Bud Light, bottles of Schlitz. A lowrider Chevy had its doors open, Mexican rap music blaring.

"How did you swing this?" I rubbed my wrists.

"I specialize in the transportation of prisoners," he said. "A contractor, remember?"

"But they're gonna tie this to you." Piper leaned in and retrieved the duffel bag full of our stuff.

"Does that mean you care, my love? Be still my heart." Milo clutched his chest. "Not to worry. I sold the business this morning to a competitor whom I detest."

A guy in civilian clothes hopped out of the driver's seat of the Honda. He tossed a small satchel to Milo and said, "We need to hurry."

"Jon, you and my future ex-wife should get in the other van now." Milo opened the bag.

"What're you going to do with the guards?" I said.

"Disarm them." Milo pulled out a small piece of cloth with the words ICE AGENT on one side and Velcro on the other.

Immigration and Customs Enforcement.

"Then I'll switch these out with the ones that say DEA."

"Sweet." Piper nodded.

"Let's go." I picked up the duffel bag and trotted to the Honda.

Piper and I got in the back. The driver hopped behind the wheel and pulled even with the white van.

Milo emerged from the rear and went to the side of the vehicle that had been our previous transportation. He tugged on a corner of the white panel, working on a tiny irregular spot. A few seconds later, he pulled a thin sheet of white plastic off, displaying a crude set of black letters: WETBACK

COLLECTION VEHICLE. DEP'T OF IMMIGRATION.

He jumped into the passenger seat of our current vehicle and tapped the driver on the shoulder. "Move it."

The crowd was growing larger. Several people pointed at the white van, angry looks on their faces.

The driver sped away.

"Ten, maybe fifteen minutes," Milo said. "Won't be nothing left but a greasy spot."

"What about the guards?" I asked.

Milo shrugged. "Left a cell phone with one."

"Thanks." Piper buckled her belt. "You saved our bacon."

"I heard the scuttlebutt, a big, top-secret transport from West Texas," he said. "After a few calls, it didn't take much to figure out who the cargo was."

Piper opened the duffel bag and removed our stuff. She placed the rifles on the floor and handed me my wallet and the cell phone I'd been using.

"Phil DeGroot," I said. "Did you send some people to the address I texted you?"

Seemed like a million years ago when I had asked to Milo to run some heavyweights over to the address where Phil wanted me to bring the witness. The entire trip to Marfa had been based on my guess that Phil was being coerced at that time. Was I right?

"He was there with his wife." Milo nodded. "Not in great shape though. Their captor was not a good person."

"Sinclair," Piper said. "That's who it had to be."

We drove without speaking for a few blocks. Milo asked a couple of questions, tried to make small talk. Piper and I ignored him, focused our stony silence on each other.

With our sudden rescue came a moment of reflection, the luxury to acknowledge the juncture of our relationship. Piper had seen Eva kiss me. I'd pointed out the kiss as something Eva initiated, which was true. But the whole truth was more complicated than that, as it usually was. I had not turned Eva away.

"The witness was really a shooter." I looked at Milo. "She killed Lazaro Morales." A pause. "Who was also her husband."

Milo didn't reply. He pursed his lips.

The driver turned on Mockingbird Lane, a major east-west thoroughfare in the city. He headed west toward the highway. The street was lined with stuff that was usually near an airport: fast-food restaurants, discount strip centers, low-rent office buildings.

I tried to imagine where my dad might be at the moment. I needed a way to find him, quickly and quietly. No ideas came to mind.

We passed between an adult bookstore and an indoor shooting range that advertised guns by the hour.

"Where do you want to go?" Milo asked. "Your wish is my command."

I told him about my father. He nodded and frowned, muttered to himself.

"Some police associates of mine." He pulled out a cell phone. "Very discreet inquiries could be made, see if he's turned up anywhere."

After brief moment of hesitation, I nodded.

"Which direction do you think he went?" Milo entered a text message.

"Don't know." I shook my head. "If he made it to the interstate and was lucid, he could be anywhere by now. Back in Dallas. California. Halfway to Canada."

"Perhaps we shall get lucky, yes." Milo sent the message.

We drove in silence for a few blocks.

"Where's the scanner?" Piper spoke to me directly for the first time in a while.

In one sense, the scanner was the cause of all our recent troubles. Sinclair had given us the device on Sunday night when we'd retrieved his cousin from the Korean whorehouse. Despite his warnings not to, we'd used the scanner the next day, which brought Keith McCluskey and Paynelowe down on us like a swarm of angry locusts.

"Scanner?" Milo said. "What are you talking about, my love?"

"Something Paynelowe is very eager to get back." I buckled my seat belt. "Hopefully it's safe."

"You hid it somewhere." Piper shifted in her seat. "Right?"

The tool shed on the rented piece of property where my sister and father lived. Where my father *had* lived.

Before I could answer, her cell phone rang.

Nobody spoke.

"A call you are expecting?" Milo said.

Piper looked at the screen. "I hired a PI to track down my mother. That's the only person who has this number."

"You gave her the number for the untrackable phone?" I shook my head.

"She's cool, not part of any of this." Piper's voice was shrill. "And if we're gonna point fingers, maybe we can talk about you giving Eva the gun."

"The witness?" Milo looked at me. "You gave her a gun?"

I started to say something but the phone kept ringing.

"Jonathan, we'll get back to you in a moment." Milo turned to Piper. "Aren't you going to answer?"

Piper stared at me and pressed the Talk button.

"Hello?" she said. "Is that you, Imogene?"

- CHAPTER SIXTY-EIGHT -

I glared at the streets of Dallas, seething, until we arrived at our destination. I didn't speak.

Milo Miller's safe house was in South Dallas, in a transitional neighborhood near a tiny but vibrant nightlife and retail area known as the Bishop Arts District. The blocks of modest brick bungalows and prairie-style homes used to be run-down, full of gangbangers, welfare cheats, and outlaw bikers. Now many of the homes had been rehabbed, occupied by writers trying to create the next Great American Something, and same-sex couples who worked north of the Trinity River but lived in the southern sector because of the cheap housing and general funkiness of the area.

Milo's place was down the street from a brewpub and a white-tablecloth, thirty-dollar-an-entree restaurant that specialized in upscale home cooking.

Six o'clock on a summer Thursday. Milo's driver pulled down the gravel driveway of the safe house, a brick home that was not fixed up but not run-down either. He parked in the detached garage behind the house. Milo directed us to the rear door, which opened into a kitchen that had been remodeled for utilitarian purposes, not as a feature for a magazine.

Double ovens and refrigerators, a deep freeze big enough to store a moose, and open shelving that displayed enough non-perishable food items—pasta, rice and beans, canned soups—to feed a platoon for a week.

Three bedrooms, each outfitted with three sets of bunk beds, closets stocked with clothes in various sizes, toiletries, and medical supplies.

Milo's phone rang, a call from his police contact; no word on my father, but they would keep looking, discreetly of course. Milo sent the driver away and tossed me the keys to the van.

"The Honda's clean," he said. "Even has an old battery without one of those tags."

Piper was sitting on the sofa, cradling in her hand the disposable cell phone that had rung. In the van, she'd told Imogene that she would have to call her back.

I grabbed a bottle of water from the kitchen and strode into the living room where I paced, drinking in little sips, hoping it would cool my anger.

"What's your plan?" Milo sat next to Piper, looked at me.

I didn't reply.

Piper put the phone on the coffee table.

"By now, there will be an APB out." Milo sighed. "Treat as armed and dangerous."

I nodded.

"Sinclair," he said. "So much trouble he's caused."

I shrugged.

Piper crossed her arms. "Aren't you gonna say something?"

I didn't reply.

A long silence ensued. Milo laced his fingers in his lap and watched our relationship enter its final, most poisonous phase.

"Ten years ago." Piper broke the stalemate. "I got into

the orphanage's files. Just for a quick look-see. Found out my mother's name was Mary. She'd be about fifty-eight now."

I finished the bottle of water.

"Imogene told me she had a lead." Piper leaned forward, elbows on her knees. "On a woman named Mary, the right age and everything."

I spoke for the first time since entering the safe house. "Where did you find Imogene?"

Piper didn't reply. She averted her gaze, bit a lip.

"You're not going to answer him?" Milo said.

Piper looked back at me. "Sinclair. He gave me Imogene's name."

"Oy vey." Milo rubbed his eyebrows.

"A couple of weeks ago," she said. "He called our number at the Cheyenne and we started talking."

"And you asked for a good PI," I said. "And the result is he's been able to track us through her."

"You don't understand." Piper shook her head. "She hates Sinclair like everybody else. No way she'd talk to him about us."

"But somehow he still managed to find out where we were?" I said. "What roads we took?"

She stared at the floor, didn't reply.

"I could have found you somebody, an investigator," Milo said. "You never asked me."

"You're always trying to get down my pants." She looked at him. "Kinda off-putting."

He pursed his lips. "A valid point, I suppose."

No one spoke. The anger built inside me, a simmering mass of rage.

Piper stood and approached me. "You kissed her."

I didn't say anything. The anger blossomed into

something else, a ring of sadness around a vast chasm of feel-
ings I couldn't express.

"We're in the middle of hostile territory." She shook her
head. "And you decide to get lovey-dovey with the witness."

I cleared my throat. "I, uh, I'm sorry. That was a bad
tactical move."

Milo nodded.

"*Tactical* move?" Piper shoved my shoulder. "What about
us? Wasn't that a bad you-and-me move?"

I didn't say anything. Words fled my mind when confronted with the weight of an emotional truth. I'd failed not
only the mission but my lover, the one person who understood me best.

"You two should get some rest," Milo said. "Clean up a
little."

Neither of us spoke. We stared at each other.

"Some food," Milo said. "I'll make us something to eat."

Piper shook her head, a rueful look on her face like a
painful long-overdue decision had been made.

"Why did you go with me to Marfa?" I asked. "You
could have gone to ground, just disappeared."

She didn't say anything.

"We both had the DA coming after us, and I needed the
money," I said. "But you, you're used to living off the grid.
You could've evaded everybody for a long time."

"Yeah, I could have gone back to the street." She spoke
softly, in a matter-of-fact tone. "But did it ever occur to
you that I didn't want to? That maybe I wanted something
better?"

I didn't reply.

"I went with you to Marfa because I didn't have anywhere else to go." She paused. "And because I loved you."

The words we could never say to each other, uttered in a dreary safe house, half the state of Texas wanting us dead or in jail. Much too late for our relationship.

Milo shifted in his seat, clearly uncomfortable with the intimacy of the scene.

I didn't say anything, at a loss for an appropriate response.

"A shower and perhaps a nap for both of you," Milo said. "Then we shall go hunting for Sinclair."

I nodded. Looked toward the back of the house.

"I won't be here when you get back." Piper paused. "But I am sorry about Imogene. That was a stupid move on my part."

"Where are you going to go?" Milo asked. "What will you do?"

She left the room without speaking.

- CHAPTER SIXTY-NINE -

Midnight on the day of my return to Dallas.

Midnight on the day after which things would never be the same.

Who was I kidding? Every day seemed like that since I'd snatched Sinclair's relative from the Korean brothel. Should have stayed in bed that morning. Shoulda, woulda, coulda. Regrets weren't my long suit. Play the ace early and roll. Don't take any prisoners; don't stop for any navel-gazing.

A quick catnap turned into a three-hour slumber that left me jittery and unrefreshed. Better than nothing. I showered, finally got all of the blood out of my hair, and slipped into a pair of brand-new Levi's that fit a little snug in the hips after the Milo-provided replacement Glock had been put in a waistband holster. A black T-shirt. The DEA badge in my pocket.

Piper was gone. She'd cleaned up, dressed in borrowed clothes, and walked out into the night, a child of the streets returning to her home.

Relationships ending were nothing new in my life. I tried to put her out of my mind, concentrate on the task at hand. Finding my father.

In the mirror in the living room, I caught sight of myself, dark circles under my eyes, smudges that underscored the sadness there.

Only Milo seemed normal, chipper and animated. He'd changed into a navy blue workout suit and a green bandanna tied around his head like a do-rag.

"I'll drive." He pointed outside.

We got in the Honda. I asked him if he thought Piper would be okay. He nodded, assured me that she could take care of herself.

Since Milo's police contacts hadn't turned up any information about my father's whereabouts, I told him that I needed to visit my sister, Tanya, and see if she'd heard anything. I didn't mention the scanner.

I entered the address of my father's trailer into the GPS, too tired and too wired to give directions. Both Milo's safe house and the family double-wide were on the south side of the county, pretty near each other as the buzzard flies but in entirely different worlds otherwise.

Fifteen minutes later, we bumped down the country lane that led to the trailer, the road as dark as Christmas morning at an orphanage. There were no streetlights, and the canopy of trees kept the light from the stars and moon from penetrating to the ground.

"How do you know they won't be waiting for you?" Milo slowed as a coyote dashed across the road.

"The trailer's a rental," I said. "I'm guessing Costco tracked down Dad by calling Tanya's boyfriend, who's a constable."

He turned down the packed dirt driveway. A gray Porsche SUV was parked behind Tanya's pickup. A single light appeared to be on in the living room, but the porch lantern was dark.

"He made it back." Milo whistled. "Amazing."

"I'll take care of this alone." I opened the door as he came to a stop by the two vehicles.

"Is that wise?" He put the transmission into park.

I shut the door and touched the hood of the Porsche. It was hot, covered in road grime. The front windshield was cracked. I jogged up the porch steps.

The ringer was broken, and I didn't want to knock, so I opened the door and stepped inside. The trailer still smelled like boiled cabbage and onions.

I strode to the living room.

Tanya sat on the sofa, staring at her cell phone. A movie was playing on the TV, Kurt Russell and Val Kilmer in *Tombstone*. She looked up, blinked. There was nobody else in the room.

"Hey." I smiled.

"Jon?" She dropped the phone. "What are you doing here?"

"Where're your crutches?" I stepped closer. "And what the hell are you wearing?"

She had on a rumpled blue uniform, cargo pants, matching shirt. The outfit looked like the clothes worn by the men guarding the Gulfstream a few hours before.

A black Sam Browne belt and holster sat on the coffee table.

"I got a job, like you told me to." She stood. "This outfit called Paynelowe. They're handing out signing bonuses."

I didn't say anything, too stunned to speak.

"They got insurance and everything. I'm on some new meds, no more crutches."

"Gee, that's swell, Tanya. When do you start?"

"Your old partner, Costco, he hooked me up," she said. "He even took Dad with him. Said he was gonna give him a job, too."

"And you didn't think that was strange?" I said. "Offering a job to a man who can't remember his name."

"You shoulda seen him, Jon." She came around the table. "How his face lit up when Costco told him he was gonna be a cop again."

I shook my head.

"Of course it wasn't a real job. But still, he got out of the house for a little and got to act like he was working again."

"Where's Dad now?"

Tears welled in her eyes.

"We even scheduled the biopsy for next week," she said. "But . . ."

"What happened? How bad is he?"

"He— I don't know," she said. "He just showed up in that Porsche about fifteen minutes ago."

The mind is a strange thing. Frank Cantrell couldn't remember his children most of the time, but he could navigate halfway across the country. He must have hit the interstate somehow and kept going.

"Is he okay?" I asked.

"I shouldn't have let him go with Costco, should I?" She wiped her eyes. "I just thought it would be nice, you know, for both of us, to get a little break."

"What's wrong with him?"

"He was really upset when he got back. Not talking right, all slurred. Had trouble walking."

"Have you called nine-one-one?"

"I was just trying to do the right thing." She pointed to the phone like that was an answer in and of itself. "Is that so wrong?"

"It's okay, Tanya." I patted her arm. "Is he in his room?"

She nodded and padded after me as I went down the hall to our father's bedroom.

He was asleep on top of the comforter, fully clothed, the same dirty uniform he'd been wearing in West Texas. A bedside lamp with a low-wattage bulb cast a depressing glow over the wood-paneled room. He appeared unharmed except for a scratch on his chin. One cheek drooped lower than the other.

"We need to call nine-one-one," I said. "I think he's had a stroke."

"Jesus, no." She sat on his bedside but made no move toward the phone. "Daddy, what have I done to you?"

I dialed the number, gave them the address, and told Tanya to stay with him. I went to the kitchen, dug around in a couple of drawers and found a flashlight that worked. Then, I left by the back door and made my way down the dirt path to the storage shed where I'd hidden the scanner.

It was still there, the same position and condition as when I'd left it.

Tanya pointed to the box when I came back to our dad's room. "What's that?"

"You only have to remember one thing." I squeezed her arm. "I was never here."

She nodded.

"Where did the money come from for the ranch?" I said. "And all the cars?"

"What're you talking about? He worked security gigs, private consulting. That sort of thing. You know all that."

"I need to know who he worked for." Even as the words left my mouth I knew the answer no longer mattered.

I touched my father's throat, felt the too-weak pulse. His skin was the color of vanilla ice cream, hanging loosely on his face. A tiny dribble of saliva pooled in one corner of his mouth.

"Why?" Tanya said. "I don't understand."

"He's not doing well." I looked at my watch. "The high blood pressure, the stress."

"You think this is my fault, don't you?" She pushed my arm. "I just wanted a break. Costco was so nice. We met him at the McDonald's, and he took care of everything."

I didn't say anything.

"So Dad took a little badge money," she said. "That any different from you?"

I closed my eyes, tired and sad and lost, like a child left alone at a bus stop. No sound but the soft rattle of our father's breath.

We were silent for a while, the weight of our emotions sitting there along with the shell of the man who had been our father. A few minutes after one in the morning, the rattle of his breath grew still and he was no more.

I stood, kissed my half sister on the forehead, and left. The ambulance still hadn't come.

- CHAPTER SEVENTY -

Back in the Honda, I put the box on the floorboard and buckled my seat belt.

"You were gone a long time," Milo said. "Everything is okay? Your Dad is there?"

I didn't reply.

"Made some calls." Milo held up a phone. "A couple of Sinclair's poker games make their payoffs tonight."

Sinclair. The cause of all this. The scanner, the missing witness, the trip to Marfa. All bore his sticky fingerprints. Payback time, Captain Sinclair.

"Where?" My voice sounded funny.

"Hillcrest Tower." Milo put the Honda in gear. "Your dad actually made it back? Is he okay?"

"Sinclair's holed up at that place?"

Hillcrest Tower was a luxury high-rise built in the sixties when flocked wallpaper and shag carpet were considered swanky. The building was near Preston Center in the heart of a wealthy North Dallas neighborhood, a lone skyscraper surrounded by a sea of expensive homes and high-end stores, just down the street from Neiman Marcus.

The Hillcrest was prestige and luxury, shellacked with faded glamour, the kind of place J. R. Ewing might have stashed one of his second-string mistresses. It was not the kind of place where you'd expect to find a slimy, gold-nugget-ring-wearing ex-cop.

"Sinclair runs a hundred-dollar-ante game on the twenty-seventh floor every Thursday," Milo said. "All his other tables drop off the take and then somebody runs it to Fat Man HQ."

"Which is where?" I coughed for no particular reason.

The dark road became even harder to see, watery. In the distance, red lights swirled.

"Jonathan, are you okay?" Milo slowed down a little. "Is that an ambulance?"

I told him briefly what Tanya had related to me. Then I wiped my eyes and said, "Just drive, will you."

Milo stared at me for a few moments, mouth slack. Then he shrugged and sped up. A few seconds later, we passed the ambulance headed to my father's trailer.

"I'm sorry about your old man." He stopped at a light. "Is he gone?"

I nodded, unable to speak.

"Here we come, Sinclair." Milo turned onto the highway, mashed the accelerator.

"This night, it belongs to us."

———

The dark hours, as it turned out, belonged to no one.

We arrived at the Hillcrest at two in the morning, parked in a far corner of the visitor section in front of the glass-walled lobby. The ground floor was empty except for two men in blue blazers behind the front counter and a security guard sitting by the door.

Milo sent and received a series of text messages, each one leaving him more agitated.

There had been no Thursday night poker game at the Hillcrest, no drop-off from the other tables. Apparently, this occurrence caused much consternation in the Dallas underworld, a rip in the time-space continuum of hoods. The Hillcrest game was a constant, starting at noon every Thursday, no matter what the date or world calamity, holidays be damned.

"Not good, not good at all." Milo shut off the phone. "Nature abhors a vacuum. Those Slavic bastards from Richardson will take over everything"

Richardson was an aging middle-class suburb to the north, home to a large number of Russian immigrants who had settled around an Orthodox church and a couple of *banyas* or baths run by *mafiya* members from the Ukraine.

"This magic scanner." Milo pointed to the box. "What does it do?"

"Lots of neat things," I said. "But when we turn it on, the bad guys can find us."

"A problem, this." Milo stroked his chin.

"Should we try the house on Tranquilla?" I asked.

Milo shook his head. "He's shut that down."

A yellow Hummer with gleaming chrome rims pulled under the apartment building's awning, and a man with close-cropped blond hair got out of the rear. He wore a black wifebeater, black workout pants, and a gold chain around his neck.

The driver's window rolled down, and he spoke to whoever was behind the wheel.

"The Russians are here," Milo said.

The guy in the wifebeater strolled inside the lobby of the Hillcrest. He had a conversation with the two men behind the counter. He handed one an envelope, what had to be a payoff. The poker game would continue, just with a different crew in charge.

"That didn't take long," I said.

"We should leave." Milo put the van in gear. "Nothing more to learn here."

"Then what?" I said.

"Sinclair has many business interests." Milo pulled away. "He leaves a trail like a slug."

We drove down Northwest Highway through the heart of North Dallas. A light rain began to fall, and I drifted off to sleep remembering my father as he had once been.

- CHAPTER SEVENTY-ONE -

Sinclair woke at dawn on Saturday. He touched the bandage on his side where the drunk vet in Brownwood had removed the tiny .22 caliber bullet and stitched him up.

The skin around the wound didn't feel quite as hot as it had last night, so maybe the infection had gotten better.

He was in a second-floor room at the Motel 6 in Denison, Texas, pissing distance to the Red River and Oklahoma. Sadie sat cross-legged on the end of the bed, watching the Cartoon Network with the sound turned down low.

This was as far north as Sinclair had ever been in his life.

For a couple days now, his plan had been to leave Texas and head for Joplin, Missouri, just over the northern border of Oklahoma, two state lines away. A cousin had moved to Joplin in the seventies, and he was going to track him down, see if he and Sadie could stay for a while and regroup.

Each morning he woke thinking this was the day he would leave Texas for good. Each night he fell into a fitful sleep on the lumpy mattress, Sadie nestled by his side.

His organization had disintegrated, scattered to the four corners of Dallas County, the scraps gobbled by the jackals of the city. Thirty years of work vaporized in the length of time it took to cook up a pot of borscht. Damn Russians.

But that wasn't the worst of it. What hurt him deep down was that he'd failed his old friend McNally. And friends like McNally—with such loyalty—were hard to come by.

He picked up the disposable cell phone he'd bought on the way back from West Texas and dialed the number of one of his few allies remaining at the Dallas Police Department.

No warrants out for his arrest yet. No serious inquiries on the street over his whereabouts either.

Both would come, though. The first of the warrants would be for the shootout at the Cheyenne, while the cartels would be scouring the back alleys of Dallas because you didn't just walk away from your job as the Shield. Even though the bigwig narco in Marfa died before taking the stand, and Eva Ramirez never testified, Sinclair was still in trouble.

He'd left his post, gone to ground like a damn rabbit. He knew the way the cartels thought. His disappearance had aroused suspicion; suspicion equaled guilt.

And guilt meant they would come looking for him. They would want answers, crave blood. He only hoped that the narco's death had somehow helped McNally.

Hopefully, none of the *sicarios* had ever heard of Joplin. Maybe they wouldn't be able to track him, and he could live out his remaining years there in relative peace.

For now he and Sadie were in a small town on the Texas-Oklahoma border famous for being the birthplace of Dwight D. Eisenhower and not much else.

A battered Samsonite briefcase sat next to his bed. The case was stuffed, the locks straining. It contained three-quarters of a million dollars in cash, everything he could easily liquidate in the one frantic afternoon he'd allowed himself in Dallas.

He got out of bed. His joints creaked and ached. The pressure in his chest was growing more pronounced, not just the acid reflux.

On the nightstand next to his revolver was a Gideons Bible.

"You ready for some Kool-Aid?" Sadie looked up from the TV. "Make you a sammy if you want one."

Sadie was quite the little homemaker, among other things. She liked to fix powdered drinks and peanut-butter-and-jelly sandwiches in the room. She also liked coloring books, throwing rocks at hobos, and giving head.

"Nuh-uh." Sinclair stared at the Bible.

When he was a kid, his mama used to take him and his old friend to church, a Pentecostal congregation in the Pleasant Grove section of Dallas, across the road from a salvage yard. He didn't remember much of those times except Mama's platinum hair shining in the Sunday sun and the fact that something big happened in the New Testament on the third day, the Lord Jesus arose from the grave or something.

Today wasn't the third day, but close enough.

He got out of bed and stretched, a great weight lifted from his shoulders, the decision made. Today was the day. He and his dim-witted travel companion would cross the Red River into a new life.

Sadie slid off the end of the bed and stood. She wore an oversized Toby Keith T-shirt they'd bought at a flea market the day before. The shirt came to the tops of her thighs.

She sauntered over and nestled up against his good side, her head on his chest.

"What are we gonna do today?" she said.

"We're going to Missouri."

"We leaving right now?" She rubbed his belly, her hand moving lower and lower.

"In a few minutes." He grasped her wrist. Stopped her advances. "We need to get us some gone from Texas."

She pouted for a moment, then walked to the desk and made a glass of strawberry Kool-Aid. She took the drink with her and padded into the bathroom.

After she was dressed, he entered the steamy room and showered. Then, he put on a fresh guayabera shirt, his nicest Sansabelt slacks, and a pair of polished calfskin Lucchese boots. He would look his best when he left Texas.

Several restaurants were across the parking lot, a Saltgrass Steakhouse, an IHOP, some off-brand Chinese buffet.

"Let's get us some pancakes." He combed back his hair, squirted a little VO5 spray on the pompadour.

Sadie packed up her meager belongings in a small duffel bag they'd gotten at the flea market. Sinclair stuck the revolver in his waistband and walked to the door. He stopped, hand on the knob.

"What's wrong?" Sadie said.

"Nothing." Sinclair stared at a spot of chipped paint on the wall. He thought about everything that was his life in Dallas and in Texas, how he'd never again see any of the places or people he knew. A lump formed in his throat.

"I'm hungry," Sadie said.

Sinclair nodded. He opened the door and stepped out onto the exposed hallway. Sadie followed him.

The shooter was to the left, two doors down.

A wiry Latino man, small like a girl, wearing a plaid shirt and jeans. He was in his early twenties and had a thin mustache just like Sinclair's. He looked like a guy who mows lawns for a living, but not as important.

Sinclair held up the briefcase like a shield, clawed at his hip for the revolver.

The shooter flipped open the plaid shirt where a silenced MAC-10 hung from a strap on his shoulder.

Sadie screamed.

Both men raised their weapons at the same time.

Sadie stood still, eyes unblinking, and the wave of bullets hit her first, ripping into her flesh. She stumbled across the hallway, bleeding from a half dozen wounds. Then she fell over the railing.

In his mind, Sinclair didn't see the spits of flame from the muzzle of the machine gun. Nor did he hear the staccato rip of the weapon's bolt as it fired.

Instead, he saw his mother right before she died. He was ten years old again, and Mama was in the kitchen of their two-bedroom house in Pleasant Grove, cooking fried chicken.

The bullets tore into his body and demolished the Samsonite, shredding the cash inside. The briefcase burst open.

Sinclair dropped to the ground, blood all over his best clothes. The house in Pleasant Grove was the color of the sun, the same as his mother's hair, and the smell of fried chicken filled his nostrils.

The last thing he saw was his mother's smile and a green cloud of hundred-dollar bills floating over his body.

- CHAPTER SEVENTY-TWO -

I spent Friday at the safe house. I rested and watched TV. Tried not to think about Piper.

The older you get, the easier the breakups were, or so I liked to tell myself. Between the two of us, Piper and I owned a half dozen issues and isms, dysfunctional behavior patterns that would preclude any chance of a healthy long-term relationship.

Milo put out the request among his network of hoods and lowlife informants: any word on Sinclair, much money would be paid. Or however that translated into Milo-speak.

Early Saturday morning, his cell rang. He had a short conversation and then disappeared down the block to use a pay phone. Ten minutes later, he returned.

"Eva Ramirez." He poured a cup of coffee. "She called you."

"What?" I paused with a mug halfway to my mouth. "Where? How?"

"She phoned the Main Street Dash," he said. "How she connected this establishment to you is beyond me."

"She's alive?"

"Apparently."

"You talked to her?"

He nodded.

"What'd she want?"

"To see you. She asked for a meeting." He added cream to his cup but didn't say more.

I made a "go on" motion with my hand. "And are you gonna tell me where?"

Milo slid a wad of currency from his pocket.

"This contains ten grand, the money you would not accept that I owe you." He held it out. "And the name of my passport guy."

I looked at the cash but didn't reach for it.

"Take a walk on this," he said. "Just disappear."

"Eva Ramirez can clear me on the two dead thugs here in Dallas."

"What about the other stuff?" he said. "The bodies in West Texas."

The media feeding frenzy had been nonstop, lurid headlines and top-of-the-hour reports about narcotrafficker violence finally spilling across the border. The fact that one of the dead *sicarios* in the hotel in Schwarzemann had been a fifteen-year-old girl only stoked the hysteria.

"I don't know what to do about that," I said. "One indictment at a time."

"A trap, this could very well be." He put away the money. "Eva could be the tip of a very big iceberg."

"That doesn't make sense." I shook my head. "I don't have anything Eva wants."

"Then why meet?" he said. "What does she have that you want?"

I couldn't provide an answer.

———

A half hour later we left the safe house. The shoebox containing the scanner was on the floor of the minivan.

Milo stayed off the freeways, drove the back streets. Fifteen minutes later he slowed and pointed to a Catholic church near downtown, the Shrine of the Blessed Sacrament.

"Here is where she said to meet."

"When?" I looked at my watch.

"Now."

This slice of Dallas was a thriving retail district, a little Mexico, more like the *mercado* section of Monterrey or Guadalajara than a city on the northern plains of Texas. The buildings that lined the street were painted a riot of different colors, reds and greens, mustard yellow and turquoise. Neon pennants fluttered from the fences around the used car lots.

The church was a traditional design, sedate in comparison. Pale brick and limestone, an ornate bell tower. The structure was a cathedral, a large, four- or five-story tall sanctuary forming the long part of a cross.

"Your scanner," Milo said. "Now is the time to use it?"

I shook my head. "Make the block."

He did as I requested.

Nothing was out of the ordinary, a handful of inexpensive cars, not new, not old either. Typical for the neighborhood. There was a two-story building at the rear of the property that looked kind of like a hotel except the architecture and design matched the cathedral.

"It's a convent." I read the sign as we drove by.

"In the middle of Dallas." Milo shrugged. "Who knew?"

"She told me her father is a devout Catholic," I said. "Maybe he arranged the hiding spot."

Milo stopped the Honda minivan on a side street, around the corner from the front entrance of the church.

I got out.

"What are you going to do?" he said.

"She wanted a meeting; I'm gonna meet her." I pointed to the scanner. "Keep an eye on that. Whatever you do, don't turn it on. Paynelowe's liable to send a cruise missile to take it out."

He surveyed the intersection for a few moments then pointed to a one-story cinder block building that was painted purple and red.

"Over there," he said. "I shall wait for you."

The structure was across the street but not directly in front of the church, a good spot to observe but still be out of the way. A Mexican-food restaurant not yet open, the sign over the door read COCINA AZTECA. Brightly colored banners and strands of darkened holiday lights draped the patio. The front wall had been painted with the image of an Aztec warrior holding a spear, glaring out at the world. A row of parking spaces ran down one side of the structure.

I opened the passenger door.

"Be careful," Milo said.

I didn't reply. I walked down the sidewalk that bordered the cathedral. Nodded at a woman pushing a toddler in a stroller. Smiled at the little girl trailing behind them. The sun felt good on my shoulders.

The main entrance of the church was at the top of a wide row of stairs, maybe twenty steps total.

I took them two at a time and eased open the door, entering the vestibule, a foyer area that smelled of candle wax and lemon furniture polish. The room was empty.

Closed oak doors led to the sanctuary.

I pulled the Glock from my waistband and pressed it against my thigh. Used my free hand and pushed open the doors.

The sanctuary was empty.

Polished marble floors, black and white checkerboard patterned, rows of dark wooden pews. At the far end an altar underneath a large wooden crucifix.

I slid to the left behind the last row of seating. Stood with my back to the wall. And waited.

Ninety seconds later, the embroidered fabric around the altar appeared to rustle a little. Hard to tell from the other end of the sanctuary.

A moment after that a figure appeared behind the altar. Dark hair in a ponytail, a white blouse.

Eva.

I eased along the wall to the left side of the room and strode to the front.

She met me in the area between the altar and the pews.

"You came," she said.

I nodded, kept the gun by my side.

She appeared rested but sad, a sense of forlornness in the slump of her shoulders. The hint of makeup she wore accentuated the weariness in her eyes. But the light from the stained glass windows made her skin glow and her hair shine, stark and beautiful against her white blouse.

I recognized my weakness. I wanted to hold her. To make everything better. For both of us.

"Thank you," she said. "I'm sorry about Marfa."

"You're under arrest." I aimed the Glock at her. "For the murder of Lazaro Morales."

"You are still acting like a *federale*?" She shook her head. "After all this?"

I didn't reply.

"Lazaro had to die," she said. "Do you know what they said they'd do to my mother if I didn't take him out?"

I pulled out my cell phone.

"They killed her anyway of course." She stared at the crucifix above the altar. "Just to make a point."

I dialed Milo.

"The money I told you about is well hidden," she said. "We can disappear."

I held my finger over the Send button. "Where's Keith McCluskey?"

"He's gone." She paused. "Where's Piper?"

"Put your hands on your head." I hit Send.

She did as requested, the movement sensuous and submissive at the same time.

"So you and I are both alone in this world." She sighed. "Me? I don't do very well by myself."

Milo didn't answer the phone.

"If we're careful," she said. "The money will last a long while."

"What about the parties?" I ended the call. "You like the good times. Won't be many of those if we go on the run."

"I like feeling safe more. And you make me feel that way."

I debated dialing 911. But the likely outcome from that move would be both of us arrested or worse.

"Let's run away." She let her arms slip from her head. "Just you and me."

"We're going out the side door." I lowered the Glock.

The entrance on the other side of the altar led to the cross street.

"My mother and sister are both dead." She didn't move. "All because of me."

"I'm sorry."

"And I can't reach my father either." Her eyes were dead, devoid of feeling. The same look a prisoner in a concentration camp has peering between the razor wire.

I stuck the Glock in my waistband. She was wearing tight black pants and a sheer white blouse. No place to hide a weapon.

"This may sound strange," she said. "But you are all I have left."

"Let's go outside." I pointed to the side door.

"You're different from the rest of them," she said. "You're a good man."

"Eva." I took a step closer. "We need to get out of this church."

She held a hand out, glided toward me. We slid into an embrace, her head against my shoulder. She smelled of fresh soap and perfume, clean and good and full of promise.

"I'm sorry," she said.

"It's okay." I stroked her shoulder. "We can go somewhere and talk—"

Noise from the far end of the sanctuary. My shirt moved.

I pushed her away, reached for the Glock.

My pistol was in her hand. She jumped back, pointed the muzzle at me.

Keith McCluskey stood in the center aisle, a gun aimed at Milo Miller's head.

She'd lied to me, again. A sense of hopelessness filled my being, despair that was only matched by the anger. At myself. I'd been duped by this woman, played like the sucker in a three-card monte game. Was my need to belong to someone so strong it clouded my sense of reason? My survival instinct?

McCluskey approached, shoving Milo down the aisle. Milo's hands were bound with duct tape in front of his waist.

"Hello, baby." McCluskey stopped a few feet away. "Any problems?"

The anger overtook the hopelessness. Something new came along: a desire for revenge.

She shrugged.

"Where's the scanner?" McCluskey said. "The last piece of the puzzle."

I didn't speak. Shook my head slowly.

Eva's face remained impassive. She looked at McCluskey, who nodded once. She squinted, lips pursed, and fired a round between my feet. The bullet ricocheted off the marble, zinging against the far wall. The smell of gun smoke filled the air.

I jumped back, hands up. "I turned it in to the police."

"No you didn't." She shook her head. "Keith knows they're still looking for it."

I'd seen cadavers that looked better than McCluskey. He appeared to have aged ten years in the last few days and lost a lot of weight, most of it from his face. His skin was the color of cottage cheese and hung loosely from the bones of his skull. His hair was thin, greasy.

"Please, Jon, don't make this hard on yourself." She brushed a strand of hair from her face with her free hand. "Tell us where the scanner is."

I weighed options. Jump Eva and take at least one bullet, probably a fatal shot, before I could wrest the gun from her grip. Milo would get shot, too. Or die later on McCluskey's terms.

Milo spoke for the first time. "It's hidden across the street. I'll show you."

- CHAPTER SEVENTY-THREE -

"Your Jew boy here is gonna be the first to get shot if you try anything," Keith McCluskey said. "So don't get tricky."

I nodded, hands raised.

"You go first." Eva pointed to me.

I walked past the altar toward the side door of the cathedral.

The four of us stopped at the exit.

"Real slow now," McCluskey said. "Open it."

I eased the door back. He pulled me out of the way, stuck his head out. Then he turned and said, "Let's go."

We exited and stopped in the shadow of the church.

"Okay, where is it?" McCluskey said.

"There." Milo, hands bound, nodded to the Mexican restaurant called Cocina Azteca. Still closed. His van was parked in the handicapped spot closest to the front entrance.

I swore under my breath.

"The device you seek is hidden in the restaurant," Milo said. "To retrieve it, two people are needed."

The scanner wasn't hidden five minutes ago, certainly not in a place where multiple people would be needed for retrieval. He had a plan of some sort, a concealed gun probably. But how did he get inside the restaurant?

"It was there the whole time when I snatched you?" McCluskey shook his head. "All right. The four of us are gonna walk over nice and easy."

The side street was empty. The woman and her children I'd seen earlier were gone. Saturday morning, more people would be out and about soon.

We walked down the sidewalk and crossed the street. Milo and I were in front, McCluskey and Eva behind us with the guns held pressed to their sides. Once on the patio, the four of us threaded our way through the tables and chairs.

"It's in the bar. Cut me loose." Milo stopped by the main entrance. "I'll get it and be right back."

"Not a chance." McCluskey shook his head. "We all go in together."

Milo looked scared. He bit his lip, frowned.

McCluskey grabbed the front door, yanked. Unlocked, it swung open. He motioned me in first, then Eva followed by Milo.

The restaurant was closed, the entry area dark. A hostess stand stood between two rooms, a dining section to the right, a bar to the left.

The waiting area was decorated with Mexican restaurant kitsch—sombreros and piñatas, pictures of smiling peasants. The air smelled like peppers and onions and pine-scented cleaner. The air-conditioner had been left on from the night before, and the temperature was frigid.

Ambient light from the front windows illuminated the empty dining area, a freshly mopped floor, tables with chairs stacked on top.

The bar was dark. A sign over the arched entryway was barely readable: CANTINA AZTECA. An image of a heavily muscled warrior similar to the one on the front of the building adorned the wall to one side of the bar's entrance. The warrior wore a ceremonial headdress and a loincloth and appeared to be gazing into the distance.

"It's in there." Milo pointed to the bar. "I need help getting it."

McCluskey pulled a folding knife from his pocket and sliced the tape around Milo's wrists.

"Turn on the lights, then come right back." He shoved Milo toward the cantina. "Try anything funny, and your buddy gets one in the foot."

Milo nodded and stumbled into the darkened room. A moment later, a thin beam of light cut through the gloom.

"All right," McCluskey shouted. "Now come back with your hands—"

Two sounds, one right after the other: a gunshot, Milo screaming.

McCluskey and Eva were unprepared, confused, as was I.

Milo had set this up. Who would shoot him?

McCluskey took a step toward the bar but hesitated. Eva grabbed my arm, then let go. They looked at each other and then at me.

No other noise from the bar.

McCluskey motioned for Eva to remain in the entry area with me.

Eva tightened her grip on the Glock and grabbed my arm again. She jammed the muzzle against my ribs.

McCluskey crept to the doorway leading to the cantina. He pressed himself against the image of the Aztec warrior and inched his head and gun in, the weapon an extension of his gaze. Everywhere he looked, the gun pointed.

He stood still for a few moments, surveyed the scene. Then he stepped away from the protection of the wall and entered the room, pistol at the ready. He disappeared from view.

Eva pushed me toward the doorway he'd gone through. We stopped in the arch, and my eyes focused.

The room had a half dozen tables and chairs, a bar along the back. Two darkened flat-screen TVs were on one side opposite the painting.

The dim light from a solitary bulb illuminated a mural on the wall to our left.

The artwork was a mountaintop tableau and took up nearly the entire wall. The subject was another Aztec warrior, this one kneeling in front of a woman asleep on a bed of rock, towering juniper trees on either side, a babbling brook in the background.

The mural immediately drew the attention of anybody who entered the bar. The warrior was oversized and had been painted in much finer detail than the warrior images in the entry area or on the exterior of the building. He had long flowing hair, ropy muscles, and an exaggeratedly handsome face, thick lashes on sleepy, half-closed eyes.

The woman was straight out of schoolboy fantasyland, humongous breasts, exquisitely long legs slightly parted. She wore a barely there two-piece outfit apparently made from clouds or translucent silk.

Milo was nowhere to be seen.

McCluskey stood in the middle of the room, swiveling his head, gun in hand. His attention kept being drawn back to the mural.

"Where is he?" Eva stepped into the bar, pulling me with her. "He's wounded. He has to be here somewhere."

I stared at the mural, shivering from the cold. The image was so vivid, I could almost smell the mountain air and the sweat on the warrior's chest.

"I don't know." McCluskey shook his head. He gave up and gazed at the mural, too.

From the side of the bar by the TVs came a faint sound. The three of us turned in unison.

Piper jumped up from behind a table. She held a pistol in her hand.

"Drop your weapons." She aimed at McCluskey. "Both of you."

Nobody spoke for a moment. Relief washed over me followed by more confusion. How did she get here? Had she shot Milo? *Where* was Milo?

"Two against one." McCluskey smiled. "You'll never make it."

The expression on Piper's face didn't alter. She didn't speak or change positions. Instead, she squeezed the trigger twice, two quick shots that hit McCluskey in the chest.

He dropped his weapon and fell to the floor, unaware of Piper's Mantra: *when in doubt, put rounds on target.*

Eva gasped. She pulled the Glock away from me, aimed at Piper.

I jumped back, out of the line of fire.

"Don't even think about it." Piper drew a bead on the woman's chest. "Drop the gun. Now."

Eva hesitated, struggling for breath like she'd run a marathon, face etched in fear. She looked at the figure of McCluskey lying at her feet. After a long moment, she complied. The Glock clattered to the stone floor.

"Where's Milo?" I bent to pick up the weapon. "Is he ok—"

"Shut up, Jon." Piper aimed at me. "And don't touch that gun."

I froze.

Milo appeared behind the bar by the beer taps, about thirty feet away. He was unharmed.

"Piper?" He strode toward us. "What are you doing? This, we did not discuss."

I shivered, not just from the cold.

"We were going to rescue Jon and apprehend McCluskey and Eva," Milo said. "Now you're pointing a gun at our friend?"

The muzzle of her weapon seemed to grow larger, and I imagined what the heat from the blast would feel like, a welcome if all-too-brief respite from the cold.

Piper was radiant, happy-looking like the day we met. She appeared well rested, at peace.

She raised the gun a notch higher, aimed at my face.

"W-w-where's the scanner?" My voice sounded hollow, far away.

She tilted her head toward the kneeling Aztec warrior, her eyes never leaving mine.

The shoe box rested on the floor by the warrior's sandaled feet. Because of the light and the background, it was nearly invisible. Hidden in plain sight.

She and Milo must have been in communication all along and worked out a plan—conceal the scanner, serve as backup for my meeting, take out the bad guys if it came to that.

Unfortunately, plans have a way of derailing when emotions got involved.

Eva gasped when she saw the cardboard container. Her dark eyes sparkled, unable to hide her hunger for the contents of the box.

"Put the gun down, Piper." Milo stamped his foot. "My undying love for you, it will wane if you do not do as I say."

Piper aimed the gun at the woman by my side and said, "You want it, don't you, Eva?"

Eva didn't speak.

"Go ahead and take it." Piper smiled. A long pause. "Just like you took Jon."

No one said anything. Her words swirled between the three of us, smoke from a condemned man's cigarette. The Aztec warrior's muscles glistened with sweat.

"They will come for us, yes?" Eva said. "Because of what has happened in the desert and what is in the box, they will never let us rest."

Stress had made her accent more pronounced. She sounded like what she was: a scared young woman from Mexico whose days were numbered, collateral damage in the wars between the narcotraffickers and the governments on either side of the border.

Piper nodded. After a moment, I did the same.

"Are you going to kill me?" Eva said.

Piper didn't reply. One side of her mouth curled upward in a lopsided smile. Milo shook his head and made a clicking sound with his tongue, a sign he was frustrated and fearful at the same time.

"Piper." I held out one hand. "Give me the gun."

My arm shook, teeth chattered.

"Choices have been made, Jon." Piper tightened her grip on the weapon. "Every action has a consequence."

"Please." I eased a step closer. "Think about all the kids you wanted to visit."

She swung the muzzle toward me. Her trigger finger whitened, and the Aztec warrior seemed to smile.

Seconds ticked by. Nobody moved. The tension in the room grew, thick enough to slice with an ax.

"Stop." Eva stepped forward. "I didn't take him from you."

Piper looked at the woman we'd driven across Texas, her expression a mix of distrust, relief, and weariness.

"Nothing happened," Eva said. "Please let me go. I just want this to end."

"You and me both." Piper rubbed her cheek with the back of her free hand.

I realized that Piper's face was ashen, the radiant image from a moment ago just an illusion like so much else. She was as spent as I was.

"Put the gun down, Piper." I sidestepped across the room, moving around McCluskey's body, and retrieved the shoebox.

Eva began to cry. She knelt beside McCluskey as Piper slumped her shoulders and dropped the pistol on a table top. Milo sighed in relief.

"We're going to leave now, Eva." I opened the box, verified the scanner was still there. "You need to leave, too. The police will be here soon."

Eva lay across McCluskey's body, cheek on his shoulder, crying.

Piper hugged herself, eyes empty.

Eva looked up at me. "You are not going to arrest me?"

"No." I paused. "I'm not a cop anymore."

A sense of relief washed over me as I spoke those words.

Piper and I were still on the hook for the two dead cartel thugs at the warehouse in West Dallas and Eva was the only witness who could absolve us. I should have wanted her to be locked up so she could testify on our behalf. However, based on the events of the past few days, I doubted she'd live more than a few hours in custody.

"You felt something for me, didn't you?" She brushed tears from her cheek.

"What's past is past."

"You thought I felt something back there, yes?"

I touched the scanner, rubbed a finger along the burnt plastic.

"You are nothing." She spat the words out. "I've been with real men—Lazaro and Keith. They know how to treat a woman."

A drug smuggler and a drug addict. Eva didn't make very good choices. No wonder I'd been drawn to her.

Milo came up behind me. "We need to roll, Jon."

"I will tell the cartel about all of you," Eva said. "And they will kill you."

"Or, here's a thought," Piper said. "I could just shoot you now." The pistol lay on the table, but she made no move toward it.

"Enough death." Milo shook his head. "Too many souls lost over this matter."

I nodded in agreement as Eva sat up and pulled a small-framed pistol from underneath McCluskey's jacket, the dead man's backup gun.

She aimed at my face. "Give me the scanner."

Milo swore. Piper's face flushed red with rage. Her gun was a long three feet from her grasp. My weapon, the one Eva had taken from me and then dropped, was on the floor nearer the entrance to the bar than to where I was at the moment.

"Okay. You win." I handed Eva the box, fumbling a little, just enough to cover my index finger turning the master switch to ON. "You take the scanner and forget all about us."

Eva grabbed the box and licked her lips, dollar signs practically swimming above her head.

"Do we have a deal?" I tried to look sincere.

Eva stared at the blinking lights, clearly not understanding what they represented. She smiled triumphantly, stood, and ran from the bar, the device tucked under her arm like a football.

When the front door slammed shut, Milo said, "That was close. Now, we should depart in an expedient manner."

I looked at Piper. "Are you coming with us?"

"You let a damsel in distress get away," she said. "How out of character."

I shrugged.

"Holy crap." Piper shook her head. "You turned it on, didn't you?"

I nodded.

No one spoke. The three of us stared at each other for a moment then dashed out of the bar and jumped into Milo's van. Eva was nowhere to be seen. Milo put the vehicle in gear, and we sped away.

A few minutes later I heard the *whomp-whomp* of a chopper's rotors over the sounds of traffic. At a stop light, I looked up and saw a large military-style helicopter flying overhead.

Paynelowe had come for its scanner.

EPILOGUE

"The chief business of the American people is business."

 —President Calvin Coolidge,
  January 1925

"This may sound trite but I firmly believe it to be true: the business of America is business, that is, making money. And money is a good thing because it provides for all of us through taxes. When I'm elected, I will make it a priority to revamp the banking laws so that it's easier for investment money to move across the border in both directions. Imagine if you will, a border without barriers."

 —US Senator and presidential candidate Stephen McNally, speaking at a private fund-raiser at the Laredo Country Club, Laredo, Texas, August 2012

- CHAPTER SEVENTY-FOUR -

Every federal law enforcement outfit except one employed private contractors.

The US Secret Service.

The man who'd knocked on the door of Milo's safe house looked like an agent in a protective detail. Average height, extremely fit, clean shaven. He wore a gray suit tailored a little loose in the middle, an attractive but bland tie. Sunglasses and a radio earpiece in one ear.

I'd opened the door but hadn't stepped outside, one hand on the Glock hidden in my waistband. I'd slept for the past eighteen hours straight, but my body felt like an old man's, my mental acuity dull as a butter knife. Piper was still sacked out in the back bedroom.

It was ten in the morning, two days after my encounter with Eva Ramirez at the Shrine of the Blessed Sacrament. We'd been keeping a low profile at Milo's. Piper was morose because Imogene's number had been disconnected, and we were both more than a little irked that we hadn't secured any sort of a payday for all the work we'd done. The lack of money was balanced out by the fact that we weren't in jail or dead.

The agent held up his badge. "Are you Jon Cantrell?"

"Maybe." I frowned. "Who wants to know?"

After the last week, nothing surprised me anymore, certainly not the Secret Service dropping by.

The media, hopped up on stories about cartel violence and a rogue group of DEA contractors, went ballistic over the discovery of Keith McCluskey's body in a Mexican-food restaurant in Dallas. Days before, Paynelowe had reported him killed in a desolate section of Coahuila, not far from Presidio, Texas, a DEA hero shot down on the front lines of the War on Drugs.

No one knew what happened to Eva or the scanner. Milo's sources indicated that the chopper had landed and a group of agents had dispersed across the streets of East Dallas. Shots had been fired. A couple of junkies claimed they saw a woman in a white blouse lying dead in an alley, a swarm of blue windbreakers surrounding the body. Neither Paynelowe nor the DEA commented.

Hollis and the district attorney's office left messages at the Main Street Dash: Piper and I were off the hook for the two dead thugs at the warehouse as well as for anything that had happened in West Texas. Apparently, Paynelowe's new contract was in serious jeopardy, and they had leaned on the district attorney, desperate to keep us off the witness stand. The Dallas police and the DA, reeling from the discovery of Sinclair's body along with a substantial amount of cash and his ties to organized crime, had been eager to play along.

"Mister Hawkins is outside." He spoke the name like it was supposed to mean something to me. "He'd like a word with you, if it's all right."

"Who?"

"Patrick Hawkins." The agent cocked his head. "You watch the news much?"

"Not if I can help it."

"This will only take a few minutes," the agent said. "And some very powerful people would consider it a favor."

"Maybe we could set something up later. It's been a rough few days."

"Nobody's going to hurt you," he said. "If that's what you're worried about."

I waited for a couple of seconds then stepped onto the porch.

"If you please, sir." He pointed to my waistband. "Leave the weapon inside."

After a moment's hesitation, I tossed the Glock on the side table by the front door and followed the agent to the two black Suburbans idling in the street. Both had tinted windows and a forest of antennas on their roofs.

"I gotta pat you down." The agent gave me a sheepish look. "Sorry."

I held out my hands, and he performed a very quick and thorough search, letting me keep my phone and keys.

The rear door of the second Suburban opened and a man in his twenties wearing khakis and a golf shirt jumped out, smart phone in one hand, a tablet computer in the other. He looked like a congressional intern or a model in a Dockers commercial.

"Don't know who you are, but you're screwing up the schedule." He pointed to the rear door. "Make it quick."

I hopped in the back of the SUV, took the only available seat. Dockers Dude shut the door and remained outside.

Inside, the air-conditioning was turned to high, cooling the rich aroma of General Motors leather and takeout food. In the front sat what appeared to be two more Secret Service agents. In the third row, a man in his forties sprawled with his feet extended, fingers tapping on a cell phone.

In the second row, in a club chair next to me, sat a pear-shaped guy with a barely there comb-over. He wore an ill-fitting double-breasted suit that had a greenish tint and looked like a Men's Wearhouse special, circa 1992.

The pear-shaped guy had a file folder in his lap, a half-eaten McDonald's Quarter Pounder in one hand, a cell phone in the other. A Bluetooth headset wrapped around one ear.

"Yeah." The man, obviously in the middle of a call, cut his eyes my way. "He just got here. We're getting ready to talk."

"Hello." I gave him my friendly but insincere smile. "You must be Patrick Hawkins."

He nodded, took a bite from the burger, and continued his phone call.

"Nebraska? That's only five electoral votes." He chewed several times and swallowed. "What the fuck do I care about Nebraska?"

I glanced around the interior of the vehicle. The agents were keeping a watch on the street. On the console rested what looked like a newer model of the scanner I'd given to Eva Ramirez, the item that had initiated all this fuss in the first place. Guess some agencies were getting the devices for field use after all. The guy in the back was still working the keyboard of his phone like a fifteen-year-old girl right before the big dance at school.

"Then you tell Rove he can suck my left one." Hawkins, still on the phone, put his burger down on top of the folder. "That backstabbing SOB picked the losing team this time."

My gaze fell to the floor where a letter-sized manila envelope rested by a grease-stained McDonald's sack. My name had been scrawled in black on the outside of the envelope.

"The demographics for the focus groups in Iowa were all fucked up, too." Hawkins snapped his fingers at me, pointed to the envelope. "There's got to be some Chinese people somewhere in that state." He was quite the multitasker.

I picked up the envelope, opened it. Removed a small packet, maybe six or eight pages.

The first sheet was on Department of Homeland Security letterhead, a job description for the position of assistant chief of staff at the Office of Counter-Narcotics Enforcement in the DC headquarters.

The suggested resume, job skills, and requirements read like it had been written with me in mind, minus of course getting fired from the Dallas Police Department and subsequently working as a hand-to-mouth contractor. The pay range was well into the six figures and included full benefits.

The next two pages were an application for the job, already filled out with my name and information. They had used the apartment at the Cheyenne that nobody had known about as my home address. Under references, they had listed three people I'd never met: the chief of police for the City of Dallas, the regional head of the DEA, and the special agent in charge of the Houston FBI office. Each name had next to it what was noted as a personal cell number.

My start date was in late January of the next year, immediately after the inauguration. The only empty space: a line for my signature.

The remainder of the packet was a near duplicate, except the open position was for something called assistant to the assistant chief, and the application had been filled out with Piper's information and resume, spiffed up like mine to remove the more blatant felonies. They'd obviously not performed a very thorough psych profile if they expected Piper to be my assistant.

"Yeah, well fuck you, too." Hawkins ended his call. He took another bite of his burger and then pulled a bulging number ten envelope from his breast pocket. "So what do you think?" He was talking to me now.

"About what?"

"The job, dumbass."

"I'm not sure what to say."

Truer words had never departed my lips. This was a big fat juicy plum being offered.

But who was doing the offering and why? Blue Dagger, my former employer, was no longer a functioning entity. And the powers that be at Paynelowe would rather poke at my eyes with toothpicks than arrange a job like this.

"Here's some moving expenses for the both of you." He handed me the envelope. "You need more, you let me know."

"What's this about?" I peered inside the second package. Two thick stacks of hundred dollar bills bound in bank wrappers, ten grand each.

"You're a team player," Hawkins said. "That's why we're here."

"What team are you talking about?"

"The one that's going to win in November."

I frowned, not understanding.

"You can go ahead and sign it now." He smiled. "Then get your girl, Piper, to ink up. And we'll be good to go."

"I might take a day or two to think about it, if that's okay."

My girl, Piper. Referring to her in that manner was a good way to get disemboweled. And was he talking about Senator McNally, the front-runner? The man whose grandson I had tried to save nearly a decade ago in the storeroom of the strip club?

"Listen to this guy." Hawkins laughed. "'Think about it,' he says. You're a comedian, you know that?"

"I'm not signing this right now. I want to know what's going on."

Patrick Hawkins paused with his burger halfway to his mouth. The atmosphere in the SUV grew chilly. He put the sandwich down and leaned toward the front.

"Agents, let's give Mister Cantrell some privacy." He opened his side and got out.

The two Secret Service men exited the vehicle, shut their doors.

The man in the third row shifted his weight, leaned forward. He had reddish blond hair, a fair complexion, and green eyes. He looked like a successful surgeon or investment banker, wearing a Polo shirt, expensive slacks, and a stainless-steel Rolex.

"Señor Cantrell. We have not met." He stuck out his hand. "My name is Raul Fuentes-Manzanares the third."

A heavy accent coated his words, at odds with the coloring of his skin and hair. He was most likely a pure-blood descendant of Spanish invaders.

Fuentes was a relatively common name in Mexico and Texas. Fuentes-Manzanares was the surname for a very old and wealthy family from Monterrey, hyphenated sometime back in the 1700s. The Fuentes-Manzanares family had interests on either side of the border, as I recalled. Banking and real estate, mining and manufacturing.

"I'm a consultant with Senator McNally's campaign," he said. "My friends call me Diego. The man who just left, Patrick Hawkins, he's the Senator's chief of staff."

I stared at the packet of money in my lap, tried to keep my face impassive. His nickname was the same as the one Lazaro Morales had implied belonged to the man at the very top of the cartel. Could this guy be the *el muy grande* leader?

"I'm in charge of what we call the border vote," Diego/ Raul said. "The Senator plans to win both Texas and California. First time one party has done that in many years, if ever."

Nothing made sense. Presidential candidates didn't associate themselves with cartel leaders, at least not in the United States. Cartel leaders didn't look like they'd just come from the country club either.

"You and your partner were alone for a short period of time with a man named Lazaro Morales."

"Yeah." I cleared my throat, voice scratchy. "What of it?"

"Morales was a sociopath and a pathological liar. Nothing he said is to be trusted."

"We didn't chitchat very much. The bad stuff hit the fan pretty soon after we got there."

Diego didn't speak. He stared at me, nodding slowly as if evaluating my words.

"Are you part of Paynelowe?" I asked.

"Oh my, no. Here is my information." He chuckled a little, handed me a card. "I do wish you would accept this generous job offer."

The item contained his name but no title or business, just an office address in La Jolla, a single phone number, and an email address. The faint outline of a golden crucifix had been embossed on one corner. The insignia appeared similar to the crude image stamped on Eva's money.

"What's with the crucifix?" My voice croaked a little.

"That's an old logo from the family business." Diego shrugged. "My grandfather is very devout."

"And you have an office in the US?" I rubbed my finger over the lettering on the card.

"We recently relocated. Mexico is very dangerous these days."

"Yeah. So I've heard. Parts of Texas are, too."

Sweat blossomed on my forehead as the thoughts raced through my mind. The next president of the United States had hired this guy as a consultant.

"You may think you know what that insignia means." Diego pointed to the card. "You may think you know how things are done on the border." He patted my shoulder. "But trust me, you don't."

I'd spent a large part of my career looking for street thugs, dealers, and pushers operating in the darkness of the netherworld that is the drug trade. And their leaders, the *jefes*, crude men suddenly awash in wealth.

"You're the cartel." I shook my head. "And the banker for the cartel. It's a perfect model of corruption."

"My family does not condone the narcotraffickers." Diego wagged a finger sideways. "But the business of being in business is a very fluid situation sometimes."

"What the hell does that mean?"

"We are most interested in legitimate economic opportunities which foster growth between our countries. With growth comes understanding."

Milo had warned me about the people above the *jefes*, the bosses of the bosses. The Diegos. Turns out he was right.

"What if, in terms of commerce, the border just went away?" Diego smiled. "Think of the growth potential then."

I nodded, understanding. "More growth means more taxes."

"And the taxes can be used for all sorts of socially responsible programs." Diego arched an eyebrow. "Like health care or education."

"Socially responsible" had become the new buzzword for the Senator's campaign, a hard shift to the center from his right-leaning roots. He'd become a true moderate, appealing to both wings of the political chicken. And he'd sold out to pay for it all, sold his soul to a fair-skinned man wearing a navy blue Polo shirt.

"The Senator means well. A truly good man," Diego said. "He shouldn't be bothered with any of this. Certainly not anything that monster Lazaro Morales might have told you."

"He doesn't know what you are?" I tried not to sound incredulous. "What you represent?"

"What am I?" Diego held out his hands, palms up. "Just a simple businessman, yes?"

I racked my brain for an answer, something that would make sense. The dark leather of the SUV's interior became overpowering, claustrophobic.

"Sign the papers, take the money," Diego said. "You've suffered greatly. You deserve it."

"Why are you telling me this?" I stared at the documents in my lap.

"Because I can." He smiled.

I didn't say anything.

"You would put the pieces together eventually." He checked his watch. "Hawkins decided this way was the best."

I began to shake, a deep rage brewing inside me.

"I wanted to handle this in a different fashion, of course." He chuckled. "But I was overruled."

I reached for the door handle.

"You hold a lot of sway over certain people," he said. "But remember, that won't last. So sign the papers sooner rather than later."

I understood then. The job would save me. No one, not even Diego Manzanares, would take out a high-ranking official at Homeland Security. It seemed that somebody was looking out for me.

"Do we have a deal, Mister Cantrell?"

I hesitated for a moment. Then I nodded and got out.

- CHAPTER SEVENTY-FIVE -

The small motorcade prepared for its journey away from Milo Miller's safe house.

I stood on the front lawn, the employment applications and envelope of cash in my hand. The conversation with Diego Manzanares didn't seem real; it had all happened so fast.

Dockers Dude and the Secret Service agents got into their Suburban while Patrick Hawkins, McNally's chief of staff, stood outside, one foot on the curb, a fingertip pressed to his Bluetooth as he talked on his cell phone.

He looked at me. I looked back, feeling tense and jittery like a cattle prod was headed my way. He reached for the door then turned around. He walked toward me.

"No, sir. I don't think that's a good idea." Hawkins stared into my eyes, obviously speaking on his cell about me, not to me. "Not a good idea at all."

I waited, not sure what my next move should be. Run inside and get the Glock? And then what? Kill a wealthy Mexican from a prominent family because of a stupid logo on his business card?

"Are you sure?" Hawkins rubbed his eyes. "Okay, you're the boss." He ended the call.

"Where did this money come from?" I held up the envelope of cash.

"Somebody else wants to talk to you." Hawkins pointed to the lead Suburban. "This is the time to act like you've got some brains. Don't start making accusations or running your mouth."

Call me dense—I've been referred to as much worse—but up until this point, I hadn't really thought about who was in the first Suburban. The Secret Service should have been a major clue, but I was physically and mentally spent after the past week, and the old brain cells weren't working at full capacity.

The rear door on the first vehicle opened, and Senator Stephen McNally emerged. He walked across the lawn with a pair of agents trailing behind him. He moved with a slight limp, a result of the Viet Cong bullet that tore into his thigh in 1971.

I stood a little straighter, held my head erect.

The Senator wore black cowboy boots polished to a mirrored gloss, a tan summer-weight suit, and a dark blue shirt open at the collar.

The boots added another couple of inches to his lanky six-foot-two frame, and the handsome but angular face that often seemed harsh in the unforgiving eye of a TV camera was softer in real life. The long, thin nose the cartoonists loved to exaggerate was less prominent. His skin was unblemished except for light crow's-feet, a minor miracle for an avid outdoorsman in his sixties.

The hair was the same as it appeared on television: thick and wavy, as brown as mahogany, tinged with gray only at the temples. His signature look, a few errant strands that fell in front of his eyes, giving him a boyish charm, was in full effect.

"Jonathan Cantrell." He held out his hand. "So nice to meet you."

"And you too, Senator." I stuck the envelope of cash and applications under my left arm, grasped his hand.

"I trust you're well." He stroked his chin, stared intently at my face. "The border's rough country these days."

His gaze was hard to describe.

Every ounce of energy he possessed had been distilled into his blue eyes. When he turned his attention your way, he made you feel like you were the most important person on the planet. Every word you spoke would matter. Every thought you expressed would be weighed and considered.

Not a bad trait for a politician to have.

In spite of myself, I began to warm to the man. He had a completely different background and temperament, but he reminded me just a little of Lazaro Morales, the charismatic drug dealer who Eva had shot in Marfa. I thought about mentioning our mutual connection, the stripper and the Senator's presumably now-dead grandson, the baby with the burned legs. Somehow, that didn't seem appropriate at the moment.

"I understand that some of my people are going to offer you a job," he said. "My hope is that you take it. We need folks like you in Washington. Honest, hardworking Americans."

The money and papers under my arm felt hot all of a sudden.

"Sir, do you know anything about a firm called Paynelowe Industries?" I decided on a direct approach.

"Who?" He frowned, genuinely puzzled.

Hawkins sighed loudly, rolled his eyes.

"They're a private military corporation," I said. "They supply contract law enforcement officers."

"Oh, yeah." McNally nodded. "Pretty small outfit. Based in Alexandria, as I recall."

Hawkins hovered nearby. He caught the Senator's eye, tapped his watch.

"Paynelowe is a tiny weed." McNally shrugged. "In a very large lawn."

I squeezed the packet of money and papers under my arm, holding on to them like a life preserver and hoping they'd disappear at the same time. I looked back at the second Suburban, wanting to ask the Senator about his consultant for the border vote.

But I didn't. I knew then that nothing I could say or do would stop the inevitable alliance between the dark and the light. This was the way of politics and the affairs of men when money was involved.

Preachers and little children saw things as black and white. In the real world, there was nothing but a misty bell curve of gray.

I may have been a cynic, but this realization made me sad and tired.

"We need to leave," the Senator said. "I have to be at a funeral in a couple of hours."

I nodded.

"I do have a small gift for you though, a token." He handed me a plain white index card. "Think about that job offer."

I looked at the card. Several lines of handwritten text: an address in a shabby Dallas suburb and a name, Imogene Boyd.

"Imogene Boyd," I said. "Who is that?"

The only Imogene I knew was Sinclair's cousin, the woman Piper had "hired" to find her mother.

"She has some information which might be of interest to your friend Piper."

"Wow." I tried not to sound overly impressed even though I was.

He smiled and pulled another item from his pocket. "Enough of that," he said. "Let's talk about your move to DC."

"What about it?" I paused. "Hypothetically speaking."

"Another thing to consider if you relocated to DC." He held up the item he'd pulled from his pocket, a picture. "You'd get to see the boy."

The image showed a child, maybe ten years old. He was Caucasian but stood between two Latino girls in their early teens. The boy was wearing a white shirt and a red-striped tie, his hair slicked back. The girls, obviously twins, wore matching pink shirts.

"You've met him before, when he was an infant," the Senator said. "That's my grandson."

The child with the burned legs who'd disappeared from his drunken mother's car. I tried to get my head around the news.

"Did you think I was going to let that addict, that whore, raise my own flesh and blood?" The Senator returned the picture to his pocket.

"He's alive." I blinked several times. "Y-y-you found him."

"I took him, is what I did." The Senator smiled but the expression wasn't warm. "He lives with a family in Virginia, has a happy life now. Those are his adoptive sisters. Believe it or not, they had a rougher early childhood than he did."

"I'm glad to know he's alive." My voice choked. "T-thanks for telling me."

"You tried to do the right thing for the child all those years ago." The Senator put his arm around my shoulders. "You tried to do the right thing for my family."

"He was a just a baby," I said. "It was a horrible situation."

"As his grandfather, I want to thank you personally." The Senator put his lips close to my ear. His voice was husky with emotion. "For that, I owe you a debt which can never be repaid."

Then I understood. I was alive because I had tried to save a powerful man's offspring years before. I would stay safe if I took the job in DC, completed the deal. I realized then the Senator most likely didn't know who or what Diego represented. Or maybe he did but didn't want to acknowledge it, even to himself.

In any event, he was genuinely trying to help me, the unseemly details regarding his campaign having been seen to by Diego Manzanares and the pear-shaped man standing a few feet away.

"Sir, we need to get going." Hawkins moved closer.

"My friend that died, the funeral today." The Senator removed his arm from around my shoulders. "I bet you knew him."

I stared at the man who would be the leader of the free world.

"We grew up together. He was a retired Dallas police officer named Sinclair." The Senator buttoned his coat. "Not exactly prudent for me to be associated with him right now, but I am very loyal to my friends, even in death."

I nodded. Clutched the application papers and money tighter.

"Remember that, Jon." The Senator brushed back his hair. "Loyalty is important."

Then he strode to the lead Suburban, slid in the rear seat. Hawkins cocked his finger at me like it was a pistol and told me to FedEx the signed applications to the campaign office the next day.

I held up a hand, asked him to wait just a moment. Everyone else was in the Suburbans, even the Secret Service agents.

The day was hot, just the two of us on the sidewalk now. No potential witnesses.

We were standing about six feet behind the front door of the second Suburban, effectively in a blind spot where neither the agents in the front seats nor anyone in the lead vehicle could see us. In fact, no one could see us but Diego/Raul Manzanares in the third row or perhaps Dockers Dude.

"What do you want?" Hawkins cocked his head. "You gonna go ahead and sign now?"

The papers and money were still under my left arm. I took a step closer and swung my right hand like I was throwing a softball, fingers aiming for his crotch.

His eyes got big, round like golf balls, as my hand grasped his genitals through the material of his tacky suit.

"Don't even think about coming after me." I gave a little squeeze.

His mouth formed an O shape, cheeks expanding in gasps. His breath smelled like hamburger meat and onions.

"If you do." I continued to squeeze. "I will hunt you down like a rabid dog. And when I find you, I will break your spine and leave you in the gutter."

With the last few words, I gave his testicles a good hard yank.

He squealed. His face was sweaty and pale.

"Do you understand me?" I eased off the pressure.

He nodded, breath very shallow.

I smiled and head-butted his nose. Then I let go of his crotch.

He remained standing, wobbly but upright. Blood streamed from his nostrils. His comb-over had gone awry, blowing to one side of his head in the wind

I winked at him, and he slowly backed away, shuffling toward the rear door of the second Suburban. Behind the tinted windows of the vehicle, I could feel Diego staring at me.

Hawkins got inside, slammed the door, and the motorcade left.

A few moments later Piper appeared by my side, yawning, a cup of coffee in her hand.

"Who was that ugly dude with the bad comb-over?" she said. "And why'd you grab his nuts and break his nose?"

"He's Senator McNally's chief of staff." I scanned the street, made sure Diego Manzanares hadn't left behind a hit squad.

"That's the rich dude running for president, right?" Piper took a sip of coffee. "What the hell did his chief of staff want with you?"

"Let's take a drive." I put the cash and applications in my pocket.

- CHAPTER SEVENTY-SIX -

An hour later, after tidying up everything at Milo's, we parked across from a tract house in Mesquite. The wood-framed structure had been built in the 1960s, when the growth from Dallas was still a long way away from this small farming town located on the eastern fringes of the county. The address had been on the card the Senator had given me.

The home was a ranch style with a shallow-angled composition-shingled roof. The attached carport appeared to be near collapse, and the exterior walls were three or four years past needing a fresh coat of paint.

We waited, and I explained as best I could. How the cartel wasn't a stand-alone entity as most people thought. It was more like another division of a family enterprise. How the real profits weren't in drugs. The real money was in money, the level of funds that banks controlled.

"So what about Lazaro Morales?" she asked. "Why would they worry about him?"

"As near as I can figure, Hawkins didn't want Morales to testify because that would harm the organization that controlled a large portion of the border."

"And the organization belonged to Diego." Piper rubbed her chin. "Who the Senator's team had made a deal with, right?"

I nodded.

Hawkins had probably encouraged the Senator to lean on his old friend Sinclair to find the witness. Sinclair, with his ass on the line anyway, hadn't needed any extra persuasion.

Lazaro Morales had referred to a "guy from Washington" who had met with him, implying that the man had arranged for his safety. That could mean only one thing: people from McNally's opponent, with the power of an incumbent in the White House, had promised Lazaro freedom and access to his money if he would take down Diego's organization, which would in turn hurt McNally's election chances.

As luck would have it, the nominal head of the cartel, the Camel, had arranged for Eva to take out her husband, so everybody came out a winner except for Lazaro Morales.

And what was the deal? A new banking system? A seamless way to transfer money one way and drugs the other? Or a border that disappeared for all practical purposes, at least when it came to money and goods. All of these options meant lots of revenue, which meant new sources for taxes. Easy to see how a suddenly idealistic Senator might look the other way as his people get in the sack with a man like Diego.

Piper pondered it all and then asked why we were sitting in front of a crappy house in Mesquite. I told her to be patient. Then I showed her the job applications and money. She read the documents once, twice, three times. Then she counted the cash.

"I don't want to work for them," she said. "We go to DC, they own us a hundred percent."

I didn't say anything. She was right, and we both knew it.

About ten minutes later a woman emerged from the house and walked down the cracked sidewalk. Her gait was slow and awkward like her bones were brittle, which, in fact, they'd become from the chemo.

She stooped and picked up the newspaper from the dead grass and weeds that served as her lawn. Then she looked across the street at the gray Honda minivan where Piper and I sat.

"I think I recognize her." Piper peered through the front windshield. "The hair is a different color though."

I nodded. The last time we'd met had been in Sinclair's poker house when we dropped off Lisa, her daughter. Her wig that night had been blond. Now it was brown.

Another figure emerged from the house, a girl in her teens.

"That's Lisa," Piper said. "The girl Sinclair hired us to rescue."

She looked different too, more her age, not at all like a prostitute in a Korean brothel in Northwest Dallas. The Tammy Faye makeup was gone, and she was wearing loose-fitting sweats and a scrunchy around her hair. She looked normal, which I suppose is the best you could hope for.

Normality, what a tantalizing idea.

"And the woman in the wig is her mother, Sinclair's cousin." I handed Piper the card the Senator had given me with the woman's full name and address, and a short message: "She has information on your girl's birth mother."

"Imogene? She's—" Piper stared at the woman. "She's the investigator I hired."

Imogene and Lisa glanced up, appeared to notice us.

"Let's see what she knows," I said.

"And then what?" Piper pointed to the money and job applications.

Our current transportation, a gift from Milo, had a battery that was untrackable and a full tank of gas. What constituted our worldly possessions filled a couple of small duffel bags in the rear.

I looked around the street at the cars with their RFID-equipped batteries. Thought about all the ways a person could be tracked. Thought about how to avoid as many of those as possible, an area in which Piper and I had a great deal of expertise.

"I don't know. We find your mother and then maybe we just take a trip."

Milo's ten thousand was in my other pocket.

"Together?" she said.

"Yes." I nodded.

We jogged across the street, reaching a tentative hand into the past on our own terms. I didn't know what would happen with the information Imogene was about to provide. I didn't know where it would take us.

The suburban street felt like a juncture in space and time. On one side lay the old. The other promised a fresh start.

After we learned what we could from Imogene, Piper told me where to go. The last known address for her mother was in Colorado, in the mountains west of Denver. But we had decided on a stop before heading that way.

I drove as she gave directions. About thirty minutes later, we parked in the visitor lot of a large complex of buildings in Southeast Dallas, not far from where Sinclair and Senator Stephen McNally had grown up.

The buildings had been constructed in the 1930s. They had redbrick walls and large windows filled with lead-paned glass. They were well-maintained but possessed a sense of weariness about them. Elderly cars in the parking lot, ill-kept landscaping.

Except for the playground equipment scattered about, the place looked like the campus of a small liberal arts college fallen on hard times.

The sign by the administrative office read PLEASANT GROVE CHILDREN'S HOME.

Piper grabbed the envelope that contained the twenty thousand from Hawkins, the moving expenses.

"Be right back." She jumped out, ran up the sidewalk to the main office of the orphanage.

I exited the minivan as well, the applications in one hand, a cigarette lighter in the other.

In an empty spot next to where we'd parked, I ignited the packet of papers.

The flames appeared insignificant in the afternoon sun. A small, white-orange flash, a puff of smoke, and the safety of DC disappeared into a pile of ash that drifted across the asphalt.

I felt better immediately.

Piper returned. We both got in the van.

"Let's go find your mother." I put the transmission in gear and headed toward Colorado.

ACKNOWLEDGMENTS

While writing is a solitary endeavor, creating an actual book for public consumption is a group effort. To that end I would like to thank Andy Bartlett, Terry Goodman, David Downing, Alison Dasho, and everyone at Thomas & Mercer for their help and professionalism.

I would also like to offer my gratitude to the following for reading early drafts and offering comments: Jan Blankenship, Amy Bourrett, Rita Chapman, Victoria Calder, Will Clarke, Paul Coggins, Suzanne Frank, Dan Hale, Thad Hill, Alison Hunsicker, Harry Hunsicker Sr., Fanchon Knott, Wade Lynton, Allan McBee, Brooke Malouf, Clif Nixon, David Norman, Rebecca Russell, Steve Stodghill, Glenna Whitley, Robert Wilonsky, and Max Wright.

Thanks to Wade Lynton for help with the technical aspects of certain firearms. Also, much appreciation to Greg Schaffer for his insight into the workings of various federal law enforcement agencies and to Kate Schaffer for her knowledge of the Washington, DC, area. Any errors in regards to these topics are mine alone.

Very special thanks to Richard Abate for his patience in reading many early versions of this novel and helping shape each into something comprehensible.

And finally, last but never least, thanks to my wife, Alison, for all her love, patience, and support.

ABOUT THE AUTHOR

Harry Hunsicker is the former executive vice president of the Mystery Writers of America. His fiction has been short-listed for both the Shamus and Thriller Awards. *The Contractors* is his fourth novel. Hunsicker lives in Dallas.